WILDE CHILD

IMMORTAL VEGAS, BOOK 7

JENN STARK

Other Books by Jenn Stark

Getting Wilde

Wilde Card

Born To Be Wilde

Wicked And Wilde

Aces Wilde

Forever Wilde

One Wilde Night (prequel novella)

For Mike, Abby, Tyson and Danielle

No longer children, but still close to my heart

Come away, O human child!
To the waters and the wild
with a faery, hand in hand.
For the world's more full of weeping
than you can understand.

~ William Butler Yeats

CHAPTER ONE

The austerely gorgeous nation of Iceland had about a dozen things to recommend it. The country boasted no mosquitoes, no strip clubs, no McDonald's...and virtually no violent crime.

Then again, the night was young.

One long strip of bars on Laugavegar Street marked the capital city of Reykjavik's sole nod to nightlife. Most of the drinking establishments tended toward hole-in-the-wall pubs and cafés versus anything remotely resembling a club. This didn't blunt the locals' level of enthusiasm, but it did narrow down the options of where Nikki Dawes and I would find tonight's star attraction.

After two days of wallowing in eerily blue waters, slathered in so much thick white mud I was sure we'd sprout, we'd finally found good reason to return to dry land: Agnar Hilmarsson, the man about to lead us straight to a million-dollar prize.

First, however, we had to get close to the guy.

"We so need to have an op when you're not dressed like a homeless person."

The voice that carried over the hustle and thrum of the 2:00 a.m. crowd was no less dubious than it had been three hours ago, when we'd started tracking our pigeon at the city's most famous luxury spa.

I glanced down at my outfit—dull black jeans, worn black hoodie, scuffed black boots. "It doesn't matter what I'm wearing. I'm just here for backup. You're who he's interested in."

"I think you're wrong about that," said Nikki, pursing her heavily lacquered lips. "Pretty sure ol' Agnar colors inside the lines."

"Not according to our intel, he doesn't."

I surveyed her with a critical gaze, but if there was one thing about Nikki I never needed to worry about, it was her sense of style. Six foot four in stockinged feet, she got an additional four inches from her black platform-heeled shit kickers. The boots contrasted violently with her flared white miniskirt and petal-pink angora sweater. Nights were cold in Reykjavik, after all, even in early September. Nikki's icy blonde hair tumbled over her shoulders in ringlets that would make Godiva envious, and her lips, eyelids, and fingernails were painted shell pink to match the lavish pearl choker stretched around her throat.

"Even if he does, in that outfit, you'd make a man change his mind," I said.

She grinned, but her eyes were flat and serious. Nikki Dawes was more than my best friend, more even than the newest hired gun for the House of Swords, a mercenary position known as an Ace. At one time, she'd been a cop covering Chicago's deadliest beat. She hadn't lost those instincts.

"Place is crawling with security, dollface. Our intel didn't mention that."

"Yeah." It wasn't for lack of the quality of our resources. One of the perks of the international syndicate I now ran was its enviable surveillance capabilities. In fact, it was in my role as head of the House of Swords that word of this artifact hunt had come across the wires…only, for once, nobody'd been looking to hire me. I must be losing my cachet.

"He's arrived." Nikki's words were low, tight. "On the phone by the Rolls."

Agnar Hilmarsson was the head flunky of Thor Bjornsson, Iceland's richest man and owner of the artifacts we were currently targeting. Thor had, of course, caught wind of the fact that the items had soared to the top of the Artifacts Most Wanted list, the call for the artifacts going out over a secure cell channel more popular among the players of the arcane black market than QVC. Agnar's arrival here in Reykjavik was undoubtedly the result of that call.

Technically, Thor's minion had one job to do in Iceland: recover the coveted artifacts the whole world was buzzing about and whisk them away to the family's main holding. But this was his home territory, far away from the eyes of his overseers in Europe. And, according to my crack research team, he had a weakness for vodka, oxygen bars, and unique dance partners.

Nikki was definitely unique.

"How do I look?" she asked now, patting down her skirt with one broad hand, her nails glittering in the streetlight.

"He saw you today with mud on your face, and he about stroked out. Trust me, he's not going to know what hit him."

He wouldn't either. In more ways than one.

We had two options to gather the information we needed—Nikki could sweep Agnar off his feet and he could take her back to his fortress with me following behind, or she could work her Connected mojo on him in plain view of his security detail. God knew there were enough of his bruisers in the bar to stage their own thug convention.

We'd agreed on option B, despite Nikki being amused enough by Agnar's instant attraction to consider giving him more than just an eyeful. But safety first.

"Go on inside," I said. "I'll head in through the back."

She gave me one last disappointed glance. "You know, you could at least have made the attempt to look hot. It wouldn't have killed you to lose the hoodie for one freaking night."

"No one's going to be looking at me." I gave her a push. "Go."

"I'm going, I'm going."

Nikki turned on one towering thick rubber heel, then strolled with eye-popping swagger to the front of the line. It parted like the Red Sea, the bouncer at the door letting her in with an easy nod. We'd paid him well to do so, but it was an effective bit of business. Across the street, standing next to his double-parked limo, Agnar pocketed his phone and watched Nikki with unmasked interest. As his gaze swept over her statuesque form, his lips actually parted.

The House of Swords' data geeks might not have pegged all of ol' Agnar's on-site security, but they'd definitely gotten the man's kink down.

That said, it hadn't been the eggheads who'd first caught wind of this particular buy. That had come through Nigel Friedman, the chief Ace of the House of Swords and a finder himself, his ear ever to the deepest, darkest ruts of the arcane black market.

A buyer who preferred to remain nameless but who'd been verified through all the usual channels wanted the Gods' Nails, a particularly mysterious Norse treasure. Thor Bjornsson, apparent owner of said artifacts, hadn't been interested in selling. Not to be diverted, the buyer announced he wanted the nails no matter how he got them. He'd ratcheted up the finder's fee on the item, and every international hunter with a need for cash — which was to say, all of them — now had the job on their radar screens.

Ordinarily, Nigel wouldn't have paid much attention to any of this — jobs went up and came down all the time. According to the rumors behind the rumors, however, the artifact was a binding tool, able to freeze anyone in their tracks...even the most powerful Connecteds. Since I happened to be a Connected with a not-insubstantial skill set, color me interested.

It'd taken some doing to take on the job myself, of course. My years as an artifact finder were, technically, behind me. I had a House to run and easily a dozen finders at my fingertips who could do my wetwork.

But some habits were proving exceptionally hard to break.

Besides, I'd never been to Iceland. A quick trip to the island sounded like just the thing to avoid all the administrative duties lingering after the untimely death of my predecessor, Annika Soo.

Nigel hadn't been a fan of me getting involved personally. He'd urged me to throw the entire weight of the House of Swords at the problem, including all our bristly bits.

I, however, wasn't keen on putting my minions at risk. I'd barely gotten them unwrapped. More importantly, the vast resources of my international syndicate were spread out over multiple continents, about to be deployed on a much bigger cause — protecting the most innocent members of the psychic community. I'd need time to figure out how to use those resources effectively, and time was in short supply on this job.

It wasn't like I was going alone anyway. Nikki Dawes was a more than capable wingman.

The artifacts on this job were also proving satisfyingly mysterious. All we knew about them was that they were an ancient Viking relic from the era of Thorolf Most-Beard, one of Iceland's founding fathers. But were the Gods' Nails actually nails? Knives? Bones? No one seemed to know. And Thor Bjornsson most definitely wasn't talking.

Fortunately, he didn't have to. His agent would do just as well.

Per the plan, I skated into the back of the bar, peeling off my hoodie to reveal the club's black logoed T-shirt. I grabbed a tray and loaded it with several complimentary drinks the bartender had just queued up, an apparent ploy to get the crowd to loosen up their wallets. I slipped into the crowd.

It wasn't difficult to find Agnar. The tall, blond, ascetically thin aristocrat had a tight knot of security that circled him at five different points, though they seemed to pay no attention to their counterparts already set up at all exits of the bar, near the restrooms, at both ends of the counter, and spread throughout the room. Thor should be paying the club extra for rental space.

I buzzed through the crowd, my tray steadily growing lighter. Every time I glanced over to Nikki, she seemed pulled further into Agnar's net, the poor sot apparently not realizing he was the one being hunted. His security detail, as fierce as they were, had no problem letting the man sidle up to Nikki. Once she got close enough to touch the man, he was hers. A few random references to generic nails, and Agnar's mind would undoubtedly stray to the Gods' Nails he'd been sent to Iceland to retrieve. After that...

"*Þjónustustúlka*?" The word barely penetrated my ears, but it was one of the few Icelandic terms I'd forced myself to learn, given the givens. It meant "waitress," and I swiveled around with a broad smile on my face, planning to nod vigorously and move off as soon as possible.

I froze.

Not because I couldn't actually speak Icelandic either. I didn't have to — another waitress had heard the request of the tall, slender man as pale as a ghost, his clipped Nordic accent right at home in the Viking capital of the North Atlantic.

However, what stopped me was...I knew the speaker. Well. He'd been one of my top competitors during the bad old days when I was more mercenary than management, and he hated my guts with impressive enthusiasm. The fact that I'd snaked more than my share of artifacts out of his grasp had nothing to do with that, of course. But if *he* was in the hunt for the Gods' Nails...

I turned as nonchalantly as I could, reconsidering the bar. The glee club of Agnar's security personnel seemed to shift in my perspective, and without the veil of my assumptions, I could see them clearly for the first time.

They weren't security at all. They were finders. Finders who even now were circling around Agnar like sharks in shallow water. These were people who knew the Gods' Nails were worth a million dollars, minimum. And if even a few of them were working together...

Crap.

Turning abruptly on my heel, I shoved my way back toward the bar, careful to avoid the two operatives from Munich who I should've recognized immediately, given I was the one who'd inflicted that nasty scar on the bigger guy's head. I slid my tray across the counter, reaching into the pocket of my apron for my cards. I hadn't read them before tonight's gig, which obviously had been stupid. But we were three days ahead of everyone else! Who needed to read Tarot cards when you had a non-metaphysical jump on the game?

Riffling the deck, I pulled out three cards, flipping

13

them up on the counter in rapid succession. Ten of Swords, Five of Wands, Six of Pents.

I groaned. So not helpful. The Ten of Swords meant betrayal; well, duh. This job was all about backstabbing. We were backstabbing Agnar, and everyone else wanted to backstab each other, either singly or in pods. Moving on.

The Five of Wands presaged an imminent fight. That wasn't technically part of Nikki's and my plan, but now that we weren't the only kids in the sandbox, it probably wasn't avoidable.

But then…the Six of Pents? That meant, what—a gift from the universe? Coins falling from the sky? People begging for help? A loan coming—

It was the tiniest movement that signaled the beginning of everything going south.

Sometimes fights happened that way, with a turn, a cough, a sigh. This one began with a startled intake of breath three people away from me, at the precise moment that the blaring music died and the throng shifted. I caught a fleeting glance of the gasping woman as her hand came up, the glint of metal flashing in the strobing lights. As I did, I realized I knew her, though I hadn't seen her since that business in Tibet.

"Gun!" I shouted in English, and across the room, Nikki stood up from her barstool, strong-arming Agnar behind her and decking the nearest thug to the floor even though he wasn't even looking at Agnar anymore. He was looking toward me…

Toward *me*.

Wait a minute.

A gun fired somewhere in the back of the room, and Agnar's bodyguard detail sprang into action while the crowd erupted into a screaming horde of running, panicked people. I twisted past two fleeing patrons and barreled straight into a tag team of mercs from Angola I recognized at the last minute, the force of my unexpected rush knocking them into a squalling trio of women who pushed them back like they were leeches. I spun the other way.

Suddenly, a second round of gunfire burst though the room, the bullets barely missing my shoulder as I launched myself over a table. Once again, these people were totally aiming at me, *not* Agnar. What was going on?

Keeping up my momentum, I tumbled to the other side and scrambled behind some chairs. That positioned me right in front of Agnar and his goons, and as a result, everyone in the room was now aiming at both of us.

Where the hell were all these people coming from? Who'd declared it International *Get Sara* Day?

Get Sara...

Everything tilted. My Tarot reading resettled along new lines in a brief, startling flash of insight. The Ten of Swords wasn't Nikki's and my scam on Agnar, or even him getting hunted down by the other finders. Those nails might have been a target, but they weren't the most important target tonight.

I was.

This entire job was a setup. A betrayal. Classic Ten of Swords.

The fight presaged by the Five of Wands was already underway in bold relief, and the Six of Pentacles...well, I didn't know what it was supposed to mean, but I knew what it *could* mean. And what it could mean...would be super helpful.

I laughed a little crazily, and behind me, Nikki caught my exact tone of nutter. One of the benefits of her being able to read the minds of those she was closest to.

"Sara?" she barked. "Don't do anything—"

"Keep him safe!" I yelled back, then popped up like

15

the jack-in-the-box I was, a shot zipping past my shoulder so fast, my brain couldn't quite process the intense wash of pain that ripped through me.

Okay, so apparently, that round hadn't gone exactly *past* my shoulder.

"Crap!" I ducked and ran for the door, grateful to finally be hearing the blare of sirens outside as cold air slapped me in the face. As expected, half the guns and their carriers followed me, tracking my zigzagging line as I reached deep inside and found an extra burst of speed. Faces vanished, traffic blurred, lights became streaks in the night as my body pushed past any normal human abilities to put distance between me and my predators—

I slammed into a brick wall. Chaos roiled around me, and I crumpled to the ground, dazed and more than a little confused.

I decided I'd hang out there awhile, see the sights of Reykjavik from the sidewalk. It was a very nice sidewalk. Flat. Cold. Sidewalk-like…

"There you are, dollface."

Nikki's strong hands gripped me, and she hauled me to my unsteady feet. She wasn't alone, I realized, blinking around as she started hustling me forward. A phalanx of men and women with semiautomatic pistols surrounded us—Agnar's actual security. Had to be. They shot a round of gunfire into the sky, effectively keeping everyone well back as we jogged along. They ran next to us until we reached a familiar-looking limo and I was dumped summarily into the backseat.

I cursed as I rolled to my back, then suddenly realized that my old friends from the arcane black market *hadn't* simply spontaneously forgotten how to shoot after all. I'd been hit, and not merely in the shoulder.

"Sweet Christmas," I muttered. I peered down at my

legs and realized they were streaked with blood, my left bicep had been clipped, and I was sporting a growing pool of crimson across my belly. "That's not good."

"Totally going to leave a stain," Nikki agreed, studiously avoiding looking at me. Though my recently acquired healing abilities meant I wouldn't be dropping dead anytime soon, it still was hard for her not to flinch when I was injured. Instead, she focused on the babbling Agnar, holding both his hands as he stared at her, wide-eyed. I pulled myself higher on the seat as one of the helpful bodyguard types passed a large white towel toward me.

"Hospital." Agnar finally used an English word, and I looked up. Nikki was shaking her head, and I tried to look less full of bullet holes.

"Through and through," I said quickly, managing a smile. "No hospital needed, just some gauze and tape."

He blinked at me, then turned to the guard opposite the one who'd given me the towel, clearly some sort of security chief. I felt the weight of the man's gaze on me, and I peered out the tinted windows of the limo.

"Maybe a drugstore?" I asked, preempting whatever the man started to say. "After that, I'm good. Then you can drop us back at our hotel. That'd be fine."

"More than fine," Nikki said steadfastly. "We don't mean to be trouble."

"Trouble!" This represented Agnar's second English word, which I thought showed tremendous progress. "You're no trouble." He glared at the bodyguard and spoke rapidly.

The man translated, a pained look on his face. "Given your assistance tonight, you must accept Mr. Hilmarsson's hospitality," he said. "You're coming with us."

Nikki sighed. "It's not necessary —"

"You must," Agnar said firmly.

Bingo, I thought. *Payment coming due.* The Six of Pents in the flesh: getting what you deserved for a service rendered.

I sank back against the plush leather seats and did my best not to grin.

CHAPTER TWO

Thor Bjornsson's house was about as close as you could get to a Viking stronghold without actually having someone blowing a mighty horn at the entrance. We passed through an honest-to-God...or, well, gods...stone gatehouse with enormous flanking walls, and the gate slammed shut behind us with absolute finality.

I didn't mind that part so much, though. If we were locked *inside*, the anti-Sara mafia would be kept *outside*, at least for a night. How we'd get off the island with the nails intact was a problem, but not my immediate concern for this evening. Right now, I needed to convince ol' Agnar and his team that I wasn't nearly as shot up as he thought I was.

"She requires Dr. Mattsson," the glowering security chief said next to me in perfect English. The limo continued gliding up the long drive toward the stone fortress that passed as the family's local pied-à-terre. "The call will be logged."

"No—I don't. Really." I managed to sit a little more upright. The heat flares had started up in my body, signaling the healing about to take place. Not as well or as quickly as when the Magician of the Arcana Council put his skills to good use, but there was no point in informing Armaeus about our goings-on. He'd just get curious, and I didn't have time for curious. The Arcana Council had been my primary client for artifact-finding missions until recently, the super high-end collection of demigods paying top dollar for anything rare, beautiful, and, above all, magical. The Gods' Nails would definitely qualify, but in this case, finder was definitely keeper.

Besides, there was nothing Armaeus could do to heal me, that I couldn't do myself, with solitude and a stiff shot of whiskey. "Just—a bathroom would be good."

"And some gauze," Nikki chimed in. "We've already been too much trouble."

"Trouble!" This word was clearly not a favorite of Agnar's, and he burst into another rash of hurried Icelandic. Nikki couldn't speak it any better than I could, so we smiled gamely as the security chief's countenance darkened. At last, he nodded, however, and relief skated through me. I didn't know what deal Agnar had negotiated, but if it kept us on the premises, I was in favor.

It took another ten minutes for us to get into the house, "temporarily" liberated of our weapons, then deposited in a bedroom with an en-suite bath attached, impressively sized by European standards and teeth-achingly luxurious. Or, it could be that my teeth simply ached. The moment Nikki closed the door behind her, I sagged against the sink.

"Well, that sucked."

"Ambush." She strode up to me and helped me out of my shirt, whistling at the state of my back. "Did you have a target printed on you? Or are you just that slow?"

"I knew the shooters," I said. "Some of them, anyway. They weren't entry-level players. And there were a lot of them."

"Uh-huh. How'd they know we'd be there?"

I shrugged, my shoulder squawking in pain. "Unless that party really was for Agnar, and we were bonus entertainment?"

"Nope. When I finally talked him around to the Gods' Nails, Agnar's frontal lobe lit up like a Christmas tree. The nails are here, and they're as big as your arm. More importantly, however, no one needs to steal jack. The family is ready to sell. They've got appointments for the next four days in London to take all bids — both from whoever ordered the hit, and from whoever's feeling lucky."

"Bids?" I paused in my peeling off of my jeans, which were now caked with blood and stiffening by the second. Black was so handy in my line of work. Pivoting, I dumped the pants in the sink, then opened the faucets. Nikki was already scrubbing my shirt in the other sink.

She looked up at me and winced. *"Dollface.* For God's sake. There are lingerie manufacturers who'd have an aneurism if they saw what you're wearing. There's no need for you to dress like a gym teacher all the time."

"Except when I'm getting shot." I gritted my teeth as I peeled off the last of my clothes, then threw those garments in the sink as well. They were made of a fast-drying fabric, which mattered more to me than pink satin bows.

I straightened, giving myself the once-over. The belly shot was the worst, black and red and puckered, but the skin was already starting to close. I hadn't been lying to Agnar about this part, though: the shots *were* all through and through, from what I could tell. My skin was a mass of bruising, but the blood loss had dropped to a trickle.

There was a knock at the door. Nikki grabbed a

21

bathrobe from a cushioned hanger and threw it to me. I'd barely lashed it on when the door opened. A female security guard stepped in, her gaze traveling from my trussed-up form to the pile of steaming clothes in the sink.

"We can wash those," she said stiffly, as she offered up a care package of what looked like antibiotic cream and enough gauze to fashion a wedding gown.

Nikki took the supplies from her. "We're good. This bed—can we sleep there?"

"Her, yes," the guard said, pointing at me. "You—Mr. Hilmarsson would like to thank you more properly, when you are finished." She squinted at me as Nikki stepped into the bathroom, depositing our gift-with-purchase. "You look much better than I would have expected."

"I'm a bleeder." I managed a weak smile. "Only a few shots hit me, but there was a lot of blood to go around, and I was on the move. I'll be shipshape in no time."

The woman didn't look convinced, but I didn't worry much about her. People believed what they wanted to believe. And nobody wanted to believe that a gunshot victim could spontaneously heal in less than half an hour. I didn't much want to believe it either, though I couldn't say I wasn't grateful for it. My healing ability was even better here than it had been in Vegas a few weeks ago.

The Magician hadn't told me it'd speed up this fast. Of course, the Magician wasn't big on sharing information if he could avoid it, which he usually could.

The guard left. Nikki helped me slather the remaining open wounds with the pungent cream, then wrapped me up with the gauze.

That took another ten minutes, along with some artful application of blood stains to make it look like I was at least somewhat the worse for wear. And the pain certainly was no picnic, so my mad healing skills weren't completely superhero-worthy yet.

"You gonna be okay while I go let Agnar fawn over me?"

I nodded. "I could use a nap, actually. Everything hurts, even if it's technically knitting back together." I focused on her, planting my feet firmly to keep my balance. "You think he'll show you where the nails are?"

"Yup. Right after he shows me his etchings." Nikki turned to the mirror and fluffed out her hair, turning first to the right, then the left to view herself at all angles. "Hmm. Not nearly enough blood." As I watched, she pulled a sodden sock from the pile in the sink, squeezing out a thin trail of red down her sweater's left sleeve.

"And that's for?"

"For Agnar to suggest he provide me with new clothes." She batted her heavily mascaraed eyelashes, which had somehow managed not to run despite the evening's duress. "Of course, I suspect nothing will fit better than one of his own shirts."

"You can't get the information you need by shaking hands?"

"Girl. I've been getting three-a-day mud packs for the last forty-eight hours. Somebody needs to appreciate the glory that is this body, it might as well be Agnar. And who knows?" she winked. "Maybe he keeps the Gods' Nails beneath his bed."

I felt a headache coming on. "We haven't discussed extraction yet."

"Nope," Nikki said. "And we're not going to until I get a load of the artifacts with my own eyes. If they're really as big as he's making them out to be, we can't exactly smuggle them out in our bras." She slid her glance to my blood-soaked clothing. "Well, you might be able to."

23

"Nice."

Nikki was still cackling when she left the outer bedroom, and I sagged in earnest against the sink this time. The pain seemed worse than it should, by a fair margin, especially if I was going all Heather the Healer with the actual gunshot wounds. Was something going wrong? Was I doing something out of order?

I stumbled into the bedroom, unreasonably glad for the oversized bed. I crawled into it, feeling almost drugged.

The bed was infinitely better than I had any reason to expect it to be. I realized that the pain was finally fading as well, a sweet and unexpected languor overtaking my bones. I hadn't rested in — days, really. Not since the last time my immortality had been tested. After helping Armaeus welcome the latest member of the Arcana Council back into the fold — over that member's strident objections — it'd taken the Magician's touch to put me back together again. But he had, and along the way I'd learned a few things about him that I suspected he didn't realize. Things I wasn't quite sure how to manage yet, but I would.

Armaeus had a particular hold on me, it was true.

But I was beginning to realize that I had a hold on him too.

I'd had no time to truly ponder the ramifications of that discovery, however. The following morning, Nigel had called me about the Gods' Nails and their unique, supposed properties. Within twenty-four hours of that call, I was here, buried in mud.

Now I was getting shot at. A lot. By people who normally didn't play together so well.

I groaned, turning over in bed, ruminating again on the spread I'd pulled in the club. The Ten of Swords meant a betrayal on a very personal level — my own. The Five of Wands meant a fight, but could also mean a minor wound, an athletic competition…

I frowned…athletic competition? That would make this, what, some sort of test? But who would be testing me?

I shook my head, trying to clear it, but it was a losing battle. In truth, I'd never felt this drowsy without the assistance of grade-A drugs, or the Magician's touch. And Armaeus wasn't anywhere near this time zone. In addition to the mental lockdown I had in play, Iceland was surrounded by water. A lot of water. That tended to dim the Magician's effects unless I opened my mind wide to him, which I categorically was not doing. Maybe someone had slipped me a horse tranquilizer.

I smiled blurrily, succumbing to sleep at last. Succumbing to…

Wait a minute.

I jerked upright. I'd been solidly on my way to recovering when we'd reached the house, I knew that. The walk to the bedroom had been a little taxing, but nothing too impossible. But then the guard had shown up with the antibiotic cream and gauze…

My gaze jerked to the bathroom. Who in their right mind spiked antibiotic cream? Who *did* that?

Against my better judgment, I lurched out of bed, then stumbled back toward the bathroom. It took far longer than it should have to unwrap myself, but once I dropped all the gauze to the floor, I staggered into the shower and flipped on the spigots. Instantly, I was bombarded with jets streaming from the ceiling and two walls, the pounding pressure enough to revive every last shred of pain I'd vanquished and bring it screaming back to life. I drew new blood from clamping my teeth into my lower lip, but the onslaught of pain cleared my head, and I flopped against the wall, gradually rejoining the world of the living as the narcotics in the cream washed off my body. Thank Christmas I hadn't used too

25

much of it.

"Think, think," I muttered.

There were any number of reasons why Agnar and his goons might want to drug me. The easiest, and most benign, was that he wanted Nikki to himself for, ah, non-life-threatening reasons. The second easiest, and less benign, was that he wanted Nikki unprotected so he could kill her, torture her, or otherwise scuff her manicure. I didn't know enough about Agnar to know which way he was going to lean, but I couldn't take the risk.

And, arguably, there was still the question of the artifacts themselves. If they actually did have magical binding powers, I'd feel much better having those particular toothpicks in *my* bathroom cabinet than in the hands of whoever it was out there who had a hate on for me right now.

It took a solid ten minutes with the hair dryer to get my underthings mostly dry, and my shirt was more or less presentable a few minutes after that. The pants and socks, however, were nowhere near workable. I left them hanging over the side of the shower door and stalked back into the bedroom, pulling on the robe again. A quick perusal of the drawers yielded no clothing, no nothing. I didn't want to walk around in my robe—but even going out at all was a problem. The guards had seen the torn clothing. They'd expect at least a few bullet holes in my person.

I scowled, glancing around for my cards. They'd been in the apron, I remembered, and I didn't remember pulling the apron off me. We'd tumbled into the car, the guards had been there, and then—

Across the room, there was a short preemptory knock. Before I could call out, however, the door opened and a man stepped through, vaguely recognizable. Not the main security guard, but one who'd been in the

26

tight-knit group. Had he been with us in the car? Given me the towel? I couldn't remember. I squared my shoulders, but the man put his finger to his lips and shut the door quickly behind him. He carried a black duffel over one shoulder, visible briefly before he turned back to me.

"Madam Wilde," he said in a clipped British voice, bowing deeply to me, then straightening and widening his stance as if preparing to do battle. "I serve the House of Swords. You are in grave danger."

CHAPTER THREE

"Danger? Me?" I frowned, trying to shake off the last dregs of my happy juice drug cocktail. "Or do you mean Nikki?"

He waved a dismissive hand. "It's one and the same. Your lack of regard for your own life is negated by your concern for your team. They become the access point to you."

I frowned. That hit a little too close to home.

"Um… Who are you again?"

"Greg Williams. I've worked in the Bjornssons' employ for the past five years, at the behest of Madam Soo."

Annika Soo, the former leader of the House of Swords, had dipped her fingers into many, many pies. A dozen or so had even been legit businesses. She'd been cunning, shrewd, and ruthless…and she'd left me utterly unprepared to succeed her. I hated being ignorant, and that was something I was trying to fix…if only people would stop trying to kill me.

I narrowed my eyes at the man. For all I knew, he was no more a friend than the haters I'd encountered in the club. "Why did she assign you there?"

Williams smiled thinly. "Mr. Bjornsson is a man of considerable influence, and Madam Soo tended to keep tabs on such people. That's not what's important, though. The call for the artifacts went out too quickly for me to respond officially through my House contacts, and I didn't want to betray my alliance in any event. But I was positioned well enough to join Hilmarsson's security detail. Your identity is well known to him, given your utter lack of attempt at concealment. It was his intention to seek you out tomorrow."

"Why me?" I asked, narrowing my eyes. "Bjornsson has fifty different people gunning for the nails." I set aside his dig at my lack of a disguise, but deep in my soul, I knew he was right. Which was why I didn't like hanging out that deep in my soul.

Like it or not, my days of slipping through crowds unnoticed were behind me unless I changed my look. And I'd have to either change it fast or become a much better shot, if today's ambush was any indication.

The guard gave a little shrug. "As it happens, Mr. Bjornsson does not know precisely where the Gods' Nails are. His first order of business, before making a tidy profit on the artifacts, is to find them. Being an efficient man, he decided that the best finder would also be someone capable of paying for the artifacts as well."

"Pay for them?" This was getting weirder all the time. "I'm not going to pay you for the artifacts." I was here to steal the stupid things, and the guard's faint smile indicated he knew that as well.

"Mr. Bjornsson believed otherwise. Of course, none of us expected you to come for the nails yourself." Williams frowned, though he wisely decided against berating me further. Instead, he reached into his bag and pulled out a familiar deck of cards, then passed them over to me. As I hefted their familiar weight in my hands, he unshouldered his bag, removing a pair of pants, a shirt, and even socks. These he placed on the bed, then stepped back, bowing again. "Please hurry,

Madam Wilde. We do not have much time."

"Right." I reached for the clothes. The guard turned respectfully to face the wall as I dressed. I eyeballed the robe that I'd dropped on the bed as I pulled on the fresh pants and shirt, but there was no point in being OCD. My DNA had been splattered all over their limo. A few skin cells sloughed off on the robe weren't going to add that much to the picture.

I refocused on Williams. "So, what's the part about me being in danger?"

"We have very recently been made aware that a full contingent of finders has landed on Iceland's shores, eager to find the artifacts." He paused. "They are even more interested in finding you, which Mr. Bjornsson plans to use to his immediate advantage. If I don't return with you in approximately three more minutes, we'll be joined by the chief of security, and you'll be coerced at gunpoint to take on the task of locating the artifacts. If you fail, you'll be held captive. Another finder will be brought in to secure the artifacts, and then you will be sold to the highest bidder as a matched set."

I snorted. "Your employer is awfully sure of himself."

"He's had a lifetime of money and influence to help him get that way."

I considered that. Setting aside my own personal issues with being sold as a toy pony, there was the Arcana Council's response to consider. Even if Armaeus would never admit it, I knew for a fact that he felt a little proprietary toward me. Sure, he'd be curious to know who was willing to go to such lengths to capture me, because that was exactly the kind of information the Magician loved to know. But he wouldn't risk me getting sold into a meetup with a firing squad simply to find out who was at the other end of the negotiating table.

Would he?

Ultimately, it didn't matter. I sent Williams a hard look. "I think trying to make me do anything by force would not be your employer's best bet."

He nodded. "It was not his original intention. He came upon it only after we realized the sudden and…vigorous interest in you. And to be fair, we had no way of suspecting that you would come to us so readily."

"Happy to help." I picked up the deck of cards, shuffling it. "The nails are here, right? In this house. You know that much, surely."

"So the family legend holds," he said. "Most of the original exterior walls remain, and many of the interior rooms are unchanged beyond those most frequently used. So if, as Mr. Bjornsson suspects, the nails were bricked into the walls, they should be here. It's simply a matter of finding them. Unfortunately, time is of the essence. No one is aware he doesn't have the nails readily at hand."

"Fair enough." I pulled three cards out of the deck in rapid succession, tossing them to the bed before bending to slip on my socks. I decided to opt for my own boots, though. Blood soaked or not, they were at least the right size.

By the time I returned to the bed, Williams was leaning over it, peering in consternation at the three cards. I understood his confusion. The Three of Wands, Emperor, and Hermit didn't look like much on the surface, and truth be told, they could fit together in any one of dozens of ways. It was never good to take the card interpretations too far before you figured out what the first one meant, though. That was where people usually screwed up.

"Throne room?" he asked, glancing up at me. "There's a receiving room near the main doors. It does contain a large carved chair, but the chair isn't original to the house."

"I'm thinking more on the water." I didn't spill any more of my candy, though. Williams said he worked for the House of Swords, which was lovely in theory, but there was no way for me to prove that while cooped up here in Castle Odin. Nigel and Ma-Singh certainly hadn't tipped me off about him as a possibility. "You got a room like that, something with a view?"

The guard nodded, then pulled out his radio and spoke in rapid Icelandic. When he holstered the device, his lips twisted with the smallest indication of derision. "Mr. Hilmarsson is the special envoy of Mr. Bjornsson because of his knowledge of this home and its passages. He has the paperwork on the nails but no knowledge of their exact whereabouts. However, he has Mr. Bjornsson's absolute trust in this regard." He shrugged. "His predilections are also easily managed and were not considered to be problematic for this venture. Mr. Hilmarsson will never handle the artifacts directly, so he would be in no risk of losing them. And as he doesn't know specifically where they are, he couldn't betray their location."

"Tidy," I observed dryly. Nikki's unique skill hadn't been necessary after all, but she'd still more than done her job. I could see many intriguing bounty hunts in our future. Assuming we worked our way out of this one.

Williams led me from the room. I followed him down long, austerely appointed hallways, eventually reaching an enormous living room that looked out onto Faxa Bay. Mist curled up over its surface—looking wholly placid at the moment.

I glanced around. The chamber appeared to have been carved out of the bedrock of the earth, but it was comfortable enough. The marble-laid floor was partially covered by a thick pile carpet, and a large fire roared at the far end, casting light upon the occupants of the room. Nikki, I recognized at a glance, mainly because she towered over most everyone else. Agnar stood beside her, and they were flanked with security guards who had their guns drawn.

Unconsciously, I slowed. "What's with the guns?" I muttered.

"As I said, your life is in grave danger," Williams replied quietly. "Succeed in finding the artifact, and you become a player in this game. Fail, and you're merely a pawn." He sighed. "I can do no more until it comes to a fight, if I'm to remain unnoticed."

"Agreed." I didn't know whether or not to trust Williams, but he didn't have to tell me anything about what was going to befall me, and his words would be proved out quickly enough.

"Miss Wilde."

It was Agnar who spoke, stepping forward nervously, his hands extended. While he might have preferred to speak in Icelandic, his English proved serviceable enough. "It appears I am in your debt twice today. I believe you can help us to locate an item of an, ah, unusual provenance...?"

I nodded, cutting to the chase. "The Gods' Nails."

Agnar inclined his head, clearly relieved at my understanding. "We are in the position to come to a fortunate financial arrangement with you, should you find the item and be able to pay for it."

Beside him, Nikki watched me with an expressionless face. If she'd gathered any new intel from Agnar, it wouldn't do me any good until this business was done.

I pointed to the large French doors opening out onto the windswept balcony. "We need to go out there. How protected is that ledge?"

Agnar's gaze darted to the balcony, and his chief of

security grunted something to the guard nearest the door. Then the chief addressed me.

"It's protected from external attack by two broad walls and an overhang. Of course, the wind can be damaging during a storm. Nothing permanent remains out there."

"It's part of the original fortress, though." Agnar clasped his hands eagerly. "It's reasonable as a location for the nails."

I didn't miss the glance shared between the head of security and Williams. Some of what the guard had told me was undoubtedly true. How much, though, was impossible to guess. Nevertheless, the nails wouldn't do me any good buried under cement, and none of these people were Connected, unless my senses were tremendously off. They wouldn't be able to wield the nails against me…I was pretty sure.

"May I?" I gestured to the door.

"Yes—yes!" Agnar hurried forward as the security chief nodded. The doors opened onto a bleak and, as I'd suspected, windswept balcony, easily twenty feet long and every bit as deep, a true three-sided room.

It was an old room too, one that clearly had served as an overlook to the wide bay below, an excellent vantage point to watch one's ships come in—which was exactly what the Three of Wands presaged. I walked toward the balcony, hugging my arms close in the stiff breeze, and peered over the barrier.

"Whoa."

Roiling ocean boiled beneath me, far more active now that I saw it up close. Momentarily confused, I turned and met Agnar's gaze. "This isn't the original temple, is it. I seem to recall that it was farther inland, over some kind of moor."

"You're thinking of Helgafell. This building was built later, by one of Thorolf Most-Beard's sons. And not as a temple, but a holding." Agnar gestured to the water. "It's well positioned for security and trade."

"And windburn," Nikki said wryly, but she didn't move from her tidy cluster of security guards. It was clear she couldn't move, in fact, without causing a mild uproar.

I scanned the space surrounding us. The stone wasn't as rough-hewn as it originally looked, but it was definitely hewn. Chairs, benches, and ledges had been carved into the wall in sharp relief, including a dais that had once no doubt held a throne of some sort. I studied the space for a few too many seconds, and Agnar fairly bounced on his toes.

"You think they're on the dais? It makes sense. That was the position for the chieftain to rest and take refreshment, gazing out over the sea."

"Where's the chair, though?" I didn't like the location, frankly. There were no pillars around the dais, or anything to echo the Three of Wands or even the second card in the reading, the Hermit. I was looking for something tall and straight, possibly with a light attached. This...this didn't feel right.

Agnar nodded happily enough, puffing up with pride at being able to answer my question. "It wasn't attached to the dais. It was carved separately, out of marble. It began to show wear within the first decade of its creation, according to the historical journals, so it was removed. It was stored for several generations in the basement, if you can believe that, and — "

"Where is it now?" The question from the security chief was clipped, and Agnar flinched.

"I — I don't know, it's been so long since I've..." He frowned, clearly trying to remember, then his face cleared. I expected him to tell us the throne was in the receiving room Williams had mentioned, but he surprised me. "The suite. Has to be — it's the only reason

35

why I wouldn't have remembered it."

"What suite?" the chief growled.

"Mr. Bjornsson's private quarters." Agnar was speaking quickly now, his excitement mastering him once again. "I rarely enter those rooms when I visit, but I'm sure—I'm positive that's where it is. Yes. Come—quickly."

We exited the overlook in a controlled rush, the men leaving the doors open as we strode across the living room and down a series of broad halls. No one held a gun on either Nikki or me, but there was still a feeling of being herded that I didn't like. This was supposed to be a negotiation, not a command performance. Of course, if I didn't find the nails, I was nothing to these people but another flavor of artifact, to be auctioned off to the highest bidder.

Something about that sat wrong with me, beyond my obvious interest in self-preservation. It hadn't been so long ago that I hadn't needed to fly so far below the radar. I'd never even *hit* the radar. In the world of intercontinental Connected static, I was barely a digitized burp. Now I was a hotter commodity than Han Solo. What had changed?

I frowned, trying to work through it. The House of Swords promotion certainly hadn't hurt my standing, but I didn't get the feeling I was going to be dangled for ransom. I wouldn't let the House ransom me anyway, I resolved. There was no way I'd be returned in any shape worth caring about if it came to that. Death would be easier.

There was also my connection to the Council. But anyone who knew about the Council knew better than to try to leverage my return to them. And, arguably, wouldn't want to risk killing me.

Yet the family Bjornsson did seem to be risking exactly that. A lot.

"Here," Agnar said triumphantly as we strode into a large antechamber. Two guys in shirts and cargo pants stood on either side of the doors that presumably led to Thor's bedchamber, both of them with guns parked at their hips.

A thought sprang to mind. A thought Nikki gave voice to immediately.

"You guys stand here like that all the time?" she asked, craning her neck to peer past her closest guard. "You know your boss isn't here, right?"

The men didn't respond, but Nikki's question had served its purpose, opening up the space between her and her entourage. Only a few steps, but those could matter.

Agnar waved the men aside, and we passed them, Nikki eyeing them pointedly. Including these two goons, there were at least six minions, the security chief, and Agnar to get past. Agnar didn't count for much, but he might be armed. Something to keep in mind.

We stepped inside the master suite. Fortunately, we didn't have to go all the way to Thor's actual bed to find the throne we were looking for. It sat in a place of honor to the right of his study, a large upright chair carved out of what looked like granite, not marble, resting on a contrasting stone dais.

"The Gods' Nails." The head of security turned to me. "They're here?"

"That's right." I nodded crisply. "It'll be the work of a half hour to free them, and at that point, I'll happily buy them from you, wiring the money anywhere in the world you would like. What's your price?"

Agnar's eyes lit with excitement, but the chief of security stepped forward.

"I think you misunderstand, Miss Wilde," he said aggressively.

It wasn't something I planned to do. The man's

abrupt step, his snide tone, his hard, cold eyes—
something here wasn't right. So when he lifted his gun
to point it at me, I could be excused from my immediate
knee-jerk reaction.

A ball of fire crackled to life between us.

CHAPTER FOUR

For a moment, nobody spoke, nobody moved. The security chief, who'd no doubt seen a few things in his day, nevertheless went white, his entire body stiffening—including his gun hand, which kept his weapon trained on me.

Nikki had shifted forward, easing away from her guards another crucial step, every muscle in her body poised for fight. I suspected that, if things went south, she'd become her usual disarming self and come up with our own guns for use.

But things didn't have to go south, I decided. I relaxed my mind more, adding to the size of the ball of flame, as I'd done so many times in Armaeus's penthouse. I wasn't much on practicing this particular form of illusory magic, because for me, it wasn't an illusion. The heat rolling off the sphere made my skin feel like it was broiling. Small crackles of flame spit from its center, dropping burning embers onto the carpet. Which began to smoke.

"Enough, enough!" Agnar finally found his words and spluttered them out, his horrified gaze on the carpet as he addressed his security chief. "We have the authority to negotiate, agree to terms. There's no need for violence—put that out!" He said this last part to me as he waved his hands at me, as if he could shoo the ball of flame away.

"Lower the gun," I said, my voice sounding hard even to my ears. Part of that was anger, certainly. The other part was a bluff, since I didn't actually know how to make the fireball go poof on its own. Armaeus usually handled that part.

My emotions weren't helping either. Rather than diminishing, the flame grew in size, now as large as my head. More scattering embers flipped into the carpet, and I held my stance as Agnar started to bleat.

The security chief finally dropped his gun, but only to gesture me toward the hearth. "If you would?" he murmured.

More grateful than I hoped I let on, I moved the fireball away from us—but it still didn't dissipate entirely. Instead, it took up residence in the fireplace, crackling merrily against the thick stone wall. Show-off.

"Your terms, Miss Wilde?" Agnar asked quickly. I considered him, then smiled as I felt Nikki's gaze on me.

Unfortunately, I didn't get a chance to play Price is Right. Beside me, the security chief raised his gun once again. I whirled to stop him but could instantly tell that his pistol was pointed away from both me and Nikki. What was he…?

My momentary hesitation proved fatal. But not to me.

With two quick shots, Agnar crumpled to the floor.

His face was caught in a perfect expression of elegant bemusement, as if he'd just been served the wrong wine with dinner. The execution had been swift and professional, and I barely had time to blink before the security chief turned back to me, making a show of holstering his weapon.

"Mr. Hilmarsson has lost the confidence of our employer," he said.

I kept my gaze on him, but the man made no more move toward me, the other guards showing no sign of aggression, including Williams. "It would appear so."

"There will be no negotiation. Find the nails, and you are free to go. Mr. Bjornsson will render whatever payment you prefer at a later time. Your quarrel with the finders is not Mr. Bjornsson's quarrel."

"Ah." I blew out a long breath, wondering when the chief had had a change of heart. Was it the ball of fire? Or had he simply grown tired of Agnar being a weenie and used the opportunity to remove him from the equation?

It didn't matter. Bottom line, I still needed the nails, and the chief wouldn't try anything until I had them. I returned my attention to the throne.

It was flanked by two large pillars, both carved with ram's horns, a clear nod to the Emperor card. But the Hermit still needed to be considered, and I narrowed my eyes, studying the throne.

In a reading where placement and pictography held more sway than esoteric meanings, there were two options. Either I'd see some sort of marking or structure that mimicked a bright light, or I needed to focus on where the Hermit was looking. While in several of the earliest decks, the Hermit looked to the right, the deck I'd grown up with had him looking left. And when the cards chose to speak to me regarding directions, I reverted to that Rider-Waite deck's imagery.

Accordingly, I moved to my left as I ran my gaze along the throne's rich velvet coverlet. A thick red-and-gold-trimmed cushion sat atop the deep seat, and a luxurious drape of more red velvet ran over each armrest and stretched down to drag the ground. Another swath of velvet, this one so heavily embroidered it could have been cloth of gold, ran up and over the chair's high back, cascading to the floor behind the throne.

I gestured to it. "This come off?"

"Of course." The security chief signaled, and a man hastened forward, slipping off the velvet covers until the throne sat in all its bare, austere glory. It looked as if it had been carved out of a solid piece of stone, but of course it couldn't have been. Not if it held the nails inside it.

"How big are these things?" I murmured almost soundlessly, but the chief was close enough to hear me.

"We don't know," he said tightly. "We believe no longer than a man's forearm, but that belief is born more from the medieval depictions of the nails of the Christian cross, not due to any Norse mythological basis."

I nodded, then squatted down beside the throne. I drifted my hand along its carved surface, an intricate design of running wolves, each of them practically leaping over themselves to get ahead, surging and straining forward.

Or — not forward, exactly.

I frowned and traced the design up, squinting to see what it was the wolves searched for so arduously. A light in the sky, I realized. The sun.

I set back on my heels, scowling. "That can't be right." I glanced up to the security chief. "See if this same design is on the other side of the chair. Wolves leaping toward the sun. Then tell me how many wolves are there."

Without questioning me, he moved to the side of the chair. When two tons of thick marble were between us to forestall the double cross I knew was coming, I punched my hand forward, my forefinger pressing hard against the circular carving of the sun.

The tiny disc sank soundlessly into the rock, and a foot-wide ledge popped out from the bottom of the throne, where two long white pointed sticks gleamed from its cold surface. As the security chief cried out, I grabbed them.

Then all hell broke loose.

As soon as I touched the artifacts, which I had to assume were the Gods' Nails, the fireball in the hearth exploded with an enormous boom, a conflagration rushing out into the chamber. I caught up one of the nails in each hand and the fire licked toward them, setting their tips alight as if I were holding tapers of wood or cloth, not what felt alarmingly like bones.

Either way, it was a great trick.

"Get back!" I yelled as I swerved around, fire now shooting from the sticks like silly string. Nikki shoved the nearest guard away from her as the remainder of the guards brought up their weapons.

The first volley of those guns was abruptly cut short. Fire arced from the Gods' Nails and surrounded the guard's pistol, binding both weapon and man together in a fiery tangle.

Binding them.

Under the hapless guard's screams, I darted across the room, and the second blast of gunfire was fortunately going in the correct direction—away from us and into the line of men. Nikki had apparently done her job and armed up, and she swept the room once, twice behind me, then followed me out.

I whirled and pointed the sticks again toward the doors. The enormous panels swung shut with a clang, instantly splintering as a round of semiautomatic gunfire pounded into them.

"Run!" I screamed, and she turned in time with me, her gun tight up against her chest.

"Where?" she demanded. "There're guards at the gate, at the—"

"Here!" We ran down one corridor, then another,

and I could tell the moment Nikki realized where we were heading by the amount of cursing that trailed me as she gamely kept pace despite her towering boots.

We burst into the main living room, where the enormous windows were still open to the stone overlook beyond. A blast of explosives behind us spurred us on. They'd be stuck with one hell of a cleanup of Thor's vacation home, but there was nothing I could do about that. We'd tried to play nice, but the security chief had made it clear they were going to screw me over, and there were way too many people in that club back in the center of Reykjavik looking for a piece of me. Negotiations weren't going to cut it. We had to get off the island, and in a hurry.

"Nigel!" Nikki barked aloud, summoning the head Ace of the House of Swords and captain of our reinforcements through the microchip embedded in one of her molars. The device was strong enough to pick up the slightest whisper, but apparently screaming was more fun. Thor's crack security team clearly hadn't thought to check Nikki's fillings.

The wind blew like mad as we bolted onto the overlook.

"Nigel, we're coming like right now!" Nikki's voice rose in panic, excitement…or maybe nihilistic glee.

I couldn't hear all of Nigel's response, but through Nikki's jawline, the indignant, furious "No" was certainly easy to pick up.

"Too late!" Nikki chortled. She reached the barrier first and leapt onto the wide railing, scanning the water wildly.

"Aim left!" she screamed at me. Then she was over the edge, undoubtedly wanting to encounter the water first so that she could help me swim, if nothing else. Swimming wasn't really a strong suit of mine, so I appreciated her foresight. I especially appreciated that she was still wearing her original clothes, which had certain technical modifications against half a dozen extremities of circumstance, one of which was: water landing.

I heard the splash below and the shouts of the men following us simultaneously. I pulled myself to the top of the barrier just as the guards burst out into the overlook, guns coming around. Williams wasn't with them. I pointed the Gods' Nails at them a final time — only there was no longer any fire to feed them. They might be tools of binding, but they apparently required source material. I scowled at the long spikes, unable to read the script carved into them. Why didn't these damned things come with instruction manuals?

Not even a breath later, an awful sound pounded out above me. An enormous fissure suddenly appeared in the rock, and the railing buckled beneath my feet. Without thinking, I threw myself backward off the stone escarpment. A thunderous boom sounded, and the first rock fell.

Seconds later, I crashed into the icy cold water of the Bay of Faxa.

"Sara!" Nikki screamed, swimming furiously toward me. The wind whipped the waves into a maelstrom, and everything seemed far too loud.

I flapped gamely toward her, the Gods' Nails like appendages now, my grip on them ironclad. Nikki grabbed me under the arms and hauled me high in the water, her other hand dipping into her bra and yanking something free.

The long, slender floatation device, black as the water around us, filled with air as soon as Nikki ripped its cord free. She kicked for the open water. With the benefit of the floatation device as a kickboard, I could help. Our escape would've been seriously hampered by gunfire raining down from up above, but that, at least,

45

didn't seem to be a problem for the moment.

I twisted back as soon as we had a rhythm going, glancing over my shoulder while Nikki bit out instructions to Nigel and the small craft he was navigating into the bay. Behind us, Thor's mansion lit up like Christmas against the pitch-black sky. Enormous clouds of smoke billowed higher and higher from gaping windows and collapsing roofs. There didn't look to be any true fire, though. It was as if the building had sustained an avalanche from its top floors to its bottom, effectively sealing everyone in, Williams included.

The rock itself had bound them.

I stared at the sticks in my hands, piercing the water like the tusks of a narwhal. They still looked more like bones than anything else, but bones of what? Or who?

Now that I had time to look at the foot-long spikes, they were far more beautiful than I'd realized. Slender white strips of…it simply had to be bone, they'd been whittled down to sharp points, and their bases, where I held on for dear life, were coated in hammered silver. I couldn't peel my fingers away if I tried, at this point, and I wondered fleetingly if the nails were binding me as much as they allowed me to bind others.

For the moment, I was completely onboard with that.

"There!" Nikki shouted the word over the thundering whitecaps, and I became aware of a light racing toward us, gradually growing stronger. A new fire began to burn inside me, a racking, almost gnawing pain, but at least it served to clear my head.

"He see us?"

"He damn well better." Nikki turned the float upside down, its bright, reflective tape glowing as Nigel's light swept over the water. "Dammit, Nigel, why're you going backward?"

The pain increased in my body until my bones

throbbed. I couldn't see Nigel any more. I couldn't see anything. I could hear the boat's engine cut abruptly, though, even over the wind. A moment later, there were several splashes.

"What the hell…"

Nikki's tone turned questioning as wet-suited Swords guards swam toward us, two for her, two for me, then pulled us apart as if we were in danger of sinking to the bottom of the ocean in the next thirty seconds. I could see again, dimly, but didn't argue as they hauled my limp body toward the back of the boat, nor as more hands reached down and plucked me out of the water. Nikki came next, protesting all the way as we were hustled up the stairs, until finally we both sprawled on the boat's main deck.

Nigel dropped down in front of me…at a distance of five feet.

"Sara?" The blond ex-MI6 agent asked cautiously.

I blinked at him, squinting through eyes that seemed permanently scrunched shut. "Yeah?"

"Can you put down the big pointy sticks?" he asked levelly. "Or at least tell them we mean you no harm? It took us three tries to get close to you because their propulsive blasts kept pushing us back."

"Oh." I looked at the artifacts. My fingers were still wrapped tightly around their bases, and a fine spray of water still clung to their tips. But as I'd already seen, the nails could bend anything to their use.

Water was bad enough. We were on the boat now. With one wrong move, the nails might condense the entire craft like a squashed aluminum can. That…would be bad.

But I had no idea what I was doing here. I didn't know how these nails worked. I didn't know where they came from. I mean, yes, okay, the Norse gods seemed to be a good place to start, but did those gods still walk the

47

earth? Better yet, did they have a customer service team?

I tried to open my hands, but a knife of pain slashed through me, shooting from my hands straight to the line of my spine, jerking me rigid.

"Dollface." Nikki's voice was high, strident.

"It's okay. I...It's okay," I managed, drawing in a shaky breath. "Give me a minute."

My mind was blank as I stared at the water, wide open and desperately seeking for *any* suggestion on how to manage this new and unexpected problem, *any* idea, *any*...

A low, sensual laugh raked across my senses.

"You never stop surprising me, Miss Wilde."

CHAPTER FIVE

It took Armaeus Bertrand, the Magician, my personal healer and all-around meddler in all things arcane, exactly three point five seconds to figure out that I'd done something different with my manicure.

"The Gods' Nails are fusing to your bone structure," he said, not at all helpfully. *"You need to release them."*

No kidding. I kept my thoughts in my own head, though, managing only to breathe slowly, in and out, in and out, as a new and unpleasant pain crept steadily through me. The sticks had seated themselves in the base of my palms, and Armaeus was right, I realized as I peered at them. During the long haul through the ocean, they'd managed to pierce through my skin deep enough that they'd need to be pulled out versus simply dropped. Whether they'd "fused" or not, I wasn't sure, but fusing sounded distinctly uncomfortable.

Either way, the slender rods now stretched up between my third and fourth fingers, then extended another six inches beyond their outstretched tips, giving me a total minimalist Wolverine look. Only I didn't think they'd be retracting into my skeleton of their own volition. Which would make playing Pokémon Go a little difficult.

Any ideas on how to release them, exactly?

Armaeus was silent for a long while, but that didn't make him any less present. I could sense him rummaging through my thoughts, learning the details of how I'd come upon the nails, how I'd used them, how I'd carried them over the last hour and change. In my current state of desperation, I wasn't quibbling about him roaming around my brainpan. No matter how distressed I was, I knew he couldn't go down the rabbit holes where I'd stored the most important of my memories. If I'd learned nothing else on my sojourn with the Arcana Council, I'd learned to protect myself from that.

"The artifact is called the Gods' Nails because it was a bony structure that grew without being attached to any human skeleton, yet was found in a druidic tomb along with other scattered bones," Armaeus said at last into my mind. *"Though the nails' binding power is great, the ancient Norse peoples learned quickly they could not be handled safely, and that was ultimately the reason the artifacts were shut into the chieftain's throne. The runes etched into their surface contain a warning, and the silver seal at the base of the bones makes reattachment more difficult for mortals. Your recent evolution into immortality has made you vulnerable to them."*

Hooray for the home team.

"That lack of attachment also rendered the nails inert, so it was a trade-off. They could be used at great cost and pain, and then retracted, but if left attached too long…" He went still again, then spoke sharply. *"Answer me now. Who do you trust most aboard the boat?"*

I blinked up blearily, and there was Nikki staring at me, her face white with concern. She stiffened as our gazes connected, and at Armaeus's obvious mental touch, she fell off the low bench she'd been sitting on, scrambling to her feet in a rush, her arms going wide.

Nigel barked something, clearly surprised, but Nikki paid him no heed. Instead she advanced toward me, and I suddenly picked up Armaeus in my mind as well. *"Release,"* he was saying. *"Repeat it, over and over in your mind. Nikki is your friend, your ally, your truth. You trust her, you believe her, she will not – cannot – harm you. Release, and she will protect you."*

"Release," I managed, and my body spasmed with an electric surge of pain. My hands clenched involuntarily, and twin jets of water pounded out of the tips of the nails, catching one of Nigel's guards off, well, guard. He screamed as he went overboard, and Nigel started yelling again.

My eyes were only for Nikki, though. She stared at me intently as she advanced across the narrow deck, never breaking eye contact.

"Release," I tried again, stronger this time. She nodded, and I realized she'd covered her hands with something dark and heavy – scuba gloves? Some sort of towel?

She closed her hands around the nails and yanked.

Another round of agonized screaming erupted. Distantly, I realized it was my own.

The sensation of having the nails ripped out was not completely unfamiliar to me. In the past several months, I'd been riven, spiked, stabbed, and shot often enough that I had a loyalty card for Extractions-R-Us. But these sticks felt like they'd sunk all the way into my spine. With a mighty haul, Nikki pulled them free, throwing the priceless artifacts to the side almost as if they burned her through her gloves. Another of the guards fell on them, and I crumpled into a ball, pain and loss and shattering wrongness crashing over me in waves.

Speaking of waves – there was something wet on me. Wet...and sticky. Blood gushed forth from my palms. A strong set of arms wrapped around me, then I endured another round of Nigel barking in my ear, yelling at someone to get me to the cabin, to get the guy

51

out of the water, to get the boat moving, and, above all, to get the *hell* out of there.

Worked for me.

I must have passed out for some length of time, because when I came to, it was…quieter. Definitely quieter. I was still wrapped in a blanket, however, sandwiched between Nikki and Nigel. Both of them looked sick to their stomachs, I noticed immediately. Nausea roiled through me as well, and I shook my head. "What—"

"Water," Nigel said tersely, and a small bottle was suddenly at my lips. I had to lean against Nikki to drink it, one of her impressively toned arms around my shoulder. It was as if I hadn't drunk for days.

"What happened?" I managed again, coming up for air.

"Just drink, dollface. You're all right. We're on the ship now, safe and sound."

"The…ship." I blinked owlishly, looking around, but it was obvious that Nikki was right. Instead of the cramped cabin of the speedboat, we were in a room that looked very much like a hospital room, only there weren't any doctors present. No one was here, in fact, other than Nigel, Nikki, and myself, all crammed together on a set of chairs. Which seemed a little odd because there was a perfectly serviceable hospital gurney not three feet away that seemed like it would be comfortable for at least one of us.

"Why are we—what's happening?"

My brain didn't seem to be making the right connections, and I couldn't move my hands, I realized dimly. There was something important about that, but it could simply be that my arms were still swaddled under the blanket, weighted down with the thick cloth.

I shifted my arms, and they responded, but sluggishly. The movement made me woozy again.

"Easy does it," Nikki said. "You toss your cookies when you lie down, and we toss them when we move too far away from you. So we're all here together, keeping all our collective cookies safe, and you're getting better. When you get better, we get better. It's a fun new game we've learned."

She said all this nonchalantly, but the content of her statement cut through my haze. I shook my head, straightening between them. "You're kidding me."

"See? More improvement still." She looked over my head at Nigel. "Your turn."

Nigel uttered a tight curse, but gamely pulled away and hauled himself to his feet. He swayed, staggered, but got all the way to the gurney before he half collapsed against it, his hands gripping the sides as his shoulders heaved.

"Keep it together, golden boy," Nikki encouraged him, her arm still tight around me. "Take one for the team."

Golden boy usually was an apt description of Nigel Friedman. He wasn't tall, but his blond, blue-eyed, British good looks and ex-special forces body made him a force to be reckoned with. Now, however, the prospect of him moving away sent a bolt of fear through me. My eyes widened in something approaching horror as Nigel managed another step. I wasn't afraid for Nigel either. I was afraid of him leaving me to fight alone.

To fight...?

A wave of sickness roiled through me. "Release," I whispered.

Nikki clenched her arms around me, hissing with what I assumed was pain. But I shook off her hold.

"Release," I said loudly, almost urgently now. "Release. Unbind. Snap out of it, whatever. Both of you, I release you — go!"

As if I'd shoved him from behind, Nigel sprawled

forward to the floor, and the pressure of Nikki's arms around me fell completely away. With a squawk, she tipped sideways, half sliding, half scrambling across the floor until she reached the opposite wall. Nigel was already at the door, his hand on it, but he whipped his gaze back to me, anxiety suffusing his face.

"Go," I croaked again, my own panic ripping through me. I appreciated the Norse and their commitment to their leaders and all, but whatever they'd inscribed on those nails, it wasn't just a warning. There was powerful binding magic here between master and minion that went beyond pure weaponry. "Go!"

They went.

The moment the medical facility door crashed shut behind them, a shudder ripped through me — then it was over. Lightness, well-being, even satisfaction flowed through me like oil tipped from a cup, and I lurched to my feet as well. I'd done it, I knew. I'd released them completely.

Best of all, I'd done it myself. Armaeus was no longer in my mind.

Slowly, carefully, I unwound the blankets swaddling me, surveying my arms. My hands were wrapped in what looked like ten layers of gauze that stretched from my wrist to the knuckles of my fingers. To my immense relief, however, there was no blood seeping through. I flexed my hands and staggered a bit, but the pain was manageable after the first flash.

"You good in there, dollface?" Nikki's voice didn't come from the door but over the PA system, as if she was watching me now on closed-circuit TV. What the hell had I done that had spooked them both so much? That was only one of my questions, and not the most pressing.

"The artifacts?" I asked.

"Under lock and key. And a few chains to boot."

Nikki's voice was wry. "What do you remember?"

"She should rest." Nigel's voice sounded tired, even through the speakers.

"She's rested plenty. She's currently coherent, however, and I'd like to keep her that way. How long until the next call?"

Call? I wondered as Nigel gave a tense sigh.

"Ten minutes," he said.

"Good enough." Nikki's voice shifted, and I could picture her turning her attention back to her screens.

"What do you remember?" she asked again.

I shrugged the blanket back over my shoulders, unreasonably cold. "You pulled out the nails, threw them. I...must have passed out."

"Close enough." I could tell from her manner that I was missing something crucial. "How are you feeling?"

"Sick," I muttered. The boat gave a slight roll, and my stomach dipped along with it.

"How sick?"

I considered that. I'd felt worse, usually after tequila, but this had a similar sense to it, all headache and nausea and wobbly limbs. I stared at the floor, then lifted my head a little, managing one step forward, then another. I made it to the gurney without falling down, and braced myself against it. "Two-day bender," I finally decided.

"Oh good. Three and we'd need you to sleep it off, but two..."

Something in Nikki's voice made me frown. I looked up at the speaker. "What happened?"

"We're sending someone down to you, ship's doctor. She checked you out when we dressed your hands, before you—well. I don't think Nigel and I should get too close till you're fully recovered. But we need you up and at 'em as soon as you can manage it, dollface."

I scowled as she signed off, torn between being irritated at her ambiguity and suddenly not wanting to know how I'd behaved under the influence of the artifacts. The doctor arrived and spent another ten minutes examining my eyes, my ears, my heart rate — and lastly, my hands. She hesitated so long about touching them that I squinted at her.

"I didn't...hurt anyone, did I?"

She blinked up at me, but her assessing gaze was level. "Hurt? No. Other than Dawes and Friedman, anyway. They couldn't leave your side once you reached the boat, without severe reactions. For the rest of the crew, it was more a pull on them, a desire to protect and defend." She smiled gently. "Arguably, that feeling was already present, but your condition drove it to manic levels, from what I observed. It diminished again once your wounds stopped bleeding, which I had nothing to do with, of course. You handled that on your own."

She paused. Clearly, someone had clued in the doc on my superglue healing ability, and she did an admirable job not asking me the million and one questions I could see burning in her eyes. "The gunshot wounds you sustained in the firefight are fully sealed, and a quick scan of your internals indicated no trace of bullets remaining in your system. If any were lodged inside you, they've been...eradicated." Her careful phrasing belied her obvious interest, but I couldn't offer her much in the way of insight. I had no idea how the self-healing worked either.

"And now?"

"I'd recommend that you ingest as much fluids as you can comfortably manage to alleviate the nausea, stay away from the artifacts for the time being, and carry on," she said. "They've put the artifacts into the hold, in a lead-lined box, and they seem to have gone dormant once more. We don't know enough about them to know how long they're going to stay that way."

"Fair enough." I stood, and she helped me to my feet, remaining at my side as I crossed to the door.

I tried to disengage her. "You don't have to go with me—"

"I do, in fact," she replied, her tone efficient and straightforward. "The protective effect isn't as strong as the compulsion that Friedman and Dawes experienced, but an echo of their separation anxiety is suffusing me as well. I'd just as soon track that and test its limits, if you don't mind."

"Great." I blew out a long breath, wondering idly if Armaeus was going to go all codependent on me too when I saw him next. The thought strangely cheered me, and I was still smiling when the good doctor finally reached a door deep in the ship, then stood away.

"You okay?" I asked as she gazed at me, a mixture of relief and satisfaction on her face.

"I am," she said. Her face split into a smile. "I feel more than okay, actually. I feel completely fulfilled at having delivered you safely to your destination. Which is fascinating, I think you'll agree. Am I dismissed?"

"Oh. Yes, you…um, you can go. You're released or whatever. Go."

"Excellent." She nodded to me, a gesture that stopped just shy of being a bow. "Good day, Madam Wilde." Then she turned smartly and moved away, not even a hitch in her step to indicate that leaving me was causing her pain. Progress.

I pushed through the door and into a hive of tightly controlled chaos.

The glowering face of Ma-Singh, the Mongolian warrior who served as head of security for the House of Swords, was on three different monitors, but his voice was only audible on one. Other monitors showed maps of what was apparently the city of Barcelona, or at least that was what was typed along its lower right edge, with bright red and yellow markers lighting up the metropolis's southwest quadrant. Still other monitors showed news feeds of what looked like a partially destroyed nightclub.

When I entered, all activity stopped for a second, and Nikki and Nigel abruptly straightened — from good ol' surprise, it seemed, not anything more insidious.

"Sorry to interrupt," I said.

"No, your timing is excellent," Nigel spoke first. "We have reports of an explosion at a club in Barcelona that hit our radar two hours ago, and information is still coming in. Ma-Singh is en route there now from Beijing, but it will take him a while to reach the site."

I peered at the screens, focusing on the one featuring an international news station, clearly covering the explosion. I scanned the subtitles rapidly. "Terrorist attack?"

"That's what they think — or what they're officially reporting," Nigel shot me a glance. "We suspect something a little different. There are Connected casualties."

I frowned. The war on magic had made everyone jumpy, but our enemies weren't the only bad guys on the planet. With militant extremist cells cropping up throughout the Middle East and into Africa, there was plenty of evil to go around. "You sure that's not a coincidence? It looks pretty straightforward on the news. And I think they'd mention it if anyone started glowing or conjuring demons or anything."

"Your skepticism is justified, Madam Wilde." Ma-Singh spoke from the screen, and I turned my attention to him. "But this nightclub is known to us in the House of Swords. It is very old, very well regarded. It attracts an eclectic clientele, it is true, but…" He shook his head.

58

"We know this attack was not merely to create panic, or to make a statement for traditional news markets. It was a deliberate hit on a specific Connected community."

"How's that?" On the screens, I could see police and fire officials crawling all over the rubble, as well as hundreds of frightened onlookers who stood beyond a thick line of police tape, many of them crying.

Ma-Singh sighed deeply. "The twelve occupants who died in the nightclub tragedy this night...all of them are Revenants."

CHAPTER SIX

"Revenants." I swiveled my gaze from Ma-Singh to Nigel. "That's not seriously a thing, I thought. We've heard of them, but we've never seen…" I narrowed my eyes at him. "Or have you been holding out on me?"

Nigel shook his head. "I've never encountered one. I also was under the impression that they were merely a story told to frighten children."

That made me feel better. From his perch on the screens, Ma-Singh continued.

"Revenants are Connecteds with appreciably longer life spans than most humans. They generally remain reclusive, forming few outside connections with their lesser-aged counterparts, and the legends that have sprung up around them, in fact their very name, is a result of both that reclusiveness and their youthful demeanor."

"People seeing ghosts," I murmured.

"Exactly." Ma-Singh nodded. "The communities remain strongest in Eastern Europe but have spread over the years to Western Europe and a few enclaves in South America, North America, and, to a lesser extent, Asia. In all cases, they remain highly secretive, and to our knowledge have allowed no genetic testing of their kind to identify the source of their prolonged life. Our own physicians theorize that their cell structure is uniquely different, minimizing deterioration, allowing them to age much more slowly while retaining an ever-youthful appearance."

A Revenant's physiological variances were a lot like my own recent enhancements due to becoming immortal, I realized, without the whole Magician-intervention protocol that had caused my personal cellular upgrade. But if the Revenants' genetic differences could be isolated...

I frowned at the screen. "I get abducting the Revenants, if someone out there is looking to replicate their genes to produce some kind of antiaging serum...that'd be worth millions. But killing them..." Another thought struck me. "Are any, um, unaccounted for? That we know of?"

"Preliminary indications are no. However, that risk remains high and has precipitated an unusual request for assistance." A new note of awkwardness had entered Ma-Singh's voice, and I refocused on him. "One which I took the liberty of answering, before I was aware of your current circumstances, Madam Wilde. Historically, when the Revenants have been in need they reach out to the House of Swords, and we have answered. It simply has not happened in a very long time."

I lifted my brows. No wonder Nikki hadn't wanted me to go nighty-night again. "Answered how?" I asked, but I already knew the answer. I glanced at my hands, wondering how long I'd be doing the whole mummy thing.

Nigel intervened. "We've changed course for Ireland, where we'll take a private charter to reach Barcelona. The ship will continue to the US, as if you're still aboard."

I thought about the welcoming party in Reykjavik.

"Is that even worth it?" I asked, irritated. "It seems like I'm the easiest woman in the world to track these days."

"You have been, with your insistence on moving around without the benefit of a disguise or a security detail," Nigel nodded, always one to take the opportunity to pile on. "But Madam Soo was the same way. It grew too difficult for her to disguise her appearance every time she went into public. So, she chose the other route."

I sighed, knowing where this was headed. "Seventy-two layers of bodyguards."

Across the room, Nikki snorted. "It's for your own protection, dollface."

"I suppose." I said the words grudgingly, though I understood Nigel and Nikki's point. I had been the primary target, back in Reykjavik. Nikki, with all her skills, could have slipped in and out of Agnar's embrace, able to identify the location of the artifacts — if not precisely, then at least down to the house. A less famous hunter might have been able to find the Gods' Nails using his or her own tricks. I was one of the best artifact hunters around, yes — but I wasn't the only one. Nigel himself had found his share of treasure without my help, and there was easily another half-dozen other finders around the globe who would give us a run for our money.

How many of them had been gunning for me in Reykjavik?

That didn't matter right now, of course. What mattered was — I was a target. If I wanted to move around the globe, I'd need to accept protection. The only trouble with that plan? Protection meant that someone else might be stopping a bullet meant for me. And I was the only one in this group who could handle that kind of wound well.

So…what, I should go out on my own? That would

be stupid.

Right?

Nigel, apparently unaware I was solving the mysteries of the world, continued. "It's settled, then. We'll adopt the same level of security Madam Soo had in place to start, and adjust down if needed. Better to be too careful than not enough."

I scowled. I didn't like this at all. "How many people are we talking about?"

"It's wiser you didn't know," Nigel said, and on the screen, Ma-Singh nodded with satisfaction.

"Madam Soo did not know the details either," the Mongolian said gruffly. "She knew she was protected, not by who or how. It allowed her to move more quickly when situations required it, rather than worry about a detail whose training ensures they are capable of defending both her and themselves. You will reach that point as well, and be a safer asset when you do."

"Fine." I spread my hands, extending my fingers wide within their bandages. "I trust you."

The spasm of energy happened so quickly, I doubled over, jerking my hands into my gut, wincing with white-hot pain as I clenched my hands. Beneath us, deep in the hold, a high keening note burst up, searing my eardrums.

It was over as quickly as it began, and the fog behind my eyes cleared as chaos erupted around me. Guards scrambled to their feet again, Nigel barked commands, Nikki cursed a blue streak. On the screen, Ma-Singh now stood, alarm writ large across his face.

"What is it?" he demanded. "What just happened?"

"Nothing—nothing!" I shouted, flapping my hands. I jerked them back as quickly, bracing myself for another keening blast. "We've got artifacts aboard—sensitive artifacts. They seem to be triggered by any sort of call to arms."

I looked around, peering into the faces of the guards. They were shining with purpose, excitement, and a slightly frenzied intensity. Nikki and Nigel met my gaze, but that same passion shone in their eyes as well. Everyone had gotten the memo to up their game, it seemed, but I wasn't sure if they realized where that message had come from.

I decided it wouldn't help anything for me to bring it to their attention. "We're good now," I assured Ma-Singh, who continued to eye the room with interest. He'd been a general in Soo's army for a long time. He knew what he was seeing, even if he didn't know how it'd come to pass. "We'll, ah, see you in Spain."

He nodded, and I didn't miss the fierce satisfaction in his face. The man was at his best when he had the possibility of some heads to knock around. He certainly was making me glad he was on my side. "I'll be waiting," he said.

Ma-Singh *was* waiting too, for all that it took us another nearly thirty-six hours to reach him. Nikki, Nigel, and I had spent most of the voyage strategizing theories behind the attack on the Revenants, as additional information trickled in via the House of Swords intelligence net. Once we'd landed in Barcelona, we all piled into a limo that wound its way toward the club. It was situated in the heart of the trendy neighborhood of El Born, and was abandoned now in a drenching rain. The cause of the conflagration had already been identified, though the crime scene was barely forty-eight hours old.

"Kitchen fire," Ma-Singh said succinctly. "Quickly spread to the main floor of the club, trapping the guests. Many escaped, twelve didn't. Those twelve have been identified with official paperwork, all of which is false. No one outside the local Revenant community seems to realize the significance of the deaths, at least not yet."

"Rumblings in the arcane black market?" I asked.

"Minimal," Ma-Singh said. "The club was very public, and its quieter clientele remained in the VIP portion, which, of course, contributed to their deaths. They were exposed to the smoke the longest." He paused. "Contributed, but does not fully explain it. The smoke shouldn't have been that thick with the ventilation the club possessed. Nine Revenants died in the inner sanctum of the club, three more on the dance floor. By the time the police arrived, all twelve were positioned in the dance floor area to alleviate questions. The building itself is surprisingly undamaged, other than the kitchen area. The new statement in the media is that it was an unfortunate fire, but not arson, and not a terrorist attack."

"And you think otherwise."

Ma-Singh nodded. "The only individuals affected were the Revenants, and they were *all* affected. Even those who escaped the worst of the fire and smoke succumbed within minutes, while their trapped non-Connected counterparts barely had any damage to their lungs or throats."

I winced. "That was the cause of death, then? Asphyxiation?"

"That was the official cause of death, yes. The medical examiner is a friend of the community. He's already signed off on all certificates. The bodies will be cremated."

I blew out a short breath, my own lungs starting to itch. "And we have no idea who started the fire, or what the purpose was in killing these Revenants."

"Not yet, but unfortunate new developments this morning confirm our primary fears." He sighed. "The community is missing two members."

"Two?" I peered at him, keeping my hands on my

lap. I'd graduated from a full mummification to a light, stretchy bandage, my palms covered in fingerless gloves. My wrists still throbbed, but not badly. "How'd they go this long without being detected?"

Ma-Singh hesitated a moment too long. "They were children. No one expected them to be in the club."

"…Children." I swallowed, shifting my glance away. The most vulnerable members of any community. But among the Connected, children paid for their leaders' greed with their lives. They were hunted and exploited for the purity of their abilities, and so many of them had already been lost. But this…this seemed so senseless. "How were they allowed in the club at all?"

"Children by Revenant standards," Ma-Singh clarified, lifting a hand. "Their appearance was that of adults in their mid-twenties, but by the standards of their community, they had not yet hit puberty. They may have been nowhere near the building. But they're missing."

"And no one knows where they might be?" Nikki asked, her voice also strained. I wasn't the only one dedicated to protecting the weakest members of our people.

He shook his head. "There is some indication of attempts to breach the building in the immediate aftermath of the fire, which the police ascribed to looters. The community began a count of their own at that point. The two's disappearance was discovered after that. They are male and female, friends by all accounts. It's hoped they weren't in the building, are simply afraid to return—or lost—but…"

"But no one knows," Nigel said, his clipped words underscoring an obvious truth. There was too much we didn't know about this community, and we were already starting from behind.

We pulled up to the building, and I peered out. The

front-seat passenger exited the limo and opened the door, enormous umbrella at the ready. Two more men emerged from the shadows of the building to stand in the downpour. They all wore heavy raincoats, opened to reveal holstered weapons.

Inside the car, no one moved.

"Madam Wilde," Ma-Singh prompted, and I jumped. I'd forgotten the routine already, as new and borderline ridiculous as it was.

"Got it, sorry. I'm ready." I gave the signal and Nigel exited first. Then I emerged from the car, allowing the two men to flank and shield me all the way up to the doorway, where they handed me off to the second set.

"Thank you," I said, grateful that they at least nodded back. The men at the docks hadn't even granted me that.

One of the guards stepped forward and opened the door to the club. "Stay between us, Madam Wilde," he said, entering the building as the first waft of charred kitchen flooring reached my nostrils.

My sight went black.

Fear. Hate. Pain. Nausea swept my body, every nerve screeching with affront. My stomach knotted, my breath stopped in my throat, my heart pounded. *Loss and endless sorrow.*

"Madam Wilde!" The shout was alarmed and far too close, and awareness rushed back over me just as quickly.

"Tripped! I just tripped," I said hastily. "I'm good."

The man behind me had caught me as I'd half collapsed, but now both guards were looking at me with stark concern.

"I'm good," I said again, blowing out a long breath, trying to regain my equilibrium despite the emotional and psychic assault. Heat seared my cheeks. It was hard to comport myself as a super cool CEO when I couldn't manage to stay upright. "Let's move along. I don't want to linger here any longer than we have to."

I didn't either. There was a stain in the very air of the place, one of darkness and spoiled meat, but the guards in front of me didn't seem to notice. The one who'd caught me hadn't been Connected, I could tell from his touch. Did the guards' lack of psychic ability make them immune to...whatever was infecting this place?

Nikki, Nigel, and Ma-Singh joined us, and to my intense relief, the guards didn't rat me out for my momentary lapse. Nikki stiffened but seemed to tolerate the atmosphere better than I did. I scowled. Time for me to cowboy up.

We moved forward silently, respectful of the tragedy that had occurred here. Another man was waiting for us inside the next doorway, this one tall and slender...and definitely Connected. He had the mournful look of a cemetery angel, and was every bit as beautiful—pale skin as smooth and white as marble, timeless blue eyes, pale flaxen hair, young, fine features. Were all Revenants so, well, ghostly? It certainly would explain a lot of the rumors swirling around them.

"My name is Jonathan Francisco," he said, his voice a clear, light baritone. "You could consider me the head of security for our collective."

Collective? I frowned at him. "Sara Wilde."

"A pleasure to meet you, Madam Wilde. I understand you know very little about our families, and for that, I suspect we should be grateful." Another odd turn of phrase, but Jonathan moved smoothly on. "I can answer any questions you may have. I've served as the security director here since I reached my majority in 1783."

I tried and failed not to goggle at him, while Nikki uttered a low, barely audible "Damn, boy."

Jonathan inclined his head, then gestured more

deeply into the building. "We appreciate your assistance." The words were polite but his face betrayed no emotion, his watchful eyes landing on me, then skittering quickly away. "You'll want to see the inner sanctum?"

"Hang on." I turned around, letting my eyes become accustomed to the dim light of the place as Nikki and Nigel entered behind me, followed by Ma-Singh and yet more guards. Nikki seemed completely unfazed, so it wasn't my Connected sensitivity that was being tweaked, exactly. It was a different ingrained memory.

Either way, I no longer doubted Ma-Singh's assertion that this fire had been a deliberate act.

"Not the inner sanctum. The kitchen," I said.

Jonathan nodded, leading us back to the rear of the building. As we went, I could see more of the place, remarkably preserved despite the recent fire, and not nearly as damaged as I'd expected it to be.

"Fire engines were on-site within fifteen minutes, and it was raining that night too," Jonathan said beside me, as if reading my thoughts. "They focused their efforts on the kitchen. That's in the worst condition."

He wasn't kidding. The cooktop and vents had been reduced to hunks of metal; the enormous wood-burning pizza hearth exploded. Radial tracks of soot seemed to indicate a blast site at the base of the hearth, but there were no similar markings near the stove. Those must simply have…melted.

"Was there anyone back here?" I asked, humbled by the brutal scene.

"We don't believe so," Jonathan said. "The kitchen had closed for the evening and had just been cleaned. All staff were in the locker room or in the main lounge.

I nodded, scanning the room, fighting the sway of nausea. "There's nothing here I can use," I said with a certainty that brooked no opposition. No one had been stolen from here. There'd been no violence of that sort. I pointed to the hearth. "The device that was in here, where is it now?"

"Disintegrated," Jonathan said. "It's been of no use to us so far. We've taken the ash for analysis, but hold little hope."

"So, what do you think happened here?"

"I believe an explosive device was dropped into the kitchens, where its detonation would wreak the most havoc through this wall"—he gestured to the gutted wall and a sumptuously decorated room beyond—"which was the VIP section of the club. The bomb had to have enough range to reach its tendrils out to those of the community in the main area of the bar. It contained a compound uniquely lethal to our kind. Beyond that, I do not have any idea."

"And the children?"

His lips turned down. "I can only pray they were not here."

I nodded. I longed to tell him they weren't, but I held off. I needed more information.

Jonathan's pocket chirped, and he reached in and extracted a slender cell phone. He put it to his ear, then stiffened.

"We should go," he said, a note of relief in his voice. "Additional assistance has arrived."

CHAPTER SEVEN

We left the pulsing center of El Born and the ruined nightclub, then continued toward the water, winding our way through streets that seemed to decrease in size the farther we traveled.

"The community lives in Gotico," Ma-Singh said as the limo navigated a particularly tight passageway. "We will walk part of the way, but first we must get people in place."

He gestured to me, and I rolled my eyes. More people in place was clearly code for the number of security personnel the overprotective Mongolian was unleashing into the streets to ensure I stayed safe. It was already beginning to chafe. Self-consciously, I closed my fingers into my palm, tracing the rough edge of the bandage through my leather glove. The Gods' Nails had proven to be powerful weapons. I didn't want them permanently affixed to me, but I could see how keeping them on my person could be useful. And keep other people safe, more importantly.

"What's this about additional assistance?" Nigel was staring at Ma-Singh, but the general merely shrugged.

"Unknown. It could be the local police, though that's unlikely. Alternatively, it could be a representative from a second Revenant community."

"Or another mercenary from the black market?" I piped up.

"Not likely," Ma-Singh said. "The Revenants have made their way in this world by hiding in plain sight among the non-Connecteds. They are no friend of the dark practitioners."

"Probably someone they've known for a long time," Nikki put in. "To a group this cloistered, any intrusion, even a benign one, has to be upsetting."

Ma-Singh nodded. "Exactly so."

The limo stopped a few minutes later. We exited onto a narrow cobblestoned street. It was lined with soaring stone buildings that were gilded with gothic touches — intricate reliefs, elaborate trelliswork, and stone carvings of every manner of gargoyle and imp staring at us from nook and corner and archway.

And no matter where I looked, there were people, despite the late hour and inclement weather. Strolling down the alleys, whispering arm in arm, milling through the central courtyard. Down one street, a band struck up, and the straggling crowd moved in that direction, for all that it was nearing three in the morning.

"Kind of crowded for a reclusive community to make their home, don't you think?" Nikki observed dryly.

Jonathan materialized out of one of the doorways, beckoning us on. He nodded to Nikki with a faint smile, clearly having heard her. "We were here first, you might say. In truth, there are advantages to living in such an old area of town — one with which we are very familiar."

He turned the corner, and a street that looked exactly like the one we just left materialized before us, lit with a succession of quaint street lamps.

"We know the byways of the neighborhood

72

intimately, and the turning of the owners of the houses. Should we have need of outside contact, we do not have far to travel, and returning on foot is always a simple matter. There is also, as you can see, ample place to secret oneself away, should the need arise." He gestured to doorway and window alike. "The virtue of very old buildings is that there are often multiple ways to get inside them, and perforce multiple ways to exit."

"Hide in plain sight," I mused, but Jonathan didn't turn to me. He seemed ill at ease with my presence, which didn't bode well for our working relationship. But perhaps we could dispense with our offer to help that much more quickly, if this "additional assistance" provider could handle the work on his or her own. I wasn't about to stay where I wasn't wanted.

"Here we are." Jonathan stood to the side as we peered up the short stone stairway to a medieval-era villa, so old it sloped over the street. He gestured for us to enter, but Ma-Singh stayed my arm, indicating that Nikki and Nigel should go first. I looked down the street, almost certain I'd seen a man step into a shadowy doorway. One of the guards? Had to be. The night was desolate, despite the grimly resilient tourists getting every moment of enjoyment out of the old city. Anyone following us would be picked up by one of our — dozen? Two dozen? — tails.

Either way, they wouldn't be following us in here. I climbed the short staircase with a strange sense of relief snaking through me.

That should have tipped me off right there, but it didn't. It wasn't until I topped the stairs and saw who was waiting for us that I realized I should have locked down my mental barriers the moment we entered Spanish airspace.

On the other side of the narrow courtyard, leaning against a rough-hewn stone arch, stood Armaeus

Bertrand, Magician of the Arcana Council.

I couldn't help my initial reaction, the warmth that started at the very core of my being and flooded outward, erasing all the darkness and fear I'd experienced in the scorched club. Following on its heels, however, was a wariness born of hard experience. Over the course of the past several months, Armaeus had taken me to heights I'd never imagined possible—only to drop me into depths I didn't know if I'd survive.

What was he doing here?

My gaze jerked from him to Nikki and Nigel. Both of them kept their mouths firmly shut. Ma-Singh, who strode in behind me, checked his stride in astonishment, but Jonathan glided up to Armaeus, pivoting to regard us. He couldn't have said *he's with me* more clearly if they were wearing matching fraternity house sweaters.

"I'm confused," I said before anyone else could speak. "If you're good friends with the Council, why'd you call on the House of Swords?"

Jonathan turned his serene gaze on me. "This time, our interest was not to draw the attention of the full House of Swords. It was to draw yours."

"Same thing," I said without thinking. Even as the words passed my lips, they gave me pause. Had I really started identifying so closely with the House I now led? When I'd first been given the job by Annika Soo, I hadn't expected to last longer than it took to put one of the generals in place. But now...

Silence hung in the air, and Jonathan seemed disinclined to break it. Then again, he'd been kicking around for over two hundred years. Taking a moment probably meant something totally different to him.

When a response finally came, however, it wasn't Jonathan who spoke it. Instead, the Magician's cool, amused voice rolled out like a red carpet through the austere stone courtyard, unraveling all the way to my feet.

"I suggested that Jonathan contact you, Miss Wilde," Armaeus said. "He had a need to find two children, and you are the best finder of lost things on this earth."

The Magician's unexpected compliment made me blink, but my British Ace blustered forward, clearly peeved.

"She doesn't belong to you anymore," Nigel said tightly, and that made me snap my head toward him. To my recollection, I'd never belonged to the Magician...or to anyone, for that matter. Irritation flared through me at the idea that anyone thought of me that way.

Fortunately, Nikki had been around all of us long enough to intervene smoothly.

"Back it up, Buttercup," she said, putting a hand on Nigel's arm. The Ace seemed to recall himself and turned an apologetic glance on me. I ignored him, instead fixing Armaeus with my gaze.

It wasn't a hardship. As always, the man was impeccably dressed, his deep gray suit and snow-white shirt looking freshly ironed. His long ebony-colored hair was swept back from his face, revealing deeply bronzed skin, piercing dark golden eyes, and finely chiseled features. He was tall, well over six feet, and deceptively slender, though his well-cut suits tended to make him seem slighter than he really was. I'd had firsthand knowledge of the power he contained within his well-maintained body...and of the various planes, dips, and curves of that...

Armaeus's lips twitched, and I forced myself to focus. "So why are *you* here? It can't be to facilitate an introduction between me and Jonathan. We've already met."

"I thought I might assist the search more effectively in person," Armaeus said, and his gaze sharpened on me. "You're still hurt."

"I'm fine," I corrected him. I wasn't sure how I felt about him being here, and I certainly wasn't sure how I felt about seeing him in person. I looked at Jonathan. "Where do you want to start?"

Jonathan sighed, looking slightly away, then back to me. "At the beginning, I suspect. If you'll follow me?"

The Revenant security leader led us into the cramped apartment, if apartment was really the right word. The space was ascetically decorated in fifteenth-century monk, its furnishings several austerity points below spartan. Beyond the foyer was a dining room with a table but no chairs, and following that, a sitting room with only a folded mat in one corner of the smoothly polished stone floor. Nothing hung on the walls, and there were no windows. A long hallway led us to the rear of the structure, where we were greeted with two large windows. They framed a double arch of lit candles that stood directly in front of the windows on a narrow side table. All the chairs from the dining room table had been dragged in here and set along the walls. Jonathan gestured to them.

He had the air of a man with a story to tell, so I obligingly sat, but before he could get started, I held up a hand.

"History lesson can come later, if it's not germane to the search," I said. "I mainly need to understand who these children are, where you think they might be and why, and any third party you suspect. And I need to know all that, like, now."

Jonathan hesitated, shooting Armaeus a look. The Magician's answering smile seemed at once a little too familiar and self-satisfied, and I found myself bristling. It was almost as if the Magician was conveying *I told you so* with that little glance, and for some reason, that cheddared my cheese.

"I apologize for being brusque, but time's of the essence here," I said coolly, drawing Jonathan's attention back to me. "The children have already been missing twenty-four hours, possibly longer, right?"

"Yes," Jonathan said at last, releasing a pent-up sigh. "Very well. The children, Lyon and Anna, were not related, and were not a couple in your parlance, but they have been good friends since their fostering."

"Fostering." I truly didn't want the history lesson, but this part might be useful. "When did that start, how long did it last, and where was it?"

Jonathan considered the question. "It began in 1950, it lasted until 2000, and they both came from separate families in Spain but were fostered in Hungary."

"For fifty years," I clarified, mildly aghast.

"That is the standard time, yes. It would be the equivalent of ages five through late teens, and encompassed the bulk of their educational years."

"Right." It wasn't my place to judge. For that, I'd need to exchange places with Nikki, whose expression showed that she was judging enough for both of us.

"What about their parents?" Nikki interjected, clearly aghast.

"They remain with the community. By the time the children are sent to fostering communities, they have already learned much. It is not as if they are abandoned unawares."

"Wait." My brain was starting to hurt. "So by age sixty, you people are roughly eighteen and — then what? You slow down?" It appeared I needed more history than I'd thought.

"Put succinctly, yes. Which brings us to Lyon and Anna. They are functionally in their late teens, having just returned from fostering, but they excelled in their studies. Excelled in all things, really. They have found the return to Gotica somewhat stifling, but have been well trained. They understand our need for secrecy and have agreed to honor our requirements."

Right. Because teenagers were big fans of rules and restrictions. "What happens to…ah, members of the community who don't, ah, honor your requirements?"

"There are other paths they might take. Some live alone, or in less urban settings. These were all options available to Lyon and Anna, in time. They were not prisoners." Jonathan's tone had turned defensive.

I smothered a grimace. Like most eighteen-year-olds, Lyon and Anna's definition of "prison" might've differed from their elders'.

"Because they gave the appearance of twenty-five-year-olds, they were free to move about the city at will, day or night," Jonathan continued. Which, arguably, did sound pretty generous. "Of course, they were also chipped."

Okay, back to prison. "Chipped," I said. "Did they know this?"

He hesitated. "No."

"And those chips are now…?"

Another hesitation. "No longer responding."

That didn't come as a surprise.

"Right." I pulled out my cards from my hoodie pocket, aimlessly shuffling them. Barcelona was an enormous city to cover on foot, even with the help of the cards. We'd better get started. I found my gaze returning to Armaeus again. What was his real interest here, I wondered again.

Then I got it.

"No," I said, sharply. Nigel, Nikki, and Ma-Singh all straightened at my tone. "No, no, and no."

Armaeus simply smiled and inclined his head. "I think you'll agree, given the time constraints, that astral travel is our only possible solution, Miss Wilde. To effect that, I am at your service."

CHAPTER EIGHT

We trooped back to the dining room with chairs in hand. I was a big fan of there being a table nearby when I was seated for an astral travel session. Mainly because I usually ended up face-planted on it.

"What *is* this process, exactly? I don't understand," Nigel groused for the umpteenth time.

"It's not rocket science, sweet buns," Nikki said, the faintest edge of irritation finally sharpening her voice. "You know what astral projection is, putting yourself someplace else, ideally to report back what you see. That's what Sara does—with a spotter, usually—only she can use her mojo to actually locate objects, people, whatever while she does it."

Nigel's gaze swung to me. "Does it hurt?"

"Like a bitch," Nikki said cheerfully, patting him on the back. "Don't worry, though. You just have to catch her when she falls over. Which, believe me, she will. Just be glad she's staying in this dimension. She's a sucker for bringing back tagalongs when she goes off the grid."

"What?" he growled through clenched teeth.

I ignored Nigel and his misplaced concern, but Ma-Singh was beginning to worry me. He seemed to get larger every time I looked at him, larger and closer, until he practically loomed over me as I settled into my seat.

"I do not like this," he said succinctly.

I didn't know Ma-Singh as well as I knew Nigel, and my second in the House of Swords had far less experience with me blundering into danger like it was a second helping of dessert. I cut him some slack and laid a hand on his arm. Ma-Singh froze. It occurred to me I probably had just breached some ancient House etiquette, but I didn't care.

"I appreciate your concern, Ma-Singh, I do. You've done everything you can to protect me, and I'm grateful for it. But you can't take this journey with me. I'm not physically traveling — I'll never leave this room."

"But your mind is traveling," he said, unmollified. "That is still too great a risk. And the Ace says you once came back…skewered."

I winced, recalling the event he referred to, an unfortunate experience in Atlantis that I wouldn't soon be repeating, with any luck. I'd returned with the weapons of another world piercing my skin, the only way I could carry them back through time and space. That little round-trip adventure had made flying coach suddenly bearable again. Ma-Singh also surely had heard about the time his own former leader had sliced me up with her white swords of doom, before we'd become friends. So, yeah, I could understand his trepidation.

"That's not going to happen here. With any luck, I'm not going to leave the city — maybe not even the neighborhood. The children will be close, I'm sure of it."

Ma-Singh folded his arms over his powerful chest and glowered. One thing about Mongolians, they were excellent at glowering.

"We should begin." Armaeus stood off to one side, allowing Ma-Singh to get his father bear on a moment longer while the others moved into place. I pulled the cards from my lap where I'd been shuffling, and glanced toward the pictures of Anna and Lyon that Jonathan placed on the table. They were two attractive young adults, sophisticated and smiling, with deep brown hair, flashing eyes, bronzed skin. They were the picture of health and vitality, and for some reason, that made me nervous.

Apprehension hung heavily over me as I drew cards in quick succession, laying them out before me. The Hierophant, Four of Wands, Three of Swords. No one spoke, but the ball in the pit of my stomach intensified.

"Church or a hospital," I said, sweeping the cards back into the deck and setting them aside. "Older the better. Maybe..." I thought about the Four of Wands. "Maybe somewhere they have weddings, if it's a church, or a hospital that overlooks a picturesque park, something like that."

"The Basilica of Santa Maria Del Mar is a popular site for weddings," Jonathan said quietly. "It's not too far either. You'll know it by its stained-glass windows, particularly its Rose Window." He glanced to the wall, though there were no windows in this room. "It would be closed now."

"Not to me," I assured him.

Ma-Singh had finally moved back, and Armaeus stepped over to me, standing to my right. At his glance, Nikki took up her position on the opposite side of my chair. I smiled at her, and she patted me on the shoulder.

"You got this," she said. "And I got you."

Nikki was my anchor when I traveled, my surefire means of getting my metaphysical butt back home. My sinking stomach made me think I was going to need more than her strong arms this time around.

I pulled my gaze quickly away, focusing again on the table as my throat worked. The dread was greater now than it usually was. It'd been a while since my last travel stint, and that one hadn't ended so well. That was all. I was simply nervous.

Beside me, Armaeus's soft, confident voice began the chant that had already sent me down several journeys across the globe. Funny, I could never quite work out what he was saying, exactly, for all that he was standing right—

I slumped forward.

My spirit detached almost immediately from my physical form, which looked strangely bowed beneath me at the table, as if the weight of the world now rested too heavily on my shoulders. Did I always look like that? I'd be sporting a dowager's hump before long if I didn't knock it off.

"Miss Wilde…" Armaeus prompted.

I'm going—I'm going. And I was. With a spurt of focus and pent-up energy, I managed to move through the thick walls of Jonathan's home with only the slightest drag to slow me down. Then I was in the heart of the oldest section of Barcelona, finally quiet in the predawn darkness. I swept through the narrow streets and around ornamental stonework and trailing wrought iron, skirting fountains and ancient cornerstones and even a few trees. Then I was moving up, up, my gaze searching for the enormous churches of the ancient city.

It didn't take me long to find them. As I scanned, I picked out several great churches—but it was the one with the giant rose window that caught my attention. Not so much because Jonathan had mentioned it…but because it glowed.

The Basilica of Santa Maria del Mar seemed lit from within by a strange, spectral light, the effect causing the enormous window to radiate with unearthly beauty. No one could possibly be in the church, however, not at this hour.

I moved toward it anyway, my feeling of dread

increasing. Based on the cards I'd pulled, the children — young adults — whatever they were, the young Revenants would be in the basilica, I was almost certain. Not wanting to disturb the light pouring out of the rose window, I skimmed toward the roof, giving over to the feeling of dropping through tile and stone and beams as I entered the enormous building.

Fortunately, one advantage of churches was they were dominated by one big room, which made the job of searching that much easier. I dropped into the center of the basilica in a rush, but the usual sense of quiet sanctuary didn't greet me here.

Glancing toward the sanctuary, I located the source of light, a strobe-like flasher atop the altar, bright and steady enough to fill the entire space, its pulse so rapid that it seemed like one continuous stream from a distance. But there was no other movement in the room.

"Search the basement?" I murmured aloud.

Armaeus seemed to hesitate, then spoke words directly in my mind. Apparently, he didn't want everyone to hear. *"What do you see?"*

Nothing — light. There's a light on the altar. Otherwise, the place is empty. I swept my gaze around the room again, relating the form and size of everything I saw. When I got to the altar, I felt more than heard Armaeus's intake of breath.

"Return to us, Miss Wilde."

I frowned. Despite his higher-level powers, Armaeus couldn't usually see more than I could, relying instead on my translation of what I saw to help him understand the situation on the ground.

Why, what's wrong?

Armaeus said something I couldn't pick up. There was the sound of people arguing behind him, arguing — or, no, not arguing. Shouting orders, first Armaeus's cool, strong voice, then others, dimmer, less controlled, more emotional. And one that was yet farther off, striking a keen note of…

Anguish.

My gaze sharpened on the sanctuary, and I drifted closer, willing myself to go quickly but somehow unable to do so. At least not until I saw the wine spilling from the top of the altar, the graceful cup overturned in one hand of the figure lying on the ornately carved surface. Confusion suffused me, and then in a flash, I understood and whipped forward, my mind working again, my thoughts flowing quickly enough that Armaeus finally stopped whoever he was talking to and returned his attention to me.

"Miss Wilde, no. Return to me, now. Return!"

But it was far too late for returning, far too late for me to do anything but will myself more toward corporeal form. I couldn't fully materialize, not completely. Which meant I could not help these children — children in everything but physical form, truly, lying on the altar, huddled together, their arms entwined as if in a lover's embrace. They were robed in pure white silk, clothes clearly not their own, and they were…they were…

My hands fluttered up to my face, covering my mouth, but the scream I silently uttered seemed to ricochet off every wall and pew in the great and terrible space.

The light that blossomed up between the two bodies of the Revenants was not that of some strobe or electric lamp. It was the dying surges of their hearts, two hearts, completely exposed in their chests, pierced through with blades. *The Three of Swords.* The two Revenants were dead — very much dead — their eyes hollow, their mouths slack. The marks of strangulation across their necks attested to their manner of death, but their violent passing was somehow not at all evident in their faces, which remained beautiful and taut, as if caught in a trance.

Impossibly, however, their hearts beat on without the need of their bodies or brains to sustain them. And the light that poured from the hearts must have taken their captors by surprise, I suddenly realized...the unholy sacrifice they were planning had been interrupted — interrupted!

I jerked my head up. *They're close!* I thought furiously to Armaeus, but he'd clearly already figured that out. *They're close! I can find them!*

"*No*," he growled back, and there was real panic in his voice. "*If they are strong enough to kill a Revenant, they are strong enough to trap you.*"

But they didn't finish the job.

I was going to hunt for them regardless, Armaeus be damned. I swept through the church and all its corners, finally hearing a sound.

"Hello?" a thin wavering voice called out.

Someone's here, saw the light. Which means it can't have been burning long. We were so close, Armaeus. I missed them by a half hour! I'm not going to miss their captors.

"*Miss Wilde —* "

I tuned him out. Flowing through the church, I felt no other forms in the pile of rock and glory, and I burst through the rose window again, circling wildly. On the glittering streets below, cars drove in every direction, too many of them to follow at once. Despair struck me anew. There was no more trail after this, I knew. I'd stopped reading cards with the revelation of the Three of Swords, too cowardly to go further. And now it was too late. To return to my inert body in the protection of my friends was to give up, and I couldn't give up. The light in the rose window was only now beginning to fade. Were the killers of those children waiting for their Revenant hearts to fade before they finished their work?

I remembered the small voice, concerned and confused. The priest! They'd be on him too fast—too fast—

I turned around toward the church as quickly as I'd burst out, and blew back into it. Mere moments had passed. The priest was still working his way up the central aisle, picking up speed, but now he was no longer alone in the church.

The priest stopped. Gasped. Then he moaned something in broken, haggard Spanish, his voice rising with panic as he dropped his flashlight and fumbled for his phone.

The attackers struck, flying out of the pews toward the old man, but I got there first.

I blasted into them with a scream that was loud enough in my own mind that even the assailants heard it. The force of my fury formed a violent punch, carrying them both back a step. I didn't normally like to go through human bodies when I was in my incorporeal form, but there was always the exception. This definitely counted as a worthwhile exception.

Realization struck me as I crashed through the first assailant, heard his scream. He could see me! See me and see me blow straight through his body, his brain scrambling to figure out what was happening to him. That his vision was so acute marked him as a Connected, but not a high-level one, I could tell at a glance. Still, he instantly whipped away from the priest, causing his partner to stumble, and then his partner spun too, catching sight of me. They both began babbling in Spanish, clearly terrified, but I could do nothing more than this, nothing more than play the part of the phantom.

Still, I could do that with fervor, and with each pass, I saw more—*felt* more of who these Connecteds were. I saw into their eyes, felt their thoughts, heard their cries — and the cries and words they'd spoken hours, even days before. Their memories were offered up to me as I shattered their body's energy. I couldn't kill them directly, certainly not in this form, but thinking of those two bodies up on the altar, I could make them wish they were dead.

Finally, they were left in a crumpled heap, nothing but screams rising from them, screams and helpless sobs. I turned to the priest, but he wasn't screaming anymore. Instead he held his hands high, his mouth moving.

Angel, he said — or I think he said it. *Angel.*

I met the man's gaze and felt him truly see me — see me, though he was not Connected in any traditional sense. Still, his faith in his God and in the hope still left on this earth for humankind was enough.

Angel, he mouthed again, a third and final time. "Go and do God's work."

We stared at each other a moment longer in utter silence. Then the sound of sirens cut through the night sky.

I fled.

The moment I burst through the church's protective walls, though, I realized something was terribly wrong. Screams were rising now, no longer from the shell-shocked killers in the church, but from every corner of the city. Revenants, I knew at once. Their wails seemed to follow me like living things, latching on to my legs, my arms, my hair. Not to pull me back down to earth, but to add the weight of their expectations to my already overwhelmed spirit.

It was too much…too much!

By the time I crashed back through the walls of Jonathan's household, I was delirious with pain and misery and the endless cries of a community I hadn't even known existed mere days ago. I fell forward with such quick violence that Nikki barely caught me in time before I brained myself on the table. As it was, she pulled me back, settling me firmly in the chair, then had to brace me from sliding to the floor. My head tipped back, my eyes rolling.

"Sara!" she snapped, her face in mine. "Sara, c'mon, girl, give me your eyes, your eyes, look at me, dollface, bring it back home. Speak to me, sweetheart. Show me you're here."

Too much! The screams wailed inside me. *Too much...*

But I already knew the truth of what I'd seen, I already knew who had sent those wraiths who'd rent asunder the bodies of those innocent Revenants, searching for their life's essence. I already knew the danger we faced—and that it would not end in Barcelona. I'd suspected it the moment I'd stepped foot in the destroyed club, if I was honest with myself, but I hadn't been willing to face it until now. Until...

"Sara," Nikki repeated, shaking me roughly. "C'mon, girl. What in the—"

"I'm back," I finally croaked with a broken, rattling cough. "I'm back."

I drew in a ragged breath. "And so is Gamon."

CHAPTER NINE

It took a few hours before Ma-Singh and Nigel would leave me alone, and even then it was only to barricade me into my hotel room. Armaeus had announced me shipshape with alarming speed, but Nikki had seen through my attempt at normalcy and had insisted we check into the nearest luxury lodging option that met Ma-Singh's exacting security standards.

For his part, the general was beside himself with what he'd respectfully termed my "rash indiscretion" in racing pell-mell into the night and not treating the astral traveling experience as the true threat that it was to my form and function. Since I didn't come back to my body able to run out of the room, unharmed, on my own two feet, he had a point. The fact that I generally didn't attempt to travel without assistance didn't serve at all to placate him. Both Nikki and the most powerful Connected in the world had been at my side, he reasoned. I still came back in virtual pieces.

It had been harder to let go of the image of the murdered Revenants than I'd expected. I'd seen so much darkness before this, the tragedy shouldn't have affected me this much. Yet, the only thing able to banish them from my heart and mind was my solemn vow to avenge them—avenge them and protect their community as my own. I'd made this promise not to my House or my people—at least not yet—but to the wailing, watchful souls who had marked my passage through the night, linking me irrevocably to their cause.

Then, at last, I slept. Or tried, anyway.

I flopped over on one side and punched a pillow into submission, flailing a little on the enormous, oversoft bed. The voluminous pillows, coverlets, and mattress tops were conspiring to drown me, but I didn't have the energy to move to the suite's second bedroom. I didn't have the energy to fall on the floor with one of the extra comforters either. I barely had enough wherewithal to keep breathing.

"You fight too long and too hard."

"Not you again," I groaned.

The chuckle that rolled over me did little to improve my mood. I slitted open one eye, and there, arrayed on the bed beside me, his body beneath the tangle of sheets and his head, chest, and one powerful arm and shoulder exposed, lay Armaeus. He rested his head in his hand as he watched me, his nearness and tone almost that of a lover. But we weren't that.

Well, technically we were, but not right now.

"We could be, if you were not so stubborn." He shrugged, the movement sending a ripple across his pectoral muscles and straight down my spine. "It would undoubtedly make you feel better."

"It would. But you'd be in trouble, trust me." I flopped over on my back, not missing the look of alarm that flitted across Armaeus's face. But since he was here…I had questions. Lots of them.

"Gamon sent those killers to harvest the hearts of the Revenants, didn't she? The timing is suspect, don't you think?" I let the sludge of emotions I'd experienced in the Revenant club and again at the church wash over me once more, my senses reviling everything that Gamon

90

was. Murderer. Torturer. Betrayer.

I'd never encountered the woman before meeting Annika Soo, so wrapped up in my own work finding artifacts and funneling money to Paris to finance my friend Father Jerome's work to protect the children of the Connected community that I hadn't really bothered to keep up with the more despicable reaches of the arcane black market. I'd heard rumors, whispers, but nothing more. Then those rumors began to be attached to a name more and more, a name at first I'd assumed was a man's, given the atrocities particularly against Connected children Gamon had perpetrated. Sexist, but true. Then Soo had lured Gamon into striking...but had underestimated the dark practitioner's strength. Gamon had killed Soo before I could reach her in time, then had fled as I'd cradled Annika's dying body.

Gamon had gone underground in the weeks since, only to resurface now. *Why now?*

"In what way is the timing suspect?" Armaeus asked blandly, though clearly he could tap into my thoughts if he really wanted to. Unfortunately, he was a big fan of making me work things out on my own. It was one of his most irritating qualities, which was saying something, considering he had a dozen.

"In the way that, if she had her ear to the ground at all, she'd have heard of the call for the artifacts," I groused. "She'd also have heard I'd become a secondary target. That's assuming she didn't place either of those calls herself. Either way, she knew I was going to be tied up, so she moved in while I was gone."

Armaeus inclined his head. "It seems a most likely scenario."

"But why now? These Revenants have been here for centuries. She could have attacked them at any point."

"It might not have been time to do so. Think of what they were harvesting."

"Blood, maybe? A living heart? I don't know what else." Other than the surgery to open the chest cavities, the bodies had been unmolested postmortem. No cuts to the head, no additional organs removed, no obvious other removal of skin and tissue. The assailants had first and foremost been after the hearts. "But why these kids? They're not the only immortals on the globe, and they're kind of hard to get to."

"True. But for all the attempts, there are relatively few immortals — or near immortals." Armaeus offered a rebuttal of my statement. "You, the Council."

"Wait," I frowned. "What about the witches and warlock sect?" I'd only met a few witches in my time, but I knew they lived well past a hundred.

"Their lifespan is longer, yes, but not as long as the Revenants. There are some who whisper that the oldest Revenant has walked the earth more than five hundred years."

I sighed. "Gamon is a Revenant, isn't she?"

Armaeus watched me with eyes that were more black than gold, a sign that his own abilities were getting triggered by the conversation. "That's never been proven."

"But it makes sense. She's held her reign of terror over the Soo family for generations. The few times we've fought, she hasn't tired. According to Ma-Singh and the House generals, her MO hasn't changed from one generation to the next. But if she is one of these…" I flapped my hand wearily, "people, she wouldn't need more of them for her own research, right? In the past she's harvested the organs of Connecteds to fuel her technoceutical development. So, what, she's on to bigger, better drugs now to feed into the arcane black market? One that requires Revenants? She wouldn't need them." I sighed, knowing my logic was running in circles but unable to stop the chase. "She could utilize her own DNA to cook up whatever noxious technoceutical she's testing now."

"Unless she doesn't want her DNA alone," Armaeus said reasonably. "And in truth, if she's searching for a heart, losing hers might be further than she's willing to go. She'd need donors."

"Donors." I winced. "Are there any other reports of Revenants gone missing?"

"They're a reclusive group."

I eyed him. "They sure contacted you in a hurry."

"I'm reclusive as well. We are, in that sense, kindred spirits."

"And yet you're not being a recluse now." I lifted myself up on my elbows, staring hard at Armaeus. "You came personally, to help them out. Why? And don't give me that bullshit about wanting to help me astral travel. Your presence here totally violates the Council's whole noninterference code, and you know it."

Armaeus didn't rise to the bait. He was annoying that way.

"It does, in the narrowest interpretations of that code," he said calmly. "But remember, paramount over even the need to remain apart from the plight of those who wield magic in this world, is our sacred charge to ensure the *balance* of magic. There is some indication that Gamon is looking to upset that balance, and we cannot allow that."

"Upset it how?"

Armaeus leaned closer to me, his intense gaze raking over me. "Tell me about the Gods' Nails," he said. "How they…attached to you. How they worked."

I glanced at him. His eyes were deep and profound, and I could feel the insidious pull of their magic. "Setting aside the fact that you're changing the subject, why are you trying to compel me to answer you? I told you what the nails are already."

"You told me what you believed." He shook his head. "But I need you to show me your memories once again, Miss Wilde. They're currently blocked to me."

"Yeah?" That surprised me. Normally I kept a pile of readily accessible memories for Armaeus to shuffle through if he ever stumbled upon my brain without me noticing, just to keep him occupied and not off sniffing into the more dangerous corners of my cerebral cortex. My adventure with the Norse artifacts fit solidly into the category of useless extraneous details—I wouldn't have blocked that.

Nevertheless, I refocused my attention on the events, letting Armaeus see them as I verbally recalled them. At his murmured insistence, I slowed down my accounting. I also relaxed deeper into the bed, my voice dropping to a low murmur. Armaeus didn't seem to have any trouble following me, even when my mumbles devolved into really loud thoughts.

I opened one eye. "You're not really in bed with me, are you?"

His own gaze remained amused, assessing. "Is that a problem?"

"Just answer the question directly for once in your life. I'm in no mood to figure it out on my own."

His laugh rumbled over me. Sounded real, felt real, the bed moving with the tremor of his body. But that didn't mean anything with the Magician. He could project himself anywhere he needed to be, even in the flesh, I suspected, though he hadn't ever owned up to teleportation.

Fortunately, he didn't make me punch him to figure out the truth. I was way too tired to punch anyone.

"I am not physically present, no. I left Barcelona three hours ago, and am now en route back to Las Vegas. There are issues there I need to address."

En route. That presupposed a plane, not a magic

carpet. Interesting.

I squinted at him. "Issues like what?"

"Council issues. By your own admission, not your concern."

I was never too tired to roll my eyes. "What, trouble in Paradise Valley already?" I prodded. "You guys have a full complement of council members now, I thought. So what's the problem?"

"There is no problem." Armaeus's answer was beyond luxury-car-salesman cool. He'd ratcheted all the way up to cosmeceutical commercial, and he purred his next words out in a way that had me rethinking my cold cream. "We could always use more council members. There remain three positions to be seated, though, unlike the rest of the council, the remaining two members are no one I know personally."

I frowned. I wasn't good at math, but even I could pick up on this one. "Three positions, but two members? How does that work?"

"You forget, there is no Empress on the council. That will likely be the easiest position to fill."

The contemplation in the Magician's voice rankled me. "I'm not taking that job, Armaeus."

He smiled smugly. "I wouldn't ask you to. You've made your choice by casting your lot with the House of Swords. It's a strong position for you as the war escalates."

A true statement, but the fact it came from Armaeus made me doubt the extent of its truth. "The war can take a powder," I grumbled. "I'm going to find Gamon. That's my priority right now."

He hesitated, then inclined his head. "I entrust you to your House. However, recall that Annika Soo tried for years to track Gamon—unsuccessfully. I would suggest you speak to Ma-Singh about what he knows and what he doesn't, and focus on filling in the gaps."

"Fair enough." I picked up the thread of his original conversation. "So who are you recruiting for the Empress role?" I totally didn't want that job, but I hadn't given much thought to the idea of someone else filling it.

"There are several viable candidates," Armaeus said, his evasion so obvious that I buried the spike of annoyance and jealousy that reared up. He was pushing my buttons on purpose, I knew. And, I reminded myself, I didn't care who he chose for his kickball team. I had my own team to take care of.

Still…

"What are the other positions?" I screwed up my face, trying to find the holes. There were twenty-one Major Arcana cards, but some corresponded more closely to humans than others. I wouldn't exactly want to try to find the human incarnation of The Sun—I suspected it didn't exist. But all this information was in the council's secret playbook, which I hadn't gotten hold of. Yet.

True to form, Armaeus put me off as well. *"You should rest, Miss Wilde,"* he murmured, and now that I was focusing on him, I realized he'd been speaking in my mind all along. It had only seemed like he was real. Like first loves and low-fat fudge.

"Uh-huh. Don't think I won't remember this question, buddy. You can't avoid me forever," I griped, but the truth was, I was already drifting off, so quickly that I almost didn't hear his last words.

"I consider the tragedy of that possibility more than you could ever imagine," he whispered. Then he was gone.

CHAPTER TEN

I didn't remember him doing so, but Armaeus must have left a parting gift of healing before he whisked away, because I woke feeling better than I had in days. That ebullience lasted all the way to me exiting the bedroom portion of my suite and encountering my assembled House team. They'd congregated in the suite's public area after I'd alerted Nikki that I'd rejoined the living, but none of them seemed especially happy to see me.

"You're recovered?" Nigel spoke first, his face unreadable as he swept a quick, hard gaze over me.

"Tip-top. What's happened?"

Ma-Singh had stood when I entered, and now gestured to a laptop on the table. "Reports of other attacks," he said succinctly. "Milan, Munich, Tokyo. No other deaths or kidnappings identified yet, but the damage has drawn much unwanted attention."

I frowned. "I didn't know we were that plugged into their community."

"We weren't," Nigel interjected with a scowl. "They're now plugged into us. After you found the two youths, additional calls hit our secure channel. The expectation is we will put the House resources in play to protect the Revenants."

I lifted my brows. "Because Armaeus told them we would?"

"No." He stared hard at me. "Because you did."

"Oh." I considered that, but he was right. I'd made that vow to myself, though. How had the Revenants heard me? "Armaeus benefits, though. He knows I believe that Gamon is behind these attacks, and for whatever reason, he's not one of her fans. The Council can't act directly to impact the balance of magic, but indirectly...." I gestured to our assembled group. "Here we are."

"Not for the first time either," Ma-Singh interjected. "Madam Soo had developed strong ties to the Magician of the Arcana Council in her final years. She committed our resources twice before on tips the Council provided indirectly, about obscure pockets of Connected souls. Once to protect a deeply hidden monastery in Tibet that had sustained a terrible attack, once to protect an extended coven in Norway."

I frowned. "And both of those were being harmed by Gamon?"

"Madam Soo believed so. We saw no evidence Gamon was behind the attacks, but once our teams were in place, those attacks stopped. We've monitored those communities ever since." He pointed to the screen, where I could see several blue dots winking across a black and green schematic of the world. "We have kept them safe. Now we must keep the Revenants safe as well."

I stepped forward to get a better view of the map. "They're almost exclusively in Europe and a handful in Asia and the Americas. Is that weird?"

"These are all the ones Jonathan is aware of, communities of at least a dozen, sometimes upwards of several hundred souls. There are outliers, solo travelers, but in terms of communities, the Revenants keep much to themselves."

Nikki made a face. "Kind of keeps the dating pool limited."

Ma-Singh made a dismissive gesture. "Madam Soo thought the same of the other communities we assisted. The monks receive supplicants every few years, even in their remote location. Those men—and they are exclusively men—are trained and join the monastery, replenishing their numbers. The covens also intermix with local populations, with the lines of power usually moving through the females. Not every child is blessed with the Gift. Those that show promise have the option of entering the community, learning the practice. I suspect with the Revenants, it's the same."

I nodded. These communities had survived for millennia far enough under the radar that they'd been protected from both the mainstream populace and arcane enemies. Clearly, they were doing something right. But any contact they had with the outside world was a risk. Had someone made a poor choice in revealing their location, or was Gamon a Revenant herself, as I thought, exploiting her own kind to advance some new drug?

Either way, she had to be stopped.

"Ask Jonathan to compile a list of recent births in the Revenant community involving non-Revenant co-parents, anything in the last ten years," I told Ma-Singh. "But I want to move forward as if it's Gamon behind these deaths. Which means we have to determine if it's a meaningful series of attacks or merely a distraction."

"And in either case, why you and why now?" Nikki asked. "This is a very public attack. Last time she did that, she killed Annika Soo. In order to draw Annika out, however, Gamon attacked Swords members. These Revenants, they're not part of the House of Swords, they're not your people. And regardless of what

Jonathan says, those kids you found aren't true children. So why does she think you'll bite on this bait?"

I sighed, studying the screen. It blinked unhelpfully at me. There was something here I was missing, something important. "We'll need people to guard these Revenant communities, regardless," I said. "She won't strike the same group twice, I don't think, but the other Revenant communities are at risk."

"As you wish, Madam Wilde," Ma-Singh's voice remained calm and controlled.

I pondered the three red blips on the screen. "There's no pattern, right? To these three locations that have been attacked?"

"None that we've been able to ascertain," Nigel said.

"There has to be a reason…" I concentrated more intently, but nothing was coming to me. "I need…" I stopped myself before I could go any further. What I needed was the Council, but I couldn't trust their help, not entirely.

Ma-Singh shifted uneasily. "We have…other resources, Madam Wilde, that can assist you."

"I know." I waved him off. The last thing I needed was more bodyguards. "I'm well protected. You're good there."

"You misunderstand." Ma-Singh regarded me soberly, and I refocused on him. The Mongolian's eyes seemed more distant. "You recall the trainer in Las Vegas, the sword master."

"Kunh Lee," Nikki supplied, and I winced.

"Yeah, no," I said. "That's not the kind—"

Ma-Singh lifted a hand to stop my rebuttal. "We have resources for the body, and for the mind. Madam Soo was a diligent student of both."

Something in his tone made me pause. Nigel was regarding him as well. "I didn't know about this," he said stiffly.

"Madam Soo did not share it with most of the House. The training she received was very specialized. Her mental abilities were never what she wished them to be, except for a very brief time after her relationship began with the Council. But through her studies, she was able to enhance her natural intuition and sensitivity." He paused and turned to me. "Given that you have more native ability, it could benefit you. But it is an arduous path of seeking."

My sense of trepidation had been growing throughout his little speech, and I seized on this last bit as validation for my reaction. "Time isn't really on our side here, Ma-Singh. And I know, I know—I get it. Speed and distraction is the enemy of the noble mind, but we can't take a time-out so I can get all Zen."

If anything, the general's scowl grew deeper. "But you have the potential to outstrip Madam Soo as a leader by relying on your abilities more than she ever could. As the head of the House of Swords, you must surely wish to use your skills to the best of their ability."

"Time, Ma-Singh," I said again, pointing to the screen. "I don't want to come back from my sojourn up the mountain and find fifteen more red flashing lights here."

"But it will take us days to mobilize forces. You could use that time to your advantage," the general pressed.

"I don't think Zen mastery is something you can grab in a drive-through." I tried to temper my voice, but enough was enough. "It's a great idea, just not a great idea now."

"The challenge that lies before us will require mastery, but you remain a novice of your own mind willfully?"

The tone of rebuke in Ma-Singh's voice and face was unlike him, but he wasn't wrong. Nigel and Nikki,

101

generally two of my strongest advocates, were remaining unhelpfully mute on the subject. Which also annoyed me.

"Fine," I snapped at length, just to move off this point. "If you know someone who can pump me up in the time it takes us to scramble our people to cover these other Revenant communities, great. And that doesn't mean technoceuticals either. For that matter, we need to start targeting the primary labs for the newest drugs on the market, find out which ones are using human tissue in their manufacturing process." I grimaced. "Specifically, heart tissue. If there's a lab that specializes in such harvesting…"

I let my words trail off, but Nikki finished the thought for me. "Then they've been using tissue from straight-up Connecteds. Powerful, maybe, but still mainstream. Heart tissue from a Revenant might kick things up to a totally new level."

Ma-Singh's phone chirped from its position at the side of the table, and he picked it up, his face tightening as he read the screen. "Another attack, this one at a temple site. Two children missing." He slanted me a glance. "True children, only appear to be around ten or twelve years old."

"Where?" Nikki and Nigel were on their feet now, and my own heart surged in my chest. Two more children! This was becoming an epidemic. As soon as we reached one site and stabilized it, another one would blow up.

"Tokyo," he said. "They're asking for you specifically, Madam Wilde, to find them—in person, not…" He hesitated, "as a wraith."

I smiled. It would take time for the general to get used to my ability to astral travel, but that was okay. I wasn't a fan of it either.

"I'll go with you," Ma-Singh said staunchly.

"We'll all go," Nigel echoed.

"No." I shook my head. "You and Nikki have to stay on call if there's another attack here in Barcelona. If there are more children to find."

"Dollface, I appreciate the vote of confidence, but I'm not you," Nikki objected.

"You don't have to be. You're a cop, and you've got those instincts. And you're Connected. Which is a skill we have in short supply." Something about that bothered me too, but now wasn't the time to revamp the House of Swords' recruiting policies.

It took another hour of logistics and arguing before Ma-Singh and I finally left the hotel, and another sixteen hours to get to Japan. Along the way, as I'd feared, another Revenant community got hit, this one in Warsaw. No immediate deaths or missing persons reported, but the mounting hysteria was clear. Eventually, someone was going to pick up on the pattern of these reclusive communities getting attacked, even if they didn't know anything about the Revenants' true nature.

If any whiff of that got out...

The thought struck me so quickly I nearly gasped. I turned to Ma-Singh, who was studying multiple screens and muttering in Mongolian into his headset mic.

"Who is Gamon afraid of?" I asked, so loud he blinked up in confusion.

"What do you mean?"

"She's flying under the radar, killing and kidnapping in such a way that *we* know what she's doing, but no one else does. Why? No way she's afraid of the police or Interpol. So who?"

Ma-Singh tightened his jaw. "To my knowledge, there is nothing and no one that she fears."

"But that's not true," I said. "She's being selective — very selective. She wants to draw me out, we got that part. But she's moving fast—quick hits, different parts of the globe... No one knows who she's going to target next. And in two places now, she's taken hostages. Not even hostages: victims. Why so many, and why now? She's acting like someone who's about to get shut down."

"Possibly." I could see Ma-Singh wasn't buying it, and to be fair, he knew Gamon and her practices better than I did. "Or she's got an order to fill."

That stopped me. "An order."

He gestured to the screens. "You ask why Gamon would move fast. The answer is that there must be a window of opportunity that is only open for a short period of time. If someone needed product, and needed it in a hurry, Gamon would scramble. If they needed prime donor tissue, then she'd have to go to the top of what was available. She clearly knows about the Revenant communities, so much about them that it's likely she's been gathering intel over time. Now she's electing to use that information. Not because of fear of traditional authorities, I don't think. She would laugh at that suggestion. But she's either afraid of some nontraditional authority that she is beholden to, or she has to fulfill a black market deal that requires an increase in her production. And to do that, she needs you distracted."

"So she's throwing missing children in my path," I said. "Nice."

"You must track her with equal duplicity." Ma-Singh scowled at me. "You cannot rely on traditional means here."

Not more of this. "Ma-Singh," I began, but it was his turn to hold up a hand.

"Hear me out," he insisted. "You are Connected, Madam Wilde. You were chosen to lead this House by the revered Madam Soo not only because of your strong heart and mind, but because of what you bring to us. Not fighting skill, though your courage is fierce. Not tactical prowess, though you are resourceful."

I frowned. "Well, when you put it like that..."

In truth, I'd never understood why Annika Soo *had* chosen me. I'd recovered family treasure for her, nothing more. It'd been a complex job, but it'd just been one job. Thrusting the reins of a multinational syndicate into my hands on her deathbed had baffled everyone. Including me. Still did. Probably always would.

Ma-Singh watched me closely. "You know why. It is because in you she saw that which she could never be. What she wanted more than anything for her people."

"I'm a Tarot reader—"

"You're not. You're much more." Ma-Singh's implacable intensity was beginning to show in his fierce, lined face. "Madam Soo consulted her own teachers after she first encountered you. Teachers in Japan. I didn't realize it at the time, but since her death, I have pieced together a timeline. She told no one, not even me, I suspect not her closest allies in the House either.

"All we knew is that she had hired you to find her mother's missing amulet. But it is now clear that she intended more for you from the start. Perhaps not quite so quickly—Madam Soo could not have predicted her own death, or she would have arranged her people so that there were fewer fatalities. But she knew you would be an asset to the House of Swords. To know that, she would have had to be told, and told by someone she trusted implicitly." He glared at me. "She would not have entrusted her House to a mere card reader, Madam Wilde. Deep down, you know this is true."

I blew out a long breath. There was no way Soo could have known about my true capabilities—not when I didn't know what they were. Heck, the depth of my weird continued to flummox Armaeus, which was no small feat.

"Let's say you're correct," I ceded, unable to resist the ferocity of his belief in me. "What does that get us?"

"It gets me the satisfaction of you taking up your mantle." He thumped his chest. "It gets you the honor of taking another step on your path. When we are finished in Tokyo at the site of the attack, you will meet with Soo's teacher. She will give you the instruction you need."

"Right." I looked out the window. "I think you're coming out on the better end of this deal. You get to keep doing what you're doing, and not suddenly have to change your ways."

He chuckled. "I am coming out on the better end, yes," he said. "Because I have you."

CHAPTER ELEVEN

The Tokyo site was a disaster, but not in the way that Barcelona had been. Tucked into a collection of houses on the edge of the Meiji Jingu forest, the Revenants had sustained no damage to their residences. There hadn't even been a bomb set off, though the shell-shocked expressions on the elders' faces made believing that difficult. Instead, the children had been stolen from their teachers in plain sight, during a ceremony at the Meiji Jingu shrine in the heart of the forest.

Ma-Singh stood at respectful attention as I met with the three eldest of the community in a hushed walled garden, the beautiful space traced over with crushed-rock pathways. In the midst of all the screaming activity of Tokyo, the oasis inspired contemplation, especially as it lay so near the vast green space of the park. The elders murmured their answers to my questions, with Ma-Singh serving as a translator.

"There was a wedding preparation underway at the shrine, maidens and priests in traditional wear, very beautiful," the Mongolian general said now, his expression stiff in the face of the elders' anguish. "The children were there, then they were not. There was no fire, no attack. They simply vanished."

"Chips?"

Ma-Singh shook his head. "They honor the old traditions, not the new. None of the community has received any tracking device nor mark of any kind to mar the body."

I considered this, taking in the stooped figures before me. These men must be extremely old, by Revenant standards. More surprising, they were Japanese in appearance, with long, thick white hair, richly toned skin, and bright, ageless eyes set into their wizened faces. They were dressed in somber black suits, hands folded over each other, and they regarded me with a kind of fatalism that was unnerving.

"They don't think I'll be able to find the children, do they?"

Ma-Singh hesitated, then shook his head, translating for the old men. They in turn shook their heads, and the sadness in their eyes was overwhelming. "They do not. They called you more as witness to assist you in finding other children. Their own are gone. They know this in their hearts."

"How?"

Another pause. Then Ma-Singh spoke again, more gently this time. "They are students of the same teacher who instructed Madam Soo. Sensei Chichiro is very wise, and all-seeing. She told them their greatest fears had been made manifest."

"Their greatest fears." I frowned as Ma-Singh explained to the elders what he had just told me. As the men spoke in another flurry of Japanese, I stared around the serene garden. They lived here, on the edge of an enormous green space, truly in the world but not of it. Their greatest fear was that one of their own would be thrust into that world without protection, forced to confront its barbarity and pain.

I refocused on the elders. "How long have they lived in this place?"

Ma-Singh interpreted their soft volley of words. "Since before the shrine was built. They've maintained their lodgings here since the early 1900s. Before that, they lived in the mountains, but it is in some ways easier to lose oneself in a city than in the country."

"How do they stay hidden now?" I shifted my gaze to Ma-Singh. "I ask because someone *had* to know about them, in order to find them at all. Someone had to see…" I frowned. Gamon had skills, Gamon was Connected. She could astral travel as I did. But she still had to have some idea of where these people lived. Tokyo was enormous, and it was only one of dozens of locations worldwide. To know specifically when and how to strike, to slip in unawares and spirit away a couple of boisterous boys—that took more than planning. That took the kind of knowledge that kept a person six steps ahead of everyone else.

Ma-Singh interrupted my thoughts with his harsh voice, speaking to the elders once more. His brows lifted in surprise at their answer.

"He says they do not remain fully hidden. The emperor has known of their existence since well before the construction of the Meiji Jingu shrine. Their community did not seek to hide from its responsibilities, merely from its neighbors."

"And the emperor has let them live here, unmolested?"

Another exchange, and the eldest man allowed himself his first weary smile. Something approaching a twinkle flashed in his eyes. Beside me, Ma-Singh grunted.

"Elder Hajime says the location for the Meiji Jingu shrine is popularly believed to have been chosen because of an iris garden that grows deep in the forest." Ma-Singh pointed to the elder. "Hajime is the one who led the future emperor to that site when the man was still a little boy, and told him that he was the one who planted the irises. When the emperor visited the site much later, as an old man, he recognized Hajime. At that moment, the emperor declared the site for the shrine to be established in the location, and for the community's names to be struck from the records, but accorded the highest honors. Those honors have remained in place since. When the shrine was bombed in World War II, it was this community that first began clearing the rubble. They do not live as they do to evade their responsibility, but their path has been straight nevertheless. Until now."

"Until now." I grimaced. "So their community is an open secret. Anyone from low-level government on up could know they're here."

"They could," Ma-Singh allowed. "But they have never been troubled before. Also, there were several children at the shrine that day, smaller and less active than the boys who went missing, more likely targets. They were left unharmed."

Which brought me back to why here, and why now, and why these boys. I fixed the elder with a hard stare. "Was there anything unique about the boys, other than that they were boisterous? Were they special in any way as compared to the others?"

Elder Hajime listened closely to Ma-Singh, then frowned. He turned and consulted with his fellows, the two of them nodding quickly at his words, then responding in a flurry of Japanese. Ma-Singh's translation pace picked up to keep up with their answer.

"They were always laughing, happy boys...inseparable...smart and funny. The best of their class. Kind and—"

"Back up there. Best of their class? You mean in school?"

Ma-Singh nodded. "They were considered top

performers."

I thought about the pair of Revenants in Barcelona. Also the pride of their community, children who'd excelled at their studies. Which again presupposed a crime of deliberation, not grabbing the easiest and first victim.

All of it led to only one conclusion, but the thought of it made me sick to my stomach. Genetic manipulation had been a practice among farmers and breeders for thousands of years, and I knew the practices of the arcane black market and technoceutical industries. Connected children had long been considered targets for their more depraved practices and products, but Revenants…

"Were these children high-level Connected?" I asked Ma-Singh, unsurprised when he translated the question to see two of the old men shaking their heads.

The third, however, Hajime, fixed me with a long stare. He spoke without dropping his gaze, and Ma-Singh supplied his response.

"He asks why you would ask such a thing."

"Because these kids were singled out. And all of you — everyone here — has the same genetic disposition toward long life. So they were taken for reasons other than that. It had to be something else, something more."

Elder Hajime frowned and stared at me a long time. At length, he sighed and spoke again.

Ma-Singh blinked at him, then swiveled his gaze to me. "They were not high-level Connected, not in the sense you mean. But they were good, he says. Pure of heart. In every generation among Revenants, there are those who are the symbols of the future, who make life in such seclusion worthwhile. These boys…they were those symbols. But he says no one knew of that. He had told no one for he was the elder, and it was his knowledge alone to bear."

I frowned, not missing the gazes of the other two men. They were not angry in the slightest, or put out, but they were clearly surprised. This information was news to them. "And he told no one about this."

"There was no purpose in sharing the information. It is transferred at the end of life from one elder to the next."

"And, so, what happens if the elder gets hit by a bus?"

Ma-Singh blinked in surprise, but I waved him on. "It's important. I need to know that. Because *someone* found out. Someone knew. Unless these children glowed in the dark, there's no other way for Gamon to single them out."

Reluctantly, Ma-Singh turned back to the elder, who now stared at him intently. I could tell the general reworked the question, but the point definitely got across. Three pairs of eyes fixed on me with flat curiosity.

Ma-Singh shifted uncomfortably, waiting.

At last the old man spoke, Ma-Singh's voice rumbling in its thready wake. "There is an oral history, handed down from elder to elder, preserved and protected by each community. It is spoken aloud once per year, by me, to a scribe, who writes the information in the scrolls, then gives me the scrolls. They have not been touched, I can assure you."

"Got it. And this scribe?"

The elder's unworried tone didn't waver. "He writes under the influence of a drug and cannot remember what he has heard." Ordinarily, this type of explanation would have sent off warning bells, but in this case, I believed the old man. I'd seen my share of powerful drugs. Memory zappers were easy to come by, and probably had been for millennia. Which left only one option. Gamon.

"The last time you did this year in review, was when — start of the year? Summer solstice? There has to be a set date for all of you, I'm thinking."

The elder inclined his head. "Solstice," Ma-Singh translated. "When the clock strikes midnight in each community, the scroll is prepared."

"Got it." I nodded. Not so difficult for Gamon to be on hand for that, hovering and listening in. I gave Elder Hajime an apologetic smile. "Next year…" Then I shook my head. By next year, Gamon would be dead. Or I would be. And if I was, the Revenants would have more trouble to worry about than someone eavesdropping on their scroll ceremony.

I turned my mind back to the problem at hand. "How old were the children?"

"Young, manifesting as children of ten or twelve years. Two boys, in this case. Good friends all. They were fascinated by the world around them, especially the beauty of the gardens at the shrine. When they went missing, at first the community thought they had gone exploring. They had not heard yet of the attacks, so they were not watching the children closely. But when they didn't return…"

I nodded. We talked a little longer, but eventually there was nothing left to say. I excused myself and turned away from the old men and their expanding circle of grief. Ma-Singh had asked after the boys' parents too. They were in the vast forest over these walls, searching endlessly for their sons. That image was not one I would forget anytime soon.

Grimacing, I pulled out my deck of cards and traced the crushed-rock path a bit more deeply into the lushly planted courtyard. I passed multiple pools surrounded by tall grasses and ornamental trees. Work had been done here recently, new flowers planted at the water's edge, an almost discordant flash of color, some sort of ornamental lily. Various tools had been arranged neatly to the side, evidence that the maintenance of this place was likely a never-ending process for the elders and their community. I sat on a low bench, watching the water as I pulled three cards.

I didn't look at the cards right away, however. I had a bad feeling about the reading and this place. Not because of the men—they were genuine, their grief unfeigned. But there was still a darkness here, the same darkness I recognized from the nightclub in Barcelona. The darkness I'd attributed to Gamon.

The cards suddenly felt heavy in my hand, and I glanced down, immediately seeing one of my least favorite cards, the Five of Swords. A card that could mean many things in a search, but its metaphorical explanation was that of an empty or hollow win. Quickly returning it to the deck, I glanced to the second card, then the third.

Dread thickened my throat, making it difficult to breathe. The Three of Swords was becoming a fast friend in these terrible days—its meaning one of grief, and also a cut to the heart. Then finally there was the Seven of Pentacles. That card showed a young man resting on his shovel, surveying the fruits of his labor. It meant a job well done, but also a caution not to rest on one's laurels, instead directing the reader to take up his or her work and start anew.

But that wasn't what it meant here.

"Ma-Singh?" I shouted. Or, I wanted to shout. The words were stuck in my throat, however, along with the breath that wouldn't come as my gaze lifted and fixed upon the newest flowers planted in this sacred space. I couldn't ask Ma-Singh to do this for me, I couldn't ask the elders to do it. And yet, I feared what I would find.

Unless I was very much mistaken, Gamon had been here, in this quiet garden. Adding a permanent insult to an even more permanent injury.

Heart quailing, I abandoned the cards on the bench and slid to my knees in front of the profusion of lilies. I decided to attempt only one small patch. I didn't want to disturb the area too much, but I also couldn't—wouldn't—defile this space with a full-scale search if I was wrong.

As I dug, a thousand questions went through my mind. How could anyone have gotten into this courtyard without being seen? Ma-Singh said everyone had left the complex to start the search, but surely they'd locked up behind themselves. Then again, picking a lock was less difficult than most people realized. And if the kidnappers had moved fast...

But why come here at all? Other than causing pain, what was there possibly to be gained?

I scooped deep into the soil, surprised at how soft it was, fresh and loose in my hands. No one had tried to conceal this burial, if that was what it was. Looking at the flowers more intently, it had to be, though. The color of the lilies was all wrong for this serene space, a discordant flash of orange and red amidst the soft whites and blues. As I pulled another clump free, then a third, I could feel a new wetness on my cheeks, but I didn't stop to brush it away.

I suddenly knew what I would find here, hidden beneath the flowers. I didn't know how much I would find, but it would be enough.

It was.

Five minutes into digging, I saw the first sign. A swath of cloth, some sort of wrapping, not pants or a long robe. But it was new fabric, a bright and bold red. The color of wedding clothes.

I didn't remember shouting, but must have, as Ma-Singh's sharp cry of alarm echoed around the walled garden. Then came the sound of rushing feet.

The Five of Swords, I thought bitterly, as the elders emerged through the tall grasses of this sacred space.

I had won, and I had lost.

CHAPTER TWELVE

Ma-Singh and I rode in silence out of the city the following day, winding our way deep into the mountains. I stared out the window of the rental SUV without seeing any of the famed beauty of the Japanese countryside.

Instead, I could still only see the bodies. Impossibly small in death, the children had been buried in a single deep grave, one on top of the other. Their perfect forms were unmolested except in one important way. Their hearts had been removed, this time completely. Gamon had gotten what she wanted.

"We're approaching the sensei's home," Ma-Singh rumbled beside me. The two guards in the front of the vehicle ignored us. I didn't know their names, or where they had come from. I didn't care either. Twice now, I'd been too late to save the children I'd been asked to retrieve. The two boys had died before I'd even landed in Tokyo, but the boy and girl in Barcelona—I'd been so close. I could have saved them, if I'd been faster. If I'd seen more, sooner.

That knowledge was the only reason why I agreed to accompany Ma-Singh on this journey into the mountains to see Annika Soo's teacher, the sensei Chichiro. No new deaths had been reported among the

Revenant communities. The House of Swords was fully deployed in their protection—so fully, Nigel was picking up rumbles of curiosity about the House's increased military presence from the other Aces assigned to the Houses of Pentacles, Cups, and Wands. I'd instructed him not to answer any questions.

Those Houses had not contacted me; I didn't know who ran them other than Pentacles, which was headed by my old frenemy and former client, Jean-Claude Mercault. And Mercault was into the technoceutical black market up to his fastidious French neck, making a fortune selling concoctions designed to augment Connected ability. He could wait until I was ready to talk to him.

Ma-Singh spoke again. "Sensei Chichiro is expecting you."

I didn't turn from the window. "You told her about the children?"

"The sensei does not require me to inform her of such things. She knew you would be coming, and now you are here. She will see you for one hour, she said, no longer. If you choose to return a second time, she will tell you the duration of that stay then."

That did make me glance his way. "I don't know if I'm in the right frame of mind for Japanese mysticism right now. This might be a bad idea."

He held up a finger. "One hour, Madam Wilde. You may choose never to return. But you can spare this one hour to see if the sensei can help you in your quest to find and destroy the assassin of your House's former leader and the killer of innocent children."

I winced. "Fair enough."

Ma-Singh smiled briefly, then nodded to the road in front of us. We'd begun to climb a fairly steep grade, switchbacking our way up the mountain. Somewhere along the way, we'd left the more modern roads too.

This one was still paved, but far narrower than it should be for such a steep incline.

"What if we meet someone coming down?"

"We won't."

I manfully resisted the urge to roll my eyes. "The sensei tell you that as well?"

"She is a very important woman, and she dictates her own schedule. She has known you would be coming and was prepared to greet you as Madam Soo's replacement."

Something in the way he made this pronouncement sent up a warning flag. "They were friends?"

"They were...well acquainted. Madam Soo began studying with her before she returned to rule the House of Swords."

"Great," I muttered, keenly aware that I was no Madam Soo. I hadn't studied anything longer than five minutes in more years than I could count. I kept this observation to myself. It was an hour, as Ma-Singh had said. It might be the longest hour of my life, but it would eventually pass.

We drove for easily another thirty minutes, long enough for me to close my eyes and imagine I was somewhere — anywhere else. But eventually the vehicle rolled to a stop, and I blinked back to awareness, straightening in the backseat. When Ma-Singh and the guards didn't move, I glanced at him.

"You alone can set foot on the ground here," he said. "She will know if we violate her rules."

I lifted a brow. "So after all your complaining, *this* is where you're going to leave me without protection?" I asked, needling him. "What if she kills me?"

Ma-Singh shook his head. "That is not the lesson you're here to learn this day."

"Well, that's a relief." I stared at him a moment longer, but when he didn't crack a smile, I groaned.

"Okay, she's got an hour. If I'm not out of there by then, and you don't come and get me out of whatever headlock she has me in, you're totally fired."

Still no reaction. I muttered something not very pro-Mongolian under my breath, then pushed the door open.

I stepped out onto the ground, which gave beneath my feet with a springiness I wouldn't have expected. Then again, nothing about this place was what I expected.

Granted, what I'd expected of the sensei's hut was born of a mishmash of pop culture images that stretched from *Kill Bill* to *The Karate Kid*, but still. The little cottage that stood before me wasn't shrouded in mists, and there were no skulls on spikes, so that was probably a good thing. The place was…cute, actually. A small stone building fronted by a flower-lined pathway, shaded by ornamental trees. The kind of place you'd expect a teacher to live in, versus, say, a ninja.

I realized I still hadn't moved, however. I determinedly took a step forward. Nothing exploded or disappeared, and I checked over my shoulder to see that the SUV hadn't dissolved into a holographic image. So far, so good.

By the time I reached the sensei's front door, I was warring between relief and flat-out panic that I was letting my guard down. Because relief was usually a signal for the ground to drop out from beneath me.

I lifted my hand to knock on the door, and it opened noiselessly in front of me. I blinked. I wasn't exceptionally tall, but I still hadn't expected to have to look down so far to take in the woman before me.

Several things struck me at once—fortunately none of which was Sensei Chichiro's fist, although it could have, as startled as I was by her appearance.

One, she was extremely compact, probably no more

than five feet tall. Second, she was young. Certainly no older than her fifties, which surprised me given how long she'd apparently been training Annika. Finally, she was smiling. At least, I think she was. Her lips were curved up at the ends and her eyes seemed warm. And not in the burning hellfires kind of way.

"Come in, come in," she said in a bright, chirpy voice. A voice that totally did not sound like it belonged to someone who could whip out a machete without notice, and that put me further on edge.

I stepped over the threshold, bracing myself for the illusion to come crashing down, but it didn't. Her house looked like a modern Japanese apartment, all clean lines and spare furnishings, painted in neutrals with splashes of pinks and blues. I could have been walking into a therapy session, and I noticed the tea steaming on the low table in front of the couch. Had Ma-Singh texted Chichiro while I dozed during the drive up? Or did she hustle up the tea while I'd stood rooted to the spot outside the SUV?

I paused and slipped off my boots, then turned in my stocking feet and bowed slightly, vaguely remembering not to hold out my hand. Chichiro startled me by holding out hers. "Your hands, Madam Wilde. Please."

Okay, this is it. I braced for impact, reminding myself that my one-hour session had already started. I'd survived a full minute of it without pain, so fifty-nine to go.

I placed my hands into the woman's outstretched palms, and she immediately tightened her grip to keep me from falling.

"Relax, Madam Wilde, truly."

That was easier said than done. Sensei Chichiro was one of the most powerful Connecteds I'd encountered this side of the Council, and her hands transmitted enough of an electrical charge that my knees wobbled. Though she must have noticed my reaction, she didn't let go, instead turning my hands over, palms up. She passed her thumbs over the bases of my wrists, and a flash of pain arced through me where the Gods' Nails had taken up temporary residence there.

Then it was gone, and her hands were back on her side of the playground.

"Better?" she asked, and I blinked, then stared down at my hands.

"Um...yes," I finally managed. I hadn't realized it, but I'd been carrying around residual pain in my hands since the nails had been yanked out. Healing didn't always mean feeling better, but I'd gotten used to the dull ache. Now it was gone. "Thank you."

She gestured to the low couch. "Sit. We do not have much time."

I sat, leaning forward as she also arranged herself on a cushioned chair at the head of the low table, not so much sitting as perching. She went about pouring the tea in a blur of action that I found impossible to follow. Then she was holding out a teacup, nodding to me. "Drink."

So far, this wasn't nearly the harrowing experience I was expecting. I took a sip of the tea, unraveling another notch of tension despite myself. The drink was crisp and clean tasting, some mixture of mint and spice, and didn't at all seem drugged. And we were still in Chichiro's front room, the SUV in clear view through the sheer curtains. Ma-Singh could leap right through the big window and save me if I started screaming, I was almost certain.

The sensei set down her own cup of tea, then studied me. "You have come to me because you cannot see clearly. It is a problem I am well acquainted with in Westerners."

"I...okay." I nodded, trying to parse a response. Technically, I hadn't come to the sensei, Ma-Singh had forced me here. That said, she wasn't wrong. I *hadn't* seen enough to rescue those children in time. I hadn't reached them before Gamon or her minions had. That needed to stop. I had to get faster — smarter. I needed to see more.

She smiled as if I'd spoken. "You do not see because there is too much before your eyes. They are veiled, and you prefer them veiled." She lifted a hand to forestall my immediate response. "Not consciously, perhaps. But that does not change the truth. When we see clearly and do not act, we have no one to blame but our own lack of courage. It is easier not to see, sometimes."

I tried not to feel defensive, but Chichiro moved on. "You do not have the luxury of not seeing any longer. You know this to be true. There is great ability within you and no discernment. I cannot teach discernment in an hour."

"Ah...well, I wouldn't think so," I said gamely. Mostly I was glad she knew about the hour limit.

"I can, however, help you see. Please come with me."

She stood, and I did as well, my heart beginning to hammer again. She turned and led the way down a narrow hallway, then opened the door at the far end. A dimly lit room lay beyond, with soft music playing. This was bad. Ma-Singh couldn't see me anymore. If I died during this operation, I would so come back to haunt his Mongolian ass.

Chichiro stepped into the room and waited for me to get my guts up enough to follow her. Though I couldn't tell in the gloom, it seemed like she was rolling her eyes at me. Snark was an international language, and I suspected she was fluent in it.

"Please remove your socks and your jacket, and lie

123

down here." She patted the table, and finally I saw the room for what it was…a spa treatment room, complete with a massage table.

Really? No wonder Madam Soo had come so often. I'd come here too if it meant I could get a rubdown, even from ol' Electric Hands.

Still, I couldn't quite allay a twinge of anxiety as I rolled off my socks and laid them and my jacket on a small teak ledge. Not giving myself a chance to think too much about it, I climbed onto the table, lying down stiffly. Chichiro covered me up to the shoulders with a blanket. I decided that if I was going to get assassinated, this was the way to do it.

"Will this hurt?" I asked, but she ignored me. I suddenly got the feeling that the room, the bed, was all an illusion, intended solely for my benefit, to calm my fears. Well, it was working. Sort of.

"I will say a prayer over you, then begin," Chichiro said, and when she closed her eyes, I felt mine naturally closing too. I would only shut them during the prayer, I resolved. Then I'd watch her every move. Of course, she probably suspected I'd do that. When better to catch me off guard and knife me in the throat?

My eyes popped open again, and Chichiro was looking down at me, her lips definitely now twisted into a grin. "It will be all right, Madam Wilde. The first time, there is no pain. When you return, that is different."

"Got it." *Note to self, do not darken this door again.*

She placed her hands on either side of my head, and the buzzing between my ears suddenly muted. She spoke then, in Japanese, I assumed, but I couldn't hear the words so much as sense their effect on me. She pressed her fingers into several points along my skull, and every nerve in my body fell limp, my bones turning to milk. That done, she moved to the base of the bed and slipped the blanket off one foot, keeping the other wrapped.

"Reflexology?" I managed, or I thought that was what I said. My eyes were slitted to half-mast, the surreal wash of relaxation dragging me down deep.

"A variant of. You..." She frowned, passing her hand over one foot, then another, but she said nothing further for several minutes. Every time she touched me, however, poking and prodding, something else seemed to unkink.

At last she spoke. "You are very damaged, Madam Wilde. Your kidneys, your ears, your stomach." Pause. "Your liver, your spine."

"Yeah, well. You should see the other guy."

"I do not have time to address these wounds. You will come back."

"Sure." I really didn't care what I said anymore, as long as she kept manipulating bones I was pretty sure had been broken more than a few times. She finally paused midway along the base of my toes on the right foot.

"There is no time," she murmured again, so much regret in her voice that I almost felt bad for her.

"It's okay, I'll—"

"Take three deep breaths, Madam Wilde."

On the second, she drove a knife through my skull.

CHAPTER THIRTEEN

"Stop that!" I screamed, or I think I screamed, yanking my feet out of Chichiro's grasp and hauling myself off the bed, scrambling into the corner of the room. My arms were flung wide, my hands outstretched, and I drove myself back, back until I came up against the solid surface of the wall.

Wall. Where there was a wall, there was a door. Where there was a door, there was a hallway, and a hallway would take me to Ma-Singh.

I needed these truths like I'd never needed anything before because—because I was blind.

"Madam Wilde!"

"Stay away from me!" I should have been grateful that Chichiro didn't finish the job right there. She could have, she should have—I would have. My brain was processing these thoughts too quickly, rampaging through pain and fear and disorientation, but all of it was superseded by a need to survive, to escape, to protect.

A flash of something in front of me made me flinch, and heat bathed my face. Somewhere there was a scream, but I focused only on the fact that I could still sense light. Light had to be good, right? It had to be.

But now the sound of crackling fire reached me, and

the acrid smell of something burning. Nothing wrong with those senses.

"Madam Wilde, you're all right, you're all right! It is simply your third eye!"

I'd used my third eye before, though. This was nothing like that — she had to be wrong about what was happening! Panic firing anew, I surged forward, my hands out to the side, banging against the wall until I reached the door. It was open, and I fell through it into the hallway, my lungs filling with smoke.

An enormous crash sounded far ahead, and Ma-Singh's voice boomed out with an appropriate level of fear. "Madam Wilde!" he roared. Then there was the sound of thudding footsteps, and the enormous bulk of something warm and unforgiving crashed into me, lifting me up in a bear hug and hauling me forward. "Sensei Chichiro-san!"

There was another round of shouting, but I couldn't focus on that, I couldn't focus on anything, as my eyelids flared wide and darkness — only darkness — greeted me. Ma-Singh swung me around, and that darkness dimmed ever so slightly, and I lurched in his arms, back toward the brightness, back toward —

"No, Madam Wilde," he shouted, jerking me back. "You can't help her."

Help...her? "I'm blind!" I nearly screamed, ripping myself bodily from him. He was so surprised, he dropped me to the ground. At least that was the explanation I was going with as I collapsed in a heap on the springy earth. When had we gotten outside?

I scrambled up and backward, swinging my head everywhere, but there was nothing. Darkness encroached all around me, and I lifted my hands to my face, running my palms over my forehead, my cheeks. My eyes were there! They should be working! I closed my lids, opened them again, and felt the tears sluicing down my cheeks.

"What's happening to me?" I gasped, shocked more that the words were no longer high and strident, but low, quiet, and filled with fear.

"Let me past!" Chichiro's voice had changed to one of absolute authority, almost palpable power, and I sensed her rushing up to me, even as I flopped myself back on my butt and tried to crab-walk away. The whistle of displaced air came a second too late for me to process it, but there was no missing the crack of a thick rod against the side of my knee, sweeping my legs out from under me and arresting my progress.

"Stop!" Chichiro commanded, entirely unnecessarily given the fact that I was now crumpled on the ground.

She crouched down beside me. "You are safe, Madam Wilde. You are not blind. Halt the fire you've released into my house."

I swung my head around toward the sound of her voice. I did feel safe, honestly, my panic instantly stripped away. But I was definitely still blind. Was this how Helen Keller had felt? Because this sucked.

Chichiro said something else, and I struggled to focus. "Fire — ?"

"My house," she said again, very calmly. "The fire. You are not blind, you aren't. I am telling you this, and I know it to be true. But I will be homeless if you don't stop the fireballs you've loosed in your panic."

Suddenly, comprehension dawned, along with a sick dread. "I don't know how to stop them," I whispered.

She spoke again as if we were discussing where to put away the Cheerios. "There is a stream beyond my house, farther up the mountain. It is fed by snows, very beautiful, very cold."

She continued on, describing the flowing water, and

suddenly—suddenly I could see it in my mind too, bolstered by her rich explanations. I knew it was there—knew it. Knew it was a place to park the fire, much as the hearth in the Viking stronghold had been. The shouts from the house abruptly stopped, then the sound of shattering glass reached my ears as twin streaks of heat flared faintly against my cheeks.

"Your poor house," I murmured, holding up my hands in…I don't know what. Shock. Embarrassment. Supplication. I imagined Chichiro's home in its beautiful simplicity, saw its clean lines, its empty spaces, its serene walls and polished floors. Even the room where I'd been blinded, so warm, so dim, so inviting. So…safe.

Ma-Singh hissed beside me, which didn't sound good, but Chichiro sighed with something that seemed much more positive.

"Good," she said simply, and her hands connected with mine, which I realized were still flailing weakly in the air, as if I could feel the space around me and give it form. At her touch, my heart rate slowed further, my breath easing in my throat. Unaccountably, tears began coursing down my cheeks, and I could feel them—I could feel the scratchiness of my eyeballs, the touch of my lids against their surface. They were there. My eyes were still right there. On my face. In their sockets.

"Why aren't they working?" I nearly moaned, hysteria mounting again within me despite Chichiro's calming touch.

"They are working," she said, tightening her hands on mine and bringing my palms together. "But they are not all you need to see."

I blinked rapidly, pulling my hands out of hers to rub my tears away. Then I focused on my hands.

"Nope, still nothing," I said, trying not to sound unhinged.

"Relax, Madam Wilde." There were more sounds of objects moving around me, the shifting of bodies, and I focused on that. I couldn't see anything, but I—I could sense the movement. Chichiro waving off the mass that was Ma-Singh; other, slighter forms in the background, also stepping away. I saw them not as images, though, but more…more as sensations. Part of the weave of the world that was still all darkness to me.

"Relax." Chichiro touched my knees, pulled my legs straight, then gradually lowered me to the ground. There was something beneath my head, some rolled-up cloth, but the grass beneath me was surprisingly dry. Hadn't it been misty when we'd driven up this mountain? Hadn't it smelled like rain?

She folded my unresisting hands over my stomach, then somehow produced a blanket. She covered me up to my chest. Dimly, I realized that this was the same position I'd been in when she'd ice-picked my brain, but Chichiro seemed so calm, so in control, that I wanted to believe she had my best interests at heart. And Ma-Singh hadn't thrown me into the SUV and fled down the mountain, so apparently he believed the same thing.

"My eyes…" I couldn't bring myself to put my fears into words, but fortunately, I didn't have to. Chichiro laid a calming hand on my shoulder, even squeezed it.

"Your natural sight remains as it ever has. You can see. But you have more than one way to see now. More than two eyes. Your brain is having to make a difficult choice, and is electing to choose neither. It happens, but not often. Only when the third eye is dominant."

"The third eye," I repeated. "There's a spot on my foot for that?"

Chichiro didn't honor that with a response. And she should have, because it would clearly be a place I'd avoid going forward.

"Your eye is open, but it is not used to seeing. It is

130

very strong, however." She laughed, a little grimly. "Very strong."

I winced, imagining the smoking wreck of her house. "So...how do I get it to close again? So I can see like a normal person?"

Another tinkling laugh. "But you are not a normal person, Madam Wilde. Why should you want to see like one? Especially when you have come all this way."

"Because —"

"Shh. Be still, Madam Wilde. Breathe deeply for me."

I'd played that game before, but since the woman was nowhere near my feet, I figured I'd be somewhat safe. I breathed in deep once...twice...and tensed, holding my breath for another long count. When nothing knifed through me, I gradually relaxed, all while Chichiro dropped a light, reassuring touch on my crown, my cheeks, my shoulders. It wasn't a massage, but simply a reminder she was there, that she was unperturbed by my blindness, and it went a long way toward reassuring me that it would go away.

"Can you picture a knotted rope?" she asked, her voice almost as drowsy as I felt.

I furrowed my brow. "A what?"

"Any item that symbolizes control to you. A rope. A chain of many links. Something you are comfortable with. Something you know well."

"Right." I imagined my gun. I don't know why, but the image formed in my mind so clear and crisp, it was as if I was holding it in my hand — except it was in front of me, isolated against the blackness yet somehow lit up and displayed in rich, perfect detail.

"That's good," she murmured. "Turn it in your mind. See it from all angles."

This was an image I could get used to. My pistol was sleek, deadly, and accurate, small enough to fit in my palm easily, its firing action so smooth that I never had to worry about my hand jerking and throwing off my aim. I loved that gun for all that I tried not to use it. It wasn't on me now, but it was in the SUV. It was a good gun. I could use more like it.

"Stay relaxed," cooed Chichiro, but she had it all wrong. With each new gun popping up in my mind, I became more relaxed, not less. A barricade of loaded guns formed around me. Guns I never wanted to need, but always wanted to have at my disposal. That wasn't a bad idea, truly. I should add more of them.

"Madam Wilde, I am laying my hand upon your brow. Can you feel that?"

The image of the guns wavered as my focus shifted, but Chichiro was right there again. "Keep the image in your mind, strong and full. See those — see what you have imagined. Is it strong?"

Piles of guns. A prepper's dream come true. I smiled, feeling my facial muscles stretch and lengthen. "It's pretty strong," I said.

Beyond Chichiro came an amused Mongolian grunt.

"I'm going to move my hands, then, here." She placed gentle long-fingered hands over my eye sockets. "Can you still see the image?"

"I can."

"Focus on the image. The safety and control it provides. The surety of it. Tell yourself you are safe, and that all that you see is safe too. That you welcome it, embrace it. That you can see all that you wish, exactly as you wish."

"'kay." This part was getting a little woo. I'd never been great at meditation, though I had to say, I'd never tried it with guns before. Chichiro was clearly on to something.

"Open your eyes beneath my hands, Madam Wilde, but do not lose the image in your mind."

"Got it." I paused a long while, gearing myself up for this. I imagined the guns, their great piles of gleaming hardware. I imagined the detail of the ones closest to me. Slowly, carefully, I eased my eyes open, expecting to see darkness.

It wasn't darkness, though. Not exactly. It was...hands. Hands covering my eyes. I could see the rosy outline of Chichiro's fingers as they eased slightly open.

"I can see your hands," I whispered.

"And the image in your mind? Focus on it while your eyes remain open."

I frowned, but that was harder to hold on to. The piles diminished, until there was only one small mound. I imagined myself kneeling over that mound, getting closer, my face right up against the gleaming weapons. That I could keep steady, even as I could see the lines grow more distinct in Chichiro's hands. She was widening the spaces between her fingers, letting additional light in.

"It is still there? The image?"

"Not as clearly," I admitted. "But it's there."

"I am taking my hand away. You do not need to hold the image in your mind. You need simply to know it is there. That it remains in your mind, your truth beyond space and time, even as you see the world of space and time around you. That it is yours to command. To keep or release as you will. You see it, and it is real, regardless of what else is real."

She'd lost me again somewhere around space and time, but I murmured an assent. Mostly I just liked hearing her voice. When she wasn't poking at my feet, she was very soothing.

"Close your eyes slightly," she said, and I narrowed my lids to half-mast.

Chichiro lifted her hands away, and I slitted my eyes

133

further, shocked at the brightness of the sun. I blinked several times, and realized she was leaning over me, silhouetted in the light, the brightness of her almost terrible to behold after all the darkness. I flinched away, and her smile grew broader, then she finally eased away from me as well.

"It will take some time, Madam Wilde. But you will learn."

"Yeah, well…" I swung my gaze away from her and was immediately accosted by the sight of Ma-Singh. He wasn't glowing bright white, but he still glowed, energy popping and cracking off him like a live wire. A live red-and-black wire, fierce and proud.

The men in the background also glowed, but less intensely, their colors blurred and muddy. I was reminded of how I could see when I was in the presence of the Magician, when he turned all the world into a mix of electrical currents. This wasn't exactly like that, but it wasn't normal either.

I glanced back at Chichiro, still lit up like a Christmas tree. "Does this go away?"

"It can." She nodded. "I suggest you remain with it a bit, however, become familiar with it. Being able to read the energy signatures of those around you is a helpful skill."

My plain old normal eyes widened. "Energy signatures," I murmured.

"And there's more." She moved completely out of the way, reached down.

And plucked a gleaming gun from the top of a three-foot pile of weapons.

She held it out to me, butt first.

"Something else that might prove helpful, I think you'll agree."

CHAPTER FOURTEEN

"No way," I breathed.

Ma-Singh looked from me to the guns, his scowl evident even through all his sparkling and snapping energy. "You couldn't have chosen swords?"

"Swords don't take me to my happy place." I pushed off the blanket, and Chichiro helped me to stand. As I did so, I made another discovery. "Your house! It's not…"

She bowed to me, her hands coming together. "I am honored that you remembered it so easily and so well."

I had, apparently. Though I'd heard and smelled the fire I'd unleashed in her domain, felt the rage of its heat, there was no apparent damage to the structure anymore. "I erased that?"

"You manifested a belief so strong, it created a reality in this world that I in turn strengthened," Chichiro said. "Your belief was required to create. Mine was required to complete. There must be the two halves to make the whole."

Chichiro was a powerful Connected, but creating something out of nothing was dangerous, I knew. Incredibly dangerous. "But is it…real? Or will it come crashing down around you tonight after we leave?"

Her laugh sounded over the mountain, swept away

on the breeze. "You tell me," she said, gesturing to the guns. "Try one."

"No. I will try it." Ma-Singh strode forward and lifted a gun off the top of the pile. He turned and took aim at a far tree, where one branch stretched out awkwardly over a tumble of rocks. He fired, and simultaneously, the branch whipped back, clearly struck.

He stared down at the gun, then shifted his gaze to me. "You will not handle these, Madam Wilde. We cannot risk it."

I shrugged. "I've got my own gun."

Chichiro spoke again. "The Sight I sought to unmask in you was solely that of seeing others for who they really are. The energy or aura about them. With something of a person's that possesses their energy signature, you can find that energy again, even in a city of two million people. This is the gift I wished you to have, the ability you needed to unlock above all others."

She gestured to the ground. "This was not. It typically takes a great mastery of meditation and focus to manifest any item, and you possess neither. And yet, without effort, you have done what even the most Enlightened cannot do." Her gaze never left me as she echoed my own thoughts. "It is a dangerous skill, so uncontrolled. You must be very cautious of your gifts."

"Yeah, I can see that," I said. Never had the warning of be careful what you wish for been more apt. "But I needed you to help me complete the circle. It's not something I could do on my own."

To my surprise, Chichiro merely sighed, her gaze lifting to the mountain behind us. "I think we have yet to learn what you can do on your own, Madam Wilde. You must take special care."

With another half hour of work—we were totally over my limit, but Chichiro didn't seem to mind—I was able to shut my unnatural eye and open it. Not easily, but it could be done. Wax on, and the whole world lit up. Wax off, and I could see like a normal person. At last, she pronounced me able to leave, and I could breathe again.

The journey back to Tokyo was very quiet.

Ma-Singh sat with his hand cradling one of the guns I'd magically summoned out of my brain, staring out the window. He didn't seem happy.

"How are you feeling now?" he asked, glancing over to me. He was as far away as possible on his side of the seat, and I quelled the insane urge of my inner ten-year-old to poke him.

"I'm…good," I said, injecting enough hesitation into my voice that his creased brow eased. In fact, I felt outstanding—better than I had in days. While he'd glared at the mountain for the past hour, I'd been playing with my wax-on, wax-off move and checking out the energy signature of the men in the front seat. They hadn't become any more interesting. Ma-Singh, however, was now an icy blue mixed with black, and I didn't need my special eyeglasses to figure out that he was battling an enormous fear.

But fear *of* me? Or fear for me? I didn't want to wait to find out.

"You didn't think this would happen to me," I said flatly, waving in the general direction of my eye. "I get the sense that you think it's a bad thing."

He stared over my shoulder a long time before finally bringing his gaze back to me. I flinched as another wave of panic slid across his face.

"What are you staring at?" I whipped my hand up to my forehead, palpating my skin, but nothing stuck out or came off on my hand. "What is it?"

"There is nothing wrong. Not anymore." The Mongolian sighed deeply, releasing the gun on his lap

137

to bring both hands up to his face. Rubbing his heavy cheeks, he seemed like he'd aged a thousand years in our trip up the mountain.

"You were blinded, Madam Wilde," he said. "For that time in Sensei Chichiro-san's house. You were afraid."

I nodded. "But I got better," I said gently.

That elicited another weary grimace. "You got better." He hesitated again, and my curiosity only increased.

"What is it? The guns? The aura readings? Why are you upset?"

He lifted his brow. "For neither of those things. You being able to discern what you see more clearly was what Sensei Chichiro had done for Madam Soo, though not to anywhere the level she achieved with you. But of course, your abilities outstrip Madam Soo's."

He touched the barrel of the gun, eyeing it appreciatively. I eyed it too. It was a beautiful replica of mine, and I found myself wondering if it also had the same serial number. That could get complicated. "And as to manifesting guns out of your mind, that is a gift that could serve you well."

"Possibly." I hadn't taken Chichiro's warning lightly, though. I could see all sorts of pain coming from bringing ideas to life, like a 3-D printer gone rogue. I knew well enough how guns worked, had taken them apart and put them back together often enough that I had a reasonable certainty that this gun I'd just produced would behave more or less the way it should. But what if I manifested a machine I didn't fully understand? Or, worse, a creature...or a person?

The thought made me slightly sick.

Ma-Singh was watching me with his mournful Mongolian eyes. "But there is more," he said. "When you were injured in Chichiro's house, it was as if I was personally attacked."

I widened my eyes. That was news. "You went blind?"

"Not at all. But I was aware of your danger, your pain, your fear. I was driven to act to help alleviate that fear. I was already three feet from the door when the fire started. The explosion of it knocked us all back on our heels, but it wasn't what spurred me first to action."

I didn't miss his changing use of pronouns. "*You* were affected by my reactions, but the others weren't. They only followed your lead and responded to that and the fire, not my fear."

"Exactly." He nodded.

"They weren't on the boat with the nails." I frowned at him. "Wait a minute, *you* weren't on the boat. You were only watching over the screen."

He grimaced. "You're correct there as well. I was a witness to your call to arms, but not physically present. I was separated by thousands of miles. And yet..."

"Well, maybe there's another explanation. Maybe you just like me a lot."

My attempt at levity didn't seem to assuage his concerns, however. "There is much about you we do not understand, Madam Wilde, and as I learn each new revelation, I am reminded that we are blessed to have you...and that we would be crippled without you."

"Aw, I love you too, big guy," I said, and this time I did reach out, punching him lightly on his arm. Ma-Singh stared at me as if I'd lost my mind, but at least his worry seemed to ease.

Still, he remained unhappy. "You are departing on a spirit journey, Madam Wilde, one which began with your recovery of the Gods' Nails. At Sensei Chichiro's holding, I saw that path curve away from me, curve and grow dark." He shook his head slightly, his skin ashen. "I could no longer see you—or help you on your journey."

"You'll always be able to help me, Ma-Singh," I said, my words gentle. "You've got enough security on me that I look over my shoulder when I go to the bathroom now. Trust me, I feel protected. I'm safe in your hands. I believe that unequivocally."

That seemed to mollify him a little bit, and we continued the rest of the way down the mountain without incident, then onto the private jet waiting for us at Tokyo Haneda Airport. Nigel and Nikki checked in, confirming that there'd been no further attacks on the Revenants, so I contented myself with practicing my magic eyeball skills with the strangers we met on the way to the plane. None of them projected the kind of intense energy of Ma-Singh, which made me wonder if he simply was that much more charismatic...or if it was because I personally knew him...or it was because he'd witnessed the aftermath of my work with the Gods' Nails. Eventually, I needed to get those artifacts translated, understand their real power.

Granted, Chichiro had lit up like a glow stick on the mountain, but she was different. She was a powerful Connected. I was beginning to realize that I should consider returning to her too. The idea didn't make me happy.

Once we were aboard the plane, however, all thoughts of using my newfound skills were put to rest for the moment. I stared in wonder at the machinery awaiting us in the central cabin, a veritable mission control. "When did we upgrade this plane?" I asked, impressed.

"This is typically the generals' transportation." Ma-Singh slid me a glance. "And Madam Soo's preferred craft as she grew more involved with the military arm of the House. At the end of her tenure, it was the only jet she would take if possible."

I thought about Soo, her almost reckless insistence on traveling into the teeth of trouble…an insistence that had ended up getting her killed. If she was used to traveling with this kind of military and technological might at her fingertips, however, I could see why she felt invincible.

"What are we tracking?" I gestured to the screens, which were already on and flashing. Apparently, the exhortation to stow all laptops didn't apply on Air Swords.

"There has been unusual activity noted in three black market sites: Bangkok, Moscow, Mexico City. New drugs coming in, flooding the market. We've acquired several samples, but the demand is excessively high." He answered my next question before I had to ask it. "It appears the drug is the same that afflicted the children at Father Jerome's holding, merely less potent. We're analyzing what few samples we have obtained now."

I frowned. "That drug is brand-new. How would people know about it? We didn't even know about it until last week."

"It's being sold as a beta test of an augment drug, and the interest it's generating is significant. Claims of reversed diseases, slowed cancers." He shot me a glance. "Most notably, however, there are reported changes in the skin tone and texture of those who take it. It's been given the name Fountain."

"Fountain." I stared at him. "As in fountain of youth." No wonder people were clamoring for it.

"There are already some issues with its release," he continued. "Apparent cases of nerve damage. It's impossible to tell how true that is. Test cases are hard to come by. But that's the rumor currently running free through the markets. Not slowing down demand, though."

"If anyone's really worried, they'll find someone to test it on first," I muttered. "They always do."

"Father Jerome is reporting additional issues with the children in his care too."

I turned on him. "What are you talking about? What issues?"

"He can tell you himself." Ma-Singh tapped his headset, sliding into one of the seats in front of the series of laptops and screens. "He called Nigel not twenty minutes ago, looking for you. Now that we're aboard, we can open a channel for conversation."

"You're sure we're secure?" I asked grumpily. Gamon had eavesdropped on a sacred Revenant ceremony, and she'd sent her killers into a church to murder children. Nothing could be safe anymore.

Ma-Singh slid me a glance. "I don't know. Are we?"

I lifted both my brows, but he was right. This should be something I could tell, right along with the energy signatures of the people around me. "Who's been on this plane recently? Any Council members?"

"No. Since Madam Soo's death, it's been used by generals only, no civilians — and definitely no gods."

I grimaced. "They're not gods. Nobody's that."

I ignored Ma-Singh's skeptical snort. Instead, I pivoted slowly, searching out the deepest corners of the cabin. With a long, exhaled breath, my third eye fluttered open.

Immediately, three locations flared with unusual energy. Could it really be that easy? "There," I said, pointing. "And there and there."

Without a word, Ma-Singh went to the corners of the cabin I indicated, finding the devices after a short search. The general scowled down at the small electronic components.

"This device is Soo's. It bears her signature," he said, indicating the largest of the three. "Doubtless spying on her own generals."

"Understandable," I said. "She'd been burned before by people far closer to her."

"Agreed." He held up a second device. "This is identical to House components but is not standard issue. One of the generals, I suspect." He hesitated. "Probably General Som."

"Ah." General Som and I had recently crossed swords, literally. That hadn't gone well. "Any way to see if it was still transmitting?"

"We'll look into it. But this one, I do not recognize." He held up a third nondescript device. I stared at it as well, almost ready to shrug it off as another one of Soo's toys.

Then I reached for it.

Ma-Singh handed it over without hesitation, and I held the thing in my hand, looking down at it with my heightened awareness. This wasn't Soo's, I realized. It was Simon's, the Fool of the Arcana Council.

Energy arced through me, quick and hot, and I dropped the device with a yelp. "Destroy that. It's a Council bug. Sweep the other planes too."

"Council?" Ma-Singh rumbled.

"Simon or Tesla," I muttered. "Has to be."

Simon and I were friends, after a fashion, but the Hanged Man of the Council, Nikola Tesla, recently returned from the ether, wasn't a fan.

Ma-Singh studied the device as he made a call on his headset, and a cabin steward came to collect the device.

"Put it in a lead-lined box," instructed Ma-Singh. "Near the engine."

After the man left, he looked at me inquiringly. I blew out a breath, nodded. "We're clean now," I said. "Patch through Father Jerome."

A moment later, the familiar but newly haggard face of the French priest filled the screen.

"Sara," he said. "It's happening."

CHAPTER FIFTEEN

"What's happening, Father?" I asked sharply. Father Jerome looked much as he always did. His white hair was close cropped, his warm eyes deep set into wrinkled skin. He wore a black shirt with a priest's collar that looked like he'd slept in it, and though his face had lit up as he'd recognized me, it quickly was slipping back into a dour expression.

"The children who'd been forced to take the latest technoceuticals? It's their hearts. They're failing." He swallowed. "Starting with the youngest."

I frowned, staring at him. "What do you mean, failing?"

Father Jerome looked like he'd spent the night crying, but he stared into the monitor with a blank, ashen face. "The youngest of our patients have all begun showing similar symptoms. Their hearts have been devolving into rapid arrhythmia, some arresting altogether. We have stabilized the children with medical comas but—we don't have any solution or any way of knowing what specifically is triggering the breakdown. And if it happens to the babies…"

I swallowed. Right now in Father Jerome's safe house and hospital, there were a half-dozen infants who'd been born to teens injected with this supposed miracle drug that was lighting up the arcane black market. I somehow didn't think the drug's vials were marked "may cause heart failure and death."

"Have any of them died?" I heard myself asking. "The babies?"

"No," Father Jerome said. "But their sleep has been disturbed, and there are some things we can't track in them. Precursor events. Even Chantal…"

Hearing the name of the pregnant girl I'd met not too long ago taking refuge in his home, made my heart grow cold. "What about her?"

"She's begun suffering from emotional breakdowns. We have her in therapy, but she has asked for us to sedate her, to stop the visions she's having."

"Visions?"

My face must have telegraphed my confusion, because Father Jerome waved his hand. "The twins had them too. They are all the same image, some sort of origin image—a hideous, complicated mask of some sort. I've tried to get them to be more specific, but talking about it brings them great fear. We're afraid the infants are experiencing the same visions. If they are…their hearts may soon be afflicted like the others, only they may be too young to endure it."

I couldn't help with Jerome's medical problems, so I latched on to how I could potentially assist. "What kind of mask? Can you get any more information—is it a modern mask, something ancient, any indication of a culture for us to start with?"

"We've gathered little but screams at this point." Father Jerome sighed, then shook his head. "We'll keep trying. There will be something soon, I think. At the start of each affliction, the visions are the clearest and the children's articulation of what they are seeing is also clear. After that, they both disintegrate." He paused, his eyes going a little hollow. "At this rate, we will have a new batch of visions and reactions within the next few days, then more comas. The twins will succumb next, I fear."

"Oh no." I'd met the twins in France, brought them into Jerome's care. In attempting to heal them, I'd taken away the hyper-acceleration of their abilities and returned them to their non-Connected, natural states, but apparently...I hadn't done enough. "But they'd been in that facility for months with no reported effects from the drug. And there would have been, right?"

Father Jerome nodded. "There should be, unless it's their interaction with other children that's causing the shared memory to implant. We've removed them to isolated quarters as best we can, but I fear the damage has already been done."

"They'd been kept apart..." I frowned hard, trying to process, then slanted a look at Ma-Singh.

"Can you get ahold of Nigel? Conference him in?" The Brit had been with me in France, had gone in to get the twins from their underground hospital bunker. Maybe he could remember something I didn't.

"Of course," the general rumbled. He began tapping on the keyboard as I racked my brain.

"What other similarities and differences exist between the twins and the other children — and are there any who haven't succumbed to the reactions yet?"

"Not in this group," Father Jerome shook his head. "Chantal is the most recent abductee we recovered prior to the twins, but she was already suffering effects of trauma. She reported the vision of the mask only as a dream, when prompted, and it had occurred to her days before we realized it was a question we should be asking. The twins haven't had any such vision that they have shared with us, and we've kept the information from them so as not to stimulate a false positive.

"Nigel is coming in on screen four," Ma-Singh

interrupted. "Both Father Jerome and he can see you, but not each other."

"Got it." I waited until Nigel's image filled the screen.

"Sara," he said, his worried eyes scanning whatever he could see of me on the monitor. "You look…well. We were sorry to hear what happened in Tokyo yesterday."

I blinked. Had that really only been a day ago? Nodding quickly, I pushed on. "Father Jerome is also on here. He told me you discussed the drug reactions in the afflicted children."

Nigel's face sobered. "He did. Has there been any change? We only talked a short while ago."

"Not yet. But when we retrieved the twins from the hospital, can you recall anything specific about their living quarters?"

"Their quarters?" He frowned.

"They'd been cooped up down there for weeks—maybe months. Much longer than some of these children who've already started showing reactions. Makes me wonder if there's something there that helped retard the process, whether intentionally or not."

"Well, it was underground," he offered. "The twins were both wearing electrical bracelets. The room I suspect was lead lined, given the sluggishness of their reactions until they exited into the hallway." He cocked a brow. "They weren't so sluggish outside of the room, for sure."

I snorted. The children had attacked us both with an unexpected ferocity, but they'd been kids—locked up, afraid. We cut them some slack.

Something in Nigel's words tripped me, though. "Those ankle bracelets. They were electrical in nature, right? That's why we had to ground ourselves to release them."

"I'm not likely to forget that," Nigel said, and I

148

pointedly didn't meet his eyes. He'd been deep-fried from the inside out from that experience, and closer to death than I liked to think about.

I tapped my chin instead, considering the children's security clasps. "So maybe there's something to do with the electrical current—maybe that stabilized them, somehow."

"Possible," Nigel allowed. "The lead-lined room would be easier to test."

"That's easy enough to check out," Ma-Singh said. "I can have one of our local contacts obtain the building schematics of the hospital. The materials used should be recorded; it is a public health facility."

"Do that. Meanwhile…" I blew out a breath. "I'll have to ask Simon about the bracelets. See if there's any possible stabilizer we can improvise. Who knows, maybe some kind of low-dose electrical current is all we need, kind of a makeshift pacemaker."

"If so, it would be a godsend. But you'll need to do it fast, Sara." Father Jerome drew my attention again. "I'm not sure how long it will be until we have another lapse here, and I'd rather avoid it. Medical comas aren't supposed to be permanent solutions."

We discussed possibilities a few minutes longer, then Jerome signed off, leaving Nigel on the line.

"Talk to me about what you're hearing in the markets," I said.

"Probably no more than Ma-Singh has already told you," the Brit replied. "Biggest influx of drugs is coming into Mexico City's arcane black market, but they're cropping up in Moscow and Bangkok too. And when I say influx, I mean a ton of product, flooding the market in the form of gateway samples all the way up to pallet-sized deliveries available for special order. And they're going fast."

"Makeup of the client set?"

"Unknown—but we're assuming across the board."

"We need Mercault's take on this," I muttered. Nigel shifted in his chair at the man's name. "What?"

"Mercault's in it up to his neck. I'm not sure how amenable he'll be to choking the trade at this point."

"What do you mean, in it? He's a friend. An ally."

"He's a businessman first," Nigel said tersely. "And this is the biggest dump of drugs in the market in five years. Everyone wants in, Connected or not, because it's not simply about augmenting your abilities, it's about becoming young again. Turning back the clock."

"But test cases are reporting nerve damage—and now heart attacks and crazy visions. Those are some pretty big side effects."

"Cases are still isolated enough to be ignored, and a lot of cash is changing hands now. If the drugs turn out to be lemons, it's not like the FDA is protecting them. Mercault will be sitting on his bags of money and watching everyone die."

"He better plan on having a ring of machine guns surrounding him and all those bags. The right sort of people start dropping, they're going to want somebody to blame." Another thought occurred to me. "Test cases were all kids. Presumably, the target users are not. Are any adults having an issue?"

Nigel hesitated, consulting a screen below the view of the monitor. "Still mostly children. Not sure where this data is coming from, though. But the skin-texture feedback—that has to be adult. Older adults, is my guess. They're testing it on someone, clearly."

"Yeah." A new thought wormed its way into my brainpan.

The last time I'd been in Vegas, we'd gotten reports of missing Connecteds—just enough to make us take notice. Gamon had been in the city only weeks before, on the hunt for Soo. Had she decided the resident

Connected community would be easy pickings for test cases of her new drug? It made a certain sort of sense. The population of Las Vegas Connecteds was transient, many of them fleeing circumstances that made it better for them to live off the grid. Especially because they weren't children, their absence wouldn't be noticed as much.

"Do me a favor, Nigel, ask Nikki to follow up in Las Vegas, see if we have any more missing persons cases cropping up—adults in particular, and Connected versus non-Connected would be good to know. We'll be there in…"

Ma-Singh spoke up. "Ten hours."

"There you have it. If she's got anything to go on, I'll be ready to look into it. Meanwhile…" I turned back to the map. "Why these three sites? Moscow isn't exactly the hottest black market. I get Bangkok and Mexico, but—"

"There's more money in Russia than there used to be, and a lot of wide open space," Nigel explained. "If you had a supply of the drug to not only test but reverse engineer, there are worse places to go off and get the job done."

"Reverse engineering. I hadn't thought of that." I passed a hand over my eyes. "Do we have any idea if the drugs causing the reaction are the original vintage versus any sort of synthetic knockoffs? And seriously, how can they already have synthesized the drug?"

"They probably haven't," Nigel agreed. "But that wouldn't stop anyone from saying they had."

"Dangerous group of users to jack around like that."

"Agreed. We've redoubled security for our scouts, but right now it's still a party. Any drug can make you feel good. Actual cellular change can't be tracked except by specialized equipment. Some of the buyers will have that equipment. Most won't. Certainly not the ones getting the gift baggies. And the reactions being noted are anecdotal. Does the drug really make you look younger, or have you simply decided it has? Are you getting better, or are you just thinking positively?" Nigel shrugged. "The placebo effect alone is going to keep the market thrumming along for a good three months at that level. At the upper levels, however..."

I grimaced. "At the upper levels, there's going to be a lot of unhappy people, unless they've spun it as an experimental drug. And you say Mercault is dealing this?"

"If there's money to be made, he'd sell anything to anyone," Nigel said tersely. "I'll get him lined up for a meeting. He's been off the radar for the past few weeks, but his fingerprints are all over these deals. We'll track him down."

"Good. See you in ten hours, then."

The rest of the flight went smoothly, with Ma-Singh testing my newly acquired eyesight in a half-dozen other ways, including disturbing the crew for impromptu aura readings. I was getting better at picking up the muddier, more muted colors of the non-Connecteds, but as Chichiro had, Ma-Singh still practically vibrated with color when he was talking to me. The announcement of our descent into Las Vegas had just come over the PA when I looked over at him, trying for casual but not trying all that hard.

"What did you do with the Gods' Nails?"

He smiled as if he'd just won some internal bet. "They're in Las Vegas at the desert house," he said, referring to Soo's original Vegas stronghold, now taken over by Nikki and, on occasion, me, as well as whatever House staff found themselves in the city at any given time. "I've sent for an antiquities expert to analyze them. The bounty on them hasn't dropped, by the way. It's still an open call, and Thor is now offering a ransom as well for their return."

"Yeah? Anything new about me?" I'd been too busy for the past few weeks to follow the arcane black market as closely as I used to, checking for the latest artifacts being sought and seeing which ones I could steal first. I missed it more than I realized.

Nigel shook his head. "There's been no further mention of you, officially or otherwise. The nails are listed as no longer for sale by the family. We've been monitoring that and put it out that you've already transferred them to a client. Whether or not they believe that is unknown, but we should assume not. We've analyzed the security tape at the club in Reykjavik, identified several of those players. If any of them draw close to you, we'll take appropriate action."

"I appreciate that." It was hard not to say something flip, but that wasn't fair. I was uncomfortable with the heightened security, but I'd also seen Ma-Singh's genuine panic when he thought I was in danger at Chichiro's mountain massage parlor. I'd thought I was in danger, but his panic both during and after my temporary blinding had fallen somewhere between heartwarming and distressing. These people had put their faith in me. The least I could do was to stay alive until I justified that faith.

We landed a few minutes later, and the first blast of the Vegas sun warmed me to the core, as it always did. Everything in the city seemed mirror bright, and I squinted toward the long gray limo that glided up to the private airstrip—then was even more surprised to see a second limo…and a third following behind it.

I frowned at Ma-Singh. "Really?"

"As I said, we are taking your security very seriously. In the wake of your query into missing persons, Nikki has advised me that she wants you to visit with the Las Vegas Metro Police Department, so she will be taking you there. The other limos are decoys. I'll have a fourth vehicle to trail you both. We'll track which of the limos are followed, and neutralize any threats."

"That...sounds great." It sounded terrible, and all my well-meaning thoughts about putting up with my security detail vanished like ice cubes in the desert. Sooner or later, if Ma-Singh insisted on sticking bodyguards this close to me, someone was going to end up hurt, or worse, dead. I didn't want that kind of responsibility hanging over me every time I turned around.

Fortunately, I didn't have too long to think about it. As we moved down the Jetway, the front door of the nearest limo popped forward, and a tall, leggy blonde stepped out and struck a pose. Today, Nikki had reverted to her old-school chauffeur uniform, but she'd paired the snappy black cap and formfitting miniskirted uniform with bright red thigh-high go-go boots and piles of platinum-blonde curls. Even passengers in the planes above us were pinned to the windows I suspected, and despite his best efforts to remain nonchalant, Ma-Singh caught his breath beside me.

"She doesn't do anything by half measures, does she?" he asked, faintly aghast.

I grinned at Nikki, feeling lighter than I had in days as she waved back enthusiastically. "Dollface!" she cried over the roar of the planes.

"No, she doesn't," I agreed.

CHAPTER SIXTEEN

It was almost like old times as Nikki held the door for me, waiting until I slid into the purring limo's oasis of refrigerated air before she slammed the back door shut. She paused outside while Ma-Singh briefed her.

Then Nikki opened her own door and took up position behind the wheel, taking a moment to ensure her hat was at the appropriate jaunty angle and her lips were freshened up before she gazed at me through the rearview mirror. The oversized cat's eye sunglasses were a good look for her, but I couldn't see her eyes.

Of course, I reminded myself, I didn't need to. Once we were underway, I could do my whole all-seeing-eye thing on her, and know exactly how she was feeling.

"You're taking me to the police station?" I asked instead. "Why, does Brody have a problem?"

That earned me a snort of derision. Detective Brody Rooks of the LVMPD and I went back a long way, all the way to Memphis, Tennessee, when I was a child psychic prodigy. I'd worked with him then to help finding missing kids, and now here we were in Las Vegas, working together again. A lot had changed since he'd been Officer Brody and I'd been Sariah Pelter, but one thing had never changed: there would always be missing people to find.

"Brody always has a problem. It's how he gets himself through the day." Nikki pointed the limo at the exit. I saw a small group of workers standing around a luggage trolley, and one of them was watching me. He was too young, I thought idly—barely more than a boy. Then again, everyone younger than me looked like they were twelve these days.

"But in this case, it's also our problem," Nikki continued. "And more of what we were worried about the last time you tripped the Strip."

I looked away from the workers, back toward Nikki. "The Connecteds who'd disappeared. There are more?"

"A whole pile of them, apparently." Nikki threaded the limo through the various gates, her keen eyes noting when each of the other limos slid off on their trajectories. "At least now we have a line on where they might be getting shipped off to."

"That's new." Ma-Singh hadn't told me that.

"What can I say? Detective Delish is good at his job. He was glad to hear you were coming home too." She lifted her gaze to me. "Between you, me, and the whipping post, he and Dixie are on the outs."

"Not my concern anymore, Nikki." And it truly wasn't. Dixie was a local astrologer of some renown, and if she and Brody wanted to read their charts together, that was perfectly fine with me. I'd been fourteen when I'd first started working with Officer Brody, and he'd been in his early twenties. I'd nursed the world's most embarrassing crush on the man—one that only worsened as we'd continued to work together. Then, when I was seventeen, I'd disappeared on him in the wake of a job gone terribly wrong...and had stayed disappeared for ten years. It was only in the past few months that our paths had crossed again, and while the zing was still there, it was more a zing of nostalgia than attraction.

156

Besides, I currently had my hands full with the Magician, not to mention my full-time gig with the House of Swords. I needed another interpersonal entanglement like a hole in the head.

In the front seat, Nikki nodded emphatically, clearly following along with my thoughts. Once she had worked with someone long enough, she could do that—no touching required to employ her Connected abilities.

"But the good detective is the cutest, can't deny that," she cracked.

I rolled my eyes. "You know, you should ask before you read people's minds."

"Not nearly as much fun that way."

Nikki turned the wheel hard and leapt forward into traffic, managing to intimidate even the hardened cabbies and tour buses hauling the newest delivery of Vegas tourists toward the Strip. I could see the gleaming line of casino hotels in the distance, bright against the midday sun—so bright that the shadows of the soaring residences of the Council that loomed above them were virtually invisible.

No, right now it was enough to see the mortal anchors of the Strip—the Mandalay Bay and Stratosphere—and draw my eye along the gleaming skyline visible at this distance. The Luxor and Paris, New York New York, and MGM, the flying ramparts of Excalibur and the stately elegance of the Bellagio.

Newer casinos had been built in the past several years, gradually becoming part of the Vegas firmament: Aria, The Cosmopolitan—even SLS, perched as it was on the sacred ground of the former Sahara Hotel. There were precious few of the early era hotels left on the Strip, but those that were seemed to still be going strong—the Tropicana, Flamingo, Caesars Palace, even Circus Circus.

A lot of magic ran beneath the Strip, the kind of

magic that drew the desperate and the hopeful, the lucky and the careworn. Every time I left, I was glad to leave, but every time I came back, I felt home. Home.

I smiled a little wearily. Only I would find a city of flash and sizzle to be homey.

"So what's the short version of what we're walking into?" I asked.

"Pretty much the payoff of what we thought was happening when Dixie worried that MedTech was being used as a cover operation meant to lure in Connecteds and snatch them. She was close. We simply didn't look hard enough. There's another medical testing center east of the strip, looks totally legit, even sounds good: Better Health Services. They advertise free day care during your office visit, regular doc-in-a-box urgent care services, as well as medical testing and—wait for it—drug research studies."

I studied her reflection in the mirror, and slipped the barriers in place in my mind. Nikki didn't seem to notice, but I'd had a while to perfect the move. As close as she and I were, I remained a very private person. A very private and occasionally twisted person. She didn't need to be witness to that all the time.

"What kind of research studies?" I asked.

"Everything from pouring lotions and shaving cream on your skin, to testing mouthwash, to getting you tripping on antidepressants, to the always popular sleep studies. The latter, just like at MedTech, went over particularly well with the young families desperate for both sleep and babysitting services. BHS was more than happy to help. But you can't just take a momma and spirit her off. You want that kind of demographic, you gotta take the whole lot."

I frowned at her. "A Connected family?"

"Family might be putting too fine a point on it," she said, shaking her head. "These were warehousers, living over in the Tanker." At my blank look, she flapped her hand. "Warehouse converted into what they call 'studio space' but is really more like squatter housing that's well below code. Owners look the other way, residents keep a low profile and don't catch anything on fire, everyone's happy. This particular mommy read cards in an off-Strip hair salon, then cleaned up after the stylists. Her husband, not a Connected, watched the kids during the day, then he worked at night. But while the Tanker is open-air during the day, at night they lock it up tight. It's a veritable oven in the summer, way too hot to sleep in there, and stuffy besides, so Mom needed to find someplace to stash the kids and catch some shut-eye. Overnight studies were exactly the ticket, and the kids got to bunk down in air-conditioning. Win-win. Until one morning, hubby comes home and she's nowhere to be found. Takes him a while to figure out what had happened—she hadn't told him she was doing this—but he goes straight to the cops. We figure Better Health Services didn't even know the woman was married. Brody caught the case, and here we are."

"She someone Dixie knows?"

"Peripherally. She's Hispanic, doesn't speak a lot of English, her documents were shit—something else the husband didn't know. One of the children is his, the youngest. The older boy came with the package. He's closer to eleven."

I got a bad stirring in my stomach as she continued the explanation. "The older son is Connected?"

"Give the lady a prize."

My third eye fluttered open. I shifted my gaze to Nikki and away again as quickly, my pupils dilating dramatically in the moment I fixed on her. She glowed nearly as white as Chichiro did, the edges of her aura sparking and snapping with other colors, all of them rich and vibrant—green, yellow, purple. I didn't know what aura colors meant, but I knew the sense I got from them. In Nikki, the bright white screamed protector to me, while the other colors conveyed her place in the world — open and engaged. All of which I already knew, of course. I could tell the value of my third eye would matter more so with new contacts than with my tried-and-true friends. Maybe if they were sick or acting funny, but otherwise, no.

"How long has the family been missing?"

"Husband came in this morning, but he hadn't seen his wife yesterday — she wasn't there in the morning, and he fell asleep, grateful for the reprieve. He knew she'd been back at some point because she'd cleaned their studio and left him food, but she was gone again when he left for work. He tried to reach her by phone throughout the night, and by morning, he finally freaked."

"So possibly two days, if we believe him."

"Yep." Nikki nodded. "I haven't seen him, so I can't speak to his mind — but Brody seemed to think he was legit."

We pulled onto the street that housed the police station, and Nikki parked in the bus slot. I blinked at her. "I don't think this is a good location."

"Sure it is. You head on in and get love buns. I'll wave at all the nice boys in blue going by." Nikki checked her lipstick again in the rearview mirror and lowered her shades to give me a wink. "Don't tell Brody what I'm wearing, okay? I do so enjoy his outrage."

I was still chuckling as I entered the police station, marveling at how similar it felt to the police station back in Memphis that I'd last entered all those years ago, before I knew enough about my life to understand how truly twisted my path would be.

Brody stood at the far end of the lobby, talking with another officer, which afforded me a second to look at him — really look at him. I blinked open my third eye and scanned the room, shocked at the muddy grit I encountered. These were not healthy men and women — they were tired, anxious, and unhappy.

Then I got to Brody, and my heart squeezed tight. His aura — or light or glow, whatever it was — couldn't be right. It was dark — too dark, a black ooze threading through what once had probably been a vibrant blue. That mixture was encased in a second layer of color, a viscous, putrid brown. I was shocked the man could still stand, that he wasn't somewhere in a hospital room, hooked up to an oxygen tank. Or morphine drip.

He chose that moment to look up, and a smile flashed across his face, so bright that it shuttered my third eye completely. Just like that, his aura winked out.

"Sara!" he called, waving as if we hadn't already made eye contact. I waved back, but I couldn't quell my concern for him. Why was his aura or whatever so depressed? Was he sick?

He didn't look sick. He finished his conversation with his fellow officer and strode over to me, his grin still in place. This was a pleasant surprise at least. I was used to Brody being irritated every time I showed up — either mad at me for leaving Vegas or mad that I came back. But he walked right up to me and gave me a quick, professional handshake-hug, never mind that I wasn't the hug type. I wasn't even the handshake type, come to think of it.

One bonus, though, touching Brody reinforced the sick, cloying sense I had about his aura, as well as the fact that he was still hitting a few Connected cylinders. Most cops did have a flare of Connectedness about them, even if they'd never admit it, but Brody's intuition had gotten unintentionally amped when he'd been trapped with me a little too close for comfort earlier that summer. While many of the other folk affected by that magical pulse had eventually lost their Connected edge, Brody clearly retained his. Which was good, given what we had ahead of us.

"Nikki said she'd be bringing you…" He looked toward the door as if surprised that I was alone. "Um, where is she?"

"Causing a traffic disturbance. You ready to go?"

"A traffic…" A more familiar scowl creased his features, and he narrowed his eyes. "What's she wearing?"

"Let's just say she's in uniform."

He trailed behind me, cursing as we reemerged into the sunshine, his gaze immediately fixing on Nikki. It was kind of hard not to, admittedly, with her leaning against the hood of the limo, one hip resting on its smooth surface. She was chatting on a cell phone, waving to everyone who went by, while studiously ignoring the bus idling behind her, tooting its horn. Loudly.

"Oh, for the love of — Nikki!" Brody strode forward, pulling an unresisting Nikki away from the car and hauling open the limo's front door, while she flailed helplessly in his arms, coming into contact with as much of him as one person could without being an Olympic wrestler. Brody finally managed to get her mostly stuffed in the front seat, then glared at me.

"Get in the damned car, Sara," he growled.

That was the grumpy Brody I knew and lo — ah, liked. Instantly, my mood lightened further, and I nearly tripped over myself hustling to the side door. I slid in as Nikki gunned the engine. With one last honk and wave to the steaming bus driver behind us, Nikki pulled away.

"Took you long enough, love cricket," she said, eyeing Brody through her sunglasses. "I was about to get heat stroke out here."

162

"Then you should have stayed in the car. Preferably in an authorized parking lot. I should have called someone to give you a ticket."

"And I would have paid cold hard cash for you to find that ticket in the same place I stow all the rest of them," Nikki replied, her grin going wider as Brody cursed.

"How is it you were in the force and you have absolutely no regard for—anything?"

Nikki sighed lustily. "Oh, how I've missed you, Detective. Now what do we have on the crime in progress? Any word from the medical facility on their surveillance tapes?"

He frowned at her. "You mean the Connected MP case, the Deguanzos? Why are you asking about that?"

She lifted her brows so far that they were visible over the rim of her glasses. "Why on earth do you think we're here?"

"I'd assumed..." He glanced from Nikki to me and back to Nikki, his brow furrowing further. "Your, uh, warehouse, Sara, over on the east side of town. It was vandalized. I assumed that's what you wanted me to see."

Now it was my turn to scowl. "My... That's empty, I thought. Isn't that empty?" I directed the last question to Nikki, my brain scrambling. Annika Soo had been something of a real estate junkie, and she owned several properties in the city, not the least of which was the enormous house on the edge of town where Nikki now lived. But the warehouse? "There's nothing in there."

"Not last we looked," Nikki agreed.

"It's not what's inside it that was damaged," Brody said, shaking his head. "And damaged isn't even the right word. You'll..." He paused. "You'll know what I mean when you see it."

CHAPTER SEVENTEEN

With that cryptic announcement, Brody clammed up, not even complaining when Nikki pulled over at the next side street and slid the privacy partition up to allow her a quick clothes change. The front of the limo was apparently more spacious than I gave it credit for, because we were back on the road within five minutes, the partition coming down shortly thereafter.

I'd been racking my brain for an opening into Brody's health, but nothing was coming to me. As Nikki sped along backstreets toward the warehouse district, I shot him another discreet look, glad to see his eyes were closed as he sagged against the overstuffed seat. He even looked tired, now that I saw him up close. How long had it been since he'd slept?

Apparently, not long enough. "I know you're staring at me, Sara," he grumbled, his voice half gravel, half sigh. But he didn't bother opening his eyes. "What do you need?"

"Nothing," I said. "You look like crap."

"On a cracker," Nikki chimed in from the front, her eyes still shaded by the cat-eye sunglasses. Everything else about her was different, though. Gone was the Lady Godiva wig and chauffeur outfit. In its place was a shoulder-length fall of auburn hair, secured by a camo-patterned bandana, and a tight black tank top paired with thick black leather cuffs. From what I could see of her arms as she hauled on the wheel to turn the limo down another street, Nikki had been working it hard in the great outdoors.

By comparison, Brody looked like he hadn't seen the sun since God was a child. "You, uh, sick?" I prodded him. I didn't know enough about auras to diagnose that definitively, but I didn't need special eyesight in this case.

"Haven't been sleeping well," he said, still not opening his eyes. "Comes with the job."

I shot Nikki a look, and she shrugged. Apparently, it did come with the job. Nikki's time on the Chicago PD might have been years in the past, but some things, I was sure, you didn't forget.

Of course, I could help him heal, couldn't I? I settled back in my seat, turning my attention out the window. I'd helped Nigel when his internal organs had been chicken fried, and I'd helped Ma-Singh when he'd been shot full of holes protecting me. But both of those cases had been situations of dire emergencies. I didn't know whether or not my abilities worked to cure the common cold. Or insomnia. Or whatever the hell was eating at Brody.

We continued another twenty minutes through the city, until gradually the houses fell away to be replaced by big-box industrial buildings of varying heights. Annika's warehouse here had served as a way station for both legal and illegal shipments into Paradise Valley, but to my knowledge, it'd sat empty for going on a year now. Why would someone mess with it? And why was Brody being so cagey about it?

In any event, he was sleeping now, and Nikki and I exchanged another glance. Clearly, she didn't want to wake the baby, but we couldn't take all day here. She made a rotation with her finger, and I nodded. A full loop around the district wouldn't be a bad idea.

I turned in my seat, suddenly remembering that we weren't on this sojourn alone. I couldn't see Ma-Singh, but I was sure he was there. It would be difficult staying hidden with so few cars in the area, but it wasn't as if he didn't recognize the warehouse district or guess at our destination. In fact, he probably would go right to the building and check it—

My cell phone buzzed.

"What?" Brody jerked awake, rubbing his hands over his face while I fished the phone out of my pocket. "Where are you going? The warehouse is half a mile in the other direction."

"My mistake," Nikki said cheerfully. She navigated the next turn, swinging us back around. I glanced down at the phone and swiped Ma-Singh's message open.

When were you here last? he'd texted.

I frowned—that was…an oddly useless question. "Ma-Singh's already at the warehouse site, and he's asking when I was there last," I said. "What's up with that? What's there?"

Brody's jaw tightened, but he gave up the ghost. "There's a—mural, I guess, is the best way you could describe it. Twenty feet tall, covering the back side of the building."

"And it's—what? Something bad? Graffiti?"

"Not graffiti. It's stylized art, pretty well done, it looks like, though I'm no judge of that kind of thing."

"Okay…" I still wasn't getting it. Nikki pulled into the warehouse parking lot, and I noticed three different cameras trained on the space, for all that it was empty. Soo had never fenced off the space because it was one of four dozen other buildings and lots—no one was likely to insist on setting up camp here versus fifteen feet down the road. "But worst case scenario, it's just paint.

What's the big deal?"

If anything, Brody looked even wearier. "You can see for yourself."

Nikki parked the limo, and we all exited it, the heat of the day shrink-wrapping itself to us until we moved into the shadow of the building. The chain-link gate was open, the lock disengaged.

"Ma-Singh's already here," I supplied, and Nikki nodded, stepping past the barrier. A narrow walkway led between some utility boxes and the warehouse, and then the space opened up again, to a smaller parking area of maybe six spaces — enough for us to step back and look up at the building.

My third eye shot open, the pain so immediate, so unexpected, I staggered back.

"Right here, dollface. I got you."

"What is it?" Brody demanded over her. In the distance, I could sense more than see another large figure striding toward us. Ma-Singh. Had to be Ma-Singh.

But I couldn't see anything but the image spray-painted on the wall.

It was…gorgeous. The detail mind-blowing, especially when it had to have been done with half a million cans of spray paint. More importantly, it was an image I'd seen before: a woman striding forth with a swinging scales of justice grasped in one hand, a sword in the other. If she'd been complacently sitting on her throne, everything still and serene, she would be a dead-on depiction of the Tarot card Justice.

But she wasn't sitting, and she wasn't serene. She looked about to break into a run, her crown tilted forward and her long judicial robes of red and gold flapping in the wind, her long dark hair flowing out behind her. She was slightly turned, as if looking over our shoulders, and her face was fierce enough to believe she was single-handedly about to go out and wreak havoc on the world.

She also looked dead-on like me.

"Sara?" Brody prompted.

"It's not me. But I've seen this before," I said slowly, all three of my eyes still wide and staring at the picture. "Not here, though. Not anywhere near here." I turned to him. "Who found this?"

"Surveillance company in the area noticed more activity than normal, though nobody reported any issues." Brody scratched his neck. "They sent a scout out anyway and talked to some kids who sent them here. It's become something of a mecca for graffiti artists in the past twenty-four hours, from what we've gathered. No one knows how it got here. No one knows who did it."

"How'd it stay clean?" Nikki asked. "If other artists have been here — they'd have added to it."

"I thought so too. But try to touch it." Brody motioned her toward the building.

Nikki shot him a look, but Ma-Singh held her back when she began to move. Instead, the general stepped forward and reached out his hand. It stopped about three inches from the surface of the wall. Ma-Singh jerked his hand back as an arc of electricity skittered out in a radial pattern.

"Force field," the general said.

Nikki picked up a rock, chucked it. No electrical jolt this time, but the rock bounced away, dropping harmlessly.

"What the hell," I muttered.

"You said that's not you?" Brody asked, pivoting toward me. "Because it sure as hell looks like it. Dressed up as Justice."

"Not Justice," I shook my head. "I saw this image on a wall in a blasted-out temple. The likeness to me is pretty good, I'll grant you. But that isn't Justice. Best I can come up with is the name Vigilance, but I don't know much about that icon. It's not standard in any decks I know. And no, I don't know why it looks so much like me, before you ask, again. I'd say it was a coincidence."

"It's not a coincidence," Nikki scoffed. "Not with it hanging here big as life on a House of Swords building."

I turned to Ma-Singh. "You didn't have any reports of this? No surveillance blips?"

"None," The general glowered. "I called the police when I first saw it, not realizing the extent of the image. The surveillance company assigned to this sector contacted us last night, and we checked our feeds, but there was nothing until yesterday morning, when the kids started showing up."

"So it popped up two nights ago and immediately had a fan club." Nikki tossed her hair over her shoulder. "How'd anyone know to look for it?"

Brody filled in. "According to the locals, people saw the electrical show, got curious, checked it out. The artist was nowhere to be found once they got here. Graffiti wars are a thing out here with the abandoned warehouses. But this — they swear none of them did this, and I'm inclined to believe them." He gestured to the wall. "If they had skills like this, they'd be in high demand on the Strip."

I walked forward, ignoring Ma-Singh's rumbled protest.

"I'm not going to touch it," I assured him, but I lifted my hand anyway. The energy of the electrical field cracked and hissed beneath my palm. "We have anyone in the House with this level of artistic and engineering skills?" I asked over my shoulder.

Ma-Singh didn't hesitate. "We do not."

"Council?" Nikki supplied. "Hanged Man's in

town, you know. Electricity is right up his alley."

"Maybe. Certainly the only viable explanation I can come up with," I said. "But Tesla didn't see that image. Nobody saw that image, except for me. There's too much detail for it to be anything but an exact replica." I scowled, thinking hard. The temple where I'd seen Vigilance had been in Atlantis, or what was left of it. The Hierophant was the only Council member who'd been alive when that mystical city was still standing, but this didn't feel like his MO.

"Gotta be some kind of message, though, right?" Brody asked. "A prompt? Call to arms?"

Something about that resonated with me, in all the wrong kind of ways. "Why do you say that?"

"It's you, Sara." Brody emphatically waved his hands at the painting. "It's clearly you. It's on your warehouse. Heavily protected so that no one'll touch it before you get the message. And it's a picture of you on the warpath."

"With a sword," Ma-Singh put in, not at all helpfully.

"That's not me," I said. I didn't know why, but I was sure of this—as sure as anything I'd ever been. "It's…"

My third eye cramped so hard, I slapped my hand to my brow, flinching away from the wall. In my flailing, my left hand arced out, raking through the force field.

All hell broke loose.

An electrical explosion burst up and away from the wall. An enormous scatter of sparks and fire threw us all to the ground. I cracked my head hard on the pavement. Lights flashed in front of my eyes, images cascading one upon the other. The hurtling trip through space and time to return to the lost city, the broken dome in the center of Atlantis, the scattered weapons I'd pulled together to bring back to this time and place. And then there'd been this image, this glorious image, stretching up on the wall above, beckoning me to see and understand. But I hadn't seen—I hadn't understood.

There'd been more nudges too, some subtle, some not. A voice in the desert wilderness when an enemy had tried hacking me up in her bid to take ownership of the House of Swords, the cryptic comments from the Hermit, speaking of times gone by without telling me a damned thing. The sense I'd had in Memphis when I'd stood on the wasteland that had been my former home…the sense of sorrow, guilt. Now this. How could it not be a message?

But a message from…?

A chill wind shuddered through me, harsh and forlorn. It's touch seemed to freeze the marrow of my bones. I felt…lost. So unbearably lost…

"Sara—Sara!" Brody screamed into my face, his breath a wash of exhaustion and coffee. I opened my eyes, and he cursed a blue streak, yanking me up and away from an equally hovering Ma-Singh.

"Oh, for the love of—let me go," I said, and they both stiffened at the tone of my voice, then cleared back and allowed me to stand.

"It's gone now," Nikki called. She stood by the painting, peering at it. "The force field. Message has apparently been received, right?"

We turned and stared up at the building. The image was still there, brilliant in the sunshine, gorgeous and powerful and full. And for the first time, finally, I knew who it was of. Not me at all.

But incredibly—impossibly—my mother.

Even as I thought it, reality rekindled in my brain. No. Not my mother. That wasn't possible.

Instead, this had to be some sort of mind freak.

Someone who knew just enough about me to know exactly what screws to turn. The Emperor, Viktor Dal, fit that ticket. Tesla, the Hanged Man and newest member of the Council to return to the Strip, loved nothing more than creating electrical light shows. The two of them were playing some game at my expense, and the mere thought of that attempted manipulation made me seethe. What was it that Armaeus had said? The Council wasn't yet at full speed? Well, he needed to get the rest of the players in place and pronto, because these little jabs needed to stop.

"We're done here," I said. I shot a look at Ma-Singh. "Get the security team on it, check the entire area, make sure there aren't any more surprises. Get a camera back here too. I want to know who else comes and goes, whether it's painters or whoever. Who comes, who stays, who does what and why."

"Who did this?" Brody asked gruffly.

"My money's on the Council," I said, twisting my lips. "Probably our old pal the Emperor, maybe with the help of one or more folks who actually saw the original version of this painting." I jabbed my thumb at the wall. "Viktor's got six guys in his employ who are likely candidates. The Hierophant could have also given him the details he needed."

"I don't know, dollface."

I held up a hand to stay Nikki's objection. "I don't fault any of them. They may not have even known what Viktor was up to, and this is pretty harmless, as pranks go. They're just screwing with me. I don't know why, but they are."

"Maybe," Nikki said, peering up. "It sure is pretty, though."

"Yeah." I joined her gaze, taking in the full power of the Vigilance image. The woman in that picture could probably have ruled the universe if she wanted to. And, while she looked like me, did that really mean anything? When I'd first visited Atlantis, I'd seen a representation of Vigilance on my palm. I'd later witnessed a more complete version of that same figure painted on the great central dome of the city—not while I was in Atlantis, but later, during a vision I'd received when I'd been playing footsie with Hell. But though the image bore a resemblance to me, the face of Vigilance might have been crafted with magic, to reflect the viewer's face no matter who looked upon it. It had been created in Atlantis, after all.

Either way, this prank had Viktor Dal written all over it. If the Emperor was ready to stage some war against me, it was fine by me. We had a lot of unfinished business between us. And with three eyes now on the job, I'd definitely see him coming.

CHAPTER EIGHTEEN

We left an unhappy Ma-Singh behind to manage the mess at the warehouse, and walked back to our car. Since Better Health Services had already been cased by the cops earlier this week and I was driving with two trained police officers, there wasn't much the general could complain about. Not that he didn't try.

A crowd of kids and granola-looking adults had gathered on the street opposite the building, clearly here to pay homage to the graffiti decorating the warehouse wall. I ducked into the limo before any of them could recognize my resemblance to the image, but continued to peer through the tinted windows at the group.

They were all sizes and more ages than I would have expected, from school-age kids to twenty-somethings, to even a few older men and women, their faces burned brown by decades in the sun. As Nikki threw the car into gear and pulled away from the curb, however, one of them caught me—for just a moment. A boy who looked...familiar, somehow. I caught just a glimpse of his face, then he was gone and we were accelerating, the ragtag group dwindling behind us.

"Make sure Ma-Singh talks to today's group of admirers," I said to Nikki. "Maybe something new will shake out, if it's not a cop asking the questions."

"Right, because he's a lot less imposing," Brody said dryly. Still, he seemed more energized than he had before, and he put the commute to good use, bringing us up to speed on the latest developments of the case. Which, sadly, turned out to be a short conversation, since not much new had been discovered.

"Okay. No one has seen the Deguanzo mother for two days now, ditto Deguanzo junior, ditto the mom's first son," Nikki said. "She's not with friends, relatives, her job, neighbors, other patients at the clinic."

"Exactly." Brody rubbed his hands over his face again, as if he could massage eight hours of sleep back into his eyes. Once again, I wondered about his aura — or whatever the haze of gunk was I'd seen when I'd looked at him with my third eye. As I watched him, I let that same Sight take over once more — but whatever I'd seen was gone now.

No, not quite gone, I realized. The murk still clung to him, not quite out of sight, dim enough that I might miss it if I wasn't looking closely enough. So — maybe he was simply tired. Or maybe my own vision was suspect when it came to someone I'd known for so long.

Or, maybe there was something more going on with the good detective. Something I'd need to figure out after we discovered what was happening to the local Connecteds.

As if on cue, Brody's next words refocused me on the crisis at hand. "The facility has been completely cooperative. It doesn't look like it was an operation that went up to the top — just sideways through the organization. Some midlevel doctor or administrative person who culled the herd. Now that we've started looking into it, we've uncovered a half-dozen other missing persons cases with potential ties to the facility over the past three months. That, we're keeping very much on the down low, so as not to spook the place.

They're back to business as usual already. We're just watching them more closely. None of the other MP cases involve kids, though."

"So why her?" I asked.

He shrugged. "Mrs. Deguanzo never used her married name, didn't want her husband to find out, and since she presented herself as an undocumented worker but who still had cash…"

"Easy pickings," Nikki nodded. "Not a bad way to conduct a sting operation too, that undocumented angle. Now more than ever, everyone's keeping their head down."

"We're already doing that to go at the drug trade — the normal drug trade," Brody said. "But that's why these MPs went unreported. Friends and colleagues who knew these people were missing were probably at risk themselves, and nobody could afford to get found by the wrong people."

"What do you have on the other victims?" I asked.

"Adults, like I said, all of them. In the clinic for anxiety meds for the most part. That's the only apparent connection. Aged twenty-four to thirty-six, healthy in the main, single, no children that they admitted to in their preliminary paperwork. All of them paid in cash."

"All undocumented?"

"No, two of the three were native-born, but they were living transient lives. No one was expecting them anywhere except their jobs, but they were day_worker positions. There's always another person standing in line to take a job like that."

I nodded. Vegas wasn't that much different from any large city. There were always those who fell through the cracks. Normally, the bodies showed up, eventually. These hadn't.

"Who on the staff is our likeliest bet?"

Brody shook his head. "They're all clean, from what

we can tell so far. Staff isn't large, and most of them have been together a long time. We've moved on to suppliers, someone walking through, striking up a conversation."

"Like that won't take fifty years to sift through," Nikki groaned. She pulled into a parking lot, the neat sign advertising Better Health Services tucked discreetly into a rock-and-cactus planter. The building itself looked unthreatening, and the lot was half full of cars.

"I don't think we need to sift through anything," I said, staring at the building. A miasma of foul colors swirled over it. "The person we want is still inside. Keep going." Obligingly, Nikki exited at the far side of the parking lot, then drove to the next strip mall opening another thirty feet down.

Brody sighed irritably. "I'm not saying you don't have skills, Sara, but we've already been through the staff. If someone's guilty, we can't prove it by normal means. And if we can't prove it, we can't get anywhere."

"You can't." I nodded toward Nikki. "But all she needs is one or two good memories to guide us. We do this right, they'll never know they've been made. We get a bead on where they took the victims, and we're out of there. We can worry about arrests later."

Brody considered that, his mouth thinning in concentration, but Nikki and I were already getting out of the car. "I don't like it," he said.

"Of course you don't. Okay, who's going to be our guinea pig?" Nikki looked at me, then Brody. "You been on site here, love chop?"

"No," Brody said. "Another officer caught this case, before we were clued into the potential Connected, um, connection."

"So they don't know you." When he shook his head, she grinned. "And you're hot and sort of pitiful looking right now. That'll help if our pointer is a chick. Can you act drunk, disabled, that sort of thing? We need a reason

177

for both of us to be with you."

"Not even that," I said, catching on. "You said the ones who'd been taken had asked for anxiety meds. So you just need to act anxious. You've already got that look down."

"Thanks," he said derisively. After another few minutes' discussion, we headed in.

The lobby of the facility looked about as exciting as the Department of Motor Vehicles, and nearly as crowded. Crying children, haggard-looking parents, and patients-to-be in varying levels of health hunched apart from each other on black plastic chairs, staring at the muted TV or paging through last month's pop culture magazines. A plump woman behind a sliding screen surveyed us as we walked in, and Brody obligingly threw up his hands.

"Darlin'. you've got it all wrong," he said as Nikki grabbed his flailing fingers and I steered him forward, even as he kept up a deep Southern drawl. "You're overreacting like you always do. Look at these people — they are *sick*, seriously sick. We should let them get the attention they need."

"Can I help you?" the woman behind the screen asked, and Brody turned his stormy blue eyes on her, giving her a smile that had melted my seventeen-year-old heart. It seemed to do the trick on a thirty-something's heart as well — it was that kind of smile.

"Well, you most surely can, ma'am. You can help me by telling my well-meaning friends that I don't need to be on meds."

"He's off his Klonopin," Nikki said succinctly. "He's fine now, but we're heading cross-country to LA, and this audition is too important for him to screw up. What will it take to get another dose?"

"I don't need another dose, I'm telling you." He turned back to the woman at the counter. Two other nurse-looking women had filed in behind her and were whispering to each other and smiling; then a tall, thin woman stepped in. She didn't smile.

A chill snuck up my spine, and I squeezed Brody's arm where I held on to it. "Klonopin," I said, low and clear. "Please, we can give you all the information you need on his condition. Is there — is there someplace we can sign in? We can wait in the car or something, I don't know…" I looked worriedly over my arm, as if in fear for the huddled mass of patients behind us.

"Nancy, please have the patient step back to examination room four," the doctor said abruptly. The woman at the counter started with surprise.

"B-but, Doctor, I haven't gotten his information yet."

"We'll take care of that later." The doctor turned on her heel.

The intake nurse gave Brody a warm smile. "A nurse will be right out. Your friends can wait in the waiting room."

"Yeah, no," Nikki said brightly, and she wheeled Brody around, the two of us clamped firmly to his arms. A moment later, the door opened and a smocked woman looked out, her eyes going wide as she saw the three of us. "Mister…?"

"We're a package deal," Nikki said, then pushed her way into the back hall before the woman could react. When the door shut behind us, Nikki offered a tight smile. "Mr. James is in need of medication. In the past, when he's been in need of medication, he's caused harm to himself and others."

"Oh, for God's sake —" Brody protested.

The nurse drew herself up. "I'm sorry, we can't allow you to do that."

"Claudia." The doctor was back, and she offered us all an assessing smile. "It's all right. I recognize the

179

symptoms. Examination room four, please. I'll take care of gathering the information."

The hapless nurse nodded and moved quickly down the hallway, Nikki and I following along. A moment later, we were in the examination room, the three of us crowding in around the paper-covered bed.

"Is she our target?" Brody asked as soon as the door closed behind us.

"You think?" Nikki said derisively. "She almost fell all over herself. Clearly, she hasn't hit quota on delivering stooges this month."

I nodded. "Or she's on to us, and we're about to get slammed for our efforts. Either way, she'll be here quickly enough. We won't need much time."

A few minutes later, the door opened again, and the doctor strode in, carrying a clipboard on which rested an official-looking form — and a white paper cup with two pills in it.

I stared at it. Surely she wasn't thinking…

Brody backed away from her, looking credibly panicked. "Now, I don't need — "

"Don't worry, I won't give these to you before I've had a chance to understand your symptoms," the doctor said with her first smile of the day, her gaze shifting to us. "The fact that you need to be escorted at all times is surely an indication that your condition is not ideal, though, right?"

"Is there something I can start filling out?" Nikki asked, moving forward. She held out a hand to the doctor. "I'm Janet Mulready, personal security for Mr. James. Trust me, he needs your help. We've been flying commando since Albuquerque, and he's going to start losing his shit in the next half hour if we don't do something. Last time he went off his meds, he disappeared for three days."

"I did not," Brody said, huffing in outrage.

The doctor gave Nikki her hand, her smile not wavering. "I'm glad you sought assistance, then."

"You ever deal with that? Missing patients?" Nikki pumped the woman's hand, then flashed her a bright smile. "Probably not. Because you can help keep that from happening."

She dropped the doctor's hand and glanced to me, but I couldn't speak, couldn't move, my third eye in so much pain, I was surprised I wasn't bleeding from the forehead. The darkness pouring off the woman was so intense, it seemed unreal. Nobody could have an aura that mired in goo and still be breathing. No one.

"Look, I've had it," Brody snapped, crossing his arms. "You can't make me take your filthy meds — none of you can."

"Whoa, whoa, there, Mr. James," Nikki said hurriedly. "It's okay, it's going to be okay."

"We have other treatments beyond Klonopin that you might want to consider, Mr. James. It's for your own protection." The doctor took a step back. Her hand stole to her pocket — cell phone? I wondered. Time to leave.

"I don't care what you have, I'm not taking it," Brody blustered. "I haven't spent the last year working my ass off for nothing. I'm going to take this trip to LA with my wits about me."

"It's not your wits we're worried about, John," Nikki snapped back. "Just calm down. It's going to be all —"

She turned away as the doctor shifted forward, and before I could react, the woman pulled something out of her coat and aimed it at Brody. He was five feet away from us — too far for me to reach. The puff of air was so slight that I almost missed it, but Brody wheeled back, almost taking the table out completely. "What the hell!"

The doctor held up an atomizer, her gaze triumphant. "Calming mist," she said. "You should be feeling better shortly. Now, if we can proceed with the paperwork?"

"Calming—what?" He shook his head like an angry bear, rubbing at his face. "That got into my mouth!" he growled.

Nikki reached for Brody as he stumbled, and hauled him upright. "Okay, we've just moved into stage two. Thanks, Doc, I guess we won't be needing you after all."

"Wait—what?" The doctor blinked, genuinely surprised.

"The dizziness and vertigo is a straight shot to violent outburst. You want that to happen here, you probably should plan on having police tape strung over your windows like Christmas lights. We need to go." She grabbed the paper cup, and held them up. "Klonopin?"

"Yes—no. You can't take that. There are protocols—"

"Fair enough. We'll stop at the nearest hospital, then." Nikki tossed the cup onto the counter. It tipped over, but nothing tumbled out. The doctor wasn't watching that, however. Instead, she focused on Brody.

"Mr. James, I suggest you don't leave," she said tersely. "It would be very dangerous."

"I'm leavin'." Brody slurred. "You can't make me stay."

"Out you go." Nikki half carried Brody to the door, which I helpfully held open as they exited. The doctor stepped out behind me, still awash in her nasty dark aura. She looked past us to a new set of men I hadn't seen before, but she didn't summon them.

"Is there a side exit?" Nikki demanded.

"Of course," the doctor murmured, indicating the beefy men. *Great.* But Nikki was already heading for it, carrying a now-unresisting Brody with her.

The doctor trotted beside us. "I must caution you that he will have a terrible episode if you don't get him

182

to a hospital soon," she said, but her voice was now at odds with the expression on her face, and she watched Brody with mirror-bright eyes.

"We'll get him there, thanks."

I held out my hand, and she took it, not seeming to mind when I dropped it just as fast. Definitely Connected. No wonder LVMPD hadn't been able to get anywhere with her.

We hauled out into the parking lot, then realized we weren't in the front lot anymore, but the back. Which meant our car was half a block away.

"Okay, love chop, you can drop the act now," Nikki grunted, stepping away from Brody. When she released him, however, he fell to the ground.

Just then, the two doors to the clinic opened, and the Twin Beefy Boys stepped out.

"This...isn't ideal," I said.

"I don't feel so good," Brody muttered, and I groaned, looking down at him.

"You all right, ma'am? Sir?" the first guard called out.

"We're good!" Nikki said, waving them off. They kept coming.

"Gun?" I asked her. Mine was still in the car.

"Nope," she said. "Mace?" she asked in turn.

I squinted as the men started pacing toward us, looking far more menacing than they needed to. "Nope," I finally admitted.

"Fireball?"

I blinked at her, then back to the men. Then I smiled.

"We can always use more fireball," I agreed.

The fight was a short one. Nikki leaned down and lifted Brody in a fireman's hold, and the men burst into a run, one of them pulling a long-nosed gun free from his side holster. I came up with my hands cupped together, with an explosive blast of fire that was barely the size of my fist. It shot out with a hissing roar, however, and exploded about four feet in front of the men, dropping them to the ground in shock.

We bolted. By the time the goons got back up to give chase, we were already a hundred yards away, and a quick look behind us indicated they were never going to catch us.

"That was kind of a sad little fireball," Nikki huffed as we ran behind the second strip of office buildings, angling toward where our car was parked. "Seems like you should be able to do better than that."

"Yeah, well, you try throwing fire on the run. It's not as easy as it looks."

But the important part was—I had done it, on demand. And we'd gotten what we came here for too.

"Where to next?" I asked, and Nikki huffed beside me, slanting me a hard look.

"Nowhere, dollface," she grunted. "Dead end. Lots of dead ends, actually. All I read from the doc were dead bodies, dumped into Lake Mead."

CHAPTER NINETEEN

We made it to the car less than a minute later and threw Brody inside. I piled in behind him. Nikki took the wheel. As we pulled out of the parking lot, I noticed a child stood on the far side of the street, watching us calmly. A young Hispanic boy, instantly recognizable to me.

Or was he? I grimaced as we shot past him. How terrible was I that he looked exactly like the kid in the warehouse — and the one at the airport? I had lonely children on the brain.

Nikki pulled my attention away from the window. "Lover boy's waking up. You wanna give him the bad news?"

"What bad news?" Brody's words were groggy, and he blinked around woozily. "Weren't we in the clinic?"

"You got spritzed to death," I needled him, but honestly, he looked better for it. Despite his disorientation, a healthy color had returned to his face, and his eyes were brighter than they had been all day. Even his aura had lightened.

"You're not kidding," he said, and he made a face as he opened his mouth, working his tongue. "I think I ate some of that stuff. No wonder I passed out."

"You got the Klonopin, Nikki, or whatever those

pills were?" I asked.

In the front seat, Nikki grinned. "You betcha. I couldn't get out of there fast enough, once she spilled her beans."

"What beans?" Brody rubbed his face and head again, leaving his hair spiked high. "She talked?"

"She thought, which was enough," Nikki reported. "First I saw images of Beefcake and Wonderboy back there loading bodies into that van we saw in the back of the building, then a view of a house up on what looked like Lake Mead. Big place too. Money."

"Oh hell," Brody groaned.

Nikki shrugged. "There's a facility inside, exactly like you thought. Testing lab. The good doc was in it up to her ears, but stressed as all hell over it, and not from guilt. She couldn't supply enough bodies quick enough. Got her ass handed to her every time she went up there."

"That explains how we got into the clinic so easily, but not the breath of doom she blew on me."

"Smelled like lavender?" I asked him, not unkindly. He was rubbing his face again.

"Not exactly," he said, palpating the hollows of his cheeks. "And whatever it was, it's itching like crazy now. She said it was some sort of calming spray? Because I'm not feeling calm."

"Well, you look a lot better, sweet buns, if that's any consolation."

"And that's very important to me, thanks," Brody said derisively. "What else did she share?"

"Dead bodies," Nikki's face hardened, her gaze fixing again on the traffic in front of her. "They were operating on live subjects, harvesting organs, killing the hosts only after the living tissue was removed and put into some kind of sealed-off container. Other areas were ambulatory test subjects—I couldn't tell if those were the same as the ones they ended up cutting, but there was easily a dozen of them. All ages, from little kid to maybe mid-thirties. Nobody old."

"You'd think they'd be testing senior citizens," I said. "These drugs they're making, they're all about turning back the clock. Nobody wants that more than those who have a clock to turn back."

"Agreed, but I got no sense that's what they were looking for. Even lover boy here turned her on, and he's — I mean, not young, but — "

"Hey," Brody objected. "A little respect for your elders. But I did get in there awfully easily. The facility, Nikki, could you see the lake around it?"

"All around it, yup. Gotta be right on the water, and there were multiple buildings surrounding it in a cluster, all painted white — but it definitely was a private residence. Didn't have a parking lot, for one, just a large garage. Did have a pier, now that I'm thinking about it. But white walls, green roof, outbuildings. Should be able to Google Earth it."

"Agreed." Brody thought hard for another minute, lifted his hand again to his face, realized he was doing that, and put it down again. "You see anyone matching the description of the young family?"

Nikki's lips tightened. "Mom didn't fare so well. She — or someone who fits what you said she looked like — was on one of the tables. The children were in the testing center, baby wailing to beat the band. It was bad. We've got to get up there."

"Need a plan first, some sort of reason to demand a warrant." He clawed at his face again. "If they've got some sort of biomedical human-trafficking thing going on, that'll take the Feds. We need at least some sort of reason for them to target and move in, ideally with — "

I reached over and tugged at his sleeves, effectively pulling his hands from his face. "Seriously, Brody, you

187

need to stop with the facial massage. You're going to rub your skin off."

"It just feels so…weird," he said. "Like it's going to start coming off in sheets."

I looked at him more closely. His skin had begun to redden, with tiny blisters just beginning to break the surface. "You think maybe you're having an allergic reaction to whatever it was she sprayed on you?"

"Ya think?" He shrugged out of my grasp. "I need to go somewhere and wash it off."

"Yeah, that's probably a good idea. And hey, I said stop that—"

I grasped his hand with mine and nearly jolted out of my seat with the surge of electricity that shot through me. "Yikes!" I dropped his hand as my third-eye vision kicked in with a vengeance.

"Holy crap." Why hadn't I seen this immediately—like in the clinic? Why hadn't I guessed?

"What?" Brody's voice sharpened as he took in my face. "Goddammit, Sara, what is it?"

"Give me your hands," I said slowly, girding myself. "Give me…both your hands. Slowly."

"Guys, this is way more interesting than traffic, which is a bad thing for all of us," Nikki said from the front. "What're you doing, Sara?"

"Hands," I said tersely.

Whether it was my face or the tightness of my voice, Brody stopped arguing. He put his hands into mine, flinching as I sucked in a sharp breath.

"What is it?" he asked, but most of the strength had left his voice. "What's wrong with my hands?"

"It's not your hands," I said. "It's you. All of you."

"Connected?" Nikki asked, her voice climbing up a notch. "He already was a little bit, remember?"

"Not Connected," I said, shaking my head. "At least, not any more than he was. And you're still that." I shifted my gaze to meet his. "But this is something else. You're um…changing."

"Meaning?"

"Meaning your body, your cellular structure. It's…it's remapping itself. Reordering. You're basically going to become younger, in terms of cellular composition. Better, stronger, faster." I gave him a wan smile. "Think the Six Million Dollar Man on steroids."

He scowled at me. "You know I'm your biggest fan, Sara, but I'm not buying that you can see my cellular composition by holding my hands."

"I…" I shook my head. "I can't explain it, but that doesn't mean I'm not right. If this keeps going and you analyze your mitochondria, I bet it's going to look an awful lot like that of the cell samples we drew from the children in Father Jerome's safe house. Which means whatever she sprayed on you…" I stared at him, shocked. "That was a *spray*. How is that even possible?"

He stared right back. "You've got to be kidding me. Nothing works that fast."

"Unless it's a poison, yeah," I said. But the Fountain elixir wasn't a poison, it was a miracle drug. A drug currently being unleashed on unsuspecting populations around the globe. "But I'm telling you, something is having an effect here. You look completely different since we left the clinic, and your…" I stopped, peering closer. I wasn't wrong. "Your, um, skin is also peeling off."

"My what?" Brody jerked his hands out of my grasp. "Don't touch it. Nikki—"

"Already there. I'm calling Dr. Sells."

"Who?"

"I said, stop touching," I corralled Brody's hands again, studying him. Nikki's in-dash phone system connected, and she barked a command for Dr. Sells's number. The woman didn't answer, of course, but the answering service had dealt with Nikki before.

"We got a low-level Connected drugged with—something new. Technoceutical on the black market most likely designed for cell regeneration. He's been sprayed with it, and it's doing a number on his skin. We're bringing him in."

"Hold, please," said the musical voice on the other end of the phone, probably IVR, probably installed by the Arcana Council. Dr. Sells might be the only Connected physician in a hundred miles, but because she served the Council in her free time, she had all the latest toys. Which meant she'd be bugged to the gills, but right now, that couldn't be helped.

Nikki glanced into the rearview mirror, then jumped when the line clicked again. "This is Sells. What's the drug?"

"No idea," Nikki said tightly. "What clinic are you at?"

"The primary. How long will you be?"

"This time of day, twenty minutes."

"And he was sprayed? How?"

"Atomizer." I spoke up. "Small, looked like an asthma inhaler as much as anything. She carried it in her pocket. I've never seen drugs..." I shook my head, cutting myself off. I had seen gas-distributed drugs before, of course, I'd been a victim of one back in the day, right here in Vegas. But that drug had been pumped into a room, not blasted into someone's face.

"One spray only, maybe two. Some got in his mouth," Nikki finished for me.

"That will speed up the effects," Dr. Sells said. "What are his symptoms?"

"Eyes clear and bright, energy amped. Flushed, itching skin, which is starting to peel. Instant reaction of dizziness and inability to walk, but that seems to have worn off." I glanced at Brody, and he nodded quickly.

"Anything else?" the doctor prompted.

"Elevated heart rate, from what I can tell." I moved my hand to his carotid, and sure enough, it was thrumming away. "Sweats, shortness of breath, mild freak-out."

He grimaced and I continued. "How bad will this be?"

"There's no way to know," Sells replied thoughtfully. "You've no idea the makeup of this drug?"

"I'll get the makeup of what we fear it is sent to you, but no, I don't know for sure." I didn't want to share any more about my suspicions over the open phone. Not with Brody and God only knew who else listening. I thought about the children in Father Jerome's safe house, the ones even now existing in induced comas. "We've got to track this down."

"No shit," Brody muttered, and I squeezed his hands, ignoring the flare of electricity.

Which was another symptom, certainly.

"Victim is also registering a higher level of Connected ability," I said, swaying into Brody as Nikki took a particularly hard turn. "No specific skills manifesting, but psychic sensitivity is definitely higher. Not sure what that means."

"It means you'd better get here in ten minutes, not twenty," Sells snapped. Then she signed off.

"Well, she's a barrel of laughs today," Nikki said into the silence, but there was no denying our uptick in speed.

"Thing is—I really don't feel bad," Brody said. "If this is the high people are paying big bucks for, I can see them thinking they're getting their money's worth, especially if the skin change looks good." He glanced at me. "Does it still look good?"

I tried to ignore the patch of skin on his forehead,

curling away from his temple. "Yeah, well, I think you got some kind of extreme dose. No way they would be spraying people like this in the rave clubs as test-run cases. There'd be a riot."

"Fair enough." He swiped his hand over his brow. A fall of dead skin cells brushed off his face, and he blinked, turning his hands over. "What the hell?"

"Just hang on, love chop," Nikki said from the front of the car. "We'll get you squared away before you become the invisible man."

By the time we reached the clinic, however, Brody had taken a marked turn for the worse. He slumped against me, electrical buzz saw be damned, and was drifting in and out of consciousness. His breathing was steady, but his heart continued to pound.

"She better have a gurney waiting for us," I muttered.

"She does. Look there." Nikki nodded toward the clinic's entryway.

Dr. Sells herself stood under the portico for incoming emergency vehicles, and she had both a wheelchair and a bed at the ready. As Nikki lurched to a stop in front of the building, an orderly hustled up to the car and opened my passenger door. At this point, Brody was practically in my lap, so the orderly helped both of us out at the same time, untangling us and lifting Brody onto the gurney.

"When did he lose consciousness?" Sells asked, leaning over Brody as he was strapped in. She used a penlight instrument to study his eyes, and she flaked a few more skin cells off his forehead. "Is it just his face losing layers?"

"So far." I dusted my hands on my jeans. "I haven't opened his shirt or anything."

"I've seen this. Bring him." Without saying another word, Sells turned and started walking fast. I waited for

Nikki to hand off the keys to another orderly, then we both strode into the hospital.

The doors opened onto an enormous sitting room, and I missed a step as I recognized the man standing within as the doors slid shut behind us. Seeing Armaeus here in the hospital made me even more nervous.

"What are you doing here?" I waved Nikki on. She paused anyway, and I realized it was in part because she was what was left of my security detail. That didn't bother me as much as it should have. "Go on," I said again. "I'll be in shortly."

Armaeus smiled at her, and Nikki jerked at what was apparently a nudge in the right direction. She grimaced and stood her ground, resisting Armaeus's mental compulsion.

"Seriously," I said. "Spill."

"Of course," Armaeus murmured. "Dr. Sells advised me you were bringing in Detective Brody, and that he might be affected by this new strain of technoceuticals we are encountering. Do you have any of the base sample left?"

"No — it was aerosolized. He got a face full of it. That seemed to be enough, though. He's out for the count. You know what it is?"

"I do not."

"Hold the phones, dollface." Nikki's face was stricken as she held up the two pills. "These pills aren't Klonopin. Or at least not officially that. No markings."

My brows lifted. "You don't think…"

She grinned. "Sure as hell worth checking out." She looked at Armaeus. "You haven't secured any of the drugs yourself yet? To hear Ma-Singh talk, they're blanketing the streets with them."

"Not the originals." Armaeus shook his head. "The knockoff market is already thriving, but the original strain eludes us." Armaeus looked at Nikki's hand, and his eyes glittered. "Until now, perhaps."

"Maybe." Nikki deposited the pills back into her bra and gave him a broad wink. "You'll be the first to know. I'm going to go find Brody and Dr. Sells."

I turned to follow her, and Armaeus spoke again. "Miss Wilde...a moment, if you will."

"I'm kind of busy here—" But when I turned around, it wasn't only Armaeus standing there. Next to him was a child.

The boy from the airport. And the warehouse. And the street in front of the medical testing building.

"He's come a long way to see you, Miss Wilde," Armaeus said.

CHAPTER TWENTY

I stood like an idiot for another moment more, staring at the boy. He was small, smaller than I'd thought from a distance, and young. He couldn't be more than ten or eleven years old, and so thin he made my heart hurt.

"Hello," I said, as he stared at me with his big, soulful eyes. To my untutored mind, he looked Hispanic—dark hair, richly toned skin, dark eyes. He turned to Armaeus and murmured something.

The Magician nodded. "English is best."

"Hello, Sara Wilde," the boy said again, in a high, perfect little kid voice. "I was sent to find you—among all the others, I was chosen. And now I am here, and you are here, and you can save us."

I stiffened, my gaze going from the boy to Armaeus. "What's he talking about?"

"Perhaps it would be better if you sat down for a minute." The Magician gestured to a seat, and the boy settled his small body into it, patiently waiting for me to sit down opposite him.

The boy drew in a deep breath, undoubtedly ready to deliver another memorized statement, but I held up my hand.

"Who are you?" I asked.

He paused, blinking at me as if he didn't understand

the question.

I tried again. "What's your name?"

"Oh." His face broke into a smile, but what came out was another memorized spurt of information. "My name is Martine Angelo Diaz. I was abducted on June seventh, transformed on July first after many others failed to make the change. I was sent to find you..." Here he faltered, glancing to the Magician, though Armaeus's face remained impassive. "I don't know how long ago. But there were many vehicles and roads, and sometimes I would walk. It was hot, though. Always hot." He looked around the sitting room, his smile full of wonder. "It is much cooler here."

"Where were you sent from?"

He shook his head. "I cannot tell you. I can only take you there."

Every alarm bell inside me that could ring started clanging with authority. I didn't care how cute the little boy's face was, this had *trap* written all over it. Somewhere on the other side of Vegas I could hear Ma-Singh growling with disapproval.

"That sounds interesting," I hedged. "Do you know how long it will take us to retrace all those roads? It sounds like you were traveling a long time."

The boy's smile broadened as if I'd just said the one thing he most needed to hear. "No! We do not start the journey from here. We start from the *casa de pájaros*."

I blinked at Armaeus, but he was now looking at the boy curiously.

"The Birdhouse," the Magician translated.

"Yes! That is what they call it. Many beautiful birds everywhere, many people. Colorful. You will like it." The child said this last so earnestly I had to remind myself once again that this was a trap.

"The arcane black market in Mexico City has a facility known as the Birdhouse," Armaeus observed, and I glanced at him sharply. He met my gaze, speaking into my mind. *"The boy's memories are consistent with that trajectory."*

Uh-huh, I thought back to him. *What about the trajectory from this Birdhouse to wherever it is he wants to take me?*

"That is a blank. I don't think he knows."

So it's a trap.

"...Perhaps."

I switched to my outside voice. "Who sent you to me, Martine?"

"You did," he said again, all smiles. "You came to me in my dreams, like in the picture I painted. On the big wall."

I stared at him. "You painted that mural? How?"

"The boys in the neighborhood, they had paint cans. I told them I would show them how to paint something small, and if I was good, they would give me enough paint. They didn't believe me, but I taught them very much. Then they helped me." He smiled. "It's a very big wall."

"But—how did you have the skill to do that?" I pressed. "Had you painted before?"

He shook his head, squinting at me as if I was testing him. "I saw it, I saw you. And I simply took what was in my mind and put it on the wall."

"But, how?" At his frown, I tried again. "Have you always been able to paint so well?"

"Oh!" He shook his head, beaming. "No, not at all. I became transformed on July first, I told you. All that I have shown and done—this journey, finding you, the painting—that has been since then. Before, I was an ordinary boy, living an ordinary life. Now I am...something more."

"Right." I swallowed. "And this process of transforming, how was it done?"

With that, Martine's face clouded, and for the first time since he saw me, he looked confused, almost lost.

"I don't—I forgot," he said quietly.

"Of course, of course," I murmured. So it was bad, at least that much was clear. "Did they give you something to eat or drink?"

"Bitter powder, like salt but it didn't taste like salt. More…" He made a face, the same face Brody had made in the car, looking like he was trying to scrape off his tongue with his teeth. "Like dirt."

July first, he'd said. They'd given him this drug July first.

"And how have you been feeling since then?" I forced a smile, trying my best to look friendly even though I wanted to launch a huge fireball—first toward that lake house Nikki had mentioned and then into a Mexican birdhouse. "You are well? Never sick anymore?"

"Never sick," he said, grinning. "I am a success, they say. Sometimes my heart is too happy in my chest, but if I am quiet and tell it to go to sleep, it does."

"Of course," I said again, adding wattage to my smile. Inside, my own heart was churning. Two months and Martine was already starting to have a racing heartbeat, just as Father Jerome had warned. He was a Connected child, a gifted one from the sounds of it, likely able to manage the effects of the pills. Brody had been hit full blast with the drug, however. How would he—and the tens of thousands of people who were given sample bags—how would they manage it? Not well, I suspected.

I had to destroy these drugs at their source, wherever they were being made, but the problem was bigger than that now. I had to find an antidote…find it and discover some way to get it to everyone who needed it. Thinking about that made my head spin, but one challenge at a time.

I circled back to Martine's original statement. "You said that I would save you, but you seem so happy. Why would you — any of you — need saving?"

"Because we are like you, but we are not you, not yet. We need you to finish the process. That's what is missing, why so many of us failed to transform, why some of those who did got sick. Because you weren't there to help us."

I looked at him, a new thread of horror twisting through me. "I'm confused, Martine. How can I help you? I don't know anything about this powder."

"But it is you who first brought us this gift, and you who complete the gift." Martine said these words with such conviction that I didn't bother countering them. Instead, I smiled. Again. This one harder to form than the last.

"You must be very tired. You've come a long way."

His eyes widened. "No! I am not tired. We can go back right away — now, we can go now."

"You could go now," Armaeus said, his tone gentler than I'd ever heard it before. He laid a soft hand on Martine's shoulder, and instantly, the boy relaxed. "But you can also prepare. When one departs on a journey, it is wise to prepare. Sara must prepare, and so should you."

The boy frowned up at him. "But how can I prepare? I have my feet. That's all I need."

"You can sleep," Armaeus said easily. "More importantly, you must sleep. It is the only way you can begin with strength and end that way as well."

"Sleep," the boy repeated, and already he sounded drowsy.

You're really good at that. You should probably have a show on the Strip.

"*I do.*" Armaeus allowed the flicker of a smile to

199

trace his gorgeous lips. *"It's called leading the Council."*

I felt his touch in my mind, seeking out the broken spaces, and by the time he spoke again, it was aloud. Martine was now slumped against him, snoring lightly.

"Go to Ma-Singh," Armaeus told me. "He'll be waiting for you with what you need."

I lifted my brows. "You knew this was what would happen? The boy coming here like this?"

"There are many possibilities that unfold in time. This was one. Not one I would have chosen, but one I cannot interfere with. Its outcome is blocked to me." He grimaced. "Blocked to the High Priestess as well."

"Good. I need her nosing around my business like I need a hole in the head."

"Miss Wilde."

"Mr. Bertrand," I countered in the same tone.

It was uncanny how Armaeus could make me feel like he and I were alone in the room when we were sitting in the midst of a crowd of people, but he did, somehow. He lifted his hand, and a light breeze brushed my hair away from my face. "You're going to be going on what is known as a spirit journey—yes." He said softly. "I'm aware that Ma-Singh used the term with you. He did so rightly. It is the path you must take, but it is one I would have avoided, out of all the possibilities. If I'd seen what was coming earlier, I could have altered the course of one, maybe two decisions…"

"You couldn't have done that, though, right?" I asked, peering at him. "There's that whole noninterference thing, which I kind of think directly opposes anything that involves altering the course of someone else's decisions."

"But the way is not clear, and it grows darker the farther away you will travel." His words echoed Ma-Singh's, and I shifted uncomfortably in my chair. "Which is not as it should be. The world as we have protected it must always be pierced with light, even if by mortal standards it seems impossible. This…is something different. And something I cannot pierce."

"Well, I'll keep you posted. It's Mexico, not Atlantis. You'll always be able to find me, even when I don't want you to." I shot him a knowing look, yet my words made Armaeus grow more somber.

When he leaned toward me, I edged away. I couldn't take the touch of his lips on me—not on my forehead, where my third eye was peeled wide as if I'd never see the Magician again, and definitely not on my lips. It felt too much like good-bye, and suddenly it was very important that this not be good-bye. Not here.

He straightened, his gaze unreadable, but I couldn't keep my cool. My voice cracked as I spoke.

"You owe me way more than a send-off in a hospital lobby," I whispered. "I should at least get flowers."

Armaeus inclined his head, but his reply was interrupted by the sound of the opening door. Nikki strode out, her head swinging around. "You should come back," she said, her words curt as she approached me.

"Sure, I just—" When I turned back to face the Magician, he was gone.

"I…right," I said, looking around the room. Fortunately, the kid was gone as well. I couldn't face the idea of babysitting him tomorrow, let alone tonight. How on earth was I going to travel with a child? The answer was—I couldn't. There was simply no way. That child needed to be cared for by the Magician, or at least by Father Jerome.

Martine had given me everything I needed, anyway. I'd head to the Mexico City arcane black market, find the Birdhouse or whatever it was, and see where my third eye took me. My eyes and my cards. It was a good combination.

Feeling suddenly cheered, I squared my shoulders and turned to Nikki. "How's he doing?" I asked.

"He's…" She grimaced. "Well, he's not good. Which is weird. Everything we saw in Father Jerome's kids indicated that the reactions took several weeks if not months to set in. Brody started failing in about fifteen minutes. I don't get it."

"I don't get it either," I said, but something in her words gave me pause. "Of course, he's not a child. That might be the key."

"But they're giving the drugs out to *adults* in those clubs. They had to be formulating them for adult usage. How badly does a kid need to grow younger?" As she talked, we pushed through to the next hallway, which was as spotlessly white as the first. "So, what, did he get a weaponized version? Also, he's Connected, at least somewhat—and the blast made him more so. According to Dr. Sells, Detective Delish is like you said: better, stronger, faster…and damned near dead."

I jolted. "What?"

"See for yourself." She pushed open the last door, and we stepped into an intensive care unit. Instantly, a nurse handed us masks, but I ignored her and moved forward to Dr. Sells, who was standing beside Brody's bed, gazing down at him. I stared, shocked. His face was covered with an oxygen mask, and his skin was the color of cement. On the nearest monitor, his heart rate was hammering at a cool two hundred and twenty beats per minute.

"What's happening to him?" I asked sharply, and Dr. Sells roused herself.

"I don't know. We've tried to slow his heart with chest massage, cooling treatments, but I'm unwilling to try medication because I'm not sure how it will interact with whatever he's ingested. We're analyzing the white pills now, but that will take time.

"Time doesn't seem to be on our side right now."

"The strangest part is — he's smiling." She shook her head. "We've even caught him laughing, though he's unresponsive to external stimuli. I don't know why. But he seems actually happy."

Immediately, Martine's words sprang into my mind. *"My heart gets too happy, and I have to tell it to sleep."*

I pushed Dr. Sells out of the way, then shoved the oxygen tube to the side, clearing a space above Brody's chest. Ignoring the bleats of the doctor and her nurses, I placed my hand on his chest. Sure enough, Brody's heart was pounding a million beats a minute, and I suddenly felt like I was too far away from him — too far.

I leaned down more closely, then turned my head, resting my cheek upon his sternum, curling my hand behind his back.

"Rest," I whispered, reaching out with my heart, my mind, with every connection point I'd ever had to Brody, every point I ever would. My third eye opened wide, but whatever had afflicted Brody's aura before was now vastly outweighed by this new threat. Everything about him was caught up in a driving, thumping race, each beat coming more rapidly than the last.

"Rest," I urged again, breathing against his chest. "Your heart will sleep and dream, your joy will wait for you, but not now — not now. Now is the time for rest. For sleep. Even the happiest of hearts must stop their dancing."

Everything quieted around me, except for the thudding of Brody's heart. It thrummed and jackhammered and banged against my ear, but I never stopped my litany of rest, never stopped reaching out. Never stopped...

I don't know how long I was at it. I only knew that when I awoke, the room was dark and still, the monitors chirping and tweeting in a soft chorus around us. Beneath my cheek, Brody's chest rose and fell with quiet regularity, his heart finally slowed to a reasonable pace. I lifted my face, and for a long moment, I just watched him sleep.

Across the room, Nikki sighed heavily. "I love you guys," she whispered.

CHAPTER TWENTY-ONE

The generals of the House of Swords assembled in Soo's desert mansion, led by Ma-Singh. I would always think of this house as Soo's, I decided, though Nikki had put her indelible stamp on the sections she'd claimed for her own. It was too large and rambling for me, roaming down endless corridors and into dozens of high-windowed rooms, their filtered shades doing all they could to bank both the heat and light from outside. Like everything else Soo favored, the house was big, complex, and damned near impregnable. Exactly like the organization she'd built so carefully, brick upon brick.

Now I sat at the head of the long table of men and women dedicated to the safety of the House, and tried to figure out how exactly I'd gotten myself here. And how I could possibly keep all of them safe.

Ma-Singh summed up his report. "The Revenants have signed the coalition agreement with our House, accepting our protection in return for serving as observation outposts at their discretion." He held the gazes of the other generals steadily, then stated the obvious. "Very lenient terms, but we are interested in building their trust, not their fear or dependence."

The group was too well trained to raise an objection

on this matter, mainly because the arguments had already been waged. And I'd conceded on enough other points that they were mollified.

One of those points was Ma-Singh's next topic. "Recruitment efforts for trained warriors have entered phase one. Early response has been strong. Training will commence in waves once initial applicant pools have been culled."

He gestured to the woman beside him, a stiff-spined Nigerian who probably would have been a warlord in another lifetime. She nodded, giving her report as well in English. "Per protocols, we are pulling half males, half females, then separating only according to skill. Fighting abilities are not a problem, but we are looking to increase our numbers of technologically savvy recruits."

"Our issue is the opposite." This man, a tall, angular Norwegian, could have been a vampire—or an elf. He was that preternaturally beautiful and pale. "Technology recruitment is at capacity but weapons training is sadly lacking. We'll expand our territory to include neighboring sectors."

The other reports were a mix of positive and negative, though I could tell by Ma-Singh's expression that he was pleased. Soo had been tapering down the size of her fighting force in the past few years, mainly because, I suspected, she'd lost control of it. But there were too many members of the House of Swords in imminent danger of a flash attack from Gamon now. If I didn't root out the source of this new drug...

Ma-Singh turned to me, interrupting my thoughts. "Your request to target Connecteds has yielded positive results as well, though more slowly."

"Keep trying." I'd been shocked to discover how few members of the House's protectors were even low-level Connecteds. That was going to change, especially since — though Ma-Singh had not tacitly acknowledged this to the other generals yet — the charter of the House was expanding to include their protection. That was our deal. I expanded our scope, he got to expand his forces. I wasn't sure it was the right equation, but it was all I could do right now.

He nodded, then moved to the more traditional opponents in the war on magic, starting with the quasi-military, quasi-religious organization that wanted to see an end to anything not of this earth — and not exclusively of their God. "Surveillance on SANCTUS has proven more fruitful as well, but the news is not good. The organization has reestablished a base in Vatican City, though it is no longer under the tacit direction of the Holy See. They have also instigated meetings with Interpol."

I winced. "Do we know why?"

"We do not. Our current speculation is that the recent interest of Interpol in the technoceutical trade has alerted them to the existence of the broad reach of the arcane black market and some of its key players. SANCTUS, with its historical charge of rooting out the non-secular threats to its religious credo, is well positioned to offer them historical data on the growth and development of Connected societies, presumably emphasizing their danger to the non-Connected public. While Interpol is in no way a threat on its own to Connected communities, they, of course, have relationships with local government and law enforcement agencies throughout the world."

"And Gamon's given them the perfect length of rope to hang everyone by," I said, following Ma-Singh's line of thought. "This new drug, Fountain. It's flooding the market through Connected channels, but because it's not specifically tied to Connected abilities, it has a broader scope. Everyone wants to turn back the clock, which means everyone's willing to try it—or at least to test it, which we can already see is not going well."

Ma-Singh nodded. "Cases involving the drug are starting to bubble up in law enforcement and medical communities, though not yet in a concerted fashion in traditional or social media, except on the deep web. However, its growing incidence rate will eventually filter up to more mainstream search engines. We don't have a lot of time."

"Where are we on drug analysis?" I asked. The faster we figured out what this stuff was made of, the faster we could destroy it.

He shifted uneasily. "Per your instructions, we have enlisted the assistance of Simon of the Arcana Council and his team of researchers. The exact chemical process is still impossible for us to replicate or even fully understand—there are elements for which there are no testing standards. Not even Simon can crack it, which has led him to speculate that it's…" Ma-Singh grimaced, clearly at odds with the Fool on this conclusion. "…a compound not strictly of this world."

I looked at him sharply. "Like, what. Unobtainium?"

Ma-Singh didn't appreciate my comment. He rarely did.

"It's not a viable theory," he said sternly. "However, one possibility is that the element was culled from asteroids discovered in prehistoric dig sites. Then again, it could be something created by an ancient alchemical process we simply are not privy to. We don't understand it, which is the primary issue, and studying the end product isn't going to get us there in time. We need source material."

"We'll get it," I said. My stomach knotted just thinking about what must be going into a drug strong enough to change someone's cellular makeup. There were some things that were meant to be unleashed into the world, and some things that were not. Just looking at the mad rush of buyers to this untested, unsafe drug was enough to convince me of that. It was bad enough what the hyper-rich were ingesting, smearing on, and injecting into themselves in an eternal search for eternal youth — this went way beyond superficial facial and skin treatments. This was screwing with humanity at a fundamental level, and that was a very slippery slope.

Beyond that, who knew what Gamon's end game was? The deaths of the Revenants continued to disturb me. There were simply too many of them who'd died in that first attack. It wasn't efficient. Whereas in Japan, only the targeted children had been killed. That...didn't add up. Why was there a different attack approach?

What did Gamon really want?

Ma-Singh's rumble cut across my thoughts. "We've deployed observation teams under the direction of the priest in Paris. With so few Connecteds in our ranks, it will be difficult to infiltrate psychic communities, but we expect to have teams in place in the next few weeks."

I didn't ask how much that maneuver was going to cost us. For one thing, I didn't want to know. For another, I didn't care. I couldn't sit on the House's enormous coffers and let people continue to be abducted and killed in pursuit of the arcane black market's endless search for riches. Gamon wasn't the only threat these people had faced over the centuries, but she was the face of their terror now. I could do something about that — I had to.

"Make sure you or your designees authorize all acts of force among your teams, no matter how small," I said, sweeping the room with my gaze. "I don't want to incite violence among these communities."

A dozen sets of coolly competent eyes stared back at me. I couldn't read their expressions, and though I didn't doubt their loyalty, I could only imagine what they thought of me. I had no training in administration or warfare—and clearly no concern for budgeting. I was a Connected, clearly so—and that had to be strange for them, didn't it?

Beside me, Ma-Singh's gaze also seemed to rest on the assembly. He directed a question to the table. "Any disruptions so far?"

A general at the far end, an older Japanese man with a lined face but fiercely cold eyes, spoke up. "The attack on the Revenant community in Tokyo has not gone unnoticed by the other Connecteds of the city. It's causing unrest. They were aware, of course, of the recluses near the Meiji Jingu shrine, but not the size of the community. I fear we will see more of this in the coming weeks—groups of people who have spent generations believing themselves to be isolated, realizing how close they are to similar groups."

"Is that a problem?" I asked.

"In theory, no," the old general answered as Ma-Singh stood and moved to a side table. "But it does underscore the need for careful watch. If these groups decide that we cannot adequately combat this new threat, they may band together and resist the intercession of non-Connected aid. That would leave them at significant risk."

"They've spent centuries surviving by hiding," I said, turning the idea around in my mind. "But this is a different world, linked in ways never before possible. If they thought they could stage an action on their own..."

Connecteds were by and large sensitives. In monsters like Gamon, that sensitivity had been funneled and honed into a brutal weapon, but for most of the community, the extreme empathy their abilities gave them blunted their effectiveness as warriors. The exceptions tended to be among arcane black market finders and the handful of assassins I'd encountered over the years.

"They'd be slaughtered," another general said, finishing my thought aloud.

The elder general nodded. "Without training, most certainly. And we have trained very few Connected warriors. It will take time to perfect the process."

Ma-Singh spoke from the side of the room. He was fussing with a long jade box. "Time is not a luxury we have, unfortunately. Instead, we can rely on loyalty and dedication to the cause of protecting our own leadership — and those like her."

I frowned at the strange intensity of his words. Working with the cast of generals was a careful balance, and I didn't want to push my agenda too far, too fast.

Then Ma-Singh turned, and my words of conciliation died in my throat. He walked over to me almost casually, handing me the wrapped packet he held. I knew without asking what it was.

The power of the Gods' Nails radiated through their meager silk covering, but the transfer of the artifacts to my hands caused no ripple of uneasiness in the group. They caused enough in me to cover anyone else, of course. Immediately upon handling them, I felt the surge of electricity roll through me, and the base of my palms ached with a keening sense of loss. Apparently, they missed being pierced through to the bone. I shuddered just thinking about it.

"Madam Wilde has not been trained in our ways, but she is a warrior," Ma-Singh continued. He gestured to me meaningfully, and I stared at him. Surely, he couldn't want me to uncover the nails in front of his generals. We still didn't understand their long-term impact, but we'd seen the short-term version.

At his glare, though, I unwrapped the silk, laying the nails bare. Of their own volition, my hands covered the bases of the long strips of sharpened bone, allowing the cruel tips to extend through my two center fingers.

To their credit, the generals did not show any reaction to this move, or to the artifacts themselves. The bones seemed to melt into my skin ever so slightly, but I focused my mind on keeping them out of my skeleton. That required my full attention, so I nearly missed Ma-Singh's next words.

"Madam Wilde will undertake great risk to preserve and protect our House and those to whom it has sworn allegiance. It is only appropriate that we will undertake a personal pledge to preserve and protect *her*, as well. As we have protected our leaders throughout the long tradition of the House of Swords."

This sounded a lot like a pinkie-swear ceremony, and I suddenly realized what Ma-Singh was doing.

"Ma-Singh," I said warningly. At the far end of the room, two people entered, swinging the door back with sharp urgency. Nikki and Nigel, the only two people other than Ma-Singh at the Vegas house who'd witnessed the strange bonding ceremony on the deck of the ship in the North Atlantic. Both of them now looked like they'd been struck with a brutal, killing fervor, their eyes flashing with intensity, their bodies rigid, ready to spring.

The generals paid no attention to them. Their gazes were on me. Not the curious artifacts jutting out from underneath my hands, but me. My face, my body. As if committing it to memory, imprinting me on their very minds.

"I know I can count on all of you to do your best whenever called to serve at Madam Wilde's request, no matter how challenging or subtle," Ma-Singh intoned.

A chill raced down my spine as the generals leaned forward. They started speaking then, but not in English. Each of them whispered words that sounded almost like a benediction, prayers wrought in their beautiful, hypnotic, and powerful native tongues. I exchanged a startled look with Ma-Singh, but he spared me only a moment's glance—a very smug moment's glance.

"I am glad to hear it," he said as the generals fell silent. They sat back, but they didn't look like people in a daze, or who'd been hypnotized into fealty. I was the only one who seemed to be fazed by the experience, and…dammit! The nails had sunk into me after all in my distraction, sharp bolts of pain lodging into my hands.

I stood quickly then, whipping my hands behind my back as Ma-Singh stood beside me. I may have had a dozen new fans, but they didn't need to see me do my hedgehog routine. "Thank you," I said, staring out at their solid, fierce faces.

I would have said more, but I didn't have the chance. As one, they stood, their backs stiff, their eyes fiery, their manner filled with pride of purpose. They bowed to me, some of them crossing their hands over their heart, then straightened.

"*Kyakka*," Ma-Singh said, or at least that was what it sounded like he said, and I recognized the lilt of the Japanese word of dismissal.

So did the oldest general, whose eyes flared even brighter at the end of the room. An expression of unspeakable ferocity chased over his face, then he turned and left.

The others followed behind them. In another minute, the room was completely empty save for Ma-Singh, myself, and the Aces of Swords.

"That," Ma-Singh said with satisfaction, "was instructive." He eyed me, his gaze dropping to my spiked hands. "I think I approve of these new weapons of yours."

CHAPTER TWENTY-TWO

With no one here who didn't know the truth, I pulled my claws out from behind my back and lifted them toward Nikki.

"A little assistance here?"

"You're going to have to come up with a better release mechanism, you know," Nikki said, but she strode cheerfully enough toward me down the long room. Her grin echoed Nigel's, but I saw as well the curious intensity in their expressions, matched by Ma-Singh's. They knew what had just gone down between myself and the generals. They'd felt the pull of the Gods' Nails too.

The Mongolian general had used this new tool in my arsenal to help build a powerful connection between me and his top military personnel, but I realized in a flash that it could be put to more personal benefits as well.

"Thank you," I said as Nikki approached. I held my hands out to her, palms up, the long bone spikes fully visible above their incision point in the base of my palm—helpfully cauterized by the magic of the Gods' Nails, and stinging like hell. The sight of the artifacts caught Nikki up short, as I expected it to. So I continued, taking them all in with my gaze.

"I'm leaving shortly for Mexico. I know you want to

keep me safe. But you can protect me best by staying here and coordinating the response to any new attacks from Interpol, SANCTUS, Gamon, or whoever else decides to come to the party. I need to do my work alone."

"No." Nikki and Nigel voiced their dissent as one, but Ma-Singh merely nodded.

"Yes," I said, curving my hands around the nails. They both stiffened, and I could see the war of outrage playing over their faces, but I didn't feel bad about it. I wasn't going to pull them into danger.

"Promise me," I said. "I can't worry about you following me where I'm going. I want to know you are doing the work that needs to be done."

"Where are you going?" Nikki asked brusquely, her hands clenched. My heart twisted in my chest, but I needed her assurance.

"Promise me first," I said. "I'll tell you, and if I need you, I will call—I will. But I need to know you'll stay here otherwise."

"Fine," Nigel said, his voice clipped. "We'll remain unless and until we are summoned."

Nikki whipped her head toward him, her eyes blazing, but she nodded tersely.

"I'm traveling to the marketplace in Mexico City," I said, bracing myself for their outrage. To my surprise, however, their faces blanked. They nodded. As if now that the promise was made, the tension flooded out of them, their path made clear.

"You will need provisions, a plane," Ma-Singh said, settling in front of the laptop open at the head of the table. "Security at least to get you through the landing site. Then they will fall away. We'll have local eyes on you as well. It would look strange if we didn't, to anyone who was watching."

I didn't like that, but I saw his point. "Fair enough.

I'm leaving today, though—tonight at the latest."

Nikki had moved in front of me. She'd picked up a couple of linen napkins from the table, and, using them to shield her palms, she placed her hands on the nails. Even through the thick cloth, I felt the jolt of awareness at her touch.

"Then you'll need these out of you," she said with a rueful grin. "I seem to recall this as being not particularly pleasant."

"I trust you," I said, remembering Armaeus's words. "I trust you, I know you are my friend, my protector, my—"

My breath caught as she yanked the nails free, and, happily, it didn't hurt nearly as much this time. Nothing like a little practice. Blood gushed forth over my wrists, and Nigel cursed, pulling off his shirt in one fast movement and catching up my hands with it.

"This job just keeps getting better and better," cracked Nikki, winking at me over Nigel's hunched shoulders. He straightened away from me, my hands now effectively tourniqueted together. Ma-Singh, for his part, had already taken the nails from Nikki, their gleaming white surfaces unblemished in the cradle of silk he used as a buffer between his bare hands and the potent artifacts. He exchanged the linen for their silk wrappings, and replaced the nails in the jade box.

"You'll take these with you," he said.

I nodded. The nails weren't ideal weapons, based on the logistics of using them, but it would be good to have them along in case I needed to turn an angry crowd. And where I was going, I suspected there would be a lot of angry people. I still needed more information, however. And for that I needed Armaeus.

"Get the plane ready. I'll be back as soon as possible." I worked my hands free of Nigel's shirt, shuddering a little as the wrist wounds pulled against the cloth. Still, the bleeding had stopped. The puckered edges of the openings stretched toward each other, the flaps of skin making me only a little bit queasy.

"I thought you were leaving tonight," Nikki said, but her tone wasn't challenging.

Ma-Singh answered for me, pointing to the laptop. "She's been summoned to Prime Luxe. A Council limo has been idling in front of the house for the past ten minutes."

I curled my lip at the idea of being summoned anywhere, but there was no point in arguing. It was close enough.

Nigel and Nikki left the room with so little fanfare, I almost felt abandoned, then quickly stuffed that emotion down. If this was going to work, I needed to remain in control of my own emotions, especially the pettier ones. Gesturing to Ma-Singh to follow me, I made my way down the long, empty halls toward the front of the mansion.

"You don't trust the loyalty of the generals?" I asked him quietly as we passed several doors, voices evident on the other side engaged in a United Nations' worth of languages.

"I trust them implicitly. I trust you implicitly," he said, with a candor that pierced me as effectively as the spikes had, resulting in an equal amount of pain. "But they know you less personally than I do. While they will protect you and follow you, I needed them to *believe* you as well. Until you earn their trust outright, I do not quibble with how I achieve that belief."

I frowned. "It kind of feels like cheating."

"Will you risk your body and all your abilities against any enemy of the House and those whom the House protects?"

"Of course I will. It's just—"

"Then it is not cheating," he said, cutting me off. "It's

217

working more quickly toward your goals. I do not know if the nails would work so powerfully with a leader who is not noble in heart. But these weapons are of the gods. So presumably not."

"Depends on which gods," I retorted, but I couldn't argue too much. I'd seen the impact of the nails already. I knew their value. I'd simply have to live up to the expectations I'd set in the minds of his — my — generals. As much as I suspected they would follow my orders into the fire, even without the nails, knowing that they'd been compelled to protect me made my own actions even more critical. I couldn't fail them. I wouldn't.

True to Ma-Singh's word, Armaeus's limo was waiting for me at the curb. I turned to the Mongolian general and shook his hand, wincing only a little at the pain in my wrist.

He noticed anyway. "You are too lax with your sense of personal care, Madam Wilde. It's no wonder you inspire your allies to be so protective and your enemies to be so rash."

The Mongolian's face was a mask of genuine, almost fatherly, worry.

"I'm working on it." I grinned. My heart seemed to expand a little as he gazed so somberly at me, and I pulled him into a quick, hard hug. He grunted with surprise, straightening quickly, and I let him go before he burst a blood vessel. But when our gazes met again, his seemed undeniably brighter.

"I'll have the plane in place this evening," he said.

"Good." I hesitated, then held out my hands for the jade box. "Let me take that to the Council."

Ma-Singh scowled, but I wiggled my fingers.

"Nikki was right. I need a better way to retract these than finding someone I trust. I have a feeling that requirement is going to prove problematic where I'm heading. If there's something they can do to facilitate

218

their use, I have to let them see it."

Not for nothing, Armaeus had likely been salivating over the prospect of studying the artifacts. It would give him something to do while I grilled Martine about everything he knew. The kid might think tagging along was a good idea, but that was a total nonstarter. Still, I had to talk with him before I left for Mexico. I needed to know what he knew.

Reluctantly, Ma-Singh handed over the jade box. "Even with the weapons of the gods, you must take care, Madam Wilde. Your enemies are all around."

I winked at him. "Thanks to you, so are my friends. I like my odds in that regard."

He sighed but obligingly stepped back. The limo driver had exited the vehicle and now stood by the rear passenger door. I dutifully turned away from the general and slipped inside the car's cool, dim confines. I realized immediately that this was a more luxurious limo than usual, even by Armaeus's exacting standards.

Right after that, I realized that I wasn't alone.

"Miss Wilde."

As the vehicle pulled away from the curb, the lights came up dimly, and I saw the Magician's long catlike form reclining in the seat opposite mine. Beside him, perched like a bobbing reed on the shoreline, was Martine.

"You guys going stir-crazy already cooped up in your penthouse?" I asked, trying to mask my dismay.

Armaeus lifted his hand to wave off my protest. "You've brought the Gods' Nails. We don't have a great deal of time. If I may?"

I handed over the box, not feeling strong enough to have the spikes anywhere near my wrists again so quickly. The boy scuttled over to my side of the limo as Armaeus took the jade container.

"You wield fire." Martine leaned forward in his seat,

219

his bright eyes fixed on the box.

I looked at him sharply. "How do you know that?"

"The pictures on the wall." He smiled. "The sword you hold—it's sharp, like these, but longer. And it's on fire."

I frowned, trying to recall the imagery on the dome of the central building of Atlantis, or even the mural Martine had painted. The sword had been held aloft, yes, by the figure in those paintings. But there hadn't been arcs of fire bursting forth. I would have remembered that.

Armaeus murmured something in a language I didn't recognize, not that that narrowed down the options much. He sighed with deep appreciation as he unwrapped first one spike, then another.

"What?" I prompted, but he ignored me for another long minute as he stared at the nails, passing his hands over them as they lay on the cloth.

Martine began to squirm beside me, and I totally was right there with the kid. I never was big on waiting. I was big on finding out what I needed to know. "So this Birdhouse," I began. "What is it exactly?"

"You're not leaving the child behind, Miss Wilde. You need him."

I waved at Armaeus irritably, as if I was swatting a gnat, but Martine apparently wasn't on Radio Magician.

"A beautiful place!" the boy said eagerly. "Everyone's dressed like birds, especially the women. There are mostly women there."

Oh, fantastic. I tried to keep the grimace from my face. "And why do we need to begin there?"

"The map back is in my heart, not my head," Martine grinned at my blank look. "I cannot tell you how it is to find the tunnels, only that I will know the way by sense. I cannot picture it, only travel it."

Tunnels?

"I told you so."

I ignored Armaeus again.

"But why?" I asked Martine. It seemed almost a foolish question, but to my surprise, the boy answered it.

"Because of the prophesy," he said, nodding quickly as I blinked at him. He drew in a long breath and recited the way any ten-year-old would a memorized poem. "Come away, O human child! To the waters and the wild, With a faery, hand in hand, For the world's more full of weeping than you can understand."

I knew that poem. Yeats. *The Stolen Child.* Oddly enough, it was one of the first things I'd learned to read all on my own. Hearing it now, from the mouth of a babe…a shudder rippled through me.

Martine pounded his chest with pride. "I am the human child. You are the wild faery. Yes? When you reach the waters, you will be our salvation."

I lifted a hand. "I've been called a lot of things, but never a wild faery."

"Really."

I glowered at the Magician. He countered with an insouciant smile and tapped the artifacts resting in his lap. A chill danced up my arms.

"These were found by the Vikings," he murmured aloud. "But they predate them. These inscriptions are druidic."

I peered at the scratches on the bones. "Kind of all the same, though, right?"

"Perhaps better stated, they did not originate with the warrior class, but with the religious. Sorcerer priests were meant to wield them, to enact the will of the gods. That they were found and co-opted by a chieftain isn't surprising, but they would never reach their full power in the hands of a non-Connected."

That made sense, given how much power they

221

seemed capable of in my hands. If they'd been truly that mighty, I doubted they'd have been barricaded up in that chair. They'd have been used as a weapon, not a symbol of strength.

Armaeus was clearly reading my thoughts. "There is also the damage they wrought to be considered. Your wrists are healing. Mortal wrists don't." He chuckled. "You could consider these nails a one-use-only venture for most. The threat of them proved to be powerful enough to serve the need in cementing the chieftain's power."

So they'd been sealed into a throne for a reason. Agony was a good reason.

"At least they didn't hurt as much the second time I used them."

Armaeus nodded. "The nails have imprinted on you, Miss Wilde, and do not give up their allegiance so easily. They'll obey—and they'll prefer to obey you."

"Yeah, well, how can I retract them more easily? I'm not taking Nikki on this trip."

"I will help you!" Martine said quickly, his eyes shining with excitement as he looked from the nails to me.

"And option B would be?" I prompted, staring at Armaeus.

"You can cast them from you, and they'll slide out far enough for you to grasp the hilts in your hands. Too far and you'll lose them, of course."

"Cast them…" I frowned. "I tried that. Those things were not shaking free."

He shrugged, returning to his contemplation of the sticks. He pointed at the lower section of the left nail. "It's quite clearly written here."

I leaned forward, but as expected, I wasn't able to translate Ogham. "Might as well be an IKEA insert."

"When the time comes, sweep your arms down and

away from your body. But the strength it will require will dim your abilities on all other fronts. Once they are affixed, I would only release them…with great care."

The limo slowed, and I glanced up, expecting to see the über-kitsch of the Luxor in front of us, the great sphinx and obelisk marking the earthbound entry into Armaeus's spectacular home of spirit, metal, and glass.

But we weren't at the Luxor at all.

"No," I said automatically. "No, no, and no."

I seemed to be saying that a lot. One day, someone would listen.

Today, it appeared, was not that day.

CHAPTER TWENTY-THREE

Armaeus didn't bother responding. He simply disappeared. The limo driver exited the vehicle and came around to the side of the car where Martine sat. Opening the door, he handed the boy out.

The door beside me opened as well, and a languid hand reached in, connected to a well-tanned forearm. The moment I put my hand in it, I knew whose it was.

"I'm not taking a child to Mexico, Kreios," I snapped as I let the Devil of the Arcana Council pull me out of the vehicle.

"Not even if you could say the Devil made you do it?"

Aleksander Kreios smiled at me with his usual devastating beauty—today he was modeling his preferred demeanor of Greek good looks—tawny hair lifting in the breeze, bronzed skin, green eyes deep set above impossibly perfect cheekbones. He was a walking cliché of what a god should look like, but he came by that honestly. He was as close to godlike as a human could get.

Now, however, I could feel his compulsion in the air. I didn't have to turn to know that Martine was being escorted aboard Armaeus's private jet.

"Why?" I demanded as Kreios ducked into the car

behind me and collected the Gods' Nails, now safely returned to their box. "Why is it so important that I put that *child* at risk? Armaeus can slip through his mind like water and tell me everything I need to know."

"He did enter the boy's mind," Kreios said, folding his arm into mine as if we were long-lost friends. And we were, after a fashion. The Devil and I had a curious respect for each other, as well as a carefully studied détente. There was something about him that I found endlessly elusive, and something about me he found endlessly challenging.

More to the point, however, he told the truth. Granted, he did that because the truth was often far more devastating than a lie, but I still found it helpful. And refreshing.

"And yet we're still here." I gestured to the plane.

"We are, albeit briefly. The Magician hates to admit his defeat, but he knows I enjoy doing so a great deal more, so allow me to explain such epic failure on his behalf." Kreios grinned down at me. "Armaeus could not, in fact, ferret out where the boy will be taking you. He tried everything, and the fact that he is not here to send you off is less about his hubris and more about his ongoing search for the reasons why. He is sending you into desperate danger, and he's aware of that, but he can't unravel a better way to get to the bottom of this mystery than for you to embark on this path. Much as it galls him."

I'd stopped at this point, never mind that the reflection of the sun on the tarmac was hot enough to cause even the Devil to break a sweat. But Kreios gamely paused as well and allowed me to stare at him. He was good like that.

"He failed," I repeated. "He doesn't know how Gamon got the kid here, or where she's located in Mexico."

"Or if she's *in* Mexico." Kreios nodded. "He's pretty certain she is, mind you. And that she's the one behind this — she's never been a fan of children." He glanced over to where Martine was delightedly skipping up the rolling stairway toward Armaeus's plane. "They are exceptionally moist for the first few years."

"And yet, he's putting the boy back in harm's way."

"The boy will almost assuredly die from the drugs he's ingested if Armaeus doesn't."

I blinked. "What? But he calmed his heart. He's showing no symptoms."

"No visible symptoms, no. And yes, he's mastered the tachycardia of his heart, much as you were able to do with Detective Brody." Kreios eyed me. "That was quite touching, I might add. Armaeus was a particular fan."

An unexpected shiver rolled through me. I'd had a crush on Brody a thousand years ago, and was still grappling with my emotions for Armaeus. The idea that the Magician might care one way or another to see me working to save Brody's life was…unnerving. And not something I could fully process right now. "Serves you right for having Brody's hospital room on closed-circuit TV."

"True, true. But at any rate, there are plenty of non-visible issues that are manifesting at an alarming rate in Martine, and in the children in Father Jerome's care, we suspect. Now that Armaeus has had the opportunity to study the boy for himself, he'll be getting in touch with the good priest to verify if the other children are facing the same issues."

"And Brody?"

"His body reacted far sooner than the children's, and he got one dose, albeit a heavy one. He'll probably fail much sooner." Kreios shrugged. "Perhaps in as little as a week."

"A week!"

The Devil gestured lazily to the plane. "You do note that Armaeus is outfitting you with the fastest transportation money can buy, short of teleportation. He's concerned about the effect of the drugs on the infected Connected communities. He also suspects that the vast majority of those exposed to the drug have, as yet, ingested small enough doses that the worst of the side effects won't manifest."

I frowned. "What about the people in the lab on Lake Mead?"

"We've looked into that. Nikki Dawes' assessments of the complicit doctor's memories were accurate. There are some survivors — the children of the woman you were tracking, though not the mother herself." Kreios delivered this information dispassionately, but my heart twisted all the same. "The police will be given the information they need to recover all those who remain, and Dr. Sells will be on hand to minister to them."

He turned more fully to me, gazing at me with his piercing jade eyes. "But there's absolutely no indication that Gamon is slowing down. Armaeus's best conjecture is that she's planning to simply eradicate a good portion of the drug-seeking world she's grown tired of.

That sounded exactly like something that sociopathic woman would do.

Kreios allowed his sculptured lips to curl delicately. "The fact that Gamon plans to take out a few batches of Connecteds while she does that is apparently all to the good."

"How is that remotely good?"

"Connecteds make terrible converts to her cause, as it happens." Kreios placed a hand over his heart, feigning surprise. "She clearly doesn't trust them to follow her while they still possess their own power, so better to simply stamp them out on an opportunistic basis."

"Starting with the Connected kids, then moving on to the elders," I grumbled.

"Once we ascertained that it was Gamon behind the killings, additional information came to light." He shot me a sidelong glance. "She is a Revenant. Like all Revenants, she was fostered."

I froze, despite the heat. "Fostered."

That she was a Revenant didn't surprise me. I'd guessed that back in Barcelona. Somehow, I'd missed the fostering link. Jonathan had said Revenant youths were fostered for fifty years. No matter how slowly someone aged, fifty years was plenty of time to develop a chip, a fair amount of baggage, and whole lot of hate.

What had happened to Gamon during those years to make her the murderous abuser she was?

"She spent her formative years in Barcelona, at Gotica. Many of the Revenants who perished in the club fire knew her — knew her and tried to restrain her darker tendencies." Kreios shook his head in dismay.

"So vengeance is hers." I shook my head, but that wasn't enough to get rid of the low-grade headache that was now buzzing through my skull. "No matter what I do, we're doomed. She has outposts all over the planet. Even if I destroy one, there are a dozen more that could release the drug into the market."

"Armaeus doesn't think so," Kreios said, surprising me. "It would appear that Gamon's had her drug cocktail at a standstill for, what, going on nine months now?" He clucked. "That's multiple lifetimes in the drug trade. But she's been stalled out until now. Armaeus assumes that she needs something else to complete the mixture, something she has not been able to gather on her own."

"Which would be?"

But Kreios didn't have to answer — and he didn't

deign to either. Instead, he resumed walking me toward the plane, as my brain tried to wrap itself around the idea that I could somehow inadvertently help Gamon complete her mad recipe. The easiest answer would be my DNA — blood or organs or muscle tissue, but despite my best efforts, I was only one woman. How could I possible give her enough to make a viable solution more than once?

At the bottom of the Jetway, Kreios handed the jade box to me. My wrists ached as my fingers scraped the box's surface. Then he bowed.

"The boy will innately know where to go. Follow him. He's bugged to the gills, so try to stay close. Armaeus cannot penetrate his mind deeply enough to know more, and that is most vexing, as I'm sure you can imagine. But we will be able to track him. And, by extension, you."

"Look, I protect kids. I don't put them in harm's way. Taking Martine with me is beyond dangerous for him," I argued. "I really don't like him coming with me at all. My cards can tell me — "

"Again, you're doing it as the only way to keep him alive," Kreios overrode me. "Armaeus was quite clear on that point. Detective Rooks is also depending on both of you getting an antidote in hand and returning with it in as close to one piece as possible.

I hated taking the kid with me. Nothing Kreios could say would make me *like* the idea. However, if the most powerful forces on this side of the veil were resolute that Martine and I were the package deal required to save Connecteds and those mortals on the fringes of their communities alike…I…I'd be an idiot to ignore them.

Maybe in Mexico, I could get one of those kid harnesses with a leash, just to keep the boy close enough to run like hell alongside me once things went to crap. It was worth a shot.

"Sara," Kreios said softly, almost sympathetically, "if you can determine what specific element of your physical form is needed to synthesize the drug more effectively — without donating that element, ideally — that would also be quite helpful. It's likely your heart will be required, based on the harvesting Gamon's agents undertook."

"So keep my heart inside my chest. Got it." This wasn't helping my headache. "And you'll tell the others I've got the kid in tow? Nikki and Nigel…"

"Ma-Singh has already been informed. He'll take on the task of informing the others. In return, Armaeus has promised to keep him in the loop on your whereabouts."

"How civil of him." I glanced back to Kreios one last time.

I'd spoken to empty air. Both the Magician and the Devil were skilled in the art of illusion, but the Devil usually needed to be in the same physical location as his better halves, or taking over some other hapless human with his features. Since he had done the poof routine, chances were good he was lurking back in the limo, and I gave the vehicle a halfhearted wave. Its lights flashed, and I shook my head. I should have known he wouldn't subject himself to this heat willingly, even if he was the Devil.

By the time I boarded the plane, Martine was already in his seat and blessedly dozing. I suspected Armaeus had a hand in that, but the truth was, I needed the sleep too. The next few hours would be the last time I'd have the chance for a while.

We traveled in silence accordingly. Even when I had the chance to ask Martine questions, he remained unhelpfully vague. As the Magician had learned before me, the boy truly didn't know where we were heading. Or what we'd find when we got there.

230

The landing in Mexico City went predictably well, with the exception that the limo waiting at the edge of the private airstrip was very definitely *not* Council property. I recognized the seal of the House of Swords immediately and collared a bouncing Martine, shoving him in that direction. Armaeus must have told Ma-Singh our destination after all. That made me feel better, at least.

"Yes, yes!" Martine announced. "A car will be much faster than feet. Much faster."

I couldn't argue that logic, and within a few minutes, we were settled comfortably in the back of the limo. It was well past midnight, but neither Martine nor I would be sleeping anytime soon, I suspected. The limo driver turned and smiled at Martine before nodding deferentially to me.

"Madam Wilde, your destination?" he asked in heavily accented English.

Martine spoke up first. "La Merced. The Birdhouse is there. We must go there."

I scowled. I'd half suspected this, since it was very near the location of the arcane black market, but the boy had insisted he had no idea where we were heading or where specifically this mysterious Birdhouse was located. When I'd asked Armaeus about it, he'd confirmed there was no specific location in the Mexico City black market for the Birdhouse — it was a movable feast, apparently. And it looked like we'd be dining late night at La Merced.

But enough was enough of the cloak-and-dagger stuff. I turned to Martine, prepared to grill him —

And stopped.

The boy's eyes had changed, going from the color of mulled bourbon to all white, as if he'd been possessed. I'd seen this look before, of course, but usually only on Starz.

"Um, Martine?"

"Birdhouse," he said again, more urgently this time. "Where the women are all like birds, and there are many guns. We must start there. It's the only way I know."

"Yeah, but…" As I frowned, Martine's eyes cleared and so did the expression on his face. He was once again the happy, bouncing boy of ten I'd met a day ago, chattering about everything he saw.

"Where are we going after the Birdhouse?" I tried anyway, but Martine merely laughed.

"The Birdhouse," he insisted. "Yes. We must go there first."

"Got it." I indicated to the driver to proceed to La Merced. "Let everyone know as well. Ma-Singh no doubt left instructions."

"Of course, Madam Wilde."

La Merced was an enormous outdoor market. It had been in operation since colonial times, and looked it. Sprawling rows of colorful tents and stalls extended in all directions, offering any number of foods, drinks, goods, and services that extended from the traditional to the flagrantly unusual. At this hour, none of the goods and services vendors were still active, but all the food and alcohol vendors were, plying their trade with frantic gaiety. Colors and sounds assaulted us, and as we approached, the driver slowed.

"Where exactly?" the driver asked. "We need to inform the spotters."

"Here is as good a place as any." Warily, I double-checked my hoodie for my trusty Tarot deck and my bag for the nails. I still didn't like any part of this. I especially didn't like having the boy in tow.

Spotters wouldn't last a heartbeat in this place—it was thronged with people, locals and tourists alike, and the trade was brisk today. I'd be lucky to keep ahold of Martine if I held him in my own arms.

"Wait until I move off and the spotter is in place, Madam Wilde," the driver instructed.

"Of course," I murmured. But I was looking at Martine. "You okay, big guy?"

"Birdhouse," the boy breathed, his head turning to look over my shoulder, into the chaos of the market. His eyes had gone milk white again. "Birdhouse."

"Yep, we're going to get you there."

I didn't understand the physical manifestation overtaking Martine, but the magic that was affecting the boy was deep, seriously deep. Unlike in Vegas, I could now feel the filth of it radiating off him in waves. It had taken someone a lot of time and effort to implant this map so deeply in his mind that even he could not access it, and when I found whoever did it, I'd make sure she never did it again.

I clicked open the box and removed the Gods' Nails still in their silk wrappings, sliding them into a deep interior pocket of my jacket. They thrummed there, giving me a confidence I didn't fully embrace. Still, every little bit helped.

The limo pulled marginally over out of traffic. Martine and I hopped out, the boy holding firmly on to my hand. I'd been half afraid that he would go rabbiting off into the crowd, but I realized I was the bigger prize here. It would do no good for him to reach the Birdhouse if I wasn't with him when he did.

That said, I didn't look around for our House trackers, but moved off smartly into the crowd, Martine pulling me along. I opened my mind as we wound ourselves into the web of intensely aromatic corridors — redolent of the smells of meat, animals, and spices too numerous to be identified. The market was suffocating under an oppressive blanket of nighttime heat and humidity, but Martine didn't seem to notice. He darted down aisles and around turns, through stalls and

233

beneath tent flaps. He seemed to be moving in a more or less straight direction. Anything that stood in his way was merely something else to be skirted or moved through.

I mentally reached for Armaeus, gratified more than I would have expected to feel his touch. Nothing like a little Arcana Roadside Assistance when you needed it.

Any ideas?

"*You're heading toward the black market, as you expected. It's the space between the Mercado de Sonora and La Merced, and it's crowded.*"

Everything here is.

The Mercado de Sonora was familiar territory for me, at least, the city's go-to market for all things occult. When I'd had artifact-hunting jobs in Mexico, more than a few times they'd originated here, where the rumors of the mystical and the profane mingled with the air of too much sweat, too much perfume, and too many high-end drugs. The arcane black market that thrived here operated, as usual, by hiding in plain sight. With a market this old, nothing was as it seemed. And when magic and illusion was your stock-in-trade, that axiom held true more than usual.

We turned, then turned again, and finally Martine broke into a run, bursting through a long butcher's shop of cuts of meat I'd never seen before and never wanted to see again. His breath coming in great, hiccuping gulps, he pushed aside the rear flap of the shop's tent, pulling me through.

Two steps later we entered a second tent so enormous, I staggered to a stop. Multicolored cloth walls, ceilings and floor-coverings greeted us, with additional strips of cloth forming makeshift walls that separated rooms within the structure. There were platforms and even stairs and a secondary floor. Through the fluttering edges of the fabric walls, I could see women of every shape and description — all of them wearing great feathered costumes, as if a bevy of Vegas showgirls had suddenly taken their boas on the road.

"The Birdhouse!" Martine said, triumphantly.

I stared, but I wasn't looking at the women, suddenly, but at a figure striding up with great vigor. A man I knew well — too well, for all that we lived in different parts of the world. There were a few things in life you just didn't forget...

And one of them was Monsieur Jean-Claude Mercault, the head of the House of Pentacles.

CHAPTER TWENTY-FOUR

"Sara! Mademoiselle Sara Wilde, I am beyond thrilled to welcome you to my humble establishment." Short, rotund, and impeccably dressed in a pale gray linen suit, white shirt and gunmetal gray loafers and gloves, Mercault spoke with his characteristic half-drunk joie de vivre, but there was something in his eyes that didn't match his ebullient smile. The slightest chill slipped down my spine, and I flicked my third eye open.

The Frenchman's aura oozed with a sick yellow hue, the color of bile. I didn't have a color-coded cheat sheet to understand all the colors of the rainbow my third eye could serve up, but bile yellow seemed bad.

Still, Mercault was a friend. If not a friend, then an ally at least. I'd saved his life not all that long ago, and arguably that counted for something, even in the cutthroat world of the arcane black market.

Granted, there was much I didn't know about Mercault or his involvement in the black market. Then again, he'd been one of Soo's fiercest competitors in drug trafficking, and used the highest grade of technoceuticals himself, to augment his fledgling Connected abilities. He was in it strictly for the money, and the kind of money that was flying through the markets right now was more than enough to kill for—

more than enough to change alliances for as well. Of course, we didn't have a formal alliance. More of an understanding.

But we did have that…right?

All these thoughts went through my mind as Mercault enveloped me in a hug, then gazed down at Martine. The boy expressed no concern whatsoever, but was that a good or a bad thing? If anything, he seemed still eager to be on his way, to move quickly to the trail home.

"Miss Wilde."

Armaeus's voice sounded in my mind, slightly staticky, and I shook my head to clear it. But Mercault was steering me into the elaborate Birdhouse, and I chose to focus on him.

"What brings you back to the market, Sara? Surely you are no longer looking for work. I could keep you well employed if that is the case."

I slanted Mercault a glance as we mounted the steps to a central platform. "I'm a little busy these days for bounty hunting."

"Too true, too true!" He laughed heartily. "And yet unless my intelligence deceives me, you were involved in exactly that sort of enterprise not more than a few days ago. Am I right? Of course I am right, no?"

I considered him coolly. "You know who was behind that job?"

"Non, non." Mercault waved his hands in negation. "As you can see, I was halfway around the world, and we are busy here in our own right."

Not an answer to the question, I noticed, but he brought up a more relevant point.

"Why here?" I asked him, surveying the gaudy but undeniably seedy Birdhouse. I gestured to the nearest flock of women. "And what's with the costumes?"

Mercault laughed heartily. "I confess, I've

developed quite a fondness for the styles of your Las Vegas since I have spent so much time there of late. And those with whom I do business…what can I say? We all have a weakness for beautiful women majestically adorned."

I slanted him a glance. "So all these women are here just for decoration? Seriously?"

"But what gorgeous decoration, non?" He opened his hands wide, and I noticed a few men flitting among the feathered figures, undoubtedly more of Mercault's guards. "They are here to keep me company, while I and my associates manage the distribution of Fountain. The most lucrative drug to hit the market in, well, ever, I suspect. And so we have to conduct our business near its very heart."

A sick dread skated through my stomach. "So you are dealing that drug."

"But of course." He kept moving me deeper into the center of his tent complex, mounting a second short set of stairs, and I willingly went along, keeping an eye on the boy. Martine remained oblivious, which was good. Or it seemed good. Then again, he was a ten-year-old boy surrounded by burlesque dancers wearing feathers. He might not be bringing his A game.

"But it's not a fountain of youth, I don't care what you call it." I eyed the Frenchman again. "You know that drug has issues, Mercault. You've got to know that."

He waggled his brows, pausing on the broad platform. We were maybe three feet off the ground now, in the center of the tent. "I know no such thing, eh? The drug is in its beta-testing stage, and production is limited. We are being responsible while still sensitive to market interest."

His word choice gave me pause. *We?* But I couldn't jump on that. Instead I asked, "Sensitive to market

238

interest? How sensitive?"

"Teasing, touching, tasting, that is all. Only a hint, the barest whiff."

"The dime bags circulating in Thailand and Russia—here too, no doubt. Those are yours."

Mercault sniffed. "Such an uncharitable description for offering a free sample of what is arguably the most sought-after enhancer to hit the market in the last decade. There is so much interest in this drug I could make billions and never provide it to the general public, you see? But I don't do that."

"You're a man of the people."

"Exactly." He patted my back. "You and I, we go back many years, do we not? Many jobs. I like to think I've helped you a great deal."

"I've helped you as well."

"You have indeed. An excellent working partnership, all in all."

Another burst of static sounded between my ears, but Armaeus could park himself on hold for the moment. Mercault was requiring all my brain cells.

"Yet now, here you are on my doorstep, all alone except for this child, but not working for me. I ask myself, are you working for someone else? Are you someone I should fear after all these years?"

"Why would you have anything to fear from me?"

"An excellent question! But you see, we French, we do not like fear, even the specter of fear. We must always work to circumvent it from bringing us to heel."

He turned and smiled, and around us, everything seemed to stop. Even the bird women stopped. And...now that I looked a little more closely...

"Sara!" Martine blurted. "This is the door! This is where we must go!"

The boy's voice sounded excitedly in the sudden silence of the room, but no one—male or female, feathered or otherwise—was looking at where he was pointing.

Instead, they were all looking at me. With the barrels of their guns.

"Don't move, my dear Sara." Mercault kept his voice conversational, his manner easy. He took a step toward me, gently pulling the boy away from me. Martine went soundlessly, focused more on the exit door than on the imminent firefight. He and a single soldier took up positions next to that far door, and I breathed a tight sigh of relief. At least the boy would be out of the way if anything happened.

And something almost certainly would be happening, I knew. Probably not something good, either.

The Frenchman gestured to the ceiling. "I have taken the liberty of installing electrical jammers, proven most successful in disrupting psychic ability. Did you know that so much of Connected abilities can parallel the behavior of electricity? I most assuredly did not, but I am gaining a renewed respect for science in all this. In truth, a renewed respect for what the human mind and body is capable of all on its own, no Connected ability required."

A part of me wanted to be aghast at his betrayal of our history. The other part of me knew this came with the territory of being a head of a House. A teeny-tiny part of me said Ma-Singh had been right and I should've brought my entire damn army. Fortunately, I only had so many parts to go around.

"Right," I drawled. "And it's in the interest of science that you have paid all these good people to be aiming their guns at me?"

"Ah! You wound me. Of course it's not in the interest of science. Merely of hobbling you." He gestured, and five of the gunmen changed their target—

focusing on Martine.

Crap.

With a quickness I wouldn't have given him credit for, Mercault stepped in toward me and deftly flicked my jacket aside. He reached in and plucked the nails from their interior pocket. So at least now I knew why the man had been wearing gloves.

"These have been lighting up our tracking devices since you entered the city. After all the effort we've gone to for these artifacts, here I should have asked you to recover them for me all along. Would have been much more efficient that way."

He held the bones in his hand, marveling at them. I felt the ache in my wrists like a visceral tug, but I couldn't risk the boy by making a grab for them. If I missed and someone shot...no. That wasn't going to happen.

With a slight gesture, Mercault drew the attention of his minions, who stepped forward to light four tiki-style torches driven into solid bases on the platform's floor. This was starting to feel very Tribal Council, but I didn't yet understand the Frenchman's end game. The buzzing in my head grew more intense, and I shook off the Magician's attempted touch. Surely Armaeus had realized already that he wasn't getting through to me.

For a moment as I stared at the flames, I considered using the skills I'd learned at the Japanese sensei to manifest weapons—weapons like guns, for example. Piles of them. Or maybe a battalion of soldiers...that would be good too. But once again, I couldn't risk screwing up with my fledgling abilities. Not with Martine so close and so unprotected. No victory of mine could be worth harming a child.

Not now, not ever.

"You've amassed a fair number of enemies, it would seem," Mercault went on. He waved his hand generously at the crowd.

New figures now stepped forward through the flock. I didn't need to take in the faces to recognize them. Some had already checked in in Reykjavik, others weren't surprises that they had a beef with me. Did I think those beefs were worth killing for? That I had a harder time with. Because Mercault wasn't going to pay all of them to take potshots at me. Surely only the successful shooter would get the bounty. How could they tell who that was?

I refocused on Mercault. "What did you want the nails for, anyway?" I asked. "We're not enemies. Well, we weren't, anyway. You didn't need to bind me to get me here."

"And yet, so many wanted me to do exactly that. How could I not attempt it?" Mercault indicated another man to stand forward, and he did, a hunter that I knew had Connected ability. Not a lot, but he didn't need a lot for the sticks to work their magic. "Lucien here has been preparing for this moment since you stole the mask of Venus from him."

I stared at the man. "That was four years ago."

"It was a costly loss." Mercault shrugged. "When I learned he'd given away the mask's location with a slip of a tongue, well…"

Lucien grinned, revealing a dreadful sight—his tongue split down the center, its end flapping in two disparate pieces. I grimaced in horror but could do nothing as Lucien grasped both of the bone shards in his bare hands. A shudder of electricity ripped through his body, and for the first time, everyone's—truly *everyone's*—eyes were on him as he flinched, the spikes sinking deep into his wrists. In a blink, the fire from the tiki torches was commandeered by the nails, arcing across the space to engulf the bone shards in flame.

I moved.

The moment that Lucien set free the power through the spikes, I hit him broadside and low, twisting him around so the arc of fire emitting from the nails blasted everyone in a five foot radius but me. Mercault got clipped, screaming imprecations in French. The first wave of shooters backed up instinctively, ducking for cover.

Lucien snarled something unintelligible, because of course how could he not with that tongue, then shrugged me off with superhuman strength. As he whirled around, however, I dove out of the way of the twin spires of fire and rushed to the far wall. The soldier was no longer standing with Martine, and my momentum took the boy to the floor.

"Are you okay?" I asked, breathlessly.

"Yes!" The boy wriggled beneath me then stared up, and his eyes were once more the color of milk. "You must not leave your weapons, Sara! You need them. They are you!"

"I hate to break it to you, but they aren't me anymore."

"No—" He struggled beneath me, so palpably panicked that despite the chaos above and around me, I could only focus on him. Time seemed to suspend, and his urgent need surged so high that it cleared my mind with brutal speed. "They are yours, you are theirs, it is how it must be!"

His words triggered a memory, something Armaeus had said, but I was having a hard time hearing over the crackling flames and renewed gunfire.

"Please!" Martine screamed, clutching at me.

I twisted around. Miraculously, no one seemed to realize I was hiding in a corner. Clearly, they didn't know me very well. As I watched, another spasm of fire leapt from the Gods' Nails in Lucien's untutored grip, and a flurry of electrical sparks showered down from above. New sounds of outrage rose up as the hair of several of the finders and angry birds caught on fire, and I huddled into a slightly smaller ball, my gaze darting around like an over-caffeinated ferret. This was bad—seriously bad. Even if I got free, I couldn't lug Martine around like a rag doll, and there were easily twelve—no fifteen people with guns slowly figuring out that Lucien was serving more as distraction than a first line of attack.

"Miss Wilde. Are you clear?"

I was so startled to hear Armaeus's clear, distinct voice again that I tumbled backward, dragging Martine with me. I practically threw the boy against the wall near the door he'd been so eager to exit, then scrambled to my feet, covering him.

Yes!

A new level of chaos blasted forth. From all sides of the tented room, black-clad men and women poured in through slashed openings, guns at their shoulders, pinning in the first and second rows of shooters. The newcomers didn't pause to ask questions but unleashed a torrent of ammo into the tented space, sending everyone crashing to the ground and rushing for cover. I scowled, whirling, but nobody'd been hit, which simply wasn't possible at that close range.

Unless...

Oh, Sweet Christmas. They were firing blanks—at least in this first round. The attack was only a distraction.

But what a hell of a distraction.

"The nails have imprinted on you, Miss Wilde, and do not give up their allegiance so easily. They'll obey—and they'll prefer to obey you."

Armaeus's words burst into my mind with an urgency I couldn't ignore.

I grabbed a gun from the floor—one of those

belonging to Mercault's people, not mine, so maybe it had actual ammo — and crawled back over to Martine. "Are you okay?" I demanded, shaking him. "Are you okay!"

"Yes!" he said, and his eyes had returned to being those of a frightened little boy.

I hesitated before shoving the gun into the boy's hands. Was this really what I wanted to do? Give a loaded gun to a boy barely ten years old? Was that what we had come to?

Then again, what would be worse — him attempting to defend himself and causing someone else harm, or him getting kidnapped by Mercault and his goons, then used for ransom or something even less humane?

A blast of very live, very close ammo shattered the wooden door over my shoulder. It was followed by another blast of phantom machine gun fire, but Mercault's shooters were figuring out the game now. I crouched down, shoving the gun back into the waistband of my pants. I couldn't make myself give it to Martine.

"Can you make yourself hidden?" I asked him. "Can you make it seem like you're not here?"

He nodded hurriedly. "You must get your weapons!"

"You don't worry about that. You go through that door and hide — hide from anyone who isn't me." I grimaced, well aware of the powers of illusion among some of the more gifted of the shooters here. "Who isn't me and isn't carrying those bones. You got it?"

I didn't wait for him to respond this time, instead turning around and scrambling forward in a crouch walk. Lucien was in the center of the conflagration, holding off all comers with staccato bursts of fire. The spikes looked so deeply lodged in his wrists that they might as well be part of his skeleton, but Lucien didn't possess the same quick-healing techniques I had, and he wasn't as strong. His forearms were bathed in his own sizzling blood, the wound cauterizing itself then reopening every time he jerked. I watched his face, his eyes, the expression of manic determination fixed there in a rictus of pain. "Not exactly what you'd had in mind, is it?" I muttered.

Another round of gunfire was abruptly cut off with a gargled scream, and the room seemed to pause for a moment, held in intense stasis.

Then there was no sound, only movement, a black sea rushing forward to take Mercault's shooters in its inky wake, and I realized what was happening. The House of Swords had struck again. Not with guns this time, but with the kind of handiwork they did best.

Two dozen blades slashed through the air.

CHAPTER TWENTY-FIVE

The screams of outrage and grunts of hand-to-hand fighting intermingled as I bolted forth, and even Lucien was apparently confused by the new form of attack. I didn't give him time to figure it out. I swept forward low, my hands out, my body tight, a gull intent on snatching its dinner from the sea. By the time Lucien whirled around, I had ducked beneath his unwieldy spiked hands and was coming up fast.

"*Release,*" I shouted, wrapping my hands around the spikes. Nothing happened except for Lucien's hands jerking forward, the Gods' Nails holding fast in their prison of bone. Lucien screamed, and I pulled again, half dragging him across the floor. More cries erupted behind my back as our awkward dance lit up the tent palace, fire slashing in unpredictable ways across friend and foe alike.

"Let *go,*" I tried again, and while I felt some give in Lucien's hands, it wasn't enough—not nearly enough. There was too much pride and pain and desire in the air between us, I could feel it like a physical thing, Lucien so drunk on the strength of his newfound toys that his gluttony seemed like it would never be slaked. He was glorying in the agony of these spikes as much as in the havoc they wrought, and that was a more powerful, headier pull than anything I could produce.

Even now, Lucien's eyes widened at whatever carnage I was inflicting, then his expression cleared and he refocused sharply on me.

"*You,*" he snarled, or almost snarled, his tongue lashing out like he was some fell mythological creature—

Just as I head-butted him between the eyes.

"Mine!" An ancient, primal surge of power thrust up within me, demanding my due. I had *found* these spikes, I had *earned* them, they were the Gods' Nails and they were—

The spikes slipped free of Lucien's wrists with a sucking pop, shucking him off like the husk from an ear of corn.

I stumbled back, wiping the dripping strips of primordial bone across my hoodie and pants. There was no way I was going to get all of Lucien's blood off the tips, but there was nothing for it, I didn't have time! More people surged into the tents, and my sword-wielding ninjas were going to be outnumbered if I didn't stop this now.

I sank the nails into the base of my palms, then roared with equal parts pain and outrage.

A fireball burst forth—no, not a fireball, but a blast of power just the same, as forceful as a sonic boom. Anyone wielding the mark of the House of Swords was battered back in the conflagration, but their opponents fared worse, screaming, crumpling, collapsing. My own eyes widened as the wave of power flowed out and snapped back just as quickly, rocking me on my heels.

And then there was nothing.

Total silence.

The whole thing had taken barely five seconds, but devastation lay all around us. Devastation…and something more.

Mercault.

Collapsed in the center of the room, surrounded with feathers, the Frenchman stared at me with shock and something approaching horror in his eyes. Fury roiled through me, and I stalked up to him, lifting one of my deadly bone shards and angling it just below his chin.

"Who are you working for, you bastard?" I seethed. "Who paid you to gut me?" I knew the answer. Of course I knew the answer. But I still wanted to hear him say it.

His mouth opened and shut like a fish, but he couldn't seem to make words. I twitched my hand forward, and a bright bead of blood appeared on his liver-spotted neck. His eyes bulged. Around me, a knot of my House's warriors stepped closer, swords at the ready.

"Who is it?" I repeated.

"You're such a fool," he spat, finally remembering how to get his mad on. "You think you are operating in a vacuum, that you can move through the world carrying all the Connected children on your back, protecting them from all comers. You are being *laughed* at, Sara Wilde. Laughed at by all of us in power. You are no head of the House of Swords. Soo must have lost her mind to give you that right."

He leaned forward, pressing himself against the edge of the nail, not seeming to mind the pain. "You speak of me as an ally, but an ally has something to give that I'm interested in having...and wants something *I* can give. Soo understood that. She gave me leeway, and I paid her for the privilege. You can't be bothered with the way the real world works. You're not paying attention."

I stiffened. There'd been a time not too long ago when the Hanged Man of the Arcana Council had instructed me to pay more attention too. Was this what he'd been talking about?

"I've been a little busy, Mercault."

"Yes, you have." He smiled bitterly, like a sullen boy excluded from the ball game. "You've been busy saving everyone but those who could be in a position to help you, if you were smart. That kind of mindset is a dangerous one. You are no ally of mine, *Mademoiselle* Wilde. I've cast my lot with another House."

I scowled at him, but despite my better judgment, I couldn't hold my tongue. "The Houses should work together, Mercault, not separately. We'll never be strong apart."

"You should have thought of that before Gamon made her offer," he sneered.

That did catch me up short. I'd thought Gamon was behind this, but...no. Surely not. It took me another second for all the dots to connect, but even when they did, I couldn't believe it. I had to be mistaken.

"Gamon," I said flatly, and Mercault's eyes glittered as he realized the truth.

"You didn't *know*, did you?" His smile was almost gleeful, as if this was a present he hadn't expected to receive. "You didn't *know*, and here I've gone and ruined her surprise."

"Gamon is the head of the House of..." The words died in my throat momentarily, my mind whirling in confusion.

Nigel hadn't warned me. And he *should have*. He should have known. He served Cups as well as Swords so he should have....

I swallowed. The Aces of the Houses did not always know their masters, granted, the legitimacy of their orders ensured by specially encoded protocols, but how could he not have...Still, there was no way he'd known and hidden it from me. No way. Not after seeing firsthand Gamon's utter lack of regard for anyone and anything. Surely...

"Cups," I finally finished. "Gamon is the head of the House of Cups."

In the deck of Tarot, Cups stood for relationships and contracts. The ties that bound. Or in Gamon's case, the ties that choked the life out of you.

"Cups, yes," Mercault's lips twisted. "Really, I thought more of your vaunted skills of deduction, Sara. It was out there plainly if you wanted to look."

"Only I wasn't paying attention," I repeated.

"Not these past few weeks, no." He read my surprise and his beady eyes lit with another surge of feral delight. "Oh, yes. She hasn't long been in power. In fact, most don't even realize that the change has occurred. She gutted the former Head of the House of Cups most effectively, though. Even sent me a video." With this last admission, the Frenchman finally paled. I could only imagine what atrocities Gamon had committed to impress him.

While my mind was churning, there was nothing wrong with my hands. I kept the razor-like tip against Mercault's throat and refocused. "How much did she pay you to bind me?"

His eyes turned crafty. "Why?"

"How *much*, Mercault? I want to know your price."

"It's not like that, exactly." His gaze flashed with the barest hint of panic, then steadied again.

"She said she'd leave you alone, didn't she?" My lips curled with derision. "You thought she'd be another Soo. Let you play in your little corner of the world without supervision, making your money off the backs of the foolish and the weak."

His wavering smirk told me I was right.

"It's you who isn't paying attention, Mercault. She'll gut you like a fish the moment you've given her what she wants. And if you don't give her what she wants, well…" My smile twisted further. "You'll get a taste of what her disappointment feels like, I'm sure."

"She won't be disappointed." Mercault showed a flare of bravado. "This wasn't a test, it was a bonus. She knew you'd come to her, bound or unbound."

"*Everything's* a test, Mercault. You think I'm lying, go to wherever you were supposed to lay your head down tonight, whether you were successful or if you weren't. See what's waiting for you." When understanding flashed in his eyes, I nodded. "And when this is done, completely done, you come to me in Vegas, and we'll talk terms."

"Terms." He fairly choked on the word, laughter contorting his face, the abrupt jerking of his body creating another slice in his neck. "You won't be alive to honor them."

I leaned into him. "You aren't going to like the fact that I'm paying attention, Mercault, but you'd better get used to it. The Houses need to stand together, or we will all fall. If Gamon doesn't see it, then she's not fit to rule. If the head of the House of Wands doesn't see it, then he or she isn't either. But when this is done, you *will* come to Vegas and we *will* discuss the terms of our working arrangement. Swords and Pents, Cups and Wands. We will stand together, or we will all die apart."

"Hardly," he sneered again. "The House of Wands hasn't shown the face of its leader in five hundred years. They're not about to start now."

"They are, and so will you." I stepped back from the man then, and a woman glided forward to my side, her face an expressionless mask. Another man stood to Mercault's right. Still others flowed around him, a barrier of silent scowls from the House of Swords. *My* House.

"When I'm gone, go with him to wherever his

residence is. Make sure nothing's waiting for him he's not expecting," I said as Mercault watched me warily. I glanced at him. "Whatever she was going to pay you, I would have met those terms and more, Mercault. I have no interest in protecting my back from my allies as well as my enemies."

I raised my voice, calling out in the now-silent space. My people had their feet on the throats of assassins and finders, but hopefully the ears of my erstwhile peers still worked.

"Mercault's bounty has been nullified," I said. "If he reinstates it, I'll pay double against whatever wager he makes. There are plenty of clients who are not of the Houses who can pay for your services. Make your money there. Should you ally yourself against Swords, against any of the Houses of Magic, you'll pay a premium for your poor choice. There will be no amount of money worth the price the Houses will exact from you."

I turned then, sharply, and took in the faces of my own black-clad warriors. Who'd summoned them to me? Ma-Singh? Armaeus? Either way, I was in their debt. More than that, I was their leader.

I bowed to them. They bowed in return, then straightened, returning to their tasks.

While I exited what remained of the tent, stepping out into the darkness.

The market alleyway was all but deserted, which surprised me momentarily, before I recalled the chaos of a few short minutes ago. I moved into the velvety night, my eyes trained on the distant lights until I could acclimate myself to the gloom.

"Martine?" I whispered, but there was no response. A shiver of dread swept over me. "Martine," I said more firmly.

For one long, sickening moment, silence reigned in

the alleyway, and a thousand thoughts crashed through me, foremost among them: *He's been taken*.

Then a soft rustling came from a patch of shadow a fraction blacker than the spaces around it, the sound of a blanket being shifted aside.

I tensed, my fingers curling instinctively around their center blade, but a moment later, the small figure of a boy stepped out into the gloom. His eyes glistened in the night, his smile quick.

"You got your weapons," Martine said happily. "We can go now. Put them away."

I grimaced as I looked down at the spikes protruding in the center of my hands, between my fingers. "It's not that easy. They're...sort of stuck this way."

"Stuck inside you?" He frowned, leaning close, and I opened my hands, showing him the path of the nails as they seated themselves in my bones.

"But how?" he asked, his voice aghast. "Why?"

"How's not so important. Why does count, though. These things really, really want to be sure that I don't let go of them this time. They don't like being lost."

"You can't take them out?"

"I can—but I'm not good at it. You could help me, though, if you wanted."

"Me?"

"Uh-huh." It wasn't that I didn't believe Armaeus and his idea for how to get the spikes to release. It was that I didn't think I would do it properly. And when it came to getting large spikes out of my skeleton, I didn't want to have to try more than once. "Get that blanket you just dropped. Wrap your hands in it—then pull them out."

He picked up the blanket, but doubt still showed in his eyes.

"I trust you," I said, focusing on him in the dim light.

254

And the thing was, I did trust Martine. I in particular trusted him not to want the nails for himself.

Hesitantly, the boy twisted the towel around his hands. Then he reached out for the nails and grabbed the ends of the bony protrusions. "They're warm!" he whispered, clearly surprised.

I was surprised as well. "Just pull your hands back, and they should —"

The spikes slid free of my wrists.

"Oh!" I slumped to the ground, more relieved than I would have expected. Martine bundled the nails in the blanket and clutched them to his chest. Behind us in the bullet-riddled tents of the Birdhouse, voices finally sounded, layered over with Mercault's fastidious snap. How had I misjudged the man so severely? I hadn't thought him a friend, necessarily, but I *had* saved his life. That really should have counted for something.

Then again, *I* hadn't misjudged him. Sara Wilde, the new head of the House of Swords, had. Apparently, there was a difference, and that difference mattered more than I'd realized to Mercault. Gamon too, it would seem.

Gamon. Head of the House of Cups. I knew nothing about that House. How much did Armaeus know about her and her involvement with House magic? Something I resolved to ask him, right after I'd made sure she never cast so much as a wish on a falling star going forward.

I sat up straighter and scanned the alleyway, noting where it emptied into a parking lot. Given the carnage inside the Birdhouse at the moment, I had my pick of vehicles.

"Which one do you want?" I asked Martine, and he stared back at me, eyes wide.

"You can take any of them?" he asked, wide-eyed. "Don't you need keys?"

"Not if you know what you're doing."

He swiveled his head and peered toward the parking lot. "That one," he whispered.

I squinted down the line of vehicles, then nodded. "Okay, then we should go." I stood and reclaimed the nails from him, sticking them back into my jacket and dropping the blanket. "And where are we going, exactly?"

"To the..." He stopped and went almost preternaturally still. When he turned back to look at me, I was ready for the milky-white eyes, but it didn't make them any easier to bear. "To the north and east," he whispered. "To the sun."

I frowned. The east was where the sun would come up, most assuredly, but it was dark now and would be for some time. And the sun never rose in the north, I was nearly certain of that.

"The sun, huh?" I asked, reaching for his hand self-consciously, unreasonably glad when he slipped his small fingers into mine. "So we should wait until morning."

"No, not the morning and not the night," Martine said firmly. "Sunset." He frowned, then darted a glance at me, apologetic. "We are too late tonight. But it must be sunset. The voice in the stones will only call out then."

"Fair enough," I said easily, hiding my grimace at this new piece of crazy. Voice in the stones? The boy was becoming overwrought, which I should have anticipated. I wasn't exactly up on my child psychology skills, however. Where was Father Jerome when I needed him? "Maybe we go now and scout our, uh, destination out, then we'll be there at sunset?"

"No," Martine said. "In the daytime, everyone will be awake. You can't be seen when you go inside, or they'll try to stop you, I know they will."

I resisted the urge to comfort him. No matter what,

I *would* probably be seen by Gamon, and at some point, I'd probably be stopped.

What happened after that, however, was what mattered.

CHAPTER TWENTY-SIX

We reached the car without incident, and after assuring Martine I wouldn't go anywhere close to the location he couldn't identify before it was time, I picked a major thoroughfare, and we headed northeast. I had walled my mind off from Armaeus again. Not that I didn't appreciate his GPS skills, but I was still taken aback about Mercault's news flash regarding Gamon. I needed time to process.

My brain churned faster the farther we drove, while Martine drowsed in the seat beside me and street signs in Spanish flashed by. Had she always been the head of the House, or had she recently overpowered the current owner? That would make at least some sense. She'd been trying to gain control of the House of Swords for some time, and there was no reason to think she wouldn't go after Wands too, whoever they were. Clearly, Mercault hadn't been worth overthrowing, not when he so quickly went down on bended knee to her.

Asshat.

A gaudy billboard rose to the right of the road, showing an enormous Aztec ruin, like a third of the billboards I'd seen on this stretch of road. Apparently this highway eventually intersected with some archeological site named Teotihuacan, and there were ruins there. Awesome ruins. Good to know.

"Too soon now, too soon," moaned Martine, huddled in the seat beside me. I frowned down at him.

"We're not going all the way there, buddy," I said, but suddenly I had a queasy feeling. I needed to find someplace for this child to sleep, didn't I? I could sleep in the car, but this boy was only ten years old. Granted, he'd made it all the way from Mexico to Vegas relying only on the kindness of strangers, but what was I, some kind of barbarian? I had to stop, find a hotel or…something. And food. At the very least, I should get him to a bathroom. Children had to pee all the time, I was nearly certain of it.

Sure, I could've called Ma-Singh and had the House of Swords swoop in and hustle us off to some five-star hotel in Mexico City, but Gamon would have every bed-for-rent under surveillance. Better to let her goons spin their wheels wondering where I'd gone while keeping my people safe from an unnecessary skirmish. Granted, the solo approach hadn't worked out so great before, but…I glanced at the nails. This time they weren't going to get away from me.

Another billboard flashed by, advertising a taqueria. Taqueria sounded like taco, so that seemed like a good place to start for food. I pulled off the highway and into what appeared to be suburban Mexico City, and the streets boasted ordinary things like drug stores and gas stations and, yes, taco restaurants. We stopped first at the gas station, where I told Martine to stay locked inside while I pumped gas, and to act like he was asleep. This proved to be a masterful decision, since he was once more passed out by the time I finished filling the tank.

I didn't have the heart to wake him when we reached what appeared to be the Mexican version of a Walmart either. But I was pretty sure I was breaking some kind of code of babysitter conduct leaving a child sleeping unattended in a car. I wrestled with indecision for a few minutes, then pulled the nails out of my hoodie, and crossed them on the driver's seat.

"Protect him," I whispered.

On the flat leather seat, the bone shards gleamed and shifted, their runic carvings seeming to glow more brightly.

I didn't know what that meant, but I felt better. The babysitter code of conduct had nothing on the Valkyries.

Inside the store, I scored pajamas and underwear that were more or less the boy's size, bath wipes and towels, and a blanket-pillow combination that might have been intended for a smaller kid but was the first thing I could find in a hurry. I realized standing in line that I looked like nothing more than a child abductor, but the sleepy-eyed old woman at the checkout didn't appear to think anything of it.

"*Mojar la cama?*" she asked, not unsympathetically. I had no idea what she said, but I bit my lip and did my best to look embarrassed. She grinned and patted my hand, then I was through.

I trudged back to the car and unlocked it, unreasonably happy to find the boy still inside. The bones were there too, and, once again embarrassed, I thanked them as well. Tossing the clothes and supplies in the backseat, I spent an extra minute putting the blanket over Martine and easing his head onto the pillow. He looked so unreasonably small, I found myself scowling at him. Was I really going to make him spend the night in a car?

I thought about Gamon and Mercault, and the mercenaries they'd bought to track me down. *Yeah, I am,* I decided. If I needed to get away, I'd rather already be in a vehicle.

The next stop was the taqueria, and I did poke the kid awake for that. If I did the ordering, God only knew what we'd end up with.

What we ended up with, however, was easily half the restaurant, the boy's eyes wide with excitement as we got back on the main road, staring from the food to the blanket and towel spread over him, then back to the food. "This is dinner?"

I eyed the twelve-pack of tacos and monster cups of soda. I wasn't going to be winning any parenting awards soon, I knew, but these were desperate times.

"It's dinner." I nodded. "We'll push on a little bit and then find someplace to hide for the night and tomorrow, okay?" I honestly wasn't worried so much about the night, but the next day might be tough.

We traveled in relative silence another thirty minutes up the road, with Martine focused on his tacos and soda, while I let my hunger sharpen my focus. The last thing I needed right now was a food coma. When the boy looked up, he seemed calmer, happier, the trauma of the tent attack behind him for the moment.

He pointed at the next sign. "We sleep."

I glanced at the cheery image of a sunrise over a squat adobe-shaped building, and I shook my head. "No can do. We might have people after us. You sleep however you need to, and I'll sleep once you're rested. Sound good?"

He agreed moodily, but within another twenty minutes, he passed out again, and I resumed my vigil. More touristy billboards cropped up as well, although now there was a new name besides Teotihuacan: *pirámide del sol*. That made me straighten. Even with my poor language skills I could tell that the first word was pyramid, but it was the second that caught my attention: sol. Sol, as in solar, meant sun. And Martine had wanted us to go to the northeast, toward the sun.

Was Gamon hiding out at an archaeological dig site?

It made a certain kind of sense. It was outside the city, and while no doubt a magnet for tourists, most of those folks would be in and out, never to return. And I'd been to my share of sites enough to know that often what had been discovered and opened to the public was only a fraction of what was really there.

How good would Gamon's security be? And what was her arrangement with the owners of the site?

I kept driving into the night, at one point pulling free my phone, which fortunately Mercault hadn't had time to divest me of. Probably hadn't worried too much about it, since he was planning on swissing my cheese. Asshat.

I punched in the number while eyeing Martine. The boy was still out.

"Madam Wilde." Ma-Singh's voice rang with such quiet authority that I almost laughed. I was glad to have him on my team.

"Sorry I didn't check in before, but I'm sure you heard what happened. Thank you for your help in getting the team in there so quickly."

A pause. "Yes. But only after the fact. The agents we had in place all had headsets. An order was given to rescue you at the tent of Monsieur Mercault, first with blanks, then with knives. I assumed it was you doing the ordering. They said it was a female who gave the command."

"That would be no." I watched another Pyramid of the Sun sign flash by. "More likely, Armaeus pretending to be me due to the tech interference." I wanted Ma-Singh to trust the Magician, but it wasn't easy. Still, the man had clearly helped when help was needed. "Either way, your team performed flawlessly. Are you tracking me now?"

"Yes," Ma-Singh said. "Heading north, northeast

out of the city. Destination?"

"Pyramid of the Sun, it would seem. One of the ruins in this giant archaeological site called Teotihuacan."

"Why there?"

"Because that's where the kid wants me to go." I grimaced, feeling the first tug of fatigue behind my eyes.

"But Gamon will not be there," Ma-Singh said, confidence ringing in his voice. "She needs a lab, medical production facilities. The ability to cart drugs in and out. This must be another stop along the way."

That gave me pause. "That's fair. It'll be somewhere past there, then. Out of the city, I'm thinking, but not so remote that vehicles in and out of the place will seem odd. Do some research and let me know likely possibilities, okay?"

I disconnected and spent a full ten minutes arguing with myself about whether or not to throw the phone out the window. In the end, responsibility won out. Like it or not, I was the leader of the House of Swords. People were counting on me. Moreover, I wasn't on a solo mission, but one with a child who didn't deserve to get killed because I wanted to play Captain America and go in alone, guns blazing. Or gun blazing, anyway. I never was good at shooting with my left hand.

We reached Teotihuacan less than an hour later, my concerns instantly put to rest about where to hide. Surrounding the ruins was a rabbit warren of streets, residences and government buildings, parking lots and shops. It was the work of fifteen minutes to find three good locations in relative shade. We'd hole up, hide out, and make our move the next evening, when Martine did his eyeball track and mapped us out of here.

I pulled into a shaded lot just before dawn and shut off the car, looking over again at Martine. He was awake again, though yawning, and I stood guard as he prepared for sleep, returning to the car to stretch back his seat and cover him. In mere moments, he was sleeping soundly. When I was ready to bunk down as well, I cradled the sticks in my hands, careful not to grasp them too hard, and breathed another word over them, the same word I'd used before with Martine. "Protect."

The shade around us lengthened and twisted, and I craned around, staring. The tree that had leaned crazily over the wall was fuller now, richer, its long limbs hanging over the wall and cascading around the car. In another minute, it looked like we'd abandoned our vehicle there sometime during the first Bush administration, never to be reclaimed.

I chuckled, weighing the Gods' Nails in my hands. It might have some codependency issues, but this was an artifact that meant business. "Thank you," I muttered, hugging the bone shards close. Illusions like these I could get used to. Then I drifted off to sleep.

A moment later, I awoke with Martine's hand on my shoulder.

"Sara," he whispered urgently. "It's time."

"Time for…" My eyes fluttered open, but instantly I saw the problem. We were still in the car, shaded from all eyes…but it was clearly dusk outside—dusk, not dawn.

I sat bolt upright. "How long have you been awake?"

"The entrance is very close here," he said, ignoring me. A second later, I knew why. His eyes had gone milk white. "You are strong, Sara. You will save us."

"So you keep saying." I blew out a long breath. "We drive or we walk?"

"Walk—no phone, nothing with…" He paused, searching for the word. "Electric. The archaeological people can track that."

I lifted my brows, but I didn't argue. We'd only be in the pyramid long enough for Martine to get his next geolocation. And the car was sweltering—it could do with a time out too.

"All right, let's go."

"Not we, Sara." Martine's eyes were no longer milky, but his smile was rueful. "You."

He reached out and took my hand, placing it on his heart. A racing staccato burst beneath my palm. "I can no longer slow its dancing," he whispered.

CHAPTER TWENTY-SEVEN

The entrance to the Pyramid of the Sun of Teotihuacan was an impressive affair, seen for hundreds of yards in all directions. The building itself was enormous, standing at the end of a street referred to as the Avenue of the Dead. This information didn't inspire confidence, but then, neither had the very sick ten-year-old boy who'd given said info to me.

I grimaced, angling past the grand entrance to skirt the building. I was searching for a nondescript square that looked like every other square of rock in this heap of ruins, only slightly raised. That was where the voices would come from. According to the boy, I'd know it when I saw it. Not trusting myself to know anything with that level of certainty, I'd kept my hands deep in my hoodie pockets as I walked, shuffling my cards.

After some back-and-forth discussion as Martine had grown dramatically paler, I'd left my phone with him, but not the Gods' Nails. He seemed pretty certain I'd need something stronger than Pizza Hut on autodial, and I wanted him to have a way to call for help. I keyed in the general's number, made the boy promise to dial it as soon as I was out of sight. I would have hated for the general to make some kind of extremely reasonable request of me that I'd have to ignore.

Now I was back in familiar territory, however. The territory of being completely lost and alone. It felt refreshingly like coming home.

I pulled out a series of three cards in quick succession, scrutinizing them quickly before dropping them back in the deck, then smoothed down my hoodie. I didn't want to draw any more attention to myself than I needed to, and it was bad enough that I was going off the beaten path. Still, there were other tourists meandering along the scrubby dirt and rocks even at this late hour, scuffing their feet along the enormous stones.

I paused in front of an informational sign, pretending to study it with great interest. Luckily, it included an English translation. The excavation had apparently not gone below the surface too deeply, with all the exciting discoveries having been made inside the pyramid itself, and even among those, the "excitement" was limited to some clutches of skeletons and a few examples of funereal pottery and jaguar statues. None of that meant anything to me.

Ma-Singh's hesitation in believing this site was the endgame rang loudly in my ears, and I had to admit he was right. This didn't look like a facility capable of producing more than a tumbleweed. There were no commercial buildings near the pyramids — at least not close enough to serve as loading stations for multibillion dollar shipments of drugs — and everything seemed geared toward archaeology and tourism. Too many eyes from too many countries. It simply didn't add up.

Like it or not, though, this was where Martine had led me, where he insisted I must go. When I'd asked if there was another destination after this, he'd stared at me, confused, and I hadn't pushed it. It was enough that I was here, at his direction. It would have to be enough.

"Focus," I muttered, scanning the barren landscape.

The rocks that were visible didn't look like escape hatches to me. They were thick pallets of stone, part of an ancient sacred road, with nary a manhole to be found. And a manhole was what I needed. The first card of the three I'd pulled was once again the Seven of Pentacles, showing a young man staring down at a series of pentacles. Those pents were in the shape of fruit on a bush, but still, he was staring down into the bushes, and by God, that was where I'd start looking.

Only there was nothing — scarcely any bushes, and those that were clustered around were set far away from the larger rocks. I wandered over to a section that looked like a miniature excavation site — pickaxes, shovels, a light — and realized it was staged, another informational placard describing the history of the place. *Crap.*

I swept the horizon with my gaze, but there was nothing. The sun was dropping lower in the sky, and all I could think of was Martine, stuck back at the car, wondering what the hell I was doing.

"Think, think."

After the Seven of Pents, I'd pulled the Six of Cups and Tower. I hated pulling the Tower anytime I was stuck underground, and the Six of Cups was frankly one of my least favorite cards to pull from a tracking perspective. It could depict anything, and since its focus was children and Martine was currently languishing in my car, it wasn't a particularly helpful draw. The cards did that to me sometimes, though, portraying my worries and concerns when I simply needed a clear-cut answer. But first things first.

"Seven of Pents." I scanned the space again. Shovel, pickax, lantern, slab, dust, rocks, bushes. Lather, rinse, repeat across the entire road, except for this little makeshift digger's gallery. For a moment, I tried to consider what it would be like to dig anything under the hot Mexican sun. Especially in the heat of the day, it would redefine misery to be out here, leaning on your shovel, mopping the sweat from your brow, wondering when the hole would ever be deep enough…

I stopped, my brain finally catching up with my eyes.

"Idiot," I muttered. Looking around to see if anyone was watching, I moved forward nonchalantly one step, then a second. By the third, I'd reached the shovel. I picked it up, only to realize it had fallen over from its casing — a shallow bucket set into the ground filled with sand. You couldn't see the bucket at all from even five feet away, but it made for the perfect base.

I pushed the shovel into the base and jumped away, bracing for impact.

Nothing moved.

Moving forward gingerly, I tried again. I wiggled the shovel a little in its sand pail, then leaped back a second time. Still nothing. I leaned all my weight hard on the shovel once, twice, in rapid succession, before jumping away as quickly.

And still nothing. The wind was starting to pick up, the sun now officially setting over the western skyline. A few more brightly jacketed official-looking types could be seen at the doorways to the main buildings, and I grimaced. My window of opportunity was narrowing, but nothing was working. There were no voices here.

I reached out and jiggled the shovel again — and no. I stepped behind the shovel onto a layer of sand, and shoved the long-handled tool down into the pail. No.

What was it I was missing? With the shovel well and truly wedged into the pail, I leaned heavily on it and stayed that way, staring at the rocks. Was there some sort of image there I was supposed to see? Some guide to opening up secret passageways? Some —

The sound tipped me off just in time for realization

to strike, but not soon enough for me to back away.

With a long, groaning shudder, sounding exactly like the haunting moan of an old man, the sand dropped away beneath me.

I plummeted.

As I tumbled down a solid surface rather than into a gaping maw, several things flashed into my mind with sharp clarity. The first was, I needed to be smarter. Even an idiot could have worked out faster that prolonged leaning on the shovel was exactly what had been needed, mimicking the young man on the Seven of Pents, who leaned on his pole while contentedly regarding the fruits of his labors.

The second was, I was falling a long way into the earth, but not on any sort of usual trajectory. This entrance was a one-way chute that funneled me somewhere deep into the pyramid, but not in a straight line. Instead, I skidded over rocks worn smooth by what had to be thousands of people before me, over hundreds—perhaps even thousands of years. Who'd built this chute into the floor, and why?

Remarkably, I had time to think about all that. It was that long a drop.

I was working out my theory of space and time when the pace of my fall picked up rapidly, and I suddenly landed on what had to be stacked bags of cornmeal. Or poured cement, as the case may be. Either way, I hit with enough force to knock the wind out of me, so much so that I crumpled to my side, trying to make sense of the odd smell in the room. Beneath me, there was corn, wheat—some sort of grain. It smelled earthy and natural. But the other scent…

I scrambled off the stacked bags and fished in my pocket for a penlight, flicking it on long enough to get my bearings. I was in a room empty of people, but by no means empty. On the near wall, where I was, were tumbled rows upon rows of bags of cornmeal, rice, or something that had once no doubt been soft but was now bruisingly hard. Against the other were pallets of…what had to be marijuana.

It simply had to be. I'd never smelled anything that could quite match the stench of the plant, acrid and rich at once. I crept over and pawed at the bricks of hash, then realized that they weren't on stationery pallets — they were on tracks, empty pallets to the left, full to the right, and a cart rail system that disappeared down an even darker corridor beyond.

At that moment, a whirr of electronics sounded, and I flattened myself on the ground. As I did so, the carts slid forward, positioning an empty cart directly in front of me. The wall on the other side of the cart slid back with another whoosh of clean, crisp pneumatics, and a robotic arm extended, neatly packing brick upon brick of pot into the pallet with blinding speed. Within a minute, the top layer was complete, and the machine paused, dipped, and the bottom layer was stacked. Over the top of the machine, I could see smooth metal panels of the room beyond, everything crisp and gleaming…for all that we were in a cave system under a two-thousand-year-old pyramid.

The doors snicked shut.

I sat there, stunned, for another minute more, then crawled forward quickly. I pulled a switchblade free of another pocket and worked it into the nearest brick of pot, slicing it longwise along the side and — sure enough, the metal of my knife hit something hard. The pot was a decoy, the medical insignia stamped on them clearly fake. It'd work to get them through the first layers of security wherever they were going, I suspected. Then they'd be redirected to places like the arcane black market in La Merced…and into the hands of dealers like Mercault.

I couldn't think of Mercault right now, though.

The doors snicked open again, and the same routine unspooled before me. There appeared to be no humans on the other side of the door, and I watched the loading procedure two more times before I worked out a plan. I'd wait until the machine had dipped down to load the bottom tray of the cart, then I'd scramble out and over the top of it, banking on the idea that no one had thought to put security on a low-level drone loading product that had already been thoroughly processed.

The doors snicked shut.

I drew in a long breath, steadying my heart rate. I'd have plenty of time—easily thirty seconds to bound up and onto the cart, scrambling over the machine. But I had no idea what was waiting for me on the other side. Still, I didn't have much choice. Here was the lab, or at least the very tip of it, that Ma-Singh was expecting us to find at some other location. It was just in no way where he thought it would be.

The doors slid open again. I crouched, counting the bricks as they were layered on the top shelf, then rose to a half-standing position as the long thick pole retracted. When it pushed forward again, I leapt. Landing briefly on the bricks of pot, I kept as low as possible and ran, dashing up the length of the mechanical arm and hurtling myself over to the other side—before crashing in a roll on a polished stone floor.

Instantly, I whipped around, trying to get my bearings. As I'd suspected, I was alone here. There was nothing but the robot loading drugs, and it was loading a *lot* of them. With the benefit of full light, I took an extra precious moment to knife through another brick, this time from the top, exposing the contents within. Six tiny metal vials gleamed up at me, filled with a viscous mixture. I thought of the spray Brody had been nailed with back in Las Vegas—was that what these were destined for? If so, no Connected was safe.

Mashing the brick back together and flipping it over, I reinserted it into the pile. The machine no doubt scanned the bricks for integrity before placing them on the pallets, but that was the least of my problems. I turned quickly to the curved ramp leading out of the room, following the trail of drugs as they were shipped down from above. That proved a rapid dead end, as the bricks were dropped via a sliding chute, not unlike the hole I'd fallen down. The place must be riddled with them, holdover passageways from the ancient civilizations who'd built these sacred spaces.

Continuing on, I darted up the corridor as it curved, all the while noting the slight upward trajectory. I was returning closer to the surface, though judging how long I'd fallen, I wouldn't get there anytime soon. I'd need to —

Voices sounded down the hallway, and I froze, then pressed myself against the thick rock walls. There was nowhere to hide here, but the sounds dropped almost as soon as they'd started, as if people had simply crossed through the corridor in between soundproof rooms. I crept forward more carefully now, noting the floors, the walls — both of them hammered stone, but not metal plated like the loading room and the corridor beyond the chute. Contamination wasn't a concern here. Hopefully, security wasn't either.

Another burst of voices. I moved forward this time to try to catch sight of who was talking. I couldn't understand them, but they were definitely speaking Spanish, and the voices were both male. The corridor turned sharply around a bend, and I hesitated, waiting for the echoes to die. Then I peeked.

The long stone corridor was fronted on both sides with a series of steel-framed windows set into the stone. There appeared to be only one set of doors, however, facing each other on either side of the corridor. Lights shone out from the rooms, those on the left a dull red, those on the right an operating-room white, too bright for comfort even all the way back where I was standing.

Seeking desperately to know more, I opened my third eye, but for once, the extra layer of sensory input proved unhelpful. If anything it obscured my vision — the sheer ugliness and pain of everything in this place proving to be an impenetrable fog.

Reluctantly, I switched back to normal vision. I waited for easily five minutes, but no one else crossed between any of the doors, so I slid along the wall, keeping well below the bottoms of the windows. When I finally reached the last of them, I inched up to peer inside.

It was a state-of-the-art drug lab, filled with centrifuges and mass spectrometers, but on a size and scale I'd never seen before. The room had to be at least thirty feet long and half again as wide, and it was bustling with techs in long white jackets. As I watched, men and women wearing masks and latex gloves worked with near machinelike speed filling and labeling vials, scanning barcodes with a wand-like device, then inserting vials into the spectrometer and sliding the trays home. By my quick count, nearly a hundred vials were shoved into the machine in the few moments that I watched, and I dropped back down, trying to process the information. How were they getting so much product, so quickly? Why were they still testing — and testing was what those machines were for, I was nearly certain. This wasn't the final packaging place where the end-unit drugs were slotted into their hemp containers. This was still…research.

I gazed over to the other side of the corridor, where the dim red light showed. That light bothered me. It flickered and danced like a fire, but with a curious

274

wavelike quality, as if there was some sort of pool in the room. None of that felt as solid and reassuring as the laboratory on my right, but I remembered Martine's eerie poem when he'd met me, referencing water. There was definitely water in that second chamber.

I moved carefully over to the last of the red-hued windows, then slowly, carefully, lifted myself up on my toes.

And went stock-still.

The scene on the other side of the window was surreal. The room was several feet below the windows, requiring a long, narrow ramp of stone to reach its main floor — but as a result, I could see nearly everything in one glance. There was a pool, a moat, actually, ringed with small torches that helped give off the wavering reflected light. Inside the moat was a platform of stone, linked to the main floor of the room by a small bridge. On the platform stood a stone table that looked more than six feet across, perfectly round, deeply carved and rutted. I didn't have to look for more than a few seconds to recognize the pattern. I didn't know a lot about Aztec artifacts, but I was familiar with that one. It looked exactly like the Sun Stone — down to its ring of jaguars, faces with gaping mouths, and arcane symbols — just smaller.

But the Sun Stone had been found in the heart of what was now Mexico City, not all the way out here in the 'burbs. And it was in a museum, a treasure of the Mexican people. What was this smaller version doing here?

Something shifted behind the table, and I stiffened further as I saw three people emerge. Two of them were masked and hooded in what looked like honest-to-god animal skins, the woman in between them dressed in a short, plain shift. Her hands were manacled and her feet might as well have been, the way she shuffled forward.

Her captors led her forward toward the table, and my eyes widened in horror.

Voices sounded from the lab, getting louder, and I jerked away from the window, darting back around the corner as the door from the lab snicked open.

My heart thundering, I shrank down against the wall, and peeked out as two white-suited figures—a male and female—stepped quickly from the bright white lab through the hallway and into the chamber of horrors. Between them, they pushed a cart filled with vials. Empty vials.

The moment the second door closed, I crossed the hallway again and inched up until I was level with the window, pressing my face against the glass. The white-jacketed pair pushed the cart down the ramp, paying no attention to the scene in the middle of the room. There, in the intervening few seconds when I hadn't been watching, the woman had already been lifted and secured atop the table, her arms and legs spread wide. All that remained on her body was a bolt of cloth over her hips, and she stared upward, clearly drugged out of her mind but not dead...definitely not dead. Her chest rose and fell, her mouth worked, though I couldn't tell whether she was praying or pleading. The figure standing at her head lifted a blade, and I flinched, ready to bolt for the door—to rescue the poor woman—to do *something*—

Only to feel the cool, steady imprint of steel against my temple.

"You're just in time for the show," came a low, guttural, but undeniably female voice.

Gamon.

276

CHAPTER TWENTY-EIGHT

Gamon wasn't alone, of course. Three beefy guards flowed up and around us, two of them holding my arms, one of them zip-tying my hands.

All the while, Gamon watched me with an expression half of curiosity, half surprise. She was a tall, hard, powerful-looking woman, with angular features that marked her as Middle Eastern — Israeli, I was nearly certain. One of the rumors about her had been that she'd been former Mossad. I could believe it, looking at her now. The last time I'd seen her up close, she'd been driving a blade into Annika Soo's body, draining the life force out of the head of the House of Swords.

Now she led a House as well. And a one-woman crusade to obliterate the Connecteds of the earth.

With her gun, she gestured me to move up the corridor, and within moments, we were entering the red-lit room, taking the same stone ramp that the lab techs had. That pair stood silently to the side as we descended, their eyes averted.

The inside of the sacrifice room was larger than it seemed through the windows. It was practically a cavern, which was no doubt why the light was reflected so strangely, but the effect was exacerbated by the blood-red pool that surrounded the sacrificial altar, and the large glass bowls situated around the altar's base. I saw those bowls up close and personal now, as Gamon pushed me forward across the small stone bridge that separated the island from the main section of the room.

The priest remained in position, with his assistant now standing back, having situated the bowls. Gamon shoved me to my knees. A guard dropped to one knee behind me, holding me fast in his meaty paws, but otherwise, I hadn't been harmed, yet. And I didn't know enough to act. Yet.

"When I was given the charge to bring you here, I had my choice of methods," Gamon said now. "You needed to be alive, though, your blood still flowing, your mind still intact. Mercault had learned of the existence of the Gods' Nails and wanted them. Promised, in fact, to bring you to me, bound. I let him try. Meanwhile, there was the boy — one of the successful test subjects before his heart weakened like all the rest." She said the words with disgust, and I blanched.

"How many were there?" I asked.

"I couldn't kill him, not outright," she said, ignoring my question. "He endured the tests better than so many of the children. Then, later, he screamed so loud and long in his sleep, racked with visions, clearly touched by the sorcerer god, that he seemed a symbol of all that would come. Afterwards, when he drew what he dreamed — and it was you — I had a second option. I could place the directions back here in his mind, and he would draw you to me. It was the consummate plan, the perfect game."

A game with children as the disposable pieces. Monster.

Gamon sighed with what sounded like genuine pleasure. "And now you are here at last. I have done all that I have been asked, and I will be rewarded."

Asked?

Who, in any frame of their right mind, would *ask* Gamon to do anything but roll over and die?

"Who'd you kill to become the head of the House of Cups?" I asked flatly, not shifting my gaze from the altar.

She ignored that too. I imagined Martine down here, or maybe somewhere close, screaming in his sleep, frail and frightened, then used for his abilities. I'd been used as a child too, the woman I thought of as my mother angling for me to be some sort of child star, visions of "Psychic Teen Sariah" dancing in her head. But not like this. Never like this.

I fixed on the young woman on the altar, who'd not uttered a word. She was still alive, I thought. But she wasn't with us anymore. Her face was set, her eyes unfocused.

"Don't kill her," I murmured, surprised I'd said the words aloud.

That, of course, generated a response.

"Her? She's already dead," Gamon said dismissively. "Though her cells are perfect—perfect! Her mind was not strong, however. She's merely a host, a husk for that perfection. Not someone who can enjoy the gifts to the fullest, and so her blood will go to the inferior drug. The bait, but not the reward."

My stomach clenched, my heart shriveling another fraction in my chest.

"It has been our biggest challenge. To find the people who can actually survive the thing they crave most of all." Gamon sighed, sounding legitimately perplexed. "We despaired of ever finding the link, in fact. Until you were given to us."

"Don't kill her," I said again. I could spend an eternity parsing Gamon's crazy. Right now, I needed to save the woman on the table.

279

"She's already dead, I told you. Her brain died before you entered this room, her body simply hasn't realized it yet. It's how we're able to harvest so effectively." Gamon gestured beside me, and the man in the jaguar skin finally moved.

The knife came down with a savage thrust so violent that I jumped in the grasp of Gamon's guard, but he held me fast, keeping me from crumpling as the knife continued its slashing, curving arcs, the movements mesmerizing in their speed and brutality. Within moments, the surface of the table was slicked with blood, and seconds after that, the blood gushed through the spigots in the base of the alter to pool in the glass bowls around its base. The second ritually dressed assistant rushed forward and expedited the process — lifting the young woman's limbs, bending and palpating body parts. I wanted to shrink away, not to look, but this was a human being in front of me, a woman barely more than a child herself, certainly no older than me, her essence rent from her with a breathless brutality.

And the ongoing gush of blood was shocking — there was so much. I stared in fascination as it filled the bowls, horrified and curious at once.

"It was a process that took us far too long to perfect. Even now it isn't quite right, I'll admit," Gamon said, her voice dripping with false modesty. "The Sun Stone that was found south of here at the central temple is larger, but it is actually the first stone, the rough draft, if you will. Not the final. It had been used in sacrifices, yes, but sacrifices only to benefit the gods, not those who served them. This stone…is something different."

"It's still sacrificial," I gritted out, forcing my tone to remain even while inside I vacillated between quailing and helpless horror.

"Yes, and if you were to study the surface, you

280

would see a marked similarity to the great Sun Stone." She spoke as though she were some Ivy League professor pontificating before his adoring students. "But unlike that stone, this one is thicker, and it is hollow, meant to take the flow of blood along its surfaces, to cleanse and purify that blood, empower it with the god of sorcery's fire and strength. If you were to look even more closely, you would see the true power of the stone. It's not in its design, but in the negative space *between* the carvings. That's what holds the mysteries the ancients knew and we subsequently lost. That's where the true magic is. And a supplicant's blood, once passed through this stone, becomes magical as well."

She drew in a deep, satisfied breath. "Introduce such purified blood into the bodily system of a mere mortal — Connected or non-Connected alike — and they would experience the same surge, the same lightness as that of a god...for a time." Gamon exhaled with a disappointed sigh. "All too quickly, however, the effect evaporates or, if the dosage is too high, the subject succumbs to one of any number of reactions. Heart attack, asphyxiation, brain death. As you can imagine, that's halted our marketing process entirely. We're completely R&D right now." She paused, and I watched more blood drain through the open mouths in the base of the altar, feeding the bowls with its life force.

Who was this girl who had died, I wondered. Where had she lived? How had she loved? And who would benefit from the blood she gave unwillingly?

A low, angry thrum awoke within me, shifting along my own blood vessels, building in strength.

Gamon continued, oblivious to my growing rage. "Quite recently, and by accident, we trapped a rogue Revenant in our snare. That was a find. No reaction to the drug, no side effects. Further testing revealed, of course, that the Revenant subspecies has no need of this drug, at least not for its life-giving properties." She gave a scoffing laugh. "They already have that in spades."

"You *are* a Revenant, Gamon," I reminded her. "You didn't need to steal the hearts of your own race's children. You could've saved this operation a lot of time and effort by testing on yourself."

"Don't be naïve," she snapped. "It's a *child's* heart that fails due to the drug, but not a Revenant child's heart. They could withstand the drug—take that another step, and you can see how reasonable it is to deduce that the Revenant children must have some cellular coding that could help us in another, more practical way. We must create a drug that people can withstand, Sara. Failing that, we must change the cellular structure of our future addicts so they can accept the drug into their systems. Surely you understand the importance of that."

We, who? Gamon was cracking around the edges and she didn't even realize it.

"The most critical organ of the human, at least when it comes to their godhood, is their hearts. Not the brain, not the glands, not the ever-elusive soul. The pure, beautiful, incredibly complex yet achingly simple organ that delivers life-sustaining energy to its hosts without any conscious or deliberate thought. It gives and gives and gives."

Gamon's voice grew hard, cutting. "And we've taken. Taken enough that we know we're on to something. The heart is the key. The ancients knew it. We mocked them for their ignorance for centuries, but they knew...they knew. The Revenant children's hearts were close, very close, but they weren't...perfect. And we need perfect. We can recreate it once we have a sample, but we can't generate that type of perfection out of whole cloth. We need a model."

She gave another low hum of pleasure beside me as she drew the barrel of her gun over my hair. "For that, you were brought to us. For that, you were given."

"I'm not a child."

She chuckled. "Not in any normal sense, no. And yet…"

I twisted away from her gun, half turning to glare at her. I'd promised Kreios I'd keep my heart in my chest. I really wanted to deliver on that oath.

"Who did you kill to take over the House of Cups?" I demanded again, trying to distract her from the organ hammering wildly under my rib cage.

Gamon's lips twisted. "Mercault should know better than to let such secrets spread to idle ears," she murmured. "Another failure added to his name."

"Who?" I pressed. "Because there's no way you've had a House for long. You're not equipped to run anything but your mouth."

Whether it was the snideness of my statement or my tone, it seemed to penetrate Gamon's fog of self-righteousness. She focused on me, and I got to see a glimpse of her soul through her dead black eyes. See it and know it had long since been eaten away. "You're a Revenant, and you killed your own," I accused her. "You're a Connected, and you've killed your own. There's no real worth in you."

"Worth," scoffed Gamon. "The Revenants abandoned me early on for not following their precious rules, for deserting my foster parents and ignoring the collective's protocols. Really, as if we didn't reach our majority in the first few years of our appreciably long lives. Their path is one of wastefulness."

Her lips quirked. "But not anymore. Now we have used their hearts to create a newer, more vibrant version of the drug, and synthesized the resulting chemical compound to a near-perfect variant suitable for the masses. For the right buyers, of course, the organic option will always be preferred."

Sick disbelief roiled in my stomach. "You're a *cannibal*. And, worse, of your own kind. No matter how few of you are left on this earth, you'll find them all to feed your sick fantasy."

"I would, yes," Gamon said. "Fortunately, I don't have to. I prayed to the god of the Toltecs who created this beautiful altar, and was granted a boon above all others, in return for a price so trifling, it made me giddy." She chuckled with manic surety. "That boon is you, Sara, if you haven't already guessed, and you are also the price."

"And you think your *god* gave me to you," I sneered, refusing to cower despite being on my knees.

"Not think, know. Tezcatlipoca heard my cry. The god of sorcerers, essence of the jaguar, giver of gifts." Her smile broadened. "How lucky that this gift proved so easy in the taking. I had merely to ask, and it was delivered."

The pistol whip came so quickly that I had no time to brace for it, no time to prepare. I was kneeling one moment, then struck to the ground and dragged upright again only by the strength of the guards gripping my shoulders and arms. As Mercault had before her, Gamon reached into my jacket with her gloved hands and withdrew the long, impossibly sharp Gods' Nails. Unlike Mercault, however, she didn't hand them off to a minion. Instead, she kept them wrapped in her hands...hands that remained very close to me. Despite the swimming in my head, I thought...that was important.

Not as important, however, as me being lifted bodily and carried forward to the altar. In some remote corner of my mind, I knew what was happening. Knew it and recognized it as bad. And yet in other corners of my mind, I saw the actions of Gamon as if through a prism. She was a usurper to the House of Cups, but who had she overthrown? How had she done it? She was having the man wrapped in jaguar skins tie me to the altar, but why hadn't she destroyed the Gods' Nails or removed them from my presence? Surely she knew their power. Surely she knew and understood their connection to me. Surely there was some rhyme or reason to her madness.

Right?

I sucked in a sharp breath as my zipties were snapped. Then my arms were stretched wide, rack-like, across the still wet and sticky surface of the sacrificial Sun Stone. I could feel the grooves and indentations of its carvings against my back. The face at the center with its lolling tongues, the mystical cats at its cardinal points. The believers who'd carved these images had been dead for centuries by the time the Aztecs had stumbled onto this site and co-opted it for their own, but that didn't change the level of the ancients' power. Their power or their sickness, in this case. Now, lying atop the stone, I could practically hear the whispers of those long-ago priests, feel the profane power of their magic.

"You're not going to get what you want," I warned Gamon.

"But you see, I already have." She laughed, looking down at me trussed up on the altar of the ancients like the Thanksgiving meal. I still felt curiously removed from the dire circumstances I found myself in, and not because I expected rescue either. I didn't. There simply hadn't been enough time. Yet I welcomed the pain at my wrists and ankles as I lay spread-eagled, mired in the blood of innocents. This was right, this was good. This was as it should be.

I shook my head, finally understanding my sluggishness. "You've drugged me."

"You're breathing it in, in this space," Gamon said.

285

She turned, gesturing toward the murky red-black pools. "We found quickly enough that those who are truly gifted can endure extraordinary limits of distress, *if* they believed that it was part of the natural order of the world. Creating a compound to facilitate that belief was not difficult. We have already synthesized it. There will never be a lack of demand for such a drug, I assure you."

My lip curled. I could only imagine the torturers Gamon was in league with for a drug such as this. Those who cared less about the information they collected and more about what the human body and the psyche could endure. There'd always been those kind of monsters — the Connected had been subjected to some of the worst that humanity could dish out. Now, it seemed we were on the cusp of an entirely new level of brutality: the worst of the worst leveled on our community by our own.

Was this what magic had come to?

I fought through the fog as Gamon leaned over me.

"You disappoint me, Sara, in all truth. When Tezcatlipoca gave me the charge to find you, to find you and bind you and lock you in place, I expected a mighty battle and the death of thousands. But no one has died except those who were already slated for slaughter, and you are here." A flicker of satisfaction danced across her face, rendering her harsh features almost attractive. "Better still, you've brought me an elegant set of knives to begin the work upon you."

She handed the nails to the jaguar-dressed man, and he took them silently, fitting them into hilts at the base of his wrists — not bone and flesh at all, but thick gray metal, locked tight against his forearms. I watched with a detachment I couldn't explain, still mired in the irony of it all.

All these millennia of spirits reaching for greater

286

truths, greater enlightenment, greater abilities, and the Connected community was on the brink of being undone...by our own kind. Did we hate ourselves so much, then, recognizing the monster within as the greatest threat? Was the war on magic not a question of us versus them at all, but us versus ourselves?

Again, was this what magic had come to?

"I envy you," Gamon said, her eyes burning with a feral intensity. "You are about to know what it is like to spill your life's essence on the altar of a god. To give the ultimate gift and receive the ultimate prize in return."

Something in her voice, the hunger in it, finally broke through.

"You're welcome to change places," I said, stretching my hands farther than she'd bound them to grasp the ropes. They weren't traditionally woven rope at all, I noted with dismay, but flexible metal strips wrapped in some high-tech fabric, probably rip proof, pound proof, and fire proof. My ankles were bound with similar straps. So much for rocking it old-school, ancient rituals or no.

Gamon straightened, waving to an unseen attendant. A bell was struck, the high-pitched, achingly beautiful tone ringing through the air.

"The heart will be last," she cried out. "A final gift to the god who brought you to me, your perfect blood that is in this world but not of it, the final ingredient to create the Fountain of eternal youth."

The priest struck, driving the nails into me and yanking them out again, flaying open my shoulders, my abdomen, my hips — too fast, far too fast for me to heal, the heat of my wounds spreading through me with fantastic agony.

Then he pierced my wrists with the brutal tips of the nails, plunging them deep.

Mistake.

CHAPTER TWENTY-NINE

Fire exploded all around me as the spikes took hold of my wrists and buried themselves into the bone. I didn't expect that, but it didn't mean I couldn't use it. Gripping the nails in my hands I yanked them out of the priest's grasp and channeled their fire straight at him, throwing him back while the heat incinerated my clothes and danced along the coils that bound me.

The coils held, unfortunately — and, worse, they caught me up in a flash of pain and electrical fire.

The paroxysm of agony that gripped me was unlike anything I'd experienced before. Everything that was rent and broken within me was cauterized in an angry surge of power and heat, leaving nothing behind but fierce and oozing wounds and charred organs. My lungs filled with smoke, my eyes with fire. The red tinge of the room was supplanted now by a glowing fireball of energy that burst forth from me and shattered against the walls, pounding against them mercilessly as if to break free. This wasn't my normal fireball either, but something almost primordial. I winced as glass broke and joists popped, and wondered for a moment what would happen if we all were buried under a pile of smoking rocks.

"No," I groaned, surging up against my restraints.

In my extremity, my third eye flashed open, and I thought of Chichiro in her mountain idyll, Chichiro's house that I had exploded and brought back into one piece again simply by my strength of will. I forced my attention to the ropes around my hands, my feet, and imagined them unraveling—slowly at first, then with greater speed, each tiny filament remaining frayed as I fought and strained against the bindings.

I kept my visible eyes screwed shut as one—two ropes broke, one foot and one hand, then I flailed upward in an ungainly lurch, reaching down with my freed left hand to pierce through the cord with the fire jutting from the bone shard. My right wrist then broke free—first in my mind, and then in truth, and for a single, blessed moment, I felt as unbound as I ever had in this lifetime, suffused with power and energy—and, above all, hope.

I sat up in a rush, but despite my newfound strength, I still had lost a lot of blood. My head spun as I brought my hands around to sever the final ties on my legs, but I couldn't move off the table.

Instead, nausea swamped me, my eyesight going in and out like a defective movie reel, and everything around me was now a kaleidoscope of bright yellow light. The moat of blood was on fire. How much of my own blood had poured through the chalice of the sacrificial altar to fill the bowls below? I leaned over, trying to force myself to slip off the table to the rock surface below. That wouldn't be so difficult, if the floor would stop moving.

Was my blood still down there? Could I somehow dump it back inside me?

I closed my eyes, struggling for composure. Six of Cups. I'd drawn the Six of Cups and the Tower. A shock and tumult—well, that had certainly happened. But the Six was supposed to have come first, and the card still made no sense to me. It showed a charming scene of children playing in a courtyard, vases of flowers all around them, the dreamy peaceful nostalgia that memories of childhood were supposed to evoke.

There was nothing dreamy or peaceful about this place.

"Tezcatlipoca!" Gamon screamed behind me, which was the only way I could tell where she was in the midst of all the smoke and fire. I lurched around, nearly toppling off the altar, and aimed my spikes at her.

Another explosion rocked the space, the equivalent of a sonic boom, sending everything flying: me, Gamon, the priest, even the altar, its top detaching and rolling toward the blood-soaked water. My own bowls of precious blood spilled and splashed in a hideous, thick spatter, and I groaned as I crunched against the wall, feeling beyond drained.

Smoke billowed into the room, and I searched my brain for anything I could recall on Tezcatlipoca. God of sorcerers, as Gamon had said, god of both war and creation, bringer of good and evil and all that was conflict in the world. Sounded right up Gamon's alley.

I didn't need to worry about Tezcatlipoca now, however. The doors had been blasted off the room, and at the crest of the ramp, I could see where the far door into the state-of-the-art lab had been as well. I longed to fill that room with fire too, but I couldn't—couldn't! I still needed the antidote for this Fountain elixir, and there was no doubt in my mind that it was spinning away in that room along with Gamon's vials of eternal youth.

Several white-coated people were approaching that door, however, carrying something in their arms, and my eyes flew wide.

This, at least, I could manage. This I could do.

I drew the nails together and snarled one word.

291

"Bind!" And twin arcs of flame jetted out, blasting into the ceiling above the door and showering down sparks and smoke. I didn't know how long that would hold, but it did the job for the moment. Nobody was leaving the lab alive until I found what I needed. Too many people were depending on me. *I* was depending on me.

Fire raged all around me. I rolled over, dragging myself through my own blood, which was not ever something I'd hoped to do, frankly. I squinted back into the depths of the sacrificial hall, trying to see more clearly, and something was definitely moving in the smoke. Was it Gamon? Her priest?

It was smoke, I realized, a smoking mirror. Had that been attributed to the god as well? The phrase came to me in a rush, and I blinked, seeing the scene before me more clearly now. The figure in front of me, swaying and twisting, wasn't the priest. It was Gamon. Only, Gamon like I'd never seen her before. Her usual thick layers of robes had been stripped from her body, and her arms were bared. In between bursts of fire, I could see she was inscribed with tattoos in full sleeves on both arms, the sinuous art writhing and moving independent of her motions, like she was being swarmed by symbols and strange beasts.

I shook my head, desperate to understand, but my blood loss had been too great. I flopped forward, dragging myself toward her. I had—to stop her. With her out of commission, with the nails blasting fire, I could bluff my way past her people. But with Gamon still upright and me so incapacitated, there was simply no way I could fight all of them.

There was also the energy suck of even using the nails—a suck I hadn't noticed before, but which was now inexorably dragging me down. Scanning my body, I saw the worst of the rents in my skin looked like they'd been cauterized shut, but I was still leaking blood and goo from my legs and upper arms. That priest hadn't been fooling around.

Gamon's manic gibberish grated against my ears as I hauled myself forward. I didn't need to get all the way to her, but there seemed to be some sort of barrier between us, the farthest trailing edge of smoke. If I could just get past that...

"Aigh!" Gamon cried. Suddenly she was there, dragging me forward and throwing me down on the same blood-soaked Sun Stone that had lain atop the sacrificial altar. The stone was now cracked down its near side, lying on the stone floor against the wall. Even with that, it had more than enough surface to support me. I couldn't seem to get away from the damn thing. I pulled my hands around, waving them ineffectually in the air, like a bug with broken pincers. But the fire of the Gods' Nails seemed momentarily banked.

Looking beyond me into the depths of the cavern, her face alight with purpose, Gamon laughed. "I bring the sacrifice to your very hands, Tezcatlipoca."

I craned my neck, my foot gaining purchase on the rock wall beside me, and twisted around to see who Gamon was talking to, but there was nothing else in the shadows but spitting, burning fire. There was no one there, no matter how she stared with wild, frantic eyes.

Gamon had completely lost her mind.

Taking advantage of her distraction, I brought my hands together, hard, braining her with my fists on either side of her temples. When the spikes connected with her skull, another burst of flame erupted from their tips, the roar nearly shattering my eardrums. Gamon instantly crumpled, and something new and powerful surged in me, a strength that seemed to flow into me from the smoke itself — which was good, because there sure was a lot of smoke.

I staggered to my feet and thrust one hand in the

downward slash that Armaeus had taught me, and to my surprise the spike slid out of my wrist and into my fingers, just as he'd said would happen. I was reeling with pain and queasiness, which he also had presaged, but there was nothing I could do about that. There was nowhere to stow the nail, with my clothes cut to ribbons, so I transferred it to my left hand and grabbed Gamon with my right, dragging her around the moat, up the ramp, and out the door of the sacrificial room. I crossed to the other door, and the sparking voltage stopped long enough for me to duck inside.

On the other side of the room, the lab was in chaos. Fire ran around the ceiling like a trapped electrical storm. The technicians had given up on their packing job and were instead cowering under tables and behind machines. The monitors blinked and chittered crazily, their circuits clearly fried.

I intended to throw a sprawling Gamon at their feet, but I didn't have the energy. Instead, I dropped her in a heap of limbs and fabric.

"The antidote," I gritted out, my voice sounding like gravel. "Where is it?"

Nobody moved.

I lit one of the bone shards like a taper and pointed it in the corner where a half-dozen techs huddled. The table sheltering them instantly caught fire, and they scattered out from beneath it, squawking in several languages.

But enough of them knew English, I was sure. It was the international language of the arcane black market.

"Antidote," I snapped again. "You have to have one, dammit."

There was another squawk of fear as I traced an arc of fire along the floor.

"They don't." Gamon's laugh interrupted my rant, her voice low and throaty. I turned, aiming my double spikes at her, ignoring the jerk of pain as the second one seated itself alongside the first in the base of my left palm.

Crap.

But Gamon lifted herself to one elbow, staring at me with a mixture of surprise and disbelief.

"You still don't get it, do you?" she rasped. "There is only one creature on this world or any other that can supply the final ingredients for the drug, and only with those ingredients could we create a true antidote. And the cost of delivering that ingredient was — simple. You. Your body, your blood. Nothing else was strong enough to summon the mirror of smoke. And once the mirror was in place, the god could be reborn."

I stared at her, my spikes still emitting pops and sparks. "You seriously have never made an antidote. Your god couldn't put that together."

"My god wanted you," she said simply.

"Well, he sucks, then. He won't even show himself."

At that moment, another explosion blasted through the earth, ripping a hole through the walls and exposing a fiery conflagration beyond. The force of it dropped me to the floor, and the techs around us dove for cover — any cover — as multimillion dollar machines cracked and exploded in the heat.

Gamon, however, kept her gaze fixed on me. "Tezcatlipoca," she murmured, her eyes bright with the fervor of the damned. "Giver of both hope and despair. The drug and the antidote. But only in exchange for your life."

I sat there a moment more, lungs heaving, hunched over, forcing myself to think. What was I missing here?

Gamon was crazy, clearly she was crazy, but I'd found in my line of work that sometimes crazy people believed things based on a kernel of truth. I had made some enemies in this world, and some enemies outside it. It wasn't completely unreasonable that my life was worth trading drug secrets from the other side of the veil. Which made Gamon not my only enemy—if she was the face of this Tezawhatever god, the go-between, even killing her wouldn't put an end to this trade. It would simply crop up again.

The heat of the fire finally broke through to me, and I turned, squinting into it.

"Who's back there?"

Gamon didn't bother turning. "You want the antidote. I want the complete drug. Both hinge on you, Sara Wilde. And the clock is ticking. You don't need me to tell you what will happen to those people infected with the highest concentrations of those drugs if they don't reverse the effects in time. You've seen it yourself."

I stared at her a long time, then finally nodded. "You can make the antidote?" I asked.

"I can," she said, and her voice was filled with certainty. Her eyes were burning with an unholy ferocity, but in this, I believed her. As insane as it sounded, I believed her. "I will."

"Then do whatever you need with me," I said at last. "Now."

She stood, and I stood with her, both of us ragged and bloody, but only one of us certifiable. So far. My left hand was unnaturally weighed down with two shards, but at least that allowed me the ability to have the use of my right. Edward Scissorhands had nothing on me.

With Gamon leading the way, we stepped out of the lab and back into the room of smoke and fire, the bright yellow light still licking from beyond the sacrificial altar, the mirror of smoke still shimmering behind it. The heat was so intense, I flinched, ducking my head as Gamon strode forth. As we walked, I searched for a way out or through this—but there was something in Gamon's manner that struck me as authentic in a way I wouldn't have imagined possible with her. She *believed* that the way to get what she wanted was by handing me over — and I believed it too.

I might not like it, but I believed it.

Gamon finally stopped, called something out I couldn't translate. The fire lifted just enough for me to peek out from my arms, and behind it, through the flickering flames I could see — something else. I could almost make sense of it too, the image dancing in the shimmering heat, scattering apart only to coalesce again.

Then it finally resolved into a single form.

I froze.

"Tezcatlipoca," Gamon breathed.

But it wasn't an ancient Mesoamerican god staring back at me, with its distinctive flat features and space alien body. And it wasn't a god of smoke and mirrors, at least not in any traditional sense.

It was a tall, powerful woman wearing robes of red and gold, her dark hair falling over her shoulders, her face impossibly cold and cruel...

And...familiar.

I swallowed, my voice cracking in my throat as I spoke.

"Um, Mom?"

CHAPTER THIRTY

The being turned to me. She was — unmistakably — the figure I'd seen on the side of the dome in Atlantis in my vision, the one Martine had painted on the warehouse wall. She was also my spitting image, a taller, better version of me — her hair longer and more lustrous, her body stronger and probably not nearly as scarred beneath all that silk.

"Sara," she whispered, and the words vibrated off the sides of the room.

Beside me, Gamon turned back, staring hard at me, then at...there was no way I could keep calling her Mom.

"Who are you?" I demanded.

That response seemed to galvanize Gamon into action and at the same time relieve her of whatever was troubling her. She faced me triumphantly. "She is the warrior god of the ancients, the sorcerer god of the new peoples of this earth, and the god of magic for today. She is all that is missing in this world."

"*Vigilance*." The voice that came out wasn't my mom's, however, as much as I would have preferred it. It was mine, and it seemed pulled from the depths of my being. The rocks shook and heaved around us, and the shards of bone sizzled in my left hand.

Gamon's mouth contorted, but it was my mother who spoke.

"Vigilance," she said, lengthening the word as if trying it on for size. "Yes, I have been vigilant these millennia, waiting for the time to return to my rightful place among you. And all it took was the simplest, frailest of humans, in the end." Her laughter swelled. "Long have I watched, looking for my chance. Long have I hunted every seam and frayed thread of the veil your precious Council has wrapped so tightly around this earth. Have you ever wondered why they have been so dedicated to the cause of that veil? Have you never considered that it is not so important what they were keeping out, but what they were allowing to remain within?"

"They cannot compare to your power," Gamon piped up, like the suck-up she clearly was.

"Why do you want back in?" I asked. Watching this better, stronger reflection of me was having a weird effect. I suspected I should be feeling intimidated, or at least a little awed, as Gamon clearly was. Instead, I felt nothing but irritation and a curious letdown. This was my *mother*. This magical, powerful being from another dimension, this creature who had so enraptured the peoples of Atlantis that they'd painted her picture on their central dome like some sort of goddess worthy of worship. This was where I came from, and yet—

She'd brought me here to *bleed*.

"Why do you want back in so desperately?" I asked again, stronger this time. My mother's gaze shifted from Gamon, whom she was regarding with clear condescension and the faintest ghost of a smile—to me.

Her expression hardened.

"Yours is not the place to ask questions. You have gone too long without guidance. You were so close in my grasp the day Llyr broke through the veil when you

299

were only a child—but you ran. You ran! To live a life without the truth. Heeding countless voices when there has ever been only one that has the answers you seek." She narrowed her eyes on me, and I felt the faintest shiver in the back of my brain, exactly the same way I felt when Armaeus was trying his lock picks on my cerebellum.

"*Mine*," she hissed.

My third eye flapped open in sudden alarm, and I stepped back, raising my hands in instant deflection. For a moment, I was too slow, and I was blasted back by the sheer force of my mother's strength, my mind filled with a cacophony of voices, screams, thundering crashes, and high, terrifying cries. And everywhere, there were words, so many words, my name chief among them, swirling and cutting and diving like weapons. I thought instantly of the torture that the Devil of the Arcana Council had endured months earlier, the endless riddle of demonic pursuit, starting and twisting back and starting again, a snake eating its tail.

"No!" I finally managed, lifting my hands higher. The twin spires of the Gods' Nails sparked with their own hiss of fury, and a burst of fire shot out, filling the space between us. In my right hand, I held my gun— though I knew it wouldn't offer any true help against my mother.

Gamon was still human, though. And, Revenant or not, she could still be killed.

"You dare defy me?" My mother had somehow succeeded in infiltrating my mind, and I could hear both her outside and inside voice. It was worse than anything I had endured with Armaeus, even at his most insidious. Her voice crawled through my nervous system, leaving a trail of violation. Across the room, her face stretched into a smile. "You are strong, Sara. But make no mistake, you are not *that* strong."

A shocking burst of pain shattered my concentration, and I staggered back. I stared down at my shoulder, confused at what I saw.

There was blood there. Crimson, shining. Welling from a hole that simply had not been there a moment earlier.

Gamon's voice cried out, high and strained, and I realized she was also holding a gun. "You are no true daughter of a god," she cried. "You bleed, you die."

"You dare!" The movement from the being on the other end of the chamber was instantaneous and devastating. Gamon screamed as she collapsed forward, pummeled to the ground by a wash of flame. Clearly, beating on me was a task reserved solely for my mother, and I didn't miss the twisted expression of outrage, pain, and forlorn need that haunted Gamon's face as she fell.

I couldn't go to her, though. I had bigger fish to fry.

"You need to go now, *Mom*," I gritted out, taking a step forward despite the gunshot wound, despite the screaming in my mind. "You need to leave."

"I am *never* leaving," hissed my mother. "I have waited too long for this, fought too hard. You are the entry into all that has been ripped from me, the *entry*, not the vessel."

"Right now, I'm the stop sign." I took another step forward, thrusting all my shock and awe aside. My mother stopped advancing and straightened, clearly surprised.

"You *dare*," she said, this time aiming the words at me. But, unlike with Gamon, there was no outrage here, no shock that a kicked dog would dare bite and thrash. There was...surprise. Confusion even.

Whatever worked. I thrust my hands forward, and from the depths of my being, a burst of fire billowed forth and blasted across the room. My mother cried out, not in pain so much as shock, and I staggered forward a few more steps, my gun forgotten, dropped behind me, my hands outstretched — one with foot-long pincers driven into it, one lost in a mass of fire.

I sensed more than felt the running of feet, the surge of emotion behind me, then suddenly I was no longer alone. Nikki pulled up beside me, machine gun under her arm, and a phalanx of black-suited guards piled in around her. She put a hand on my shoulder and held me — held me fast, the blow of crushing horror emanating from my mother's form somehow blunted and shunted aside but not yet dead, not yet —

"*No.*" The masculine voice sounded in my ears, in the air, and in the very rocks around me. I knew that voice. Nikki hadn't just brought the reinforcements of the mortal kind, she'd pulled the strength of the Magician to her side. As Ma-Singh had said, no one could accuse her of doing things by half.

And that the Magician was here — again — struck a keening and unfamiliar chord within me, momentarily drowning out all other thoughts, all other truths. He had come here, he had followed me, through the water and the wild. He'd sent reinforcements when I'd been in danger, and when I needed more — so much more — he'd stepped into the breach himself, lending his immortal strength and otherworldly magic to my aid.

If he wasn't breaking the rules of his own Council, he was bending them pretty far. I didn't know why, but right now…right now I was just desperately glad he was here.

"*No,*" Armaeus breathed again, and in the center of my being, I felt lighter, brighter, the darkness that Vigilance had brought with her easing its hold on my heart — the heart, which even Gamon had known was the central force in all this. The heart that Gamon had pierced and I had hardened.

"No." I added my voice to the throng, Nikki's protecting presence beside me, and with a Herculean thrust, I rejected all of my mother's darkness, hurling it toward her with a scream of loss and outrage that had first begun building inside me twenty-seven years earlier, when she'd apparently brought me into existence not as a child to love and help grow...but as a tool, a pawn. Her pawn.

But I wouldn't be that for her — couldn't be.

"No!" I cried again.

And that seemed to do it. The sudden sound of rushing wind jetted through the chamber like a reverse tornado, dropping the House of Swords warriors to their knees, Nikki and I stumbled forward, also going down. Armaeus — I didn't know where Armaeus was, exactly, but I knew he wasn't here, wasn't caught up in this maelstrom. Was he the one causing it? Or had I done that?

It didn't matter. Everything was wind and pain, and even Gamon's broken body was lifted and flung forward, her long legs and arms flailing until she finally gained her balance — then she was running, sprinting after the disappearing visage of my mother. I realized too late Gamon was getting away, but I had no more breath in me to stop her, no more strength to do anything but breathe.

"No," I gasped one last time, then there was nothing at all.

Silence blanketed the room.

Nikki and I crouched together, staring at the hole that had been blasted into the wall, while Ma-Singh barked something in Spanish and several black-clad warriors sprang forth, running pell-mell into the breach.

They wouldn't find Gamon though, I knew. They definitely wouldn't find my...

I swayed.

"Whoa there, dollface, easy does it."

Nikki steadied me as some unseen person wrapped a blanket around me. She held me in the crook of her arm, speaking over my head.

"She's got multiple lacerations and a fairly fresh bullet hole in her, and I don't want to test her superhuman healing skills on this. Someone find the way out of here and pronto, because we sure as hell aren't getting out the way we came in."

That last made me laugh, and I choked a little, realizing with some surprise that my throat had been burned raw. "Martine?" I managed.

"Sent up the alarm exactly like you instructed. We were already in Mexico City, Armaeus sent us right after he lost contact with you the first time in the black market."

I frowned. "When was that?"

"Don't know, don't care. Something didn't sit right with him, and I wasn't going to argue." Nikki turned me gently. "Here we go now. We'll get you out of here and back to the—"

"Wait," I stopped her. We were passing the shattered Sun Stone, still slick with my own blood. I picked up the largest chunk I could carry, a section that bore the face of a jaguar, its mouth open, the hungry maw a hole meant to capture the blood that even now was stained inside it. "We're going to need this," I managed. "For the antidote."

Nikki paused, but knew enough not to ask unnecessary questions. "Just the one chunk?"

I sighed, looking down at it. I had only so much blood to give, not so much that we'd need more of the infernal stone than this to strain it. "Just this. If it works...when it works...we'll need to destroy everything else in this place."

"Consider it done," she said, and in her voice was

the strength I no longer had, the certainty I might never have again. In her hold was the power to keep me on the path I must follow, and the warmth and security that she would cradle my broken body, when all was said and done.

"Thank you," I whispered, tears running down my face for no reason at all.

"Thank you right back, dollface," she said, patting my shoulder. "And thank you for not dying. Saves me from dealing with a heartbroken Mongolian. Ain't nobody wants to see that."

She turned me gingerly toward the door, and eased me out of the room.

CHAPTER THIRTY-ONE

"I should have had this idea myself. I could have made millions with the blood I've drawn from you."

Dr. Sells's dry words accompanied the unhooking of a bag of thick red liquid from a stand. Working quickly and efficiently, she lifted another one into place, unclamped the tube trailing from it, and checked my vitals for the eleventy-millionth time.

I tried not to watch the thin line of red trace its way to the empty plastic sleeve, focusing instead on the tray of cookies arrayed next to the paper cup full of Tang. I didn't even realize they made Tang anymore. "How much more do you think you'll need?" I asked, trying to keep my voice steady.

I wasn't weak, exactly, and I was certainly motivated. But after today's one-woman donation drive, I didn't think I'd be looking kindly at needles again for a long time.

"Not much. These supplies are enough to treat the children, the ones who received the most significant doses. With your concentrated blood additive filtered through the sun stone, combined with the antidote mixture Gamon had already created, the resulting product requires only a few milliliters in an atomized form to do the trick. Aerosol doesn't normally work so well, but for this particular chemical mixture, it is proving remarkably effective. We'll release it to the known distribution points of Gamon's Fountain drug and its variants. Word is already circulating that the antidote gives a better high than the original drug."

I stared at her. "You're kidding."

"I'm not." She tapped the bag again. "Blood of an ancient goddess, if you believe the stories." Before I could protest further, she waved me off. "Anyone not infected who wants to buy whatever we have left of the mixture after the current caseload is exhausted will be required to donate to an anonymous fund Armaeus has set up to support Father Jerome's work."

"Oh." I sank back against the pillow. "Well, that's okay, then."

She smirked. "I suspected you'd think so."

"And the local cases?"

"Martine is fully recovered. He's still quite gifted. He'll be someone to watch as he matures. But his heart is no longer enlarged, its arrhythmia fully stabilized. He no longer complains of it dancing." She smiled. "He's asked after you many times, you know. I think he's bonding to you."

I nodded wearily. "Yeah, well, we can't find his family. So he's going to need to bond to someone— someone who isn't me. What about Brody?"

"Detective Rooks recovered with remarkable speed. Per your instructions, we didn't explain to him the exact nature of the compound that made up the antidote."

"Good. The last thing I need to have is him thinking he owes me anything. If it wasn't for me, he would never have gotten sprayed in the first place."

"Perhaps," Dr. Sells said, though she looked ready to argue the point. She tapped the bag, straightening it slightly, and I fought the slow queasy roll of my stomach. "This lot will complete Europe. There are isolated cases still coming in, but the side effects reported are not dire enough to warrant intercession. The fewer people who know the truth, the better."

"There's already enough of those." I thought of Gamon, running into the fire after the fading image of her god. The god who'd used her, then betrayed her, all to get at me. There'd been no sign of Gamon in the abandoned corridors of the Sun Pyramid, which was far worse than finding her body. She'd either escaped into the world, or she'd been carried out of it bodily. Neither idea particularly appealed, for very different reasons.

The door to my room burst open, and Nikki strode in, a small figure in hospital scrubs trotting beside her. In fact, Nikki was dressed in hospital scrubs too, her auburn hair swept back in a ponytail, her statuesque form somehow filling out the usually shapeless garment in all the right ways.

"Dollface." She grinned, beaming at me. "You have a visitor."

"Is that a tailored set of scrubs?" I asked. Nikki smirked as Martine approached cautiously, looking from me to Dr. Sells, then to the blood bag slowly filling its way to the brim.

"Are you all right?" the boy asked.

I nodded. "You were right all along, Martine. I was the solution, just not in the way I'd thought."

He still frowned at the bag. "They're taking so much."

"The human body is an amazing instrument," Dr. Sells told him briskly. "Especially Sara's version of it. For all the blood she loses, it's replenished within her, faster than it is for most people. She'll be a little dizzy for a while, but not too dizzy, and not for very long. She'll be her old self in no time."

The doc adjusted the bag again, and I grimaced. Nothing like being good to the very last drop.

"You're synthesizing everything on-site?" Nikki asked, casual as all hell. Since she'd shown up at the Pyramid of the Sun, she'd stuck to me like white on a whalebone, questioning every move made by anyone who wasn't herself, Nigel, Armaeus, or Ma-Singh. Dr. Sells wasn't exactly known for her scruples when it came to running side tests on me.

"We are," Sell said.

Fortunately, we didn't have to take her word for it entirely. Armaeus was monitoring the amount of blood taken from me and synthesized into the antidotes. The resulting compounds were handled with the kind of security the NASA space program didn't merit. I wondered if he let Sells create the organic version of the drug as well, for testing purposes only, but I couldn't think about that right now. As long as I didn't have to give up a milliliter more blood than necessary, I was all for it.

At last Sells was satisfied. She unhooked the bag, then took apart the entire apparatus. Next she covered my much-abused arm with a bandage. The wounds I'd sustained on the altar had mostly healed as well, only the long white slashes where the Gods' Nails had inserted themselves remained visible.

I glanced over to where the nails now sat, once more ensconced in their jade box. I wasn't in any hurry to use them again, but they were mine in a way that Soo's jade amulet or the other symbols of her position simply weren't. I'd earned these, and they had literally become a part of me. That meant something.

"This is the last of it?" Nikki asked, drawing my attention. She eyed Sells skeptically. "You're not going to come in and draw more in the dead of night or anything?"

"Sara can be released long before that." Sells turned to me. "As soon as you can walk without dizziness, in fact. But I would like to insist you get as much rest as possible in the next few days. And food high in antioxidants wouldn't hurt. Maybe a vegetable or two if you're feeling really crazy."

"I'll eat," I said tiredly, but I didn't rise to her vegetable challenge. The kind of problems I had were not going to be solved by a spinach salad.

Sells nodded, then turned toward the door.

"Millions," she murmured again as she walked out of the room.

Nikki watched her go with narrowed eyes. "You good with Martine Short here? I need to make sure the doc doesn't make a detour."

"Go." I waved her on. The truth was, I didn't trust Dr. Sells either. She'd been in Armaeus's pocket since forty years before I was born, and she seemed truly dejected on missing out on her chance to roll the dice on my blood for her own personal profit. Then again, this was Vegas, and she'd been here since the 1950s. Living that long in this city probably did something to you.

Nikki tousled Martine's hair, then went off in search of the good doctor.

Meanwhile, I focused on the boy. He'd taken up position on a chair by the door, leaning so far forward that he almost fell over. "You're allowed to drag that chair closer," I said, laughing when he scrambled to his feet, then crept forward, suddenly seeming shy.

He put the chair as close to the bed as he could, then slipped into it, leaning forward once again to brace his hands on the bed. He looked into my eyes with the kind of searching expression that only a kid could manage.

"You nearly died," he said, far too seriously.

I nodded but didn't try to brush off the question. "I did. So did you."

"Yes, but I didn't choose it." His eyes seemed to grow bigger in his face. "You did. Miss Nikki said you always do."

"Miss Nikki?" I asked, as levelly as I could. "She tell you to call her that?"

"It just seemed like I should." He smiled broadly. "She looks like a Miss Nikki."

"She does indeed." I matched his smile with one of my own and raised a brow. "So how come she's a Miss Nikki, and I'm plain old Sara?"

To my surprise, Martine frowned, and he glanced away. When he looked back, his face seemed somehow smaller...or his eyes bigger. Whatever it was, it made my heart lurch.

"Can I ask you something?" he mumbled.

Panic riffled through me. I'd somehow stumbled into a child emotional zone, with no one close to bail me out. Father Jerome was still half a world away; Nikki was on the hunt for Dr. Sells before she sold me out to *Shark Tank*. Even Nigel would have been useful here, and he was worse with kids one-on-one than I was.

Still, I stiffened my spine. "Of course you can. We're friends, and friends can ask each other anything." Well, almost anything. If Martine was about to lay something on me seriously deep, he'd be better off shouting down a hole.

"Do you remember your family?" His voice had dropped almost to a whisper, and a single tear dribbled down from his left eye, which he brushed away brusquely. "I mean, their faces? Their names?"

"I..." I swallowed. This was potentially dangerous territory. Because there were two types of family in my world, the kind who made sense and the kind who apparently ate worlds for a living. But the tortured look on Martine's face told me what he was truly asking, and for that, I did have an answer.

"I do," I said. "I grew up in a little town in the southern part of this country, called Memphis. And there, my...my mother raised me the best way she knew how. She cared for me and fed me and told me everything she could about how to be successful in the world, how to stand up for myself and face my troubles squarely." I didn't mean for my voice to waver, but it did all the same. Martine's eyes grew wider, almost rapt.

"Was she pretty?" he asked, and I almost choked on the laugh that burst from me.

"She was," I said. "She didn't look much like me, come to think of it now. She was blonde and blue eyed and always smiling. She told me I had my daddy's looks, but that he'd gone away and it was just the two of us, making our way in the world. And we did, you know." I gave him an encouraging smile. "We did okay for a lot of years."

Please don't ask me to explain where she is now, I silently prayed, but Martine lowered his gaze and studied his hands for a moment, the small, slim fingers laced together. "She died, didn't she?" he said.

"She did," I replied. And then more words suddenly came, words I didn't expect, about a group of people I'd not thought of in a very long time. "But after that, you know what happened? I found a new group of people who were almost like family. They took me in and loved me more than I ever thought anyone would."

He lifted his head again, his eyes still too large. "They did?"

"They did. They all lived in RVs—sort of like houses on wheels—and they traveled throughout the country, seeing everything they could. The mountains and the desert, the oceans and the swamps. And, in time, they became my family."

I blinked, startled at the strength of the memory. I'd been seventeen, on the run, hitchhiking at a rest area just south of Memphis when a stout, blonde, grandmotherly type had bustled up to me, clearly seeing me for what I

312

was, shell-shocked and hurting. An hour had flown by before she'd finally gotten me to talk to her. Then she'd announced she'd be my first ride, and I could get my second whenever I wanted to leave their group of RVers. I smiled, now, thinking of it. It'd taken me five years before I'd decided I was ready to leave. They'd been my family, at a time when no one else wanted the job. And they'd been good at it.

Martine sighed, watching me. At length he spoke again. "I don't remember my family."

I stiffened involuntarily, and he tensed too, clearly afraid he'd said something wrong.

"I try to!" he blurted. "But I...whenever I try to think of them, there's nothing that comes back. No pictures of my mom or dad, or whether I had brothers or sisters or a dog or..." He pursed his lips. "I think I would have remembered a dog, but there's nothing there. Nothing at all."

I reached out a hand toward him, not knowing what else to do, and he slid his over as well, our fingers interlocking on the bleached hospital sheets.

"What do you remember?" I asked, as gently as I could. "What's the first thing?"

He sighed, shrugged. "Waking up in a cave. I was a boy—I looked like this, and I could talk and write and run and I knew how to eat and be respectful. But I didn't know how I knew these things. The general..." He shook his head slightly, forging on. "The general, she said that it was okay that I didn't remember. That sometimes memories made us weak, and I was in that place to be strong. That she needed me to be strong."

He dropped his head again, but not before I saw the blush staining his cheeks. "I wanted to be strong for her. So I didn't...I didn't try to remember. Even in the early days when there was...something, something almost there I pushed it away." He brought his gaze up to me, and his face was ashen, haggard, the face of a boy far older than his years, who'd already seen so much, traveled so far. "It was there, and I could have reached for it, and instead I pushed it away!"

Tears were running freely down Martine's face now, and I gripped his fingers more tightly, reaching over awkwardly with my other hand to grasp his shaking shoulder. He was trembling all over, and my first worry was over his heart—but I couldn't stop the words tumbling out of his mouth if I'd wanted to, couldn't interrupt the flow of his pain.

"I might have had a sister, a mother. I might have had a father or he...or he might have been gone like yours. I might have been alone with my mother, or had three brothers and I don't know. And now I will never know. The memories are all gone, gone away so far that I can't bring them back."

"That's not true, sweetheart. That's not true." I patted him more fiercely, still awkward, my heart breaking. It couldn't be true, I resolved. He was just a little boy, a little boy with all his truths locked up inside him. He deserved to find his way to those truths, to find the family he'd lost—if there was still a family to find.

"And then I saw you in my dreams and I painted your picture, and when the general told me I had to go find you and I thought...I thought: you could be my sister. My older sister who would let me call her Sara, like a brother would. If you were coming anyway to save us, to make us better, maybe...maybe you could stay with me. You could be my family, and I wouldn't forget you!"

He said this last with such renewed fierceness that I jumped, but it was Martine's turn to grip my hand fiercely, his little ten-year-old face screwed up with resolve. "I wouldn't forget you, Sara. Not ever!"

"I know you wouldn't, Martine, I do," I assured him

hurriedly, and I didn't stop him as he lunged toward me, enveloping me with his thin, spindly arms. He was still so much closer to being a little boy than a full-grown person, and he sobbed in my arms inconsolably, letting out all the fear and anguish and pain he'd probably blocked from his mind during his months of incarceration with Gamon, whether on his own or with the help of her drugs and loyalty tactics. He sobbed until he had no more tears to cry, and then he kept his head ducked, his small body shaking, his hold never loosening until he fell asleep.

"We'll find your family, Martine," I whispered as his shoulders finally eased, his tiny exhausted body relaxing at last. "We will."

And if we didn't, I knew of another group of souls who made up a family as big as the open road. I could find them again, I thought, and ask them to do for Martine what they'd once, a little over ten years ago, done for me.

Because that was what families did.

But for now, I let Martine sleep, long after the time when I could rightly have left the hospital and returned to the world outside. Long after Nikki returned to me, even, taking up her silent watch by the door, her eyes suspiciously bright in the room's shadowy depths.

CHAPTER THIRTY-TWO

Armaeus didn't send a car for me at the hospital. I appreciated that.

When I left, Nikki and Martine waved to me from the posh cafeteria, the boy's distress at me leaving leavened by his astonishment at the food he was being served. There were still many more tests he would need to undergo, and I needed time. Time to find his parents, if they were still alive. Or time to find a second family to open their arms to him. Either way, Martine would never have to forget that people loved him, ever again. No child should ever go through that.

Pushing out to the sidewalk of Sells's private clinic, I was surprised to find Ma-Singh waiting for me. The Mongolian stood in the half shadows, but his mournful expression lightened as he met my gaze.

"Ma-Singh!" I looked around. "Tell me you haven't been out here this whole time. Why didn't you come inside?"

The big man shrugged. "You have many who would protect you from the threats of magic in that place. You didn't need me there. Eventually, though, I knew you would slip their bonds. I only had to be ready."

I sighed, but in truth, I didn't mind. If ever there was a man who would save me from myself, it was this one.

"I'm only going to the Strip."

He gestured to a car, which pulled out of the line and cruised forward. "And so I will take you. And await your call whenever you are finished."

Something about his gruff loyalty made me blink hard, but I looked away quickly. I'd already hugged the general once this year. If I did it again, he might spontaneously combust.

Ma-Singh and his driver accompanied me to the Palazzo, though I knew the Magician would be waiting for me in his towers at the far end of the Strip. I needed to build up to that, though. I stepped out into the bright morning, two and a half miles from my destination, glancing across the street at the pink skyscrapers of Treasure Island as it soared over its faux pirate's paradise of palm trees and murky lagoon. I needed the sun, but perhaps more importantly, I needed the walk.

"I am capable of walking, you know," the Magician said, falling into step beside me out of nowhere.

I jerked involuntarily to the side, almost falling as Armaeus reached out a hand to grasp my arm, steadying me.

"Stop doing that!" I hissed, though no one paid us much attention. Early morning runners swerved around us, their minds on whatever music was pumping through their headsets. Sidewalk cleaners pushed brooms alongside their rolling trash cans, and all the fountains along the Strip were silent, their mechanics exposed for checks and repairs. The maintenance of Las Vegas Boulevard always took place in the early morning like this, when the majority of the city was sleeping off the effects of the night before.

Armaeus settled into his long-legged, easy stride, matching my pace. He released my arm, and I missed the contact instantly, but I folded my arms against my chest, twitching at the fabric of my sleeves to hide my awkwardness.

After we'd passed the line of gondolas parked at the edge of the still waters of the Venetian's harbor, the Magician spoke again. "We haven't found any trace of Gamon's body, nor indications of her death. We can only assume she's still alive."

I nodded. I'd assumed as much. "Mercault?"

"In a panic." Armaeus's voice dripped with derision. "Ma-Singh has confirmed that the House of Swords is not responding to Mercault's outreach, and Simon has been tracking all of Mercault's incoming and outgoing communication. He's had no contact with Gamon that we can ascertain. His story seems to hold — she reached out to him, revealed her position as head of the House of Cups, entered into an alliance with him. A short-lived alliance, it would seem."

"Who'd she kill to get the spot?" It was unbelievable that between technology and magic, we still couldn't identify two of the four leaders of what were supposedly the last organized syndicates of magic in the world. During my convalescence under Dr. Sells' care, I'd spoken with Nigel about it, but he'd confirmed he'd only received orders from the House of Cups via coded messages. He'd never once seen the leader of the House or any of his or her generals. And now they were…gone. Vanished.

"Unknown. And no one's talking — yet. Cups were not players in the arcane black market, but there will be a leak somewhere, it'll simply take time."

"Time and leverage," I said grimly. "I suspect Gamon's pretty convincing on the importance of keeping quiet."

"Gamon has long kept a tight hold on her people, and there's no indication she's easing that now. Folding in her own network with whatever exists of the Cups' infrastructure will make her…quite powerful. And quite dangerous."

"Yeah, I got that part," I muttered. I also got something more, something I wasn't quite sure how to process—Gamon's face, stark and staring as the goddess...alien...guardian of the galaxy or whatever the hell my mother was flexed and stormed before us. I didn't know what my mother truly wanted in me, but Gamon would have gladly given it—might still give it, if my banishment of my own flesh and blood didn't hold. "Gamon's not the poster child for mental health, Armaeus. And she's running a House."

"Houses that have remained on the sidelines for generations," Armaeus countered. "Not even with the resources of the Council were we entirely sure about Soo's operation until very recently. Mercault's position slipped only because he prefers his vices over his need for secrecy. Even if Gamon is, in fact, leading Cups, we don't know the impact—there may arguably be none."

"There's some." I shook my head. "She didn't take on that role merely to lull Mercault into a side deal. She's got an end game." My lips twisted. "And, let's face it, I haven't been discreet about my role in the House of Swords. So from a collection of Houses shrouded in secrecy, the entire system is now all but revealed. Especially if Gamon is still alive. I think if we figure out Wands..."

Armaeus completed my thought. "If we determine the leadership and structure of Wands, then yes, the puzzle will be complete. We'll know how, or if, the Houses can work together to protect their own."

I snorted. "Well, based on the fact that Gamon is now one of the players, I wouldn't hold my breath on that."

We moved up the stairs of one of the innumerable pedestrian walkways that now shuttled people above and along Las Vegas Boulevard, cutting down dramatically the traffic jams and accidents that had plagued the city in earlier years. At this hour, the escalators were almost all nonoperational, another victim of the Strip's maintenance cycle. I glanced down the Strip, past the glittering glass fronts of the newer casinos, to where Prime Luxe hovered over the sphinx and obelisk of the Luxor. Even in the full sunlight, if I looked exactly right, I could catch sight of its towers and ramparts of glass and steel, rising over the end of the Strip like a sentinel.

"There's more to discuss than the Houses, though," Armaeus said. "I lost contact with you at odd moments while you were traveling—sometimes at your discretion, which was always clear, but sometimes at other times, even when you weren't deliberately blocking me." The words were said without heat. Armaeus, more than most, understood the challenge I had with allowing him access to my brain. Mainly because I could never fully trust what he was doing when he was scuffing around inside it.

Still, this was news to me. "Like when?" I asked, genuinely curious.

"It was obvious, once I considered the problem." He lifted a lazy hand, tapping the front of my left shoulder, where the slender bone shards of the Gods' Nails rested inside my jacket. "When these were deeply set in your bones, or when you tapped their power, you were lost to me. Not at first—I could still connect with you when you were in Reykjavik. But as you grew more accustomed to the power of the artifacts, as you welcomed it…" He waved his hand as if batting back a fly. "Your mind was rendered completely blank to me, off-limits. It was quite unlike your focused intention to keep me out. This was…as if you were on another plane altogether, utilizing magic I have not encountered in all my years on this earth."

320

Since Armaeus had been kicking around the planet since the 1100s, this was saying something. "But you analyzed the shards. You gave them back to me. How did you not know this already?"

"As I said, at first, it wasn't even something I thought to check. Even now, the magic within the shards is inert. When they were used by Mercault's assassin, I could plumb the depths of his mind easily, shattered though it was. Not so yours, when they were rightfully returned to you. I'd assumed you were blocking me, or that Mercault's defenses had strengthened once more." He shrugged. "I was wrong."

I frowned down at my chest, as if I could study the bone fragments through my hoodie. "Which means, what? That these aren't from earth?"

"That is the simplest explanation, yes. They are, quite legitimately, of the gods. Or the gods as prehistoric man knew them."

"You're sounding like that *Ancient Aliens* guy again."

Armaeus actually chuckled, and something hard and fierce squeezed in my chest. It somehow was so much more difficult for me to be with him when he acted remotely human. I was used to him being an ass. He was good at it, and I understood it. But moments like these, when he seemed...almost normal...these were the hard times. These were the times that made me wish for something different for us, some alternate balance of power.

He stopped and pointed to one of the towers down the Strip, and I squinted at it. Excalibur was a particular favorite of mine, for all that it was redolent of early '90s Vegas kitsch. Its brightly colored domes and ramparts made it a favorite of families and young, less jaded couples, and it was just far enough away from the true center of the Strip to give the illusion of peace and quiet…as quiet as Vegas ever got, anyway.

"There is a great deal I seem to have not been paying attention to," he said. "That will need to change. Your concerns about Interpol's interest in the Connected community were well-founded, and they have sent a ripple through the intelligence community that is already generating alarming reports of psychic profiling and targeting. As a Council, we have lived through waves of such targeting in the past."

"The Salem witch trials?"

"That's one of many." He nodded. "As was the Roman occupation. The Spanish Inquisition. The massacre of the Templars. More recently, state-sponsored genocides from extremist regimes in various pockets throughout the world. Those, we managed to get through. This, I'm not as sure we can. Coordinated at an international level, yet carried out just beneath the surface of public awareness, these communities could be expunged without anyone knowing they were gone. The very anonymity of the Connected community could lead to its undoing…an undoing we anticipated from outside the veil, not within it. Which…changes things."

"Changes them how?" I didn't mean my question to come out so pointedly, but any mention of the veil took me perilously close to thoughts I couldn't quite process yet. The keeper of the veil, the Hermit, was a well-known Council member…and my father. Beyond that, all I pretty much knew about him was that he kept the veil stitched together. Not why, and not for how long. I'd assumed that was predominantly because he needed to keep a low profile, given that his enemies included creatures like Llyr, the ancient ruler of Atlantis whose banishment had precipitated a little historical gem of a story known as the Great Flood. But now I knew who else the Hermit had been keeping out of late: my mother. I just didn't know precisely why.

Armaeus wasn't an idiot, of course. He sent me a cool glance that communicated that he knew what I was thinking about, then waved again. The ramparts above Excalibur seemed to extend upward far beyond its last fluttering flag, not a tower at all but a double curving staircase of easily a million stairs, shooting up into the clouds. At its top was a single domed building, more like a cell than anything approaching a residence.

"That appeared on our horizon last night, while you were recovering in the hospital. But I have been expecting it for some time."

"You..." I swallowed. "You got a new member of the Council to turn up?"

"Not a new one, and not for long, I suspect. But the Hermit of the Arcana Council has remained on the other side of the veil long enough."

I stared, barely willing to believe it. "The Hermit...my father...is coming for a visit. And you made up an extra bed for him. Because Prime Luxe is too small for him to stay in one of its seven thousand rooms."

Armaeus's smile was thin. "The residence of the Hermit was his own creation, and subtly done. None may touch him there, affording him an oasis of calm in the chaos that his return is sure to bring."

"Oh?" I asked. Chaos didn't sound good, but Armaeus merely shrugged. He turned again, gesturing. We were forced to mount another pedestrian walkway, this one taking us directly in front of Excalibur and its Hermit's perch.

"It's inevitable," he said at length, after we'd cleared the stairs and moved out over the street below. "It is not every day that a Council Member is made to answer for his crimes."

I stopped short, halfway across the pedestrian bridge, and stared at Armaeus. "Um...what crimes

323

would those be, exactly?"

"His decision to bring a child into this world is not one that we took lightly, but when it was discovered, it was determined there was no true harm. You were raised without knowledge of the Hermit's actions, you were valuable to the Council, and he continued to do a job that very few people in this plane are capable of doing."

"You let it slide, in other words."

"We let it slide. However—he also did not disclose your true mother, merely assured us she would never pose a problem. As you can see"—Armaeus waved toward me—"that is most assuredly not the case. Her interest in you is concerning, though, in its way, inevitable. Her interest in the power she might wield in this plane, however, and the fact that she was able to penetrate what I suspect were highly fortified barriers…is far more problematic."

"And who is 'she' exactly?" Forcing these words past my lips was more difficult than I expected. It was one thing to learn your mother was a pain in the ass—a drunk, a drug addict, a criminal. I could handle that. I'd grown up with that, if I really looked hard enough at the truth. But this…

Armaeus sighed, then shook his head. "We don't know. In the time of Atlantis, the pantheons of gods that warred over earth was richer than you can imagine. The records of that time were deliberately expunged over the years except for the barest crumbs of information."

"But you don't need records. You've got Michael. He was around then."

"The Hierophant withdrew into seclusion at approximately the same time your mother burst through the veil. He has been unresponsive since."

"Unresponsive?" I stared at him. "That's not seclusion, that's a coma."

Armaeus didn't reply to that and I grimaced, feeling a renewed headache coming on. "So whatever Mom is, it's bad enough to send the Archangel Michael into hiding. That's...that's not good, right? That can't be good."

"It is neither good nor bad, until we know more. But your mother is definitely outside the realm of what we understand, and her ability to penetrate the veil at this particular time is disturbing." Armaeus glanced coldly at the spiraling staircases atop Excalibur, faintly outlined in the bright, sunlit sky. "There's far more going on within the Council than I suspected, and I think I have more than the Hermit to watch."

"Tell me about it," I muttered. Armaeus wasn't the only one with personnel problems, though. Gamon was out there, Mercault was flopping around like a fish on a dock, and somewhere in the shadows lurked the House of Wands. If we stood apart, we should surely fail. But if we joined forces...and didn't kill each other...maybe we wouldn't need the intercession of the Council to fight our battles. Maybe we could fight them ourselves.

I looked at Armaeus as he stared hard at the spiraling stairs of the Hermit's domain. In fact, if we played this right...maybe for once the Council would be in *our* debt instead. I really liked that idea, I realized, and I liked the options it gave us. Options not only for the House of Swords, but for all Connected people everywhere, struggling to preserve their place in this world.

A fierce emotion surged within me, quick and hot. I let a grin curve the corner of my mouth as I considered all the angles.

This was Vegas, after all.

You should never bet against the House.

CALL OF THE WILDE

Join Sara in August, 2017 as the war on magic flares to sudden, brutal life, requiring her to summon the four Houses of Magic for an epically contentious summit. Together they must forge an alliance to preserve the Connected world as they know it—if they don't kill each other first. Meanwhile, Sara must grapple with who (and what) her mother truly is, unearth a growing threat within the local Connected community…and come to terms with the newest member of the Arcane Council: a powerful, provocative sorceress hand-picked by Armaeus to serve as the Council's new Empress.

Want to keep apprised of the latest news of Immortal Vegas, get sneak peaks and free books? Sign up for my newsletter at www.jennstark.com/newsletter!

A NOTE FROM JENN

Sara's reading in the opening chapter of Wilde Child begins as a bit of a misdirection—showing that there's always more than one way to read the cards. Those cards' general interpretations are below, which fit most situations…unless you're about to walk into a fight. In that case, keep your wits about you and your eyes sharp!

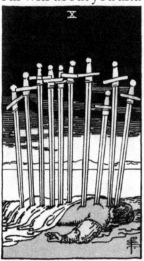

The Ten of Swords

The Ten of Swords is always a nasty bit of business

to draw in a reading, symbolizing the feeling of being stabbed in the back, or utter defeat. While the dawn breaking on the horizon offers a hopeful note, typically this card indicates that you are facing an irrevocable ending, one that generally is accompanied by pain, regret, and sorrow. In a medical/health reading, this card does not signify anything more than you're about to go under the knife (or are experiencing pain in your back/midsection)—it's not a negative card in medical readings so much as an indication of pain. When you draw the Ten of Swords, be willing to let go what you must (or brace yourself for an ending you might not be ready to make), and know that you are strong enough to survive this ending. Better things are waiting for you on the horizon!

The Five of Wands

Get ready for action! The Five of Wands is all about jumping into the thick of things, whether as part of a sporting event, competition, or flat out fight. You could have several people vying for your attention (or your services/products) or you could feel like you are in a tightly competitive market. Minor injuries can result from moving too fast or acting rashly, so be careful out there! When you draw the Five of Wands, make sure you're psyched up for action. You may find that the competition is fierce—or simply that you're thrust into the middle of a very active day, with lots of rushing activity that keeps you on your toes. You've got what it takes to make the most of your opportunities if you're willing to play the game—but this card puts you on notice that you can't sit on the sidelines any longer!

The Six of Pentacles

The Six of Pentacles is one of the most reassuring cards in the minor arcana, because it's all about getting what is due to you. Granted, if you have been loaned money you may find that this loan is coming due, but most of the time this card symbolizes that whatever you've put out in the universe is coming back to you three-fold. Positive thoughts, forward-moving action, and sincere effort is all rewarded here, with the universe showering you with gifts. When you draw the Six of Pentacles, consider your own situation. If you don't have any outstanding debts that you've been avoiding, you will almost certainly receive the blessings of the universe in some way. If you do have a debt, you may find the funds to repay it appear in an unexpected way. Pay attention, too, to how you can help others who are less fortunate. Anything you give is ultimately a gift to yourself.

ACKNOWLEDGMENTS

Once again, I am grateful to readers who expressed a strong interest in the series continuing with Wilde Child. I was able to peel back some layers of Sara's history with this book, and I hope it holds some interesting discoveries! My thanks go once more to Elizabeth Bemis as well for her tremendous work on my books and my site—only 351 sleeps 'til our next island adventure! Gene Mollica again gave me a beautiful cover for this book, capturing the story's fiery climax—very much appreciated! My editorial team of Linda Ingmanson and Toni Lee actually made me cry with their amazing work and attention to detail...I'm in awe of their craft, and any mistakes in the manuscript are, of course, my own. Edeena Cross once again provided an exceptionally helpful beta read—thank you for your time and your relentless good humor! Kristine Krantz saved my skin once again—and my sanity, for which I'm forever grateful. And as always, sincere thanks go to Geoffrey—with every book, I appreciate you more. It's been a *Wilde* ride.

ABOUT JENN STARK

Jenn Stark is an award-winning author of paranormal romance and urban fantasy. She lives and writes in Ohio. . . and she definitely loves to write. In addition to her "Immortal Vegas" urban fantasy series, she is also author Jennifer McGowan, whose Maids of Honor series of Young Adult Elizabethan spy romances are published by Simon & Schuster, and author Jennifer Chance, whose Rule Breakers series of New Adult contemporary romances are published by Random House/LoveSwept and whose modern royals series, Gowns & Crowns, is now available.

You can find her online at http://www.jennstark.com, follow her on Twitter @jennstark, and visit her on Facebook at http://www.facebook.com/authorjennstark.